CREEPIN'

CREEPIN'

Edited by

MONICA JACKSON

L. A. BANKS, DONNA HILL, MONICA JACKSON, J. M. JEFFRIES AND JANICE SIMS

CREEPIN'

ISBN-13: 978-0-373-83060-2
ISBN-10:   0-373-83060-2

© 2007 by Kimani Press

The publisher acknowledges the copyright holders of the individual works as follows:

PAYBACK IS A BITCH
© 2007 by L. A. Banks

THE HEAT OF THE NIGHT
© 2007 by Donna Hill

VAMPED
© 2007 by Monica Jackson-King

BALANCING THE SCALES
© 2007 by J. M. Jeffries

AVENGING ANGEL
© 2007 by Janice Sims

www.kimanipress.com

Printed in U.S.A.

CONTENTS

Veteran bestselling African-American paranormal romance and erotica authors serve you up a collection of strange and sexy tales with werewolves, demons, voodoo, vampires and avenging angels—*oh my*.

We've stirred in love and tenderness, and spiced liberally with scrumptious *raw* sex.

Lemme tell you, these dishes are even better with unexpected delicious twists of betrayal, infidelity, jealousy and revenge, topped off with dollops of old-fashioned cheatin' and gettin' even.

L. A. Banks takes us into the world of werewolves when a wronged wife shows her man what being dogged really means in *Payback Is a Bitch*.

Donna Hill delves into a risqué addiction, when a lonely woman becomes obsessed with an unseen lover in *The Heat of the Night*.

Monica Jackson knows how a woman can feel when her man's too fine for his own good. It's easy to get a bit jealous, but a girl should be careful not to bite off more than she can chew in *Vamped*.

J. M. Jeffries shows us revenge can be a dish with a high price, at least it is when voodoo is involved in *Balancing the Scales*.

Janice Sim's angel spreads a bit of heaven on earth, until hell decides it wants her for its own in *Avenging Angel*.

Don't expect the same ol' boring dishes or any reheated leftovers. Dig in to this quintet of hot and spicy stories and try something new, something fresh and something different.

But I warn you, we might get a little dirty up in here. It'll be worth it.

Enjoy,
Monica Jackson

PAYBACK IS A BITCH
by L. A. Banks

Dedicated to the readers who make it possible and the authors who took the time and effort to contribute their muses.

chapter one

Cherry Hill, New Jersey

"Oh, Douglass...*get it,* baby."

"You know I'ma wear it out—just open your legs a little wider."

"Save some for me, too, lover."

"I've got enough for both of y'all."

The long, toffee-hued, brunette beauty leaned back on her elbows with her lids half-closed as he carefully sprinkled another line of cocaine on her inner thigh and then dragged his nose the length of it to her crotch, licking up any tiny particles he'd missed. He powdered her bud as she opened her legs wider for him, and then numbed his tongue and lips suckling it off. Her deep moan brought the blonde away from his shaft, the loss of warm, wet mouth-contact made him thrust against air while he watched her dust the brunette's dark nipples with the expensive white powder. Visual ecstasy claimed him as her small pink tongue laved at the sugared teats, causing the woman beneath him to writhe and buck as his tongue plunged into her swollen pussy.

Blonde hair mingled with brunette hair as the blonde slid her body above her prone friend's. An agonized expression captured her face as she offered her tight pink nipples to her girlfriend, her finger working against her slippery slit.

"Just suck them," she murmured to the woman beneath her. "This shit has me so horny, I can't stand it."

He watched the brunette struggle to lift her shoulders so she could lap at the double-D sized silicon breasts swaying in her face. The blonde arched and moaned as her friend flicked the pad of her thumb against one nipple and drew the other into her mouth, then finally pushed both creamy breasts together so that she could suckle the sensitive tips at the same time. The brunette's hips bucked against the attention his tongue was giving her clit.

Pussy and ass were in his face, his hand furiously stroking against the cock-ache both women produced. Need finally forced him to his knees to plunge into pink, hairless blonde pussy from behind for a few strokes, and then hot, bushy, toffee-hued pussy in the next. Withdrawal and reentry was driving him crazy. The coke had thoroughly buzzed him, keeping his dick so hard that tears were in his eyes. It didn't get any better than this...the bitches were moaning, begging for him not to pull it out, snorting hits while humping each other beneath him while he fucked them both. Damn—this was living!

But he was so close to the edge, he couldn't pull out again. He'd slipped out of the brunette's tight snatch, the need to cum making his balls contract, and the blonde had dropped down low to grind her bud against her friend's. Blonde ass was the target, whatever orifice was open would do. Female tongues were in a wicked dance, fingers working in and out of each others drenched vessels in jerky near-orgasm motions. The blonde's legs were wide open, her rectum supple, ready, tight. The thrust made him holler; the explosion in his groin put lights behind his closed lids. His deep guttural wail fused with the cries from the two women beneath him. He pulled out hard, splattering the blonde's ass with seed, and then collapsed.

Who needed an uptight wife when the perks of being a sports management mogul offered all of this? He loved cheerleader wannabes!

Mainline, Philadelphia—Radnor...

Sidney Coleburn-West remained as still as stone within the darkened living room of her expansive Radnor home. An eerie half moon bathed the large bay windows of the Tudor in a wash of luminescent blue-white hue. The exterior flood-lights had been turned off per her contact's instructions. No porch light. The house sat idle, dark and vulnerable—like her. Now she'd wished she'd agreed to meet somewhere other than her home.

She could hear the large, antique grandfather clock in the open, cathedral foyer ticking its warning with a solemn echo off the polished hardwood floors. The Oriental rugs didn't mask or absorb that ominous sound. Her eyes remained fastened to the window. Her best friend Leonora was a cop, and she knew some people who knew some people in the hardball business. Leonora wouldn't have steered her wrong, and she wouldn't have gone here unless it was absolutely necessary. Douglass West was out of control. Her husband had to get out of her life. That was non-negotiable.

Sometimes justice wasn't just, and most times, the wheels of justice ground too slowly and very unpredictably. Evidence was often hard to come by. Getting it to be admissible was a whole other can of worms. Her husband had high-powered, sports legal team connections, people who'd do a lot of his work pro-bono. She would have to pay every step of the way, even though she was an attorney. Her contacts weren't as high-profile as his. Therefore, since the high road wasn't an option, she would fight for her dignity by way of the low road this time. Yeah…by any means necessary.

Sidney drew the hurt around her like a blanket and glimpsed the thick envelope on the Queen Anne oval coffee table. The image became blurry from tears she refused to allow to fall. Thirty-nine and soon to be single again. No children. Her time was running out, ticking away like the large grandfather clock down the hall. Fear of that reality had made her ignore the signs and overlook certain truths until they were so bold and so ugly that there was no way to turn a blind eye.

She'd been used to building up her husband's sports management career…her hard-earned assets siphoned into his enterprises, her name used to block his child support payments and hide his debt, she'd later learned. Then an LLC reversed her fortune again, and silent partnerships and hidden trusts ripped the foundation right out from under her.

Nothing in her life had prepared her for her lover, her husband, her best friend, to become a financial predator. Book learning didn't equal intrinsic knowledge of betrayal. That was something hard-learned by experience, and her loving family didn't even have that in their experience base to draw from...not like this, not this insidious. It was her good name and contacts that had been absorbed, picked over and then discarded, her hopes of a real family shattered along with her heart.

Sidney shuddered and blinked back the tears. How could he have been selfish enough to go away on what was supposed to be a business trip and get a vasectomy, just to keep from having a family with her? So cruel that he'd smiled at her sobs and told her he already had three children from a previous marriage and he'd decided that was enough for him—but he'd never given her real access to even those children, citing they were *his*. She was an outsider.

But what about her need to nurture, to feel life grow within her, or to have a tiny new life to love? How did the man sleep at night? she wondered. No soul. Now the bastard was having an affair? Plus, he had laughed in her face and told her he'd walk with half of all she'd worked hard to acquire, when he'd brought nothing, not even real sweat equity to the table...would ransack her life for her future earnings, too, as though he'd built her fast-track legal career? Oh, hell no. This was war.

A shadow moved across the window and Sidney tensed and stood. She picked up the envelope and headed toward the grand foyer, her destination the front door. But a deep, baritone male voice spoke from the darkened hallway within the house, paralyzing her.

"Put it down on the table and step back from it."

A thin sheen of perspiration instantly covered her body. Her heart beat in mild arrhythmia as fear nearly strangled her. How did the shadow get into the house and into the foyer *that fast?* Leonora said the guy was good, but damn...

Sidney dropped the envelope on the crescent-shaped table in the hallway and quickly backed away. How had he gotten into the house? The question gnawed at her as her eyes strained to see into the darkened corner to no avail. She didn't even hear a car pull up in the driveway or on the street. After tonight, she'd call the alarm company and have motion detectors installed throughout the second floor, too!

He sniffed the air, her fear was doing irrational things to his brain. No fraud detected, this lady was the real deal. He watched her fists balled at her sides and the way her soft ivory Mohair sweater clung to her curves. Camel-hued slacks hid her long, graceful legs. Even in the darkness he could see her regal bone structure beneath satiny, cinnamon skin, thick tresses washed her shoulders in auburn...her pretty brown eyes held a strange combination of fear, indignation, hurt, and the most profound rage he'd seen in a very long time. She smelled good enough to eat. Later, he told himself. Yeah. This one was good, and he'd take the job.

He stepped out of the shadows and picked up the envelope, weighing it in his hand. He didn't need to open it to tell that all his cash was there.

She tried not to gasp when she saw a hulking six foot six frame exit the hallway darkness and reach for the envelope. The size of his hand alone made her stare. His skin was the color of midnight—nearly blue-black, just like the leather jacket and pants he wore. A pair of haunting, dark eyes with a strange reflective quality to them roved over her body, making her fight not to shudder. It was impossible to tell whether or not the sensation was fear, bizarre desire, or both. It had been a very long time since she'd been this close to real testosterone, and had never truly been in the company of what Leonora called, "an enforcer."

For the briefest moment she wondered how he'd moved through her house with such silent stealth at his size. It didn't matter how, though—as long as he was on her side. If Leonora hadn't sent him, she would have hit a security system panic button in the house and tried to dash behind a locked door to call 911.

"It's all there," she finally said in a quiet tone, her voice coming out in a dry, husky rasp. "Twenty thousand."

A low chuckle was his initial response. "Cool. You want me to sic 'em…or just bring you evidence that might make him back down from a court battle?"

She simply stared at the source of the baritone voice. "You do more than investigations?"

"Not all the time," he said calmly, folding away the envelope into his jacket breast pocket. He looked her up and down with a level of appreciation that began to melt her bones. "Let's say that sometimes on a job, a man can get inspired. After seeing you, and hearing about what he did to you—I'm inspired."

For a moment they both stared at each other.

"Thanks," she murmured, and finally looked away. "I haven't inspired anybody in a long time. But, I can't have blood on my hands."

He nodded and let out a slow, weary breath. "I hear you, was gonna tell you to let it be on my hands. However I take it you're a lady through and through. But when I see shit like this…it pisses me off."

She smiled sadly and captured his intense gaze, her eyes now never leaving his. "Yeah, well…welcome to the club and thanks for the offer, anyway. I don't want that on my conscience, though."

"You still love him?"

She hesitated. "No. I feel robbed. Like I'm in mourning. He's already dead to me, really." She tried to laugh it off, but the sound that came from her was a shallow, brittle tone. "You're already looking at a widow. The love and what used to be my husband died early on in this travesty of a marriage. There have been so many indignities and so many horrible things said…" She turned away and hugged herself as her voice fractured. "No. I'm not still in love. What's left here is in name only."

"Good," he said quietly through his teeth. "Then anything that happens will be on my conscience, not yours."

She turned around quickly, her gaze very steady now. "Please. I just want the man investigated, to be able to take some video or get photos—something that will make him just back off, go away, and give me a clean, no-fault divorce. I want my life back, that's all. I figure God will get him back, I don't have to do it. I just don't want to be used any more."

"Yeah, God will definitely get him back…maybe by sending an angel of death for using a sweet sister like you. Or maybe The Almighty will release a demon that's bigger than him, something with a bad attitude that will eat his ass alive? Maybe something wild and carnivorous like me, one night? The possibilities are endless, when you go supernatural."

The man in the shadows chuckled low in his throat. It was a deep, sensual release of sound that partially frightened her but also drew her in.

"As much as he probably deserves it, still...I can't..."

"Yeah, I know. I was just playing with the concept on my palate...seeing as how Leonora told me what an asshole he really is."

She watched the tall, ominous male begrudgingly nod, and only then did she relax. If only there really was such a thing as supernatural champions. Sidney sighed. She had to stop tripping. If there were, she'd be out of a job and there'd be no legal profession or need for courts. Besides, for all of Leonora's superstitions and psychic counselors—like Madame Irvinia up in Reading, PA, and whatnot, she *knew* her police officer best girlfriend would *not* have sent a hit man to her Radnor home. This guy quietly worked with the cops on out-of-jurisdiction cases, so a lot of the fear evaporated just knowing that. It made perfect sense that he had to test her to be sure she wasn't down to try anything shady. That's right. He was just testing her character.

"I don't want him hurt," Sidney said, lifting her chin, "just...neutralized by truthful information. Please. That's all. I'm an attorney and can't do anything illegal."

"As the lady wishes. Leonora's good people, said you'd only want it this way—but I had to check for myself, first. The name is Brick," he said, stepping out of the shadows so she could finally see his face. "I can track anything, and I do a lot of off-the-books work for the cops." He glanced around. "You got a shirt or something that he recently wore? An article of clothing, whatever?"

Although she'd passed his test, her vocal cords were temporarily frozen. Leonora hadn't explained what she'd encounter. Sidney could only nod in reply to Brick's request. Her gaze was riveted to a ruggedly handsome face, the smoothness of ebony skin with a gash in one thick eyebrow from some long-ago fight, no doubt...the way an expertly barbered beard created a velvet matt finish against his strong jaw...then sheer size overwhelmed her—massive shoulders, a stone-cut chest straining against a black cotton t-shirt, a torso that undoubtedly gave him his name. Brick. Yeah...no lie. Eight cinderblocks in a neat builder's stack of abdomen. She'd dared not lower her gaze beyond that, but reflex won out and made her jaw go slack. Where was this champion when her husband was talking shit and needed his punk ass kicked?

"So, lady, what do you wanna do?" the mysterious male standing in her hallway said in a low, sensual tone, cocking his head to the side.

For a moment she couldn't move. There were two ways she could answer his question. Embarrassment singed her as her body tried to respond, swelling the valley between her thighs. Her face was hot. It had been so long. Celibacy was kicking her natural ass. Raw, animal sensuality oozed from the man's pores, with an indefinable undercurrent of danger.

Why didn't Leonora tell her about this hunk, when she'd been starving for two years while battling an asshole husband? Brick was going to help her right a serious wrong, in a way that was just and non-violent...but there was also a look in his eyes that said he wasn't above a little emotional-even-the-score comeuppance, if she needed him to make love to her. It was written all over his face, the question: do you wanna? For the first time in way too long, someone had her back—even if she'd had to pay dearly for the privilege. Still. She wasn't totally alone.

Brick opened his hands in a gesture of impatience. "The shirt—sometime tonight?"

"Oh, yes, my apologies," she said quickly, wrenching her thoughts away from the carnal. "I…I just was wondering how you got in here. Frankly, it made me nervous," she said, going toward the steps.

He watched her retreating form, the way her lovely ass sashayed up the wide, curved staircase. The snide remark he'd lobbed at her was designed to get her to move and move fast before the wolf in him started to growl. He could already feel a sense of territorial imperative stirring within him. Females in distress always did that to him. It was the way she was looking at him. He could see the need for her to settle the score with her trifling husband on several different levels etched deep inside her wide brown eyes. Yeah, no problem. For this sweet beauty, he'd gladly oblige. But Leonora said that wasn't part of the package, and Sidney seemed like a woman that would make him mess around and bite her. Not good. She didn't need to catch the Lupine madness from him.

Brick glanced at the moon through the double-high Pella windows in the foyer, glad that it wasn't yet full. Leonora should have warned him—and being a female that had a propensity for other females, Leonora knew fine when she saw it. This Sidney female had caught him way off-guard. She was *good-Gawd* fine and had started to warm in his presence. He could smell swollen, wet female anywhere. His mind was bouncing off the crown molding and eighteen foot ceilings...he wondered when the last time had been for her, given she was married to a complete idiot.

"Seriously," she called down to him from the floor above, "how'd you get in?"

"The big oak outside the west end of the house. Need to get trimmers to cut some of the larger branches back from the windows as a security measure," he called out from where he stood.

He didn't bother to tell her that it was highly unlikely any average human male could hit that upper limb he'd used from a running jump, let alone a standing power leap, or even reach the distance from the branch to her window with enough remaining upper body strength to hang on with one hand and open the window and then flip in. But the lady needed some kind of explanation so she could sleep at night.

Besides, it was time to get out of here. He could feel all sorts of impressions making the hair on the back of his neck bristle. Heat trails soon became visible within the darkened space; he could see them like summer heat waves rising off asphalt, the hue crimson, emotions embedded within every band. Sidney Coleburn-West's tears. Cruel laughter. Shady deals. A bewildered woman. It didn't make any sense!

Brick dragged his fingers across his close-cropped hair and shook his head, forcing his canines not to lengthen. Why was it that some brothers had it all, but were such fuck-ups?

He peered up the stairs, hoping his new client would hurry. He would have given his eye-teeth for a normal life like this; a good wife, plush home, solid community rep, cash flow, the ability to have normal kids...Brick's eyes narrowed in the darkness. Leonora had told him all about it, had given him the female play-by-play as she'd begged him to take on her best friend's private case. Normally, he didn't do private matters like this—strictly corporate and municipal side deals—that way there was never anything personal involved. Now he was half sorry he'd relented, because Leonora didn't tell him how fine Sidney Coleburn-West would be, or how honest she'd smell, or how her soft, vulnerable scent would fill his nose and make him wanna howl...or that she'd been faithful, hadn't been touched during the two year divorce drama. Yet, now that he was here, he could smell it.

Sidney's footsteps brought him out of his thoughts as she came to the top of the landing.

"Mostly everything has been laundered and boxed from the cleaners or under plastic. That's the thing...he lives here on a legal basis to keep his ability to come and go as he pleases, but he doesn't *live* here." Her voice held a shaky quality of repressed rage and humiliation. "That's why I'd asked you to come as discreetly as possible and leave fast, because I never know when he'll come in or if he's having me trailed by a detective." She let out an exasperated breath. "That's all I'd need, would be for him to accuse me with having an affair, on top of everything else, when I've been a Girl Scout."

Sidney walked down a few steps and then stopped, as though afraid to come any closer to him. "Leonora told me you rarely meet and do business in public, so, I figured a brief meeting here so you could get whatever you needed could work, but..." She suddenly let out another ragged sigh. "All I found was an old brush and comb set. I don't know if you work with dogs, bloodhounds, or whatever, but—"

"The brush will do," Brick said, alighting the stairs in one fluid lope. He held out his hand, she tossed the brush down to him and he caught it with a quick grab. "That's enough, and I've seen the old wedding photos Leonora had. I know what he looks like, where he works, his favorite watering holes, and now I know what's at stake." He glanced at Sidney, his hot gaze traveling up and down her body and then he caught himself, and tore his gaze away. "My dogs will be on it. We'll find the rat bastard, where he hangs his hat at night, and what he does, who he does. We'll get it all on tape. No problem."

"Thank you," she said quietly, breathing out the words and beginning to twist the bottom edge of her sweater with nervous hands.

He definitely had to go. Brick began walking toward the front door. The breathy, sad resonance of Sidney Coleburn-West's voice had given him wood.

chapter two

Sidney stared at the front door for a long time. She'd watched it open and quietly close, and had witnessed an imposing presence gracefully glide through it with the stealth of a wolf. Whew…

She rubbed her hands down her face and quickly dashed down the stairs to turn on all the exterior flood lights and porch lights, double-checking every door and setting the alarm before going back upstairs.

But she stopped at her second floor office and peered at the wide-open window, studying the two-hundred year old oak tree beyond it. Pure amazement washed over her. Damn…if he could do that. It looked like an impossible divide, though? The nearest branch to the ground was something like twenty-five to thirty feet up…how in the hell? Too many questions battered her brain as she quietly closed the window, latched it, and made a mental note to call a tree surgeon in the morning.

Crisp fall air made her want a fire, even though building one always brought on the blues. She paused at what was now only *her* bedroom door and stared at the impressive mantle and fireplace. This was where she and Douglass were supposed to make love and make beautiful children. This was supposed to be their sanctuary. Now it was an abandoned place with a deadbolt lock on the door so he couldn't come in and possibly bug it while she was out— or come into her bedroom to start any crap while she was asleep. His mock living quarters were down the hall. She'd spent a mint checking and rechecking for electronic listening devices. Maybe he'd given up, as none were ever found. Paranoia was rife; his clear goal to make her lose her mind and break her spirit.

She didn't bother turning on the light as she entered the bedroom and simply disrobed in the dark, flinging her clothes to a nearby chair. Her body ached for a hug as she pulled her pastel pink chemise over her head and stepped into her lacy pajama boxers. She knew her way around the room by heart, blind. Nothing moved, and everything stayed the same; it was only her rattling around in the huge house…maybe she should sell it. In fact, she would, she told herself, as she slid beneath the soft white cotton linens and goose down comforter. That is, if Douglass would ever stop fighting her for it and would stop arguing over his so-called interest in it. But she'd bought this before they were even married as an investment property! Every piece of furniture in it was an heirloom handed down to her from her family. He had no right to take what her relatives had left her. Greedy SOB.

Sidney punched the pillows behind her and sank against them, trying to keep her focus on the moon beyond the large, leaded-beveled glass windows. Her eyes had adjusted to the shadows and she could make out most of the images in the room that were now bathed in blue-gray. Leaves from the trees made moving patterns against the sheer curtains as the fall wind blew. It was so pretty, so serene when the house was still. Once winter set in, the snow was gorgeous...that first pristine snowfall always did her in.

Yet as quickly as the peaceful thought swept over her, melancholy chased it away. The snow piled high outside, wood burning in the fireplace, brandy spiked hot chocolate, a lover's kiss, sweet and slow...that's what was supposed to fill this house, this home. Fall leaves burning in the yard, laughter. Spring flowers budding and beautiful, color-rich azaleas, the smell of fresh mowed grass, and sitting out on the deck with ice cold wine, planning a future together.

Isolation crushed in on her, making the comforter feel like a sarcophagus. Deafening silence smothered her. She glimpsed the clock but refused to wake up any of her friends at this unreasonable hour. Everybody had to get up and go to work the next day. She had to cope. Period. Obviously, the only reason she was tripping was because a tall, fine, male specimen had entered her home and that had triggered her memory of what it was like to want and be wanted. Under normal circumstances, she didn't even give those types of feelings a second thought. She was done with men for the time being. She focused on her career, her commitments, her friends, her social responsibilities, anything and everything but how robbed she felt...or the hole Douglass had left in her life.

"Brick." The random thought leapt out of nowhere.

She said his name with a sigh. Sidney shook her head and laughed quietly as she snuggled further under the covers. What kinda crazy nickname was that? A man named Brick, of all things, was gonna bring Douglass West down, just like the NBA players he managed. It was always something stupid, something from around the old neighborhood that was the Achilles' heel. Dang, what, besides his fabulous body, led to Brick being given that name? She could only imagine.

Her mind on fire, Sidney let out a deep sigh and closed her eyes, hating that her body had begun to warm again at the mere thought of the sexy mystery man that had appeared in her hallway. Mentally she stripped away his jacket and then his shirt. A slight shiver claimed her as she wondered what his chest would feel like, or how his tight nipples would feel beneath her palms. She swallowed hard as her own nipples tightened at the thought. Was he the silent type in bed, all steel jaw and control, or a howler? she wondered, allowing her fingertips to gently circle her breasts.

A stinging ache deep within her canal opened her thighs and brought her thumbs to slowly flick at the overly sensitive tips of her breasts. Her mind fastened upon his mouth while drawing out the sweet agony of pleasuring herself. Tonight she wanted it to last, rather than to have it be a quick and feral release.

Beneath the thicket of covers, she eased her chemise over her distended skin, allowing the silk to graze it in a gentle sweep. A quiet moan escaped her lips, and she hastened to lick her thumbs, and then brought them back beneath the covers to tease her nipples.

The sensation of wetness against the angry, pebbled

surfaces made her arch and lift her hips. Hot liquid seeped between her engorged folds and slid down the crack of her butt, causing her plump slit to throb. Unable to withstand the building sensation, one hand slowly traveled down her abdomen, while the other continued to tease her breast, her mind fixated on the intense eyes that met her in the darkened hall...the deep, rich timbre of voice that asked what she wanted to do...she wanted to do *this*. If she'd had more courage she might have breathed out the truth...might have said she wanted to be loved hard and made to feel whole for just tonight, have someone be her champion in more ways than one.

Her fingers slid across the plump lips slicked by her juices, her bud now almost too sensitive to touch. A gasp cut through the night, followed by a gut-deep moan. Her mouth hungered for a kiss, for the press of heavy flesh against flesh as timid fingers opened her lips, causing a shudder...a hand grasping at her breast, a cry renting the room the moment her clit was found. Flicks maddening, still the need for penetration bringing tears of frustration, drawing both hands to the cause in a frenzy...one to attend the over-ripe bud, the other to shove too-short fingers into a sopping, aching place too long ignored.

The orgasm came so fast and so furiously that it drew her up in halting jerks, tears streaming, but left her awash between half-satisfied and half-crazed. On her belly in moments, a wedge of pillows between her legs, a hand there beneath her, riding her fingers, trying to find the right spot, needing them deeper, thicker, and wider, moving against anything that would provide friction, her eyes shut tight, one image before her, driving her...Brick.

When she came this time, the covers had fallen away. Her body was left damp, cold with sweat. Her chemise was pulled over her breasts, pajama bottoms were askew, hair all over her head like a banshee's, and she was out of breath. Acute loneliness made her hide her face against the sheets and weep.

Brick remained very, very still in the shadow of branches, a part of the trunk. This was complete bullshit. He lowered himself down from the maple adjacent Sidney's window. He'd heard her call him, and had only doubled back to be sure her jerk husband hadn't come in on her to start some mess. At least that's what he told himself. And, yeah, it made sense for him to be sure she was okay...to just put a cursory eye on her to be on the safe side. No sense in scaring the woman to death, just a glance, then he was gonna be out.

Yeah, okay, so a glance turned into a little more when she snuggled down under the covers and got that look on her face...and the smell of her need hit his nose. And, although he wasn't completely human, he was indeed male, and what brother could just turn away from a woman in that condition, huh?

But she'd called his name...and oh, damn, was she hot. If he wasn't afraid of scaring the mess out of her, he would have gladly come through the window—but that would have been very uncool. Ringing the doorbell seemed like a better answer, especially since she was crying. Damn. Note to self, bare canines and rip that SOB's throat out if he blinks wrong.

Brick rounded the house and rang the bell, shifting

from foot to foot on the landing. The acute hard-on was giving him a headache. He could hear Sidney standing and moving through the house, but attempting to be quiet to act like she wasn't home. He leaned on the bell, knowing she was trying to be sure it wasn't Douglass playing games, or coming home drunk and high without his keys just to torture her.

Part of him knew this was a bad idea. He should have taken the money and walked, and not doubled back for drama. But seeing Sidney touch herself like that...the image was burned into his brain now and forever. Her rapid response, the way she'd turned over in agony, frenzied, gathering the pillows beneath her, then her lovely brown ass bobbing up and down. He closed his eyes and leaned on the bell, finally rewarded by having the front door crack open.

"Yes?" Sidney said, slightly out of breath, her eyes searching as she hid behind the huge oak obstruction. "I was asleep. I didn't hear you."

She wiped her face with the back of her robe sleeve and kept smoothing down her hair. The scent of her sex rendered him mute for a moment.

"Can I come in?" he said quietly after a brief pause, "before the neighbors see me?"

She immediately backed up and allowed him in and hurriedly shut the door, then hugged herself, looking self-conscious.

"I can't take your money," he said with a rush of breath, and then dug into his jacket pocket and handed her the envelope.

"Ohmigod," she said, her voice quavering. She thrust

it toward him, but he held up both hands refusing to take it. "You're not going to take my case? What did I do wrong...why—"

"I'm gonna take your case, and should have something within a week or so, but I'm not going to take your money. This one is on the house."

"Why?" she asked softly, her eyes searching his in the darkened foyer as she slid the envelope onto the crescent table nearby.

"Because you've been abused enough. I tripled my fee, what I told Leonora you should pay, because I don't generally do personal cases of the domestic variety. I hate 'em. Too messy. I didn't want this one."

"But..."

He nodded. "But I got involved. Now I sorta don't feel right charging you like I did."

Sidney nodded. "You want a drink or something?" She let her breath out hard. "I could use one."

"Yeah...sure. What do you have?" The scent and sight of her was giving him blue balls.

"What do you want?" She just stared at him for a moment.

He swallowed hard and didn't immediately answer. "Whatever you're offering." He wanted to kick himself.

"I've never done this before," she finally said in a quiet rush.

"I know," he murmured and came closer to her. "You're a beautiful, kind-hearted woman with a good soul...and this whole thing has been really messed up." He brushed a stray wisp of hair behind her ear but kept enough distance between their bodies as not to crowd her too quickly. "I'm not a permanent solution, Sidney…but I can be a temporary fix, if you want that."

She briefly closed her eyes as his hand slid against her ear. "I just want it to stop hurting for a little while."

"I understand anesthesia," he murmured, closing the gap between them and deeply inhaling her scent.

Two large tears welled in her eyes and spilled over her pretty lashes. She shook her head no. "I don't need anesthesia…I need morphine, this hurts so badly."

He wasn't sure if it was the build-up of what he'd witnessed, the close proximity to her soft skin, her fragrant sex, the tears, or the wavering sound of her voice, but he lost it, then and there. His mouth covered hers, and the kiss she returned was so eager that his hands swept up her five foot seven frame to lift her against him, his mouth devouring hers.

The taste of her soft tongue made his eyes cross beneath his lids. The softest hands he'd ever felt brushed his cheek, and then graceful fingers raked his hair. A whimper escaped from her mouth into his, and he began walking, blind, following her house floor plan by memory, taking the stairs in three foolish bounds. He had to chill, not really freak her out…but, damn, she was all that. He could still smell her essence on her fingers as her hands petted his face. The warmth of her mound against his stomach made his shaft fill as he walked, the wetness seeping through her silk boxers, dampening his t-shirt, his hands kneading her supple ass. Her skin felt like *butter*. Her hair pure silk. Every gasp she released sliced at his reason. If Douglass's stupid ass put a key in the door now, he'd be a dead man walking. There'd be no way to hide the canines.

He lowered her down onto her rumpled sheets, yanking

off his jacket while she worked at his shoulder harness. As much as he hated to, he leaned away from her softness, and slid off the holster, carefully dropping the Glock nine on the floor before stripping off his T-shirt.

She stared at him and breathed out the words "Oh... my...God..." in a very tense whisper.

He almost closed his eyes as her gaze raked down his torso and she leaned forward to unbuckle his pants. Somewhere sanity kicked in and he managed to get his Timberlands off so he could take off his pants. She was even more beautiful in the moonlight up close. The way her hand slowly went to her mouth when he finally got out of the leather made him look away. But as she pulled the flimsy fabric over her head and allowed her petite breasts to bounce free, he had to return his gaze.

His semi-callused hands seemed huge as they covered her breasts and she held his wrists, her head dropping back as the moan worked its way up from her depths. That sound she made was his undoing. He had to taste her, had to pull the small, bittersweet chocolate kisses between his lips...had to make her arch for him the way she had only a half hour prior. It was pure madness, moonlight inspired—a skin against skin inferno, his weight making her cry out and clutch his shoulders.

Her skin was a salty, creamy confection, his jaw dragging across the surface, then under swollen lobes down her quivering belly to wash his face in her sweet cum. Damn...this woman was fine, he'd lost all reason. Slick, burning inner thighs clenched his jaw as though trying to break it. Her voice had become another layer of aphrodisiac. He had to put it in. Then he froze.

"Baby, tell me you've got—"

"Oh, no!"

Sidney scooted out of his hold so quickly that all he could do was watch her. Disbelief claimed him—a gorgeous, naked, ready woman began ransacking drawers and had then disappeared into a walk-in closet. She came out clutching a purse, dumping the contents before she attacked another one. The sight of her frenzy was driving him to the brink. He couldn't stabilize his breathing. His voice was a ragged pant. Need carved at his testicles. The skin along his shaft and the head felt like it was splitting. It seemed as though the sound of his labored breaths was making her work harder. He tried to close his eyes against the sight of her to pull himself together, but couldn't.

Her firm, smooth, wet ass glistened in the moonlight. Her small, cone-shaped breasts swayed as she worked, riffling through purses. Her eyes were wild, her hair a beautiful sweep of tussled auburn, her long legs calling him, the prospect of them being wrapped around his waist enough to cause tears to form in his eyes.

She raised her fist and dropped a purse to the floor like a woman who'd hit lotto. "Got one!"

"How old is it?' he asked, still breathing hard.

"Oh, shit…"

He stood and went to her, and took her mouth in a hard kiss. "I'll work with what you've got for now, but we'll need more than one while the moon's still up."

She placed the foil packet in his hand. He studied it for a second and said a quick prayer.

"I'm sorry…I didn't expect—"

He captured her mouth again to stop her awkward

apology. In a strange way, he was pleased to know she hadn't lied about the abstinence. "I didn't expect this, either," he said in a hot wash against her ear, and then began to open the foil packet with slightly trembling hands. The quiet chant in his mind begged for the latex not to have dry rotted.

"I went out with Leonora and crew to one of our friend's bachelorette parties…they were throwing these at all of us and I kept one as a souvenir. Until now, I really forgot it was even in there."

"Glad you have a good memory," he said, struggling to fit it on.

"That was maybe eight months to a year ago." She looked up at him anxiously. "You think it's still good?"

Her breathy voice was kicking his ass as he worked to sheath himself. He was beyond answering her; she'd have to read his eyes, tell from the hard kiss, hear that it was okay in his breath and stop babbling apologies. "Baby, it's all right," he finally whispered, and gathered her into his arms to walk her back toward the bed while steadily kissing her.

"It only went halfway on, though," she murmured, her breath hot against his neck as she broke the kiss when they fell against the duvet.

"Most of them do." He looked down at her and gently spread her legs, loving the expression that washed over her face. "Towards the end, I'll have to hold it."

She closed her eyes. It was the sexiest thing he'd seen in a long time, the way she turned her head away from him and slid her eyelids shut as though the information was too much to bear, then she arched. He'd read her right, had heard her loud and clear, and positioned himself between her thighs, then entered her in one hard thrust. Her voice rent the room, his chasing it. She was so tight she'd left him twitching for a second.

Long, silky legs wrapped around his waist in a death grip. The need to move put him on all fours, her waist clutched in one massive forearm, the mattress leveraged by the other. He had to will himself not to shape-shift on her...but, damn, it was so good. She was human and it wasn't even a full moon, yet the sensations tearing at his groin had almost put hair on his knuckles.

Common sense dictated that he had to get his hand between their bodies, feeling the pending pleasure seizure begin to dredge his sack. She was sobbing, cumming hard again, her nails digging into his shoulders—just the way he loved it. He had to drop his head back to breathe and to make sure he didn't mess up and break her skin or cause a cut that could give her Lupine madness. His mind cried out what his mouth could never utter: *Sidney, sweet Sidney, you have to stop up-thrusting and bucking, sending slick spasms down my shaft!*

He caught the slippery rim of the condom nearly two seconds past two late as his body convulsed hard in a shuddering gasp, her cry threading through it. He needed to sink deep within her, but couldn't risk it with shaky latex. Instead he pulled out with a gasp, still heaving, his face buried in the crook of her neck, her sobs of pleasure making him want to throw caution to the wind.

Finally collapsing on his side, he pulled her to him and kissed her forehead, then sprawled out.

"You okay?" he asked through ragged breaths.

She nodded and laid her head on his chest, panting. "Yeah. Morphine...this was definitely morphine."

He smiled with his eyes closed. "Good. Lemme run to the store and I'll keep you anesthetized all night."

She leaned up on one elbow. "Here?"

He chuckled. "Yeah. Why not?" He reached over and yanked several tissues out of the box on her nightstand, and removed the condom, balling it up in the soft wad and tossing it in the trash.

She sat up slowly. "What if..."

Brick sat up with effort and slung his legs over the edge of the bed. "He's gotta prove it, just like you do. I hear real well and move real fast in the dark." He grabbed up his boxers and pants, and slid them on, then found his T-shirt, donning his shoulder holster and Glock. "But if you'd feel better, we could make a quick run up to King of Prussia and find a nice hotel?"

She smiled as she watched him dress. "This was a good temporary solution, Brick. I'm glad you came back."

"But..." He smiled and buckled his belt, knowing she wasn't about to leave her house tonight, and him coming back to rock her world for the rest of the evening was out. Once the edge had been taken off, clarity had set in. Sidney Coleburn-West was not going to be caught wrong in her own home.

"I don't want you to think—"

"It's cool," he said, sweeping her mouth with a gentle kiss. "Just don't over-process what just happened, all right?" He stroked her hair. "Promise me that."

She held his wrist and pressed a deep kiss into the center of his palm in a way that lowered his lids. "I won't," she breathed against his hand. "No guilt, no regret, just an awful lot of appreciation."

He found himself sitting on the edge of the bed. "Sure I can't coax you out for one more round?" he teased, kissing her bare shoulder.

She shook her head no and stroked his chest as she laid her head against it.

This woman was doing something weird to his normal love 'em and leave 'em philosophy. It felt very strange, indeed. "All right," he finally said. "You need me, for *anything*—especially if he comes in here off the wall—you call me. You know my cell number."

"I promise," she said, and kissed his mouth fully, her tongue sliding over his teeth. She pulled back and cupped his cheek for a moment and then looked at the moon. "Maybe when I'm really free...once this is all over, one whole night—no pressure...if you want to?"

Wow...that was supposed to be his line. If he wanted to? He swallowed hard, feeling his body responding to her all over again. "Yeah. Then lemme get moving on that information."

He stood, glimpsed the window, then remembered it would be better for him to not freak her out and simply slipped out the back door.

chapter Three

The moment Brick walked into the private after-hours wolf club, Leonora spotted him. She removed her arm off the shoulders of the lovely redheaded female she'd been with, kissed her cheek, and issued him a sly smile. He watched his buddy slip her lithe, athletic frame off the bar stool, her chiseled features and her short, curly black hair catching glints from overhead lighting as she approached with her beer in hand. The amusement in Leonora's large brown eyes almost made him head for the door.

Before Leonora had sauntered too close to him, he held up his palm to warn her not to start. It was all in the way she raised her nose just a tad, nostrils slightly flaring, and then laughed. He tried to focus on the back slap greetings from his fellow dawgs and to laugh with them, but his nerves were wire taut. Even though he smiled and seemed friendly enough, they sensed his unspoken tension, and backed off.

"Wow," Leonora said, coming closer to him. "I'm jealous. If you weren't the alpha male of the pack, I'd call you out for a challenge."

"So you got jokes," he muttered, one eyebrow raised, trying to get to his private table in the back. He could feel Leonora following him, her mirth making him jumpy. Sidney's touch, and the need for more of it, rubbed his emotions raw…just like the need to protect her from any harm suddenly had.

"Who's joking, brother?" Leonora flopped down beside him against the black leather cushioned booth with a wide grin, eyes beginning to glow with mischief. She plaintively ran her hands down her tawny suede lapels and brushed invisible lint off them. "I've been crazy about her for years, but she's straight as an arrow and a living doll. So…? Divulge all."

"C'mon, Leo. You know that's not my style." He accepted a Hennessey neat from the beaming waitress who brought it, and slid a twenty on her tray. "Thanks, baby."

"Any time, Brick," she crooned, and then made the international sign to call her with thumb and pinky extended next to her ear.

He just raised his glass to the over-friendly waitress without committing, glad for a distraction from Leonora's probing. But Leonora would not be dissuaded, and she tugged on his jacket sleeve like an excited puppy.

"Didn't I tell you she was all that?" Leonora leaned back in the booth and let out a sigh.

"She's real good people, Leo. Gotta give you that."

Leonora smiled. "And *fine*."

"Okay," he said, laughing. "And fine." He took a swig of his drink to try to quell the smile that thinking about Sidney had produced.

Leonora waved her hands in front of her chest. "No, no, no, no, no. Not fine. Fiiiooonne," she howled.

They both laughed hard.

"A'ight, so you want me to howl up in here, girl? Yeah, she's real fine."

"Now, I'm satisfied. Thank you." Leonora shot him a sideline look. "But don't mess over her, Brick. You might be the top dog, but I'll die trying to rip your throat out if you—"

"Hey, hey," he said, not offended in the least. "I said she's good people. I didn't say she was good tail." He looked at Leonora hard. "There's a difference."

Leonora finally relaxed and nodded. "Sho' you right," she muttered. "I had to finally accept that she was oblivious, didn't see me like that, but always had my back as a best friend…so…I just want the best for her. You feel me?"

"I feel you." He clinked his short rocks tumbler against her beer pilsner. "Much obliged."

"You owe me," Leonora said with a wink.

"For the rest of my life," he said, taking a deep swig of Hennessey.

"Whoa…that good?"

Brick just closed his eyes and set his glass down very precisely. "Talk me outta going back over there, Leo."

"Oh, *snap*…" Leonora murmured. "If I'm not mistaken, am I hearing that 'this is the one' tone in your voice—the tone that I've never heard before? The Mitchell Brickland, felled by a human female? Stop, *playin'!*"

He opened his eyes. "Keep your voice down, and no, I haven't been felled. She's just real nice. I gave her back her money."

"Damn, dawg. You're a goner." Leonora cocked her head to the side. "And it wasn't even a full moon yet."

"I know. But I'm cool. She just caught me by surprise— you didn't say how nice she'd be, and you shoulda warned a brother, for real." He could feel his hair beginning to bristle on the back of his neck the wider Leonora smiled. It made him testy. "You ain't right, Leo. Now I've gotta hunt that bastard down, but she doesn't want bloodshed. That ain't our way, and you know it—once we go on the hunt, shit, anything's liable to kick off." Brick dug into his back pocket and flung Douglass West's old brush onto the table. "Got his scent in my nose, picked up his foul vibe from the house, but all she wants is pictures."

Leonora looked at him very hard, her eyes meeting his. "Now you know why I asked for the pack alpha to check this out...why I'd begged you to look into this for years? I met him. Hated him from the start, but my girlfriend was in love, wanted to be married so badly she went deaf, dumb and blind for a minute." Leonora leaned forward and covered Brick's forearm with her hand. "I would have savaged that son of a bitch a long time ago, but you said no human kills in the territory so authorities wouldn't get jumpy. But you see how he's doing my girl?"

Brick polished off his drink and set it down hard. Thinking about Sidney still made his balls ache. "Yeah, I saw. But I feel like you set me up, Leo, 'cause you also understand why the rule is no domestic disputes. We settle the big shit. The domestic, we don't touch because half the time the victim falls back in love with the perp and then would wanna start a wolf hunt for the so-called murder

of the guy who was gonna put her in her grave, anyway."
He stood quickly, making Leonora bolt up with him.

"Yo, yo, yo partner," Leonora said, landing a hand on
his shoulder. "Easy, man. You okay? You're showing
canines and got half the bar bristling and ready to follow
you out the door."

Brick rubbed his palms down his face and let his breath
out hard. "I'm cool. That's why I came here, first, and
didn't go looking for him tonight."

"Lemme buy you another Henny," Leonora soothed.
She looked Brick up and down. "I thought you got some
and were chill?"

"I said I was all right," he snapped, hailing the waitress
to refill their drinks, and then sat down again with a thud.

Leonora chuckled softly and spun his empty rocks glass
around on the table. "Yeah, I feel you. A little taste just
left a brother hankerin' for more."

Falling asleep was next to impossible now. Sidney lay
awake staring at the ceiling, her life in complete chaos.
What had she just done? This was the craziest, most spon-
taneous, and possibly most dangerous thing she'd ever experienced. Leonora was out of her mind. No...*she* was out
of her mind!

Bolting out of bed, she raced across the bedroom and
down the hallway, then ran downstairs and snatched up
the envelope that she'd left on the table. Then, slowly but
surely, she retraced her steps like a thief, making sure that
nothing was out of order, and that all traces of Brick's
home invasion were gone. Finally back in her bedroom,
she stashed the wad of cash in the safe within her large

walk-in closet, and then rushed out, suddenly remembering the condom-filled tissue ball in her wastebasket.

She stopped short and froze. Douglass was leaning against her doorframe with a satisfied smile.

"Took you long enough, Sid," he said, straightening his French cuffs beneath his navy Armani.

"Leave my bedroom," she said, going to the telephone and calling his bluff. She picked up the receiver and held it, her fingers poised to dial, but she dared not look at the wastebasket. DNA evidence; she'd really be screwed.

"Neighbors have eyes, even in this very shrub-intense, single family, tree-lined environment." He chuckled and pushed off the doorframe, standing just outside it.

Her heart was beating so hard it made her ears ring. But just like he could never be nailed for circumstantial evidence, neither could she. Seeing a man enter and leave was one thing, proving any wrong-doing was another. After all, Brick was a licensed investigator. He had indeed been hired and had a right to be here...now what he did once he'd arrived was an entirely different question.

Sidney lifted her chin. How many women had Douglass screwed from the month after they'd been married onward? She'd gone for counseling, then papers, because the man refused to stop. Now he was using? Fuck it, this was her house.

"You need to watch your back, Douglass," she crooned as sarcastically as possible, after the brief pause needed to collect herself.

"Oh, my, my, is that a threat I've caught on tape?"

"No," she said evenly, setting down the phone to go to the door. "He's security because I was feeling threatened by you. The neighbors will be seeing a lot of him. Do let them know so they won't be alarmed." With that, Sidney slammed the bedroom door in Douglass's smug face and flipped the deadbolt.

Shaken, she crossed the room and hugged herself and stared out the window at the moon. Whoever the neighborhood stoolie was, she was just thankful they hadn't been able to call Douglass home sooner. An hour earlier and she would have had to leave with her tail tucked between her legs. But there was no guilt. The marriage had long been destroyed and Douglass was no angel. He was obviously still high, and didn't need to know that she'd hired an investigator. But she did like the little lie she'd told him about Brick being her bodyguard, even though Brick didn't do that type of work. However, she sorta liked the sound of it, and man oh man did Brick guard her body well tonight. But leave it to Douglass to even ruin her most private thoughts.

Sidney picked up the wastebasket with a sigh and headed for the bathroom to flush the contents.

Someone was banging on the front door like the police. The sun was blinding her. Sidney rolled over, glimpsed at the clock and shrieked. It was 10:00 a.m. She hadn't called the office, hadn't set her alarm clock the night before, and in her fury with Douglass, hadn't set the phone back in the cradle properly—so it was off the hook.

Snatching her robe, she unlocked her bedroom door and called out that she was on her way down, yanking on the baby blue silk cover-up while still running. When she got to the door, it was the police—Leonora.

"Can I help you, officer?" Sidney said laughing as she flung open the door. "Do they teach that scare-you-to-death banging at the Academy, girl?"

Leonora's expression didn't change as she responded, her eyes hidden behind dark aviator sunglasses and the bill of her hat set to perfection. "I was worried. You didn't come to work, didn't call in, phone was off the hook. It's not like you to just be AWOL."

"Girl, come in," Sidney said, breezing out onto the porch landing and hugging Leonora. "I can explain all, and if you have time for a cup of coffee...I have some really, really juicy stuff to tell you," she added with a giggling whisper. "Ohmigod, Leo...it's...just let me check to see if Douglass got out of here, and we have to talk and have our coffee in my bedroom, because who knows if he's tried to drop another device in here."

Sidney watched a slow smile come out of hiding on Leonora's face, then Leonora took off her hat, stashed it under her arm, and nodded.

"Fifteen minutes, then I go back to chasing bad guys."

"Okay, let me case the house," Sidney said, feeling like she could fly as she dashed around to every room checking for signs that Douglass had left.

She couldn't stop giggling as she buzzed into the kitchen, satisfied that he'd gone, and then quickly began making coffee while talking a mile a minute in code.

"I'll call the office after you leave and cite a migraine. This morning, I just needed time to really sleep in and rest...and I feel sooo relaxed, more than I have in years, girl!"

She took down two huge mugs from the wall and fixed Leonora her brew just the way she knew her best friend always liked it, four sugars and black, and then she fixed hers with one sugar and lots of cream. The only thing that puzzled her was that while she prattled on, Leonora was extra quiet this morning, when normally her home-girl was as boisterous as all get out. The only thing she could chalk it up to was the fact that Leonora had obviously been so worried that Douglass had finally done her some real bodily harm, it was taking her a minute to recalibrate herself.

Leonora watched Sidney zoom around the kitchen, her robe moving over her soft, pretty skin...breasts unfettered, swaying beneath a wash of blue...the lovely, smooth lobes of her butt brushed by silk...long, gorgeous legs flashing out, graceful hands preparing coffee for two, her mouth still looked kiss punished—hair a tussle of auburn velvet all over her head. Even just out of bed the woman got her aroused. Plus, Sidney still faintly smelled like sex, and she'd never picked up that scent on her before. It was always a fantasy, one locked deeply away and never allowed near the surface where a friendship could be destroyed by overstepping bounds.

But then Brick had opened Pandora's Box by coming into the club looking pained, no—starved was a better word...like a man who'd just been given a sniff and then sent away. It fanned the flame of the fantasy, caused a hunger that was hard to ignore.

Leonora steadied her breathing as she watched Sidney from behind. She understood what Brick was going through...knew that feeling well, that ache, that need produced by one totally unaware. And although her friend knew she was open to alternatives, she didn't know to what degree she'd been the object of secret desire for years.

"So, let's go where we can talk," Sidney said brightly, coming up to Leonora and giving her a big hug. "I love you, girl!"

Leonora held her close for a little longer than advisable and nuzzled her hair. "I love you, too, lady."

Sidney broke away. "I'm all right—now. Don't worry." She beamed at Leonora and handed her a mug and then danced away, crooking her finger for her to follow.

Leonora pushed off the counter. Her body still burned where Sidney's had pressed against it. If she'd done this to Brick, she now understood her pack-leader's condition. By the time she'd reached the top of the stairs, after watching Sidney's bottom bounce up and down before her, she could barely breathe. But once in the bedroom, where the lingering sex scent was more pungent, even though normal humans wouldn't have been able to detect it, the ache between her legs was so acute she couldn't sit down.

Sidney latched the door behind them, took a huge slurp of coffee, and then set her mug down on the dresser. "Girl…" she said, her voice a hiss of excitement.

Leonora closed her eyes and held onto the mug with both hands.

"I know, I know, you think I'm crazy, Leo…but that guy, Brick, you sent over here to do the job…whew!"

"I told you he was awesome," Leonora said flatly and then took a long sip from her mug.

"No, no, no—you did not tell me he was *all that* and smack-yo-Momma fine. No. You left that out, girl. You just said he was good at what he does, and you did not tell me how good he was at *that,* either!"

Leonora begrudgingly smiled. "He's good people, and yeah, the man is fine."

"Are you blind?" Sidney rushed up to her friend and suddenly kissed her cheek. "Leo, you know I haven't been laid in two years...you know how bad Douglass treated me before that." She held Leonora by both arms, threatening to spill her coffee. "I was so horny last night, I thought I'd lose my mind...then he came back, and well...I lost my mind."

Leonora's mouth opened and closed. "You actually went all the way...and did him?"

Sidney looked both ways and leaned into Leonora so she could whisper into her ear. "Ohmigod, gurl, it was so freakin' hot that I was in here sobbing. He gave me my money back, but somehow I wanna give it back to him for what he did last night...but I don't want him to feel like it's a slap in his face—like I'm saying I'm paying for *that,* but I also don't want him to feel like I'm trying to get over on him...I don't even know this man or his whole name—this guy who peels out of the shadows like he's the dag-gone darkness itself, and can jump a tree limb from thirty feet at a dead stand." She pulled back from Leonora, their bellies still touching and stared her in the eyes. "I know I sound crazy, perhaps I am, but now getting with him is all I can think about. Do you know what I mean?"

"Yeah," Leonora said, her voice a gravelly rasp. "When you want something so badly, it's right there, and you're so hot you don't know what to do because it's been so long. I feel you."

Sidney nodded. "But I have to keep my perspective.

He's here to do a job, not to get all complicated in my crazy, lonely life—I know that. What happened was probably just an accident on his part...and mine, because I was in such a bad way. But I really like this guy—although, I don't know anything about him."

"You're gonna have to ask him to divulge all, because he's my buddy, too," Leonora said, caressing Sidney's cheek with the pad of her thumb.

Sidney captured Leonora's hand and pressed a hard kiss into the center of her palm. "I know. I respect that." She sighed and broke their embrace, and went to fetch her cooling coffee. "But I'm not going to lie. I'm just so..."

"Horny right now," Leonora breathed out and took a healthy slurp of her coffee.

"Yeah, girl," Sidney said, laughing. She flopped down on the bed and held her cup with both hands. "I need some *so* bad. Just one more time. Do you hear me?"

Leonora nodded, the ache between her thighs now almost unbearable. She was so wet that she feared it would show through her uniform pants. But she tried to keep a steely grit, even though every breath made her nipples sting. "It's been a real long time for me, too, girl. I know. I can't even talk about it."

Sidney sighed. "Life shouldn't be this hard."

Leonora didn't move, but continued watching Sidney as she popped up from the bed and abandoned the coffee mug on the nightstand, then went to her underwear drawer. Leonora's eyes followed her around the room as she hunted for a clean bra and panties she would wear that day after she showered. She knew the routine by heart, it had fueled so many fantasies that she'd begun timing her appearances at Sidney's door just to be able to watch her get dressed. By rote, Sidney kept talking, the words becoming more distant as Leonora watched her disrobe.

But she could barely hold her black coffee as Sidney casually stripped blue silk away from her body, and the sunlight from the windows bathed her petite breasts in golden rays. Leonora could feel her lids lowering; it was almost too much to take in and not be able to go to touch her. Sidney's caramel-hued nipples were relaxed and she wished for a cool breeze to make them tighten in her sight. If she could just lick them, pull them between her lips, just once...feel Sidney's tongue against hers, taste her pretty mouth...feel her damp, silky hair as her hand slid over her mound. Just the thought of that was causing her breaths to grow shallow. Coffee notwithstanding, between every sip her mouth went dry.

Leonora allowed her gaze to slide down her friend's flat abdomen toward the thatch of dark, silky hair that she'd do anything to taste. There was no doubt about it; she'd have to stop home for ten minutes alone in the bathroom after seeing Sidney like this.

"I'll be out in a second," Sidney called over her shoulder. "Or you can come in and sit on the toilet like we always do, so we can still talk—like I have a million questions—just say, 'no, I can't go there,' or 'yes, I can answer that.' I *promise* to respect your boundaries, girl, really, really I will—but this man is...wow."

"No problem," Leonora murmured, sipping her lukewarm java. "Brick, you're one lucky SOB," she whispered, and then pushed off the dresser to go watch Sidney shower.

* * *

Leonora was practically panting by the time she'd gotten back into the police cruiser. Watching the water cascade down Sidney's naked, cinnamon body...seeing her lather herself through the glass shower door, the steam a sensual cloak making her hotter as she watched...then the whole process of her girlfriend toweling off, applying cream to her skin...then putting on the sexiest, sheerest, ice pink bra and panties.

She understood Brick's dilemma very well. Leonora swallowed hard, got out of the vehicle, and bound up the steps of her apartment building. She was gonna lose her job for sure, as she'd been where she wasn't supposed to be all morning. She was just glad that it had been relatively quiet. By now, her normal lunch break time, she was near insane.

Fumbling with her keys, she hurried into the building and didn't wait for the elevator. She hated being single. Her last girlfriend break-up still stung, and six months was a very long time to be solo...especially with Miss Sidney prancing around naked.

As soon as Leonora opened and slammed the door behind her, she headed for the bathroom, tossing her hat on the sofa like a Frisbee as she passed it.

Her starched, blue shirt felt like it was strangling her, and she fumbled with the tie and buttons at her neck just to get it partially opened. The moment she did, she let out a quiet groan and covered both breasts with her palms. Her nipples stung so badly that she couldn't immediately bring her hands away from them; they'd ached to be touched for hours. As she flicked her thumbs across them, coaxing them out over the edge of her bra, the long-awaited sensation made her rhythmically squeeze her thighs together.

Panting, her hips undulating against nothing, she finally brought her hands to her belt and slacks fastenings. She was so swollen and so wet that the slightest caress, even through the fabric, made her gasp. Her bud was throbbing, agony rippled in waves up her canal—she dug her hand into her pants, fingers instantly sliding against her drenched slit, causing her to swoon against the door, and almost cum the second she touched herself.

Steadier now, Leonora leaned against the door for a few minutes, catching her breath, her eyes closed, clothes disheveled. Slowly she peeled herself away from the shut door and approached the sink to wash her hands and splash cold water on her face. She peered up into the mirror and stared at her reflection. "Damn, Brick. How'd you walk away, man?" In fact, how did Douglass West just walk away?

She splashed her face again with water and grabbed a towel, sheepishly looking at her backside to see if she'd wet her pants through. That's the last thing she'd need, as she didn't have time for a whole uniform change. Maybe she could just shimmy her slacks down and wipe several times with a wad of tissue.

Then it hit her as she bent over the sink to clean herself up. The only way Doug West would have been able to really walk, was if he wasn't even into Sidney in the first place.

Leonora stood very slowly. All the cheerleaders and extraneous booty in the clubs…a cover-up. The brother was on the DL. Damn. Time to get Madame Irvinia in the mix.

chapter four

"Madame Irvinia is the only way!" Leonora argued, grabbing Brick's arm.

"The woman said she didn't want her husband hurt," Brick yelled, wrenching out of Leonora's hold. "You know that old lady's got enough mojo to make a werewolf heel, so—"

"The girl said no violence, but she didn't say—"

"She didn't say plagues, boils, cancer, a stroke, a car accident by way of an eighteen wheeler collision off a cliff, a—"

"Okay, okay, I hear you," Leonora grumbled. "But you oughta let her throw the bones and kill a chicken to save us some time and aggravation in finding out when and where the trail begins on West's secret life."

Brick stopped pacing in his Center City apartment and bristled. "What's with the 'us'? I thought this was my case, my kill? I thought you'd brought the alpha in on the job to bring closure to the problem, once and for all?"

Leonora looked away. "Yeah, well, she's still my best friend."

"She'll always be that, but you best be clear where the line is."

Leonora's eyes still didn't meet Brick's as she spoke. "I thought you said last night that she hadn't taken you there...permanent-like. That you were *cool*."

It was his turn to look away. He couldn't answer Leonora right now, not about this Sidney thing he hadn't figured out. "Let's go see Madame O," he said in a near snarl. "We'll pick up the trail, and get this bad guy out of the woman's life...then later, me and you can squabble over the bones."

Leonora begrudgingly nodded. "Fine."

She'd been jittery at work all day. Once she'd gotten there. Sidney looked up from her stack of briefs and stared out the window for a moment. Sure she'd risen like a rocket to become one of the youngest partners in her firm, but she was still a long way from the corner office. She was still the new kid on the block. The older attorneys had dug in like ticks and sucked primo resources off the top, first.

Yet as she watched the sun set, sending a rose-orange light to reflect off the high-rise panes, she suddenly realized that the thrill of the chase, the adrenaline rush of the corporate climb had quietly died within her. Winning, losing, it didn't feel like it mattered. It was all a game. Pointless. A secret part of her just wanted to roam free...feel the rush of exploring new lands, new sensations, feel the sun on her face and wind at her back. Brick.

Sidney set her pen down very slowly and took off the reading glasses that were poised on the bridge of her nose. She closed her eyes and gave herself strong counsel. *Don't go there.* She'd worked too hard for too long to allow one wild night to destroy it all. There was too much invested, her life was too orderly. For the same reason she'd fight Douglass tooth and nail to protect what was hers as a matter of principle, she wouldn't let a tall, fine interloper tear out her soft underbelly. No one would ever get that close to a sure kill again.

She opened her eyes and quickly stood, wondering where the horrific imagery of being surrounded by wolves came from. She hadn't had those types of terror-filled thoughts in years.

An hour and a half on the road in rush-hour traffic left him feeling penned in and trapped. Now inside the little clapboard house in Reading, Pennsylvania, a sense of claustrophobia was strangling him. He needed to run and run hard.

Brick kept his gaze sweeping as they waited for the old woman to get done in the next room. Normally, he and his pack members came to Madame Irvinia late—after the human regulars had gone. But this was an impromptu visit.

As inconspicuously as possible he tested for scents, his line of vision trapping bundles of herbs, Gris Gris pouches, bones and feathers stashed over doorways. Rickety tables with matchbooks to level them out held tasseled shade lamps. Overstuffed chairs covered in tattered crimson and gold velvet drew one in, but he sat on the edge, not sure what powder or potions might have been shoved deep within the cushions.

From a sideline glance he studied his road partner. Leonora's ears moved ever so slightly, picking up the faintest sound. She was a very cool alpha female, as much

as she got on his nerves. Mild chaos tumbled in his gut—
friends weren't supposed to fall out with each other over
a woman. As long as the object of desire was unclaimed,
then the rivalry would go on, hot pursuit eminent. But
once she'd been claimed, then…yeah, competitors would
chill and go back to being buddies.

Problem was, it was too soon to tell, and he wasn't
trying to stake a claim—yet. And it just wasn't protocol
to run hard after your best friend's hunt, and then not
really want it. He had to know for sure, 'cause him and
Leo went way back. Brick stared at the door, willing
Madame Irvinia to hurry with her divination. Sidney
Coleburn-West was becoming a problem.

After forty agonizing minutes, the parlor door flung
open, and a nervous-looking young woman clutching her
purse and a tissue slipped out with Madame Irvinia not
far behind. Brick and Leonora were instantly on their feet.

"Now you remember what I told you to feed him, right?
You want him back, that's what you gotta do. You want him
dead, come back and I'll give ya something different." The
older woman dabbed sweat away from the scoop neckline
of her purple and yellow flowered housecoat. "Don't change
my recipe, either, or ya might accidentally neuter that fool."

The young woman wiped at her tears, nodded quickly,
and then mumbled her thanks as she rushed out the
front door.

Brick gave Leonora an I-told-you-so glance, which his
friend ignored. Madame Irvinia issued him a jaunty pout
and folded her arms over her sagging bosom.

"Now I know its gots ta be bad for you ta bring yo' rusty
behind to see dis ole lady." Madame Irvinia smiled a tooth-

less grin, her wrinkled, dark face stretched wide from the effort. She opened her scrawny arms, flabby biceps wiggling like a rooster's comb as she went to Brick for a hug.

Laughing, he bent and pulled the elderly woman close. "Been a long time, Mom Irv."

"You watch out for my wig, boy," she said, swatting him away with mirth and adjusting what looked like a matted, dead gray cat on her head.

"Oh, so I don't get no love," Leonora said, bumping Brick out of the way to sweep Madame Irvinia into a hug.

"Aw, baby, don't you be jealous," Madame Irvinia crooned. "You know you my pumpkin." She kissed Leonora's cheek. "C'mon into the kitchen—my conjurin' room. Y'all look like you both need some real mojo tonight."

Douglass pushed the envelope across his polished oak desk toward two thick-bodied street mercenaries. Dark shades hid their eyes, but the bomber jackets couldn't hide their physical bulk.

"I want her hurt and scared, not dead. If she's killed, it'll seem too suspicious given our long property settlement battle. I can't afford that."

Both henchmen nodded.

"We got you," one said, standing and tucking away the envelope into the breast pocket of his jacket.

"Anybody could get mugged in Center City." The other henchmen shrugged with a wicked smile. "Parking lots are dangerous at night."

They watched the old woman flop down at her yellowing linoleum kitchen table, putting strain on an elderly, plastic-covered dinette chair. Brick eased himself into one, noting that Leonora did the same, half afraid that their weight would make their chairs give way.

"Y'all want some tea?"

"No," Brick and Leonora said in unison, and then backed off to mellow the response.

"Just ate, Mom," Brick said, glimpsing Leonora.

"You know me, Ma—I'm good. I don't eat much till after midnight," Leonora said.

Madame Irvinia sucked her teeth. "I wouldn't root y'all—you's good as kin. 'Sides, what would the point be? Ya already got more on ya than you can practic'ly bear. Humph!"

"Now don't get testy, Mom. We're just sorta in a rush," Brick soothed, reaching across the table to grasp the elderly woman's hand.

Still salty from the rebuff, Madame Irvinia withdrew her hand. "That's my conjurin' hand, best be careful, and it got Arthur—so don't be grabbin' it with your big paw."

Leonora swallowed away a smile. "He didn't mean no harm, Ma. He's just all messed up over this human female, and needs a little advice."

"Speak for yourself," Brick muttered.

Madame Irvinia narrowed her gaze but the smile tugging at the corners of her mouth gave her away. "Seem like ya both is hankerin for the same bone, but that ain't my business."

Leonora looked away. Brick gave the elderly woman a sheepish sideways glance and chuckled.

"That's not why we're here, really. See, we can't just hunt down this guy that's been giving our client the blues,"

Brick explained, trying to reason with Madame Irvinia while eying Leonora's agitation.

"Why not?" Madame Irvinia fussed. "If he's a complete horse's ass, which he'd have to be if y'all took the case, then…"

"The lady said no violence," Leonora groaned, throwing her hands up in the air with disgust.

"Then why'd y'all take the case!" Madame Irvinia pushed away from the table and grunted.

Brick raised an eyebrow and looked at Leonora. "Because it was *a friend* of Leo's—*that's why.*"

"So, how long you been going with this girl, Leonora?" Madame Irvinia asked, standing in a huff. "How she got your nose so wide open as a human dat she kin tell you not to hunt down a threat as a wolf? You tell her what you was yet, baby? You shape-shift on her so she could see? 'Cause there was no reason to get this big lug all up in it, if you was gonna make him repress his hunt. You don't call in an enforcer for minor squabbles, ya know dat. I don' know if I got anything in my cabinets strong enough to keep his wolf down, once a threat scent is in his nose, baby, so—"

"I'm not sleeping with her," Leonora said quietly. "She's straight…just my best friend."

Madame Irvinia glanced from Leonora to Brick. "Well she done slept with somebody up in here, and it weren't me, I tell ya, 'cause I picked up a nookie aura the moment you two crossed my threshold."

Brick looked out the window over the sink. "We've gotta get pictures, track him, come up with enough evidence to pin on him, so the lady can get out of the sham of a marriage she's in," he muttered, deflecting the charge.

"What!" Madame Irvinia rounded the table and stood before Brick with her arms folded. She then shook her head. "Whoooo boy. Fresh, too. Not even twenty-four hours old since ya got some, is it?"

"Mom..."

"Uh, huh. And she wants *you* to be non-violent? She know you a wolf?"

He looked at the floor. "No. Just a tracker. She doesn't believe in the supernatural."

"What!"

Both Leonora and Brick cringed as the old woman's voice hit a decibel that hurt.

"She's *real* straight," Leonora said. "As in mainline suburban."

"Aw, Lawd." Madame Irvinia slapped her forehead. "Mitchell Brickland, lemme tell you somethin', young man." She pointed a gnarled finger toward his chest, but her voice was gentle. "This ain't nothin' but heartbreak, ya hear me? She ain't gonna be able to deal with you howling at no full moon." She then looked at him hard when he turned away from her, and cupped his cheek. "Baby, you best stop messin' with her right now 'fore you give her what you got. Understand?"

Brick shrugged out of the caress and stood. "It ain't about all that. We're just here to get a clean line on where to sniff. It's more efficient than running around for a few nights trying to pick up the trail. All we need is a start point."

"Ma...what he's saying is, after being with her, he can't go tracking to all the places our client's threat has been. The longer Brick hunts, the worse the urge to bring West down like road kill will get, and within a few nights when the moon goes full, he might not be able to keep his word to our client not to rip the bastard's throat out—especially if that jerk steps wrong."

Leonora sighed and leaned her head back against the kitchen wall while sitting with her eyes closed. "This was my fault, really. I never shoulda introduced the two of 'em."

Madame Irvinia waved her hand. "Aw, ain't no blame, ain't no fault. It is what it is. Humph. She must be a pretty lil' thang to have y'all all messed up like this." She sighed and sat down again on the creaky chair. "All right. Whatchu got? Something from the threat, something from your client. Thas what I need to go to work."

Panic swept through Brick. "I only brought what she gave me of his." He produced the brush and slid it across the table towards Madame Irvinia.

But the old woman cut Leonora a glare. "Give it up. I needs it to get a bead on thangs."

A rush of rosy pink flushed Leonora's cheeks as she kept her gaze on the sink ahead and dug deep into her pants pocket to produce a pair of lacy, pink boxers. The low growl that rumbled in Brick's throat started way down deep in his diaphragm. Leonora's lip curled into what was beginning to be a snarl. Instantly, both potential combatants were on their feet. Madame Irvinia snatched the garment and banged on the table.

"She met her first, Brick—and if ya start some crazy dog fight up in my house, I'll root ya both. Now sit!"

It took a moment, but after a bit, Brick and Leonora flopped back down, ignoring the shaky condition of the furniture and smoothing the hair at the napes of their necks. Madame Irvinia gave them both a warning glare and sucked her teeth, then pulled a small pouch of stones and bones from her cleavage and cast the contents on the table amid the brush and panties.

"He's a real smacked ass, ain't he?" the old woman said, studying her bizarre spread. "Yeah, I can see the attraction y'all have for 'er. She's got a heart of gold and a little wolf in her, too." She looked up to stunned expressions with a smile. "Uh, huh. Got bit by a stray dog that lived through a Lupe attack when she was an itty-bitty thang. Had to be a Beta or maybe one of the pack's adolescent pups that tangled with it, but the mangy creature lived to bite that sweet thang. She's scared ta death of dogs. Y'all know that?"

She-scent wafting off Sidney's panties and the information Madame Irvinia had just given him, made Brick stand and pace. His heart was suddenly thudding too hard within his chest and he needed to run, be outside, wanted to feel the fall air rushing through his coat.

"'Nuff to almost make ya shift on the spot, ain't it, boy?"

He ignored Madame Irvinia's chuckles and went to the sink so he could stare out the window.

"Go, 'head. You can open it. Ya look like you need you some air—don' be passin' out on my floor, my kitchen ain't dat big."

Leonora stood and leaned against the wall, seeming faint. "I knew she was scared of dogs all her life…she told me she'd been bitten…showed me the small scar from the stitches once…on her calf. I just never knew the dog was a carrier." Her voice drifted off becoming a murmur of appreciation. "Damn, no wonder we both have it so bad for Sid."

Brick glanced at Leonora over his shoulder, annoyed

that he'd missed the scar in the dark despite the intimate encounter. Now he wanted to touch that place she'd been nipped…kiss it, find it on her shapely cinnamon leg. "Me and you have got to get to a place of peace on this, Leo."

Leonora nodded. "I love her…but she told me she was flip-top over you when I stopped by there this morning."

Brick pushed away from the sink, knowing the information Leonora had given him was a peace offering. The part about Sidney's reaction to him almost made him hyperventilate. Still, the fact that Leonora had gone over to Sidney's so soon after they'd been together bothered him. "You saw her this morning?"

"Get over it," Leonora snarled. "It's our routine. She makes me coffee, I have it in her bedroom so we can talk like girls—while she gets dressed and takes a shower."

It took everything in him not to lunge. Just the idea that Leonora got to watch Sidney get naked and shower in broad daylight, and he hadn't, made him irrational. "From this point on, that's out!"

"You making a claim on that territory—or is it still wide open and up for grabs?"

"It's claimed!" he shouted before his brain could consult his mouth.

"Good!" Leonora shouted back. "And you'd better not mess her over, either! She deserves the real deal, permanent mate bond! You got that?"

"I got it, you got it. Leo? Don't fuck with me, I'm serious!"

"Whooowe," Madame Irvinia exclaimed, shaking her head, and making the two wolves remember that she was in the room. "Boy, you just made you a declaration with a witness."

Brick ran his palm over his bristling hair and turned back toward the window. Somehow the half smile he glimpsed on Leonora's face just before he turned away made him feel like he mighta just gotten set up. But still, there was no doubt about it; Sidney Coleburn-West definitely had his nose wide open.

She said goodnight to the evening guard by rote and got on the elevators that led to the parking garage. It seemed like she'd worked insane hours her whole life, and ever since her marriage had crumbled, she'd taken it to an entirely new level of workaholism. But what else was there to do? she mused, digging her keys out of her purse. Now was not the time to slack off. No telling what Douglass would do or what he would take and she needed to be shielded with a nice nest egg if he got half of her assets.

The urge to call Brick was making her palms itch, but she held her head up and clutched her purse, car keys, and briefcase, refusing to go for her cell phone as she crossed the concrete divide. An eerie sense of being watched made her hesitate, glance around, and then hasten her steps. When she reached her silver BMW, she froze.

"Hey pretty lady," a deep voice said, as a man with a ski mask and large gun stepped out from behind a steel column.

Her voice and breath were trapped in her throat for a second, and then logic quickly swept through her as she held out her purse.

Another figure stepped behind her, boxing her in between her car and the adjacent vehicle.

"Smart, too," the man behind her said, and then suddenly yanked her against him.

The gun leveled at her forehead kept the scream inside her chest. But feeling the hard body behind her with an erection gouging into her butt cheek made her terror impossible to hide. Panic sweat made the fabric of her blouse and slacks instantly stick to her. Pinpoints of light were beginning to dance before her eyes. She felt nauseous, couldn't breathe.

"Please, don't hurt me," she whispered as a huge forearm crushed her windpipe. "Just take the money—please...there's credit cards, everything in my bag."

"Don't you like it when they beg, man?" the man holding her asked his accomplice.

The gunman ripped Sidney's purse from her shoulder. "Love it, 'specially when they're this damn fine."

A low growl made the gunman whirl around. The man holding Sidney backed up, dragging her as a body shield. From the shadows a large, black wolf stalked out, head hug low, canines glistening, eyes a strange, reflective gold. It moved forward slowly; its shoulders the height of the BMW's hood. Her scream echoed through the lot, but neither the gunman nor the man half-strangling her seemed to care.

"Shoot it!" the man holding Sidney yelled, pulling her further away as his partner backed up.

Appearing almost paralyzed with fear, the man holding the gun lifted it ever so slightly for better aim. Sidney saw it in slow motion; the minute movement of his arm. The enormous animal before him leapt to the right in a blur, landed on a car hood, then zigzagged to the roof of her Beamer as the mugger spun and squeezed off erratic rounds. Before she could blink, the gunman had lost an arm and she shrieked and turned away as he fell between the cars with the wolf standing on his chest.

It was the sound that made her dry heave and her ears ring with terror-induced blood pressure spikes; a man's high-pitched scream of agony; the sound of bone, tissue, wetness, then silence…followed by an ominous growl.

Suddenly she was falling. The man who'd been holding her thrust her forward as the beast stalked toward them. She hit the concrete on her hands and knees only to look up into strangely familiar eyes before flattening herself to the ground and covering her head. A whoosh of fur skimmed her back; she felt it through her blazer. But she dared not turn to invite the thing to chew off one of her legs. She heard it land, a man yelling. Snaps, gurgling cries, then silence.

Sidney held her breath. She could sense something close to her, could feel its body heat fuse with her own. *God save her, it was coming back!* A cold nose nudged her cheek. She stopped breathing as warm breath flowed over her hair. She bit down on her lip to stifle the fear whimper bubbling within her. Then the presence was gone.

chapter FIVE

He splashed his face clean, washed his hands in the men's room sink, and adjusted his leather jacket sleeves. Stupid bastards. This wasn't supposed to get violent, but Madame Irvinia was rarely wrong. He could just imagine what might have happened to Sidney if he hadn't gotten the lead to check her boss out. It was gonna be impossible to hold Leonora back, and he just hoped that she wouldn't lose her mind over in Jersey while tracking West.

Brick hurried out of the bathroom and slipped into the exit stairwell. Now it all made sense. Sidney would work herself to death, land plum projects, while her rotten ass boss spilled the beans and bent over for her husband. The deal was so wrong it couldn't ever get right…so damned foul that it had put blood in his nose, and now Douglass was trying to rough Sidney up to make her sign? He'd kill him.

Making a vertical leap to level one of the parking lot once outside the building, he ran to the stairwell and quickly came out on the fifth floor. Sidney was still cowering on the ground, clearly afraid to move in case the wolf came back.

His footfalls made her look up, and bless her soul, she tried to motion him away for his own safety. Tears streamed down her face, and he came to her more quickly than he'd intended.

"It's okay, it's all right," he said, gathering her up into his arms.

"Ohmigod, get into my car—it's a beast, it's huge," she said between ragged breaths as she clutched his biceps and tried to push him toward her vehicle.

"I know," he said calmly, ushering her to her car. "It's mine."

She stopped short and stared at him. "You let something that lethal run loose in a public parking lot to guard me?" Her voice was an incredulous whisper. "Are you insane?"

He hadn't thought about her having that reaction. Truth be told, he still had a bit of defense adrenaline surging, along with the very sated hunt sensation. She wasn't supposed to get all legal and technical…right about this time he would have appreciated a nice long stroke down his back and an "atta boy." But, hey. Women.

"Well, uh, it's expertly trained to only go after criminals that show deadly force, and uh, it wouldn't have hurt a civilian that—"

"Where is that beast now?" she asked, her face pale and voice becoming shrill. She glanced around and then averted her eyes to the ceiling. "There's two dead men in this parking lot, and I think they've been mauled so badly they're partially eaten."

He watched her cross herself and back away from the BMW he was leading her towards. "Leonora got him… uh, she was downstairs with a cruiser…uh, the animal has a GPS chip embedded in it, plus something they put under his collar to tell us when he attacks—she got him chained up, don't worry, okay, baby. The cops will come, Leo will explain about the potential robbery and the guard dog— uh…we'll just say she was going on rounds with a canine unit and two perps jumped out and tried to mug her, the dog went ballistic, and she never even pulled her nine. But you should get out of here, feel me? No need to have your name connected with this."

Sidney's eyes searched his. "You're sure Leonora is cool with all of this? I've never been involved in anything like this in my life," she whispered, her tone holding so much trauma that he pulled her into his arms. "But you two sound like you've done this before and have this whole routine all worked out."

Brick kissed the top of her head and hugged her. Sidney had no idea how many times he and Leo or other members of the pack had to work around the aftermath of a hunt. "Counselor, there's a lot of bad shit that goes down on the streets that the average law abiding citizen and media doesn't need to know about. Unfortunately, sometimes there's no way to follow the rules—because the rules don't have all the variables accounted for."

He body-blocked her line of vision to the carnage and turned her to face away from her car. "Lemme find your keys and pull your car out—it's also probably better if I drive, 'cause you don't seem in any condition."

She just hugged herself and nodded. He hurried with the task, trying not to run over any body parts. He'd hose down her vehicle in his garage later. That was the only way. He and the pack kept chemicals for just such occasions. He'd have to leave Leo a voicemail to double back, get the security tapes, and black 'em out just after the perps entered. They could easily blame it on muggers who were casing the building. Then just as he got it all worked out in his mind and opened the door for Sidney, she puked.

Leonora crouched down in the bushes with a telephoto lens. The slight smile on her face belied her intense concentration she required as she juggled a digital video recorder with a still shot Nikon, noiselessly following the movement within the Cherry Hill home. So this was Douglass West's other home, hidden so sweetly in Sheldon Randolph's name. It was such a lovely evening for a photo shoot, too. Not a cloud in the sky. A little dinner, an expensive wine, cocaine for dessert, now to retire to the family room before the fireplace for some two-way head. If Sidney couldn't use these, then the judge was on the take. Leonora chuckled and bit her lip.

Payback was most certainly a bitch.

"No more arguments," he said in a firm but gentle tone. "In the tub, now. Your clothes go in that bag on the floor. By the time you get out, they'll be washed and dried. Toothpaste and mouthwash is in the cabinet—have at it." He handed Sidney a glass of merlot and turned her around by her shoulders to walk her through the bathroom door. "Both Leo and I have done this drill before. You gotta trust me on this."

Sidney took an unsteady sip from the glass and closed her eyes. "I don't even know your real name, and you're asking me to trust that I can leave two mauled bodies in a parking lot?"

Okay, maybe the lady had a point. He stepped around her. "Mitchell Brickland. Me and Leonora were in the Marines together. She got her education and got out, and went into civilian life as a cop. I got out and now I do what I do. Does that help?"

She smiled into her glass as she took another sip. "A little. Leonora is a good reference."

He smiled. "She's probably my only reference, but I couldn't let you just walk around without security."

She looked up at him, now placing her hand in the center of his chest. "I never want to witness a human being die, but I have to admit that for a moment there was a primal...I don't know," she said quietly. "A me-or-them feeling gripped me, and I desperately wanted it to be them, not me. Does that make sense?"

"Hell yeah," he said with a shrug, allowing the pad of his thumbs to graze the line of her jaw. "Two punks had a gun at your head, would have done more than rob you from the looks on their faces, and you got out with just a few bruises and scraped knees. Them or you, baby. I picked them, too."

There was something in her eyes that made him know that maybe he'd said too much. After all, Sidney Coleburn-West was a skilled attorney and most likely used to reading between the lines in a person's eyes.

"How did you know what expression they had on their faces, Brick?"

He glanced away, his mind scrambling. "I don't wanna upset you."

"Tell me, Mitchell. I need to know."

Aw…maaaan…she'd messed around and called him by his birth name, all honest and tender and whatnot. He cast his gaze to the white tile floor.

"I closed their eyes for them, okay." That's the most truth and the best answer he could give her.

"They didn't have terror on their faces at the last?"

Her question was so logical that it made him stare at her. "You've never seen men die, have you?" He was going for naïveté and the fact that he knew she probably wanted to drop the topic worse than he did.

She shook her head no.

"Good. You don't want to," he said with no fraud in his tone. "The evil in their hearts is always the last thing you see. Only the righteous keep the look of horror, then that slips away to peace."

She shuddered and fell mute.

"Get in the tub," he murmured. "Wash it out of your system, and after I clean your car up and do your clothes, I'll get a shower, too—then we'll talk more…or just chill. Your choice."

He was glad for something constructive to do with his hands. Washing the car, throwing the blood solvent on there that Madame Irv gave him and the boys, was a very good thing right now. He just wished he had something equally as compelling to do with his mind.

Her body felt like someone had beat on it with a crowbar. The tension from being grabbed, then holding her body so stiff that every muscle felt like it had pulled

away from the bone, made her wince as she stepped down
into the large, ivory porcelain Jacuzzi and leaned into the
jets. Her knees and palms ached and stung. Bits of gravel
were still in the heel of her hand from when she'd been
pushed to the concrete ground. A criminal had pointed a
gun in her face. Wild shots had been fired. If it weren't
for Mitchell Brickland's beast of a dog, she could have
been killed, or worse. The most frighteningly majestic
creature she'd ever seen in her life had come to her, sniffed
her, and yet bypassed her to let her live.

Sidney sunk down deeper so that only her neck was
above the fragrant bubbles. Warm merlot was making her
heady, and Brick had been astute enough to leave her the
bottle to go with the glass. This man who she just met
seemed to innately know what she needed, and all of it
was basic, like instinct. Protection, pleasure, relaxation,
and space to sort it all out. He didn't crowd, but was like
a mysterious presence—there, yet not, but there when she
needed him most.

After the third glass of wine, the problems of what might
happen in the parking lot investigation slipped further and
further from her mind...just as her body slipped deeper into
the warm bubbles, her legs and arms bobbing in complete
surrender to the sensation. She didn't even start when Brick
tapped on the door and peeked his head in.

"Hey," she said lazily.

"Your clothes are dry...want me to leave them in the
bedroom, or put them on the bench in here?"

"Oh, yeah, I guess I should get out of your tub." She
chuckled softly and sat up to reach for her glass to refill it.

"No, you can stay in the tub. I've got a robe you can

borrow...as long as you don't mind me jumping in the shower?"

She glimpsed him from the corner of her eye as she poured herself another glass of merlot, sloshing it a bit. "Now why would I mind that?" she murmured.

His mouth went dry. "Cool" was all he could say. He'd tell her later about the link to her boss. Now didn't seem like an opportune time to bring her focus back to her troubles, not when she was so relaxed and her skin was glistening under the bathroom lights...damn she was beautiful.

The way she was looking at him made him turn around to strip off his gear, and grab a towel. He tried to seem casual as he dropped his pile of dirty clothes in a hamper and tossed his shoes into the bedroom somewhere.

Suddenly feeling awkward as hell, he almost got into the shower with his towel on. There was nothing practical left to do but drop it as he turned on the spray. Maybe it was the way her eyes hunted his body, just seemed to lick right over it as she slowly sipped her wine. Might have also had something to do with the fact that he'd come as close as he ever could to showing her his wolf, and he didn't want to get shaky to let her see any hint of it now. Then again, it could've had a lot to do with the fact that he was trying to seem cool and nonchalant, but had wood so bad it was making his temples pound. She didn't need to know all of that and might take it the wrong way... never could tell with women.

"I love your condo," she said out of the blue as he lathered his chest.

"Thanks." Okay, he had to do better than that, but it

was really hard to think and he was so hungry it didn't make sense.

"Have you been here long?"

He turned into the spray. "'Bout ten years. I'm not here much, though. Job keeps me in the streets at night."

"Oh," she murmured in a tone that ran all through him.

She watched him rinse off, mesmerized. It was like witnessing water rushing over stone—like a dark, rich, near black volcanic rock. Conversation was failing her, just like her breath. They'd never even spoken on what had happened the night before. Somehow they'd both seemed to know that the topic was off-limits. But he was clearly thinking about it—his body couldn't lie about that...and just witnessing his arousal without really being able to do anything about it, was making her crazy. The wine didn't help.

"You want some wine?" she offered, lifting the half-empty bottle and hoping he'd turn around, just a bit, to look at her. She wanted to see his phenomenal physique again full frontal, not just the teasing profile he offered as he hid part of it in the five-jet spray.

"Uh, yeah, I'll get another glass when I get out—thanks."

Need and tipsy misjudgment made her lift up a little higher than she'd originally intended. "If you tell me where the glasses are, I can dry off and go get you one."

He glanced over his shoulder, paused, and then turned to stare facing her. His eyes followed the bubbles sliding down her breasts. Her hand clutched a bottle, holding it mid-air. His eyes never left hers as he turned off the shower, opened the glass door, and stepped toward her unconcerned about the water he tracked on the floor.

Something in his eyes made her simply hand him the

bottle. He took it from her, still staring at her, took a long swig and then set it down on the rim of the tub.

"How are your hands?" he murmured, collecting her palms within his, and then turning them over.

The action made her stand, his gentle upward tug all the encouragement she needed.

"They got torn up a bit," she said quietly, and then watched him lower his mouth to each one to place a gentle kiss on the scrapes.

"In a couple of nights it will all be better," he whispered, placing her injured palms on his shoulders. He stepped in closer. "It was already in you."

"What was?" she whispered, her body trembling from the heat wafting off his. She turned her face up, her mouth hungering for a kiss, her wet body aching to have his brush against hers.

"The ability to protect yourself," he murmured, making their bellies touch and causing a swift burn to race through her.

She couldn't answer, the gasp was complete. The hard length of him felt like it had been soldered to her pelvis, and an eerie tingling had begun in her palms. From nowhere the need to climb up him and take his mouth made her do it. His response was just as primal and immediate, lifting her from the tub, he wrapped her around his waist, kissing and blindly walking her out of the room.

"I wanna see where you got nipped," he breathed out, making them both fall hard on the bed. "Leo told me...you also skinned your knees."

His hot lick down her neck, between her breasts and over her belly arched her so hard she sat up. When he just kissed her mound and trailed his hands down her legs, she thought she'd lose her mind. He found her banged-up knees and gently kissed them, and something about his attention there sent that tingly sensation through her again...but this time it burned more, made her hotter. Then he kissed down her legs and found where she'd been savaged as a child. The small scar ached now to the throbbing rhythm between her legs. His nip there broke the skin and made her cry out. Confusion, pleasure, and a dizzying level of want shot through her. He was so much bigger than her, thicker, heavier, but she felt like a madwoman, crazed and struggling to get him to mount her.

Yet it was impossible to twist into the right position— he had her by her legs, his face lowered to nip her inner thigh...then he found the place that made her cry out and grab the sheets.

Head back, crown dug into the pillows, panting open-mouthed, she didn't care about the frenzy in her voice as he lapped at her till she convulsed. Her hands couldn't feel enough of his skin at once, her mouth couldn't capture his. She wanted to taste him, but right now had to have him inside her. He obliged for two hard thrusts that put tears in her eyes, and then pulled out with a groan, making her almost fight him.

He moved to reach a nightstand drawer, she rolled over and pushed herself up onto her hands and knees and dipped her spine low, watching him, breathing through her mouth. If she wasn't mistaken he'd released a sound that was so low it sounded almost like a growl—but she could definitely relate.

If he didn't calm down, he'd howl for sure. His hands

were shaking as he sheathed himself in latex and almost ruined it with too-sharp nails. This was crazy, what had been on his mind? Kissing an open cut—him? New Lupe virus from the exposure was now running through her, making her wild, sending her through changes like she was in heat. He could see the repressed wolf in her stirring; it had been dormant for a very long time. Her eyes were beginning to change, her breathing was becoming erratic...it was the sexiest shit he'd ever seen.

Within two seconds he was on her, the mount a hard thrust. When she threw her head back and howled, he almost busted a nut. He couldn't help it, she was burning him up. Every snap jerk of her spine called his wolf home. Her body was hollering, "Baby, come get it." But he couldn't go there on her, not until she'd gone through her first phase. She'd never know how close to the transition edge he was the moment she let out a low, mourning wail when he dipped low to find her spot. Her nails dug into his hip to hold him there, to let him know, oh, yeah, he'd found it.

"Right there?" He rasped, sweat rolling off his nose and down his back, splattering linens.

"Yes!" Her voice was an a cappella shriek.

"You sure?" he asked, just to distract himself to keep from cumming too soon.

"Yes!"

"Want me to take it out so you can—"

"No!" Her voice dissolved into a sob as she tried to link her ankles behind his knees to hold him in place.

He needed to let it go so badly he was seeing stars. "Tell me when you're there, sweet Sidney. You right there, baby?"

"Brick!"

Okay, he couldn't play it off any more—his name at that pitch was a definite yes. He came so hard he bit his tongue and only a very thin margin of restraint kept his wolf at bay.

They both collapsed with him still joined to her. He gathered her against his chest and stomach and spooned her, breathing hard. She covered her face with her hands, and he watched full-blown hysteria overtake her.

"I've never felt like this in my life," she wailed, beginning to rock with him still lodged deep within her.

He just held her and petted her hair away from her face, remembering his first time before the phase shift.

"I don't know what's wrong with me, I can't get enough," she panted, her voice bottoming out to alto and making him lift his head.

"I got you," he said in a low rumble next to her ear. "Till you drop, all right?"

She reached back and held him by the jaw, peering at him over her shoulder. "It's your voice, too...that..."

"Growl," he said as low as he could from deep within his chest and then chuckled, thoroughly pleased.

She shuddered and leaned back to kiss him hard. "Yeah. Like I said, I'm off the chain tonight."

chapter six

It was mid-morning before either one of them could summon the energy to make the necessary calls. She called her office and feigned another migraine, which was not at all far from the truth—he called Leonora to come over and to bring whatever grub she could lay her hands on.

Sidney paced in front of the large picture window staring out at Philadelphia's majestic skyline with her cell phone pressed to her ear. Maybe she was having a nervous breakdown, some vast departure from reality? Right now she felt so wild and free that if her boss said the wrong thing, she'd tell him to go fuck himself, career consequences be damned.

As she waited for Sheldon Randolph's executive assistant to come back onto the line, elevator music drilling a hole in her brain, the feeling of absolute entitlement swept through Sidney like a wild fire, threatening to consume her logic. She didn't care what was protocol or not this morning. She didn't care about whatever was going on at the ruthless office or the politics therein. The right to be free ate at everything rational within her, so did the right to retaliate, the right to deliver swift and sudden justice...the right not to have to mew excuses to a self-important asshole of a boss about why she'd be out again—she'd be out because that's what she fucking felt like being—*out*.

"I'm calling to say I won't be in today, Marie," Sidney snapped as soon as her boss's assistant came back on the line.

"Oh, no..." Marie said with a desperate gasp. "You know today is when Sheldon leaves for his annual deer hunt up in the Poconos with his VIP clients. I'm afraid he's already gone, and he had expected you to be the manager on duty to handle any crises while he's away." Marie paused, allowing her voice to convey the guilt trip with just the right amount of sugary emphasis.

"I have a migraine," Sidney said through her teeth, trying to temper the flare of aggression that shot through her.

"And, as you may have heard on the news this morning, there *has* been a crisis of sorts, Sidney. I know you have a migraine, but two robbers got mauled in our building's lot by a police K-9 unit, and now the building tenants want to meet to discuss greater security measures for all staff working late given this could have been a real tragedy if an innocent person had been attacked by those horrible men they found. This time, the dogs will get a medal, but next time it might be someone in the building that gets stalked by muggers. We—"

"Will have to have someone else on staff to deal with the security meeting and whatever other crap Sheldon threw my way while he's out playing in the Poconos," Sidney snapped, cutting off her boss's assistant. "I'm not in the damned mood."

Pure silence strangled the line for a few tense moments.

"Well, all right," Marie said curtly. "If that's how you want it, then I'll just let Sheldon know when he calls in."

Sidney hung up without answering, not bothering to wait for the next volley of messages and instructions that Marie no doubt had. Not today. For some odd reason she felt like she could possibly rip the woman's face off. Truthfully, she felt like she could do that to anyone who crossed her right now.

Glancing at Brick across the room, Sidney stared at him with quiet appreciation. He'd pulled on an olive-hued mock turtle neck sweater that fit his form to a T with a pair of black jeans. The color added an earthy richness to the dark earth color of his skin. Plus, despite her temporary annoyance, she loved the way the gun holster fit around his wide shoulders and broad, muscular back. Of all the people she really needed to talk to today, this person seemed to instinctively know that the sound of a voice would be like someone scratching their fingernails down a blackboard at the moment.

His eyes asked a silent question as he looked up at her while lacing his black Timberland boots. *Was everything cool at the office? Hell no,* her mind screamed as she clutched the cell phone in her fist. She'd have to beg forgiveness later. Making a real doctor's appointment would be wise. It was the weirdest thing, though. Brick simply nodded like he knew the thousand thoughts running through her mind, but was so quiet she almost sighed out loud.

But when his condo buzzer sounded, she snarled. Actually snarled! Sidney covered her mouth with a hand and paced away to steady herself. Tears immediately filled her eyes.

"I don't know what's wrong with me," she whispered.

"It's just Leonora," Brick said in a mercifully quiet voice. "I'll buzz her up."

Without turning, Sidney just nodded and then braced herself for the intrusion of more sound.

For some strange reason, not wanting to be in Brick's bedroom when Leonora arrived, she melted into the living room. It was the most bizarre feeling in the world...her walk felt like a glide...a lope. The hair was standing up on the back of her neck. She could smell a cheese steak coming down the hall outside the condo unit. She could smell Leonora's distinctive scent! At the same time, something irrational in her made her want to fight something, anything, although not Leonora or Brick. Sidney covered her face and breathed into her hands for a moment as Brick glimpsed her from the corner of his eye and opened the condo door. Her stomach growled so loudly she was embarrassed.

Sidney spun on Leonora and licked her lips. Her best friend looked at Brick then at Sidney, flung the greasy bag across the room, and squared off on him. Brick backed up growling at a decibel so low it had wet Sidney's draws.

"How long has she been like this Brick?" Leonora shouted, tears standing in her eyes. "She was never supposed to be brought into the life!"

"Don't fucking lecture me, Leo!" Brick shouted back. "It was already there, dormant—you know what Mom Irv said!"

Leonora backed down and strode into the living room, her eyes steady on Sidney. "How you feeling, baby?" she asked, her voice cracking.

"I thought we were clear," Brick growled. "That's mine."

"Friends till the day I die," Leonora said, lifting her chin. "You bit her, didn't you?"

"That ain't your business, last I checked, and if it's to the death—"

"I'm hungry, dammit," Sidney said, crossing the room and going for the bag. "Chill, people. Whatever your beef is, handle it after we eat. Shit!"

Leonora cast a hard gaze on Brick. "Listen to her. She doesn't even sound like herself." She swallowed hard. "Sid was always so…soft." Leonora's voice caught in her throat as she watched Sidney tear into the bag with abandon and eat standing up over the counter.

"She'll get back to that," Brick said quietly. "It's just working through her system…that's all. But she's…" He closed his eyes.

"All alpha," Leonora murmured with appreciation.

Brick just closed his eyes and nodded. "I couldn't help it…I nipped her."

Leonora nodded as she watched Sidney begin to polish off the second cheese steak, hands and chin running red with ketchup. "I wouldn't have been able to hold back, either, brother."

Brick steadied himself. "Let her have the bag…then, maybe after she eats, show her the pics."

Leonora nodded and unconsciously licked her lips, speaking to Brick without looking at him as they both stared at Sidney. "Okay," she said quietly. "Then I've gotta go."

Brick simply nodded. "Yeah. Then, you've gotta go."

Halfway through the third two-foot long sandwich, Sidney took a breath and looked up at them. Paper was everywhere, a lot of it eaten right along with the cheese steaks and her hands, face, and blouse were a mess.

"I'm so sorry," she said, looking mortified. "I've never done anything like this in my life."

Both Brick and Leonora drew shuddering breaths, accidentally saying the same thing at the same time in the same timbre: "I know, baby."

"So, what do you want me to do?" Leonora said, collecting the devastating array of digital images off the coffee table along with the video camera. She ignored Brick's arched eyebrow.

"Don't you mean, what do you want *Brick* to do?" he said, tilting his head to the side to give Leo a warning to back off.

But the contest was lost on Sidney as she stared down and stopped Leonora from pulling the images away from her sight. "No. The question is, what does Sidney want to do about this?" She stood and walked to the window and looked in the direction of her firm. "They played me. The whole time I was working like a dog, trying to do my best—they played me. Took my best clients, gave me the hardest cases and shittiest workload, and the whole time, I worked like a damned dog." She turned slowly. "And the both of them were in cahoots all along."

"Baby, what do you want to—"

"I want to go to the Poconos," Sidney abruptly said, cutting Brick off. "I want to confront them while they're in their cozy little cabin and tell them to their faces that I'm not the one to be played!" she shouted, beginning to pace. "I want to dig my nails into their faces and rip them off! I want to tear out their lying tongues—just yank out their fucking windpipes!" she shrieked, then picked up a lamp and threw it. "I want them to hurt like I hurt, pray for someone to come to their rescue like I did!" The couch went against the wall. "I want blood!"

Brick had stood and was walking in a circle. Leonora was hyperventilating and had begun to rock.

"I'll take you to the Poconos, baby. We can drive up this afternoon, if you want?" Brick's voice held a timbre of expectancy that made Sidney stop ransacking his place to stare at him.

She was breathing hard, her eyes wild. "I have to… I have to…" Her words trailed off as she stared down at her hands.

"The full moon is tonight," Leonora said with a thick swallow of palpable desire. "Maybe that's not a good idea, if she really doesn't want blood on her hands?"

"We're tight, Leo, but you gotta go," Brick said, his full gaze on Sidney as she began rampaging throughout his condo again. "I love seeing her like this."

He'd pulled the rented SUV off the side of the road, rolling as far as they could in the semi-dark over dirt, grass, brightly-hued leaves, and twigs. Night was just about to make an entrance, her dark gray cloak of near sundown dusk slowly lowering over tall pines and oaks. The change-over between day forest noises and scents and those of evening had begun just as surely as Sidney would go mad with transition the moment the full moon shone upon her lovely face. All reason would be eclipsed. She was nearly insane already.

Brick touched her cheek to make her wait. Douglass and Sheldon had rifles and were probably fairly decent shots, not that it would kill her, unless their bullets were silver, which he doubted. But the pain of recovery during a transition would be like an agony she didn't need to know. Sidney looked at him, anxious.

"I know," he murmured. "But you have to wait to make your move. You can't just roll up on a hunt, wild, without stalking it right. That's a good way to get hurt."

She nodded. "I'm not going to kill him, just...I don't know. I want to just punch him in the face...but I know that's not legal. I just want to tell them both where they can shove it—probably where they already have." She whirled around in her seat. "Did I just say kill?"

Brick traced her cheek and didn't answer, watching the gradual shift between human and Lupine sensibilities overtake her wide irises.

"I don't know what came over me in your apartment," she whispered. "You must think I'm mad...I swear I'll pay for everything and will replace it—I think I need a shrink...the repressed rage for years...oh, God, Brick, what's happening to me?"

His hand caressed her throat as he watched her skin become damp with perspiration. "It's normal, after what's just happened to you."

"I don't feel normal, I feel like I'm about to pass out at the same time I'm about to leap out of this truck!"

Her chest had begun to heave as she battled to breathe. To keep her occupied and her focus away from the cabin, he let his hand slide down to capture her breast. She closed her eyes and released a moan that ran through him.

"Stay with me a little while till it gets dark," he said quietly watching her eyes roll beneath her lids as his thumb caressed a nipple through her sweater. "Wait until they can't see you roll up on them, all right?"

She nodded quickly and released her answer on a rush of breath as she brought his other hand to the neglected breast. "All right."

"Isn't this a lot better than fighting right now?"

He took her mouth hard, not waiting for her answer. The moan she released over his tongue was enough of one. It had been so long since he'd been with an alpha female of his kind, and had never had one during a first phase, that he'd become slightly irrational. Just witnessing her first primal rush, the way she yanked at her skirt to bring it up over her hips, and just as quickly began struggling with his pants was enough to make him forget about hunting Douglass's stupid ass.

Sidney's lithe body had slipped across the gear-shift, one knee perilously wedged between the driver's seat and the door, the other trying to find anchor against the center seat divide, her breaths frantic pants as she tore away the sheer fabric obstruction of hose and panties between them. Their gazes locked. Her eyes had begun to turn a lighter hazel from the inner wolf glow behind her normally dark brown irises. Just seeing her that way made him throw his head back and beg his wolf to stay put.

"You know what you are?" he gasped, trying to prepare her in case he couldn't hold a phase-shift back.

"Starved," she breathed out in a warm rush against his cheek, stroking him while touching herself above him.

"She-wolf," he gulped, kneading the firm lobes of her ass. "Alpha." Her touch was maddening, her pulsing grasp and release just right. Not too hard, not too timid, pressure at the exact point... "Do you know what that means, Sidney?" he asked, painfully trying to force himself to get her ready for a life altering event.

"She-wolf…" she repeated, her words deep, resonant, and making his stomach clench. Then she lowered her body and dragged his dripping head along the length of her slick slit, making him release a groan from inside his chest. "Gentleman's way of calling me your bitch?" she gasped, taking his mouth, devouring it, and then pulling away breathlessly. "Is that what you want? Me to talk dirty to you? Is that what you mean, Brick—'cause right now, I have no problem doing that."

He was losing his mind and she didn't get it. He shouldn't have waited this long to try to make her understand, but all day long her body had been having this same conversation with his. "Yeah." He dropped his head back against the seat rest. "I mean, no…" His mind was fracturing between the wolf and the man, her slippery, warm gyrations against his head, the grip of her hand, her bud feeling like the tip of a tongue…a howl scrabbling at his dry throat for release. "Oh, damn, baby" was the only thing that came out as she mounted him and withdrew.

Knowing that neither of them could take the frenzied touches any longer, he simply tilted the steering wheel up and out of her way as she mounted him again hard with a deep groan. He'd tell her later, would have to hope she didn't freak when he showed her. But the rhythm spoke a thousand words: I'm sorry, I'll make it right, I didn't mean for it to go down like this, but oh, shit, girl, it's so fucking good! A howl ripped up his throat as her eyes turned gold. Her canines were cresting for the first time as she threw her head back and howled when she convulsed.

He grabbed her tight around the waist to ground her to stay a moment in human form, then looked her in the eyes and kissed her fast, breathing hard. "Remember who you are. Don't let the first moon break you." He then let her go, opened the vehicle door before she panicked and felt trapped, and watched her flee his lap in one fluid wolf move.

It was the most amazing transition he'd ever witnessed. Her clothes were in his lap; she stood almost three feet at the shoulders...a gorgeous chestnut silvery brown, with wide, seeking eyes as she slowly backed away from the vehicle unsure and snarling. His wolf couldn't stand it, the SUV was too confining as he watched her. Soon his clothes pooled on the SUV floor, and he met her on the leaf strewn ground, threw back his head and howled.

When her voice joined his and she eased closer to him sniffing, and then nuzzled him, that was all she wrote. He was done. Whatever she wanted, whomever she wanted. Fresh deer meat was in his nose, wafting from the cabin. They both looked up as two human fools came out on the deck with Chardonnay in hand.

"They have wolves out here?" Douglass said, looking out toward the nearby mountains.

"Guess so, but in all my years hunting up here, I'd never seen them. They sound beautiful though."

Before Brick could stop her, Sidney had rushed low along the side of the house and in one bound was over the deck rail snarling. He loped over and watched as a glass of Chardonnay slid from Douglass's hand with a crash. Sheldon slowly backed up. Brick couldn't take his eyes off Sidney. She was gorgeous...canine's saliva slicked and glistening under the moon, a sure kill in her sights, primal fury in her eyes. Sheldon was a fool to try to back up to get a rifle. Brick's mind calculated the lunge distance—*twitch, motherfucker, and you're mine.*

Sheldon twitched. Brick pinned him, but waited, only knocking him out from the fall. This was his woman's night, she had first kill rights. Brick looked at her as Douglass screamed. The sound of his voice made Sidney's coat bristle along her spine. It didn't take her three seconds after that. The man's throat was gone before he'd blinked. There was nothing to do but join the lady for dinner. Venison could work as an entrée; it was still strapped to the top of their appetizer's Jeep. Then again, she didn't seem to be interested in eating either rat bastard, just ripping them into tiny shreds...fine by him. Damn, women could be so cold when done wrong.

Several full moons later...

Her attorney sat back and spread an array of papers across his desk. "Well, Mrs. West, it seems as though your husband's plan to take you for everything backfired. You were still his legal wife when he and your boss met an untimely death while hunting in the Poconos. Who knew they had beasts out there like that?"

"Well, what can I say?" Sidney offered coolly with a shrug. "Shit happens. Douglass had bad karma. So did Sheldon. Funny how that worked, that they both left me richer when the money was always their driving force, not mine. My issue was always a matter of not submitting to having someone just take what I'd worked for. Ironic." She sat back in the sumptuous leather chair and stopped talking before she went too far, feeling a primal surge waft through her.

Her attorney sighed and nodded. "Ironic indeed, but I sure hope the authorities catch that bear or cougar, whatever the hell it was that ripped them to shreds. But maybe this was just their bad karma, like you said. I always thought it was very inappropriate for Douglass to be on such familiar terms with your employer, especially given the circumstances. Then the pictures." He shook his head. "We didn't even need them. Lucky, too, that we didn't use them to force a quick resolution…because this way you get it all."

She fought not to smile and kept it widow-appropriate. "Well, Wallace, you know what they say…payback is definitely a bitch."

L. A. Banks, the author of The Vampire Huntress Legends series, has written over 17 novels and contributed to 7 novellas, thus far, in multiple genres under various pseudonyms. She mysteriously shape-shifts between the genres of romance, women's fiction, crime/suspense thrillers, and of course, dark vampire huntress lore. A graduate of The University of Pennsylvania Wharton undergraduate program with a Master's in Fine Arts from Temple University, one never knows how or when this enigma will appear...her forms are many, her secrets of crossing genres vast, and she does this with a husband, four children, and a dog from some remote, undisclosed lair in Philadelphia. Leslie lives in Philadelphia.

Find out more about L. A. Banks and her upcoming works at http://vampirehuntress.com

THE HEAT OF THE NIGHT
by Donna Hill

chapter one

Agggg, God...yesssss...yessss! Noooo! Ooooohweee! Ahhh, ahhh, ahhh...

The four-poster bed banged up and down, literally leaping off the floor each time that thing pounded into me. The head of it was the size of a fist and the length and breadth of it like a forearm. I craved every inch it. If my thighs were stretched any wider I'd split right in half. I didn't care. I had to have it, needed it. Each time it rammed up inside my throbbing pussy, lights exploded in my head. My body heaved and trembled violently while scorching tears streamed down my cheeks, the steam from them rising to surround the tainted bed.

I thought I heard myself screaming but the sound was only in my head. The cock was—and no pun intended—out of this world, but it was killing me night after night, day after day. Still, I never wanted it to stop. Never.

In the distance I heard a ringing. The darkness in the room slowly began to clear. The veil that had clouded my vision drifted away like morning mist. The ringing continued. I felt it slipping out of me, the pressure lifting off my body. I sucked in a deep breath, my first one for what seemed like hours. Whatever held my arms and legs in place released me.

A sudden sickening emptiness pushed up inside my now hollow tunnel and filled my insides with a wretchedness that I could not explain. I wept. Not tears of joy but of a deep sorrow.

I reached across the nightstand and turned off the alarm. Slowly I glanced around my room. Everything looked the same. The off-white curtains still blew gently in the breeze of the early dawn. The pictures still hung on the wall. My clothes for work were where I left them, laid out on the chaise lounge. My jewelry box, a gift from my grandmother, still sat on my dresser.

On the surface things looked so very ordinary. I pushed myself into a sitting position in my bed. I glanced downward. My gown was in shreds, slashed from top to bottom. Through the holes in my nightgown I saw long red welts beginning to form on my skin.

I shook my head. Covered my face with my hands. What had happened?

I knew the answer, at least I thought I did, but I could never admit it. Not even to myself. It was simply too bizarre. The only explanation was that I was losing my mind. That possibility was more palpable than the unthinkable.

With great effort I pulled myself from bed. My legs felt like spaghetti and I had to grab hold of the nightstand to keep from falling.

Through sheer force of will I slid one foot in front of

the other until I finally made it to the bathroom. Exhaustion gripped me by the throat, cut off my air. I sucked in oxygen through my nose and plopped down on the commode, the exertion of the short walk taking its toll.

A hot shower always made me feel better after one of these *incidents*. Incidents. That's what I called them for lack of a better term. These things that kept happening to me, night after night for the past few months—*incidents*. I'd heard somewhere that's how crazy people get started being crazy, with little incidents. Guess I was a little crazy and getting crazier by the day.

I leaned forward, pushed the shower curtain aside and turned on the faucets full blast. When I was finally able to pull myself together I stood up to take off what was left of my gown that hung in tatters from my shoulders like some alien flag.

Then out of the blue I started to laugh—laugh hysterically. I laughed until I was doubled over and my gut hurt. Who would believe this shit? I didn't even believe it most days. But then my pussy would start humming and my nipples would stand up straight, my muscles burned and a hazy kind of feeling took over. And all I'd want is that crazy, big-ass crooked dick pounding inside of me to put me out of the mad misery.

Christ! What was happening to me? I don't even like dick to be truthful. At least I didn't think I did. The men I'd been with were few and far between, and they left much to be desired.

I'd heard women talking about the Big O and how great it was. And some G-spot. Ha. It was like listening to a foreign language. But I'd play along like I'd had plenty of Big O's with some to spare. All lies. I didn't have a clue. Until recently. Now I had the whole alphabet on lock!

I ripped the rest of my gown off and tossed it on the growing pile with the others. Yeah, maybe some hot water and soap would do the trick.

By the time I arrived at work I was feeling much better. Almost like myself.

"Hey Christine," Melody, my best friend, said when I walked into the office.

Me and Mel had been friends since high school—tenth grade. For a long time I had a real thing for Mel, right from the first moment I saw her naked in the girls' locker room when she came out of the shower. Her body was like that of a goddess, perfectly sculpted. Even back then her breasts made my mouth water. They were full and round with dark brown nipples against cinnamon brown skin. To this day she still has that tiny waist that you can put your hands around and that nice high ass that…well…you get the picture.

Simply put, Mel was gorgeous *and* sweet. Sometimes when I was around her my heart would race so fast I could hardly breathe. And my clit would swell and harden like a little…well, you know. But I knew Mel was strictly straight. She had more men in her life than the line for free cheese. So, I comforted myself with just being her best friend.

Then this thing started happening to me and all thoughts of one day kicking and licking it with Mel evaporated. I was consumed by dick. Shit!

"Damn girl, are those suitcases under your eyes or what?" She looked at me askew.

"I haven't been sleeping too well lately."

"I can tell. Have you tried chamomile tea? That usually helps me. I can get you some if you don't have any. I have tons."

"Thanks."

I took my seat in the cubicle next to hers, powered up my computer and checked my To Do list.

We worked at a small but growing casting agency on the lower east side of Manhattan. I really liked my job. It was great to be able to find that perfect actor for a role and see them rise to stardom. It didn't happen very often but at least we got a lot of potential stars in front of the decision makers.

"So what did you do last night?" she called out over the partition that separated us.

My mind went blank for a minute.

"I called you a couple of times but I kept getting your voicemail."

What the hell was I doing last night? Oooh, yeah...the *incident*. The thing is when it starts happening, I seem to lose all sense of time and place.

"Huh, what time did you call?"

"Around eight, then again about ten."

Shit, twelve hours screwing! "Not sure how I missed those calls. Sorry. Answering machine has been acting kinda funky lately."

"I know how that can be. Maybe I'll get you one for your birthday next month." She laughed.

"Want to catch a movie after work?"

"Girl, I really need to get some rest. I'm just so tired lately."

"You're right. I can bring over dinner from that restaurant we like if you don't feel up to cooking."

I'd love to have Mel over. But, to be truthful, I was terrified that whatever it was that was happening to me would happen in front of her. No matter how much Mel may have liked a good stiff cock, I don't think she was ready to see her best friend with her legs gapped open, being humped by something she couldn't see and begging for more.

"That's so thoughtful, Mel, but I'm good. I have plenty of stuff in the fridge that I can heat up." I looked up and she was standing over me.

Her arms were folded beneath her breasts which gave them even more lift. I averted my gaze from those luscious tits to her dreamy brown eyes.

"What's up?"

"That's what I want to know. You've been acting really weird lately. You hardly ever answer your phone, you look like shit and you never want to hang out anymore. Is Lucas back and you didn't tell me?"

My throat was suddenly dry and the room got really warm. Something was squeezing me between my legs, not hard but just enough to get me instantly wet. A moan escaped my lips. I felt lightheaded. And it took all I had to keep my eyes from rolling to the back of my head in delight. I gripped the edge of my desk. Not here. God. Not in front of Mel.

I pushed up from my desk and darted down the hall to the ladies room. Thankfully I worked in an older building with one toilet. I locked the door behind me and took deep, quick breaths.

I can beat this, I chanted over and over. It's all in my

head. I can beat this. But even as I wished it away, hot, steaming breath burned along my neck. Hands or something like hands pushed me against the wall—hard. I banged my head and saw stars.

It was clawing at my clothes, trying to get them off. With what little ounce of sense I had left, I had the presence of mind to pull my sweater over my head and take off my pants. If we were going to do this I'd be damned if I was going to walk back to my desk with my clothes turned to rags.

No sooner than I got out of my pants I felt my panties rip and something long and slick lapped at my cunt. My legs wobbled. I held onto the sink to keep from collapsing from the pleasure. That tongue or whatever it was, licked and lapped and sucked until I came with such force I fell to the floor.

Before I could recover I was hoisted up by my waist and I felt something like claws dig into the soft flesh of my belly. I was turned around and forced to bend over. My feet didn't even touch the floor as that magnificent thing rammed inside me, over and over and over...

Everything went dark.

When I came to, I heard banging on the door. Maybe it was the banging that brought me back.

"Chris! Chris! Are you okay? Open the door."

Damn, it was Mel. I pulled myself up off the floor and came face to face with my reflection in the mirror. My hair was standing up on my head, my eyes were glassy and I was naked as the day I was born. My bra was hanging on by one raggedy strap, didn't see my panties and ugly purple bruises dotted my body like a freak rash. I gripped the edge of the sink and pulled in huge lungfuls of air to try to clear my head.

"I'll, uh be out in a minute. Not feeling too good."

"You need help?"

Yeah, but not the kind you think. "I'm okay. Really. I'll be out in a minute."

"All right. If you're sure. Maybe you should go home. You've been in there for a half hour."

Shit. A half hour? "Yeah, um maybe I will."

I turned on the faucet full blast to discourage any further conversation then splashed cold water over my face.

This had never happened before. The incidents always took place in my bedroom and only at night. Had my wild hallucinations broken free from the mental chains that held them in place to run rampant night *and* day? The thought terrified me.

Being ravaged or imagining that I was being ravaged in the privacy of my home was one thing. But here...at work? My mind began running around in circles like a frightened mouse in one of those stupid mazes. I didn't see any end in sight either.

I stared at myself in the mirror. What was happening to me? Oh, no, not again. In the mirror I could see what it was doing to me. What my mind was doing to me. My nipples were rock hard as I watched them being sucked by something I could not see. I saw the skin get pulled, the tender flesh massaged and kneaded right in front of my eyes.

But heaven help me there was nothing else in that little ass room but me.

I tried to move, swipe the unseen mouth and hands

away but I couldn't. I couldn't do anything but submit. Something grabbed the mounds of my ass, squeezed then lifted me off the floor as if I weighed no more than an infant. Then it was inside me again, not as forceful this time, almost gentle in comparison to what I'd just been through. That thick, knobby thing moved in and out, growing fat and slender, long or short at will. It moved slow and the things that stroked my flesh didn't scratch or tear but rather they caressed—caressed so tenderly that it brought tears to my eyes.

Then just as suddenly as it began, it was over. I felt myself sliding down the cold tiled walls until my butt was on the floor.

My pussy throbbed, gripping and dripping madly, needing desperately to have something stiff and big to wrap itself around. I shoved two fingers inside, three, four. In and out, faster and faster. It didn't help. It wasn't enough. I couldn't cum. I couldn't. A delirious need overtook me. I felt a scream building from deep down in my toes. I shoved my sweater into my mouth to keep the words that I thought I'd never say spewing from my lips: Come back! Don't leave me. I need you! Please.

That's when I knew for sure that I had gone over the edge.

chapter two

Needless to say, I had every reason to leave work early that day. I was a wreck, physically and mentally. Mel did all but carry me out to the cab that was waiting for me and promised to call later that evening.

By the time the cab pulled up in front of my house, I was beginning to feel a little better, not as lightheaded and woozy. My pussy was hollering like a banshee, opening and closing like a barn door. And the welts and bruises on my breasts and stomach were beginning to sting. I needed a hot soak for sure.

I was so incredibly tired as if all the life was being drained out of me. Melody was right, I looked like crap. My skin was dry as leather, my hair was breaking off and I bore a close resemblance to a raccoon.

Trust me, I have to make light of this. If I don't I'm sure I will go out of my mind. If I haven't already…

I put down my coat and purse on the table in the hall and inched my way to the bathroom. I turned on the tub and let it fill with hot, steamy water, then I added some Epsom salt to help with the aches and pains.

Standing in front of the bathroom mirror I slowly stripped out of my clothes and stopped breathing. What I saw brought a new fear to my heart. My body looked as if I'd been in battle. Bruises and scratches covered every inch of my tender flesh.

What was happening to me? This couldn't be my imagination. It simply could not be. This was real. I touched a raging red spot on my left breast and even as much as what I saw repelled me, I was oddly turned on.

The incidents through were unlike anything I'd ever experienced. Although they were wild and unexplainable, they were the greatest sexcapades I'd ever had. And the more it happened, the more I feared it, the more I wanted it. How sick was that?

Sighing deeply I turned away from my damning reflection and got into the tub.

The hot waters enveloped me like an old favorite blanket. I slid down up to my neck, rested my head against the back of the tub and closed my eyes.

Three months earlier my life was as ordinary and mundane as a nun's. I wasn't seeing anyone, hadn't for months. My life was pretty much consumed with work, doing the whole party thing and lusting after Mel when she wasn't involved with whomever her latest beau was at the moment.

"You need a guy in your life," Mel said to me one afternoon while we were hanging out at her apartment.

She was wearing these skimpy shorts and a cut off T-shirt while she was reaching and bending, watering her cornucopia of plants.

I was trying to pay attention to what she was saying and

not how her shorts hugged her ass or how her nipples poked up in the T-shirt. I wiggled in my seat and turned my attention to the stack of magazines on the coffee table.

"My life is just fine. Having a man in it doesn't guarantee anything."

"At least you'd be getting it regular." She giggled. "Quite frankly I don't see how you manage to get through the droughts." She spun toward me, hands on her hips, tits jutting forward. I swallowed. "I gotta tell ya, if I don't get a good stiff one at least three times a week I turn into a real bitch. I don't know how you do it, girl."

"I manage. Besides, sex isn't everything."

Her right brow rose in a perplexed arch. "It isn't?"

I shook my head and chuckled. "We're just different that's all." I tucked my bare feet under me. "I enjoy a good fuck just as much as the next one."

"What you need," she wagged a finger at me, "is someone to rock your world. Then you'd have a new attitude. Believe me."

"I'm starved," I announced, needing to change the subject. "Whatcha got in the fridge?" I hopped up from the couch and marched off toward the kitchen.

"Some cold chicken and potato salad," she called out to my retreating back.

That's another thing about Mel, she could cook her ass off. One of these days if she ever settled down she'd make someone a great wife.

"You ever think about getting married, having kids?" I asked her when she followed me into the kitchen.

She shrugged. "Hmm, sometimes. But I'm enjoying my freedom. I don't know if I'm ready to be tied down to the same man night after night. Know what I mean?" She snatched a chicken wing from the plastic bowl and began munching. She hopped up on the kitchen stool. "What about you?" she asked over a mouthful of chicken.

I took a plate from the overhead cabinet and set it on the counter, then loaded it up. I was suddenly starved for real.

"Me? When's the last time you really looked at me? I'm overweight and contrary to popular opinion about light-skinned chicks and good hair, mine isn't." I plopped a dollop of potato salad on my plate. "Most guys only want me for a minute and then move on."

"I wish you wouldn't say things like that about yourself. You're a good looking woman. Intelligent and fun to be with. But you never want to fix yourself up. You don't wear makeup and when is the last time you splurged on yourself? Besides, men don't really want Barbie dolls, they want a woman with a little junk in their trunk." She winked at me and my heart skipped a beat.

"According to you," I grumbled.

"Tell you what, next Saturday, let's have a real girlfriend day. We'll get manicures and pedicures, get our hair done, buy some makeup and then go shopping." She grinned. "How's that sound?"

A day with Mel, no matter what she had in mind, sounded fine to me, even if I could care less about what she wanted to do. The truth was I was a plain Jane. As plain as they come. And no amount of shopping and makeup was going to change that.

That following Saturday me and Mel had our girl's day out. That crazy broad dragged me from one end of Fifth Avenue in Manhattan to the other: Bergdorf Goodman,

Neiman Marcus, Chanel, Lord and Taylor and of course, Victoria's Secret. Until that Saturday the closest I'd ever come to anything in those high-end dens of inequity was the Sunday sales section of the newspaper.

"You must have the perfect day-to-evening suit," she'd said as we strolled the aisles, me in awe of the price tags and her with the eye of a connoisseur. When Mel's eagle-eyes landed on the perfect garment she'd zoom in like a missile on lock and snatch up the unsuspecting outfit with a triumphant flourish.

By the time we were finished—four hours of non-stop shopping later—I had two suits, three pairs of shoes, jeans, sweaters and enough lingerie to open my own small boutique.

I was filled with a giddy kind of excitement, albeit tinged with my ingrained Catholic guilt and about two thousand dollars poorer.

"The first thing that attracts a man," Mel went on with her lesson as we toted our designer shopping bags to The Cookery, a restaurant inside Rockerfeller Center, "is outward appearance. They're all visually stimulated creatures."

Like I didn't know that.

"So the first thing is to get your outside together. You have the outfits, next is hair and makeup."

"Mel," I groaned, "I hate makeup. It makes my face itch."

"That's because you always use that cheap drugstore shit. We're going to Bloomingdales!" She smiled with glee.

Needless to say I plopped down another two hundred bucks on makeup by MAC, whoever the hell that was. At the rate I was going I'd have to work so many hours to replenish my bank account I wouldn't have time or the energy for Mr. Dick.

On the sneak, Mel had booked an appointment for me at John Frieda, the same guy who does all those television commercials about hair care.

His salon is what you would call swank. It was in a building with an elevator, a real receptionist, a cushy waiting area that had refreshments and a salon floor right out of America's Next Top Model. None of that storefront crap that I was used to in the 'hood—big windows where anyone walking by on the street could see your stylist slapping perm on her head or gluing in your new hair. This was an experience. Not to mention that while I sat under the dryer, a manicurist did my nails and my feet. I felt like a million bucks. Maybe all this girly stuff wasn't so bad after all.

By the time Mel pulled up in front of my apartment building, courtesy of her leased Mercedes Benz CL, I was bone tired, but Mel insisted that I try on my outfits with my new look.

I obliged and I must admit, I actually looked pretty damned good.

"Girl, you look like a completely different person. If I was a guy I would sure give you a play."

If only.

She walked around in me in a slow appraising circle.

Mel was barely inches away from me, so close that the hairs on my arms stood at attention. She stopped in front of me and ran her tongue across her lips. The pointy tips of her titties brushed against mine and I almost came in my brand new Victoria's Secret thong.

"Humph, humph, humph." She shook her head, reached out and tucked a stray strand of hair behind my left ear. Her breasts pushed up against mine and my pussy started hollering in a foreign language.

She was so close, I thought. I could smell the softness of her chocolate skin. What would she do if I reached out and gave her pouting pussy a friendly little squeeze.

"Are you okay?"

I blinked a half dozen times in a nanosecond. "Huh?" I focused on her face.

She put her hand on her hip and stared at me with a cocked brow.

The air that I'd suddenly gulped in got caught like a fish bone in my throat. I started coughing and couldn't stop.

Mel ran into the kitchen and returned moments later with a glass of water. She held the back of my head and lifted the glass to my lips. It was at that point that I wanted to fall down and die of something sudden and rare.

"I'm f-fine," I was finally about to sputter.

"Had me worried there for a minute."

I forced myself to smile and moved away, then headed for the kitchen. Mel followed.

"So, uh, what was going on back there?"

I went straight to the fridge for some ice. "What do you mean? The coughing? Chile something got caught in my throat." I dumped ice in my cup and started sucking.

"Don't hand me that shit, Chris. Your eyes were closed, your head arched back, mouth open with your little pink tongue flicking in and out from between your teeth. If I was into women that little show would have turned me on." She grinned like she knew my secret. Then she wagged her finger at me. "You were practicing!"

Huh? "Oh…that. Yeah. I was sorta. You know think-ing…that's all."

She nodded in understanding.

"Pretty realistic, huh?" I asked, thankful for the reprieve.

"Sure had me fooled." She stretched and yawned. "I'm beat. I'm going to head on home."

I breathed a quiet sigh of relief. Mel started for the bedroom to retrieve her bags and her purse. "I need to get in a quick nap. I have a hot date tonight."

"I'm just going to take a nap that lasts until tomorrow morning."

Mel giggled. "You are too funny." She walked to the front door. "Call you tomorrow."

"Sure. I'll be here."

She walked out and I closed and locked the door behind her.

I slapped my palm against my forehead. How stupid was that little episode? I needed to get my mind off Mel, that was for sure. One thing was for certain, I was using up the best years of my life lusting after someone that could never be mine.

There had to be someone out there for me. Somewhere.

chapter three

It was shortly after that Saturday extravaganza that I started feeling kinda funny. Not sick funny, but weird funny as if something or someone was always in the room with me, following me around my apartment. I find myself stopping and looking over my shoulder, checking the door and windows, opening closets. It was making me crazy.

One night I literally jumped up out of my sleep because I swore someone was sitting on the end of my bed. I switched on the light and blearily searched the room. Not a soul there but me. I attributed it to some crazy dream. But it kept happening, night after night.

Then one evening I dreamed that I was struggling for air. I couldn't breathe and was gasping for breath. I tried to wake up but I couldn't. It felt as if a weight was sitting on my chest holding me down. When I was finally able to break free, throwing my arms and legs around, once again I was alone in the room. I sat in the chair for the rest of the night peering into the dark, looking for whatever it was that was plaguing my nights.

For about a week, I spent my nights sleeping in the chair and the weird shit finally seemed to stop. I got my first decent rest in ages. And it's a good thing, too, I was about to get some holy water or a priest up in there.

Finally feeling chipper I bounced into the office ready to make a star out of someone. I was humming a John Legend song when Mel sidled up to my desk.

"Guess what?"

I looked up from my call log. "What?"

"I hooked you up with a great guy. He's a friend of Tony's. That's the new guy I'm seeing. Anyway he has a friend, Mitch. And he's dying to meet you."

I squeezed up my face. "Dying to meet me? How can he be dying to meet me if you just started going out with Tony?"

"Look, if I say he's dying to meet you, he is. I talk about you to Tony all the time." She smiled. "So, get your outfit together. We have tickets for Friday night to *Caroline's Comedy Club.*"

"Friday? How do you know I don't have plans already?"

"Because I'm your best friend and I know everything about you. You *don't* have plans."

I heaved a sigh. "All right," I conceded.

"Hey look at it this way, you get a night out, some good company and this might be Mr. Right!"

I rolled my eyes. "Okay. What time?"

"Be ready by seven. Show starts at eight."

"Fine."

Friday arrived a little too soon for my liking but in a crazy way I was excited. It had been longer than I cared to admit the last time I'd been out on a date. So I planned to make the most of it.

From the moment I got home from work, I began preparing. I took a long hot shower, bumped my hair and meticulously applied my makeup exactly how the salesgirl instructed at Bloomingdales.

Those tasks out of the way, I hunted through my lingerie drawer for the perfect undergarments. Hey, you never know. I picked out the hot pink set and did a few twirls in my full-length mirror to see the effect. Not bad at all. Then it was off to choose an outfit. I didn't want to be too dressy or too casual, so I settled for in between: a pair of jeans, my caramel-colored cashmere turtleneck sweater and my caramel ankle boots.

I was standing in the mirror taking in the full effect of my outfit when it started.

At first it felt like something had passed by me, like a light breeze across the back of my neck. But none of my windows were open. Then there was a distinct presence behind me, a kind of heat. But like I said, I was standing in the mirror and all I saw in the glass was me.

I shook it off as my over-active imagination and nerves about meeting Mitch. I turned away from my reflection and I swear to the heavens, something squeezed my breasts.

I yelled and backed up, stumbling over my feet and fell right on my ass. My eyes darted around the room and I was breathing so fast I got dizzy. Then the doorbell rang.

My date. Shit.

I scrambled to my feet and darted toward my bedroom door. And it slammed shut. Slammed shut right in my fucking face.

"What the f—"

Something pushed me back into the room until I wound up on my bed. The bell rang again. I tried to get up and couldn't.

Then just as suddenly as all the weird shit happened, it stopped. I looked across the room and my bedroom door was open. That funny feeling that I had that something other than me was in the room was gone. The bell rang again.

Cautiously I got up. I had no intention of being knocked down again. I inched toward the door then bolted out before it could shut, but nothing happened.

I kept looking over my shoulder as I headed for my front door. I drew in a breath, fluffed my hair and pulled the door open. And damn if it wasn't Mr. Right himself standing there with a smile bright enough to light up a dark room.

Damn, damn, damn.

"Hi, I'm Mitch Walker."

"I'm Christine. Sorry for the wait."

"Not a problem. Ready?"

"Uh, yeah. Let me just get my jacket and bag." I took a quick glance over my shoulder. "Come on in."

I stepped aside to let him in. Dang he smelled good too. I inhaled deeply.

"Nice place."

"Thanks."

Good thing my jacket and purse were in the front hall closet. I didn't want to take any chances on going back into my bedroom and not being able to get out.

"All ready," I said, joining him in the living room.

He turned from studying the family photos on my mantle. "Mel and Tony are downstairs in his car. Me and you are going to take mine if that's cool with you. I hate being dependent on someone else for transportation."

"Great. Then let's go."

He stepped out into the hallway first. I peeked my head inside the door one last time before closing and locking it. My imagination was on overdrive. There was no other explanation.

At least I thought there wasn't.

The car ride to the club was pleasant enough. Mitch was pretty talkative, telling me about his job as a computer programmer for IBM, and his love of all things sports related. He confessed that he'd never been on a blind date before but his good buddy Tony had convinced him and so far he wasn't disappointed. That admission definitely boosted my ego.

"How about you? Ever been on a blind date?"

"This is a first for me, too. I've always heard such horror stories about blind dates."

He chuckled. "You and me both." He cast a quick glance in my direction. "So, do I pass the test so far?"

I turned to him and smiled. "So far..."

As our evening continued I'd all but forgotten about the weird stuff that happened at my apartment. I was truly enjoying myself and Mitch was the perfect gentleman, seeing to my every need.

"I told you he was a winner," Mel said when we made a quick dash to the ladies room.

"Hey he has it going on for sure. Thanks."

She patted me on the shoulder. "You know I wouldn't hook you up with some loser. You're my girl." She leaned closer to the mirror to reapply her lipstick. "So you think you gonna give him some?"

"What? I barely know the man."

"So? He's fine, available, you can tell he likes you, you're both consenting adults. What's the problem?"

I shrugged. "On a first date, Mel?"

"Hey, it's the easiest way to tell if there should be a date two. Why waste time with all the preliminaries when you can find out up front if it's worth pursuing."

Her logic was questionable, but it seemed to have worked for her.

"We'll see."

"You got on your new undies, right?"

I felt hot all over. "Yes," I said in a hush.

"Good. And be sure to do that move you did that day in the kitchen." She dropped her lipstick back in her purse and sauntered out.

I shook my head and followed.

When Mitch and I returned to my apartment there was, of course, that awkward "what now" moment. If I let him in how long should he stay. If he tried to get some should I give it up? What if he didn't want to come in? What did that mean?

"Are you going to ask me in? If not, it's cool, you know."

I lowered my gaze in embarrassment as if he'd been reading my mind. "It's been a while. I don't even know the protocol anymore."

He stepped closer and tilted my chin up with the tip of his finger. "Let me help you to remember."

He lowered his head and his lips touched mine, gently

at first then with just a little more pressure. I held my breath and savored the feel of his mouth against mine. Then his arms slipped around my waist, slipped a sweet tongue in my mouth and pulled me close. I felt his dick pressed up against me and it was rock hard. Oh, my.

"Hmm," he murmured against my lips, then slowly eased away. "Just like I thought, sweet." He looked down into my eyes and let me go. He braced his hands above me on either side of the door frame. "So is it coming back to you now?"

I swallowed. "I seem to be recalling a few things." I stepped back and let him in.

We never made it to the bedroom, which was intentional on my part. Too much freaky shit was going on in there that I was in no position to explain to an almost stranger. In any case, Mitch didn't seem to care one way or the other. It was clear that he wanted what I had and damn if I didn't want to give it to him.

Mitch and I were tangled up together on the couch which had us both giggling like high schoolers. Through a series of twists and turns and some moves I didn't know I had, I was out of my clothes and showcasing my hot pink Victoria's Secret. Now that I was showing my stuff I wanted to see his package.

I pulled his sweater over his head and came face-to-face with his white wife-beater T-shirt. He had a strong chest and nice muscles, not overly pumped up but definitely in shape. I leaned close and kissed his neck, inhaling that luscious scent while running my fingers down his chest to the thick buckle at his waist.

"Let me," he murmured against my hair.

I felt him fiddling with the belt then the sound of a zipper being lowered. He took my hand and pushed it inside the opening of his pants.

"Feel that? It's all for you. Ready and willing."

I wrapped my hand around his cock, imagining it in my mind. It was thick, not long but long enough, and smooth as butter and it pulsed in my hand every time I gave it a little squeeze.

"Stroke it," he said.

So I did and he rotated his hips against my hand. I ran my thumb across the thick head and felt the first dew drops forming. Yeah, he was ready alright, but his ass better wait for me.

I let him go and reached behind me to unfasten my bra. My heavy breasts popped out in greeting.

Mitch's eyes roved hungrily over my tits before sucking a nipple deep into his mouth.

Whew, my pussy started yammering. Mitch must have heard her calling because he expertly pushed two fingers inside me to pacify her. That only made her jump and holler some more.

"Damn girl, you're hot and wet up in there and I can't wait to get inside you."

He somehow managed to shift our positions so that I was beneath him. I threw my right leg over the back of the couch and braced the other one up on the coffee table. Yeah, it was all coming back to me.

Mitch was heavy but I didn't care. He leaned over me and dug around in his pants pocket coming up with a condom.

Tearing the packet open between his teeth, he sat up on his knees and pushed the condom along the length of his dick. He looked down and at me, slid his hands under my ass to lift me up then pushed himself inside me.

I just knew that first big thrust after not having dick in ages was going to be mind-blowing sensational.

I didn't feel a thing. Nothing. I knew he was moving in and out of me, but it was as if it was happening to someone else and I couldn't enjoy it. I knew my hips were bumping and grinding with him but I couldn't feel shit. It was like my pussy was dead or had been shot with Novocain. I felt something inside me but it was like in the distance.

Mitch was moaning and muttering my name, telling me how good my hot juicy cunt felt.

"Oh, shiiiit baby...give it to me...yeah, just like that... open up some more sugar..."

He pulled me tighter and I worked my hips like a hula dancer. My legs were cocked wide open, my feet straight up in the air, my ass at least four inches off the couch. I had to feel something...had to. Sweat was rolling down my forehead. My tits had swollen to the size of small melons and I knew at any moment that Mitch was going to explode. So I worked faster, harder, digging in my heels and my nails.

"Ohhhhh, Goooooodddddddd!" he roared and rammed in me with such force I knew we were going through the couch.

For several moments he shook, trembled and pumped until he finally collapsed on top of me.

I stared up at the ceiling in disbelief, Mitch was weeping.

He pulled himself up and turned away from me. "I... I never felt anything like that before," he whispered in a strange voice. "It was so good it was terrifying." He turned and looked at me as if he expected to see someone else. He started going for his clothes. "I think I better go."

I was so numb I didn't give a shit what he did. I watched him get dressed. He leaned down and kissed me, mumbled something and walked out.

I'm not sure how long I sat there, but it was long enough to get a chill. That's when I finally pulled myself together and got up.

I looked down on the floor to my heap of clothes and the discarded condom pack, the only indicators that some sexual act had taken place, because I still hadn't felt a thing.

I know there are plenty of women who say they don't feel anything during sex. But this was different. This wasn't just about not coming, not having the Big O, this was about not even feeling his dick inside me. Period. At all. It was almost like he wasn't there. I'm sure I was aroused. My pussy was still dripping wet. My nipples were hard as rocks, but I sure has hell didn't feel like I'd just been fucked for the past hour.

Maybe my pussy was dead from non-use, I thought as I dragged myself to my bedroom. Or maybe I'd been lusting after Mel for so long that I really couldn't enjoy a dick. What other explanation could there be?

Resigned to my dickless, cumless life I crawled into bed, turned off my light and prayed for sleep.

chapter Four

I had just dozed off, at least I thought I had when I felt something heavy settle down on the edge of my bed. I tried to open my eyes, but I couldn't. And then began what I thought must be a dream, a hot, erotic dream.

I wanted to participate but it was as if I was a happy bystander that only needed to enjoy.

My entire body was humming, an internal heat coursed through my veins. Even though I knew I was fast asleep everything felt so real: the tugging and sucking of my tits, the hot kisses along my neck, the slender finger that slid in and out of my cattrap tickling and teasing me. I writhed and groaned for more. I bent my legs at the knees or rather they were bent for me somehow and spread wide.

And then something like I've never felt was inside me—thick, nobby, long and so hard it couldn't have been real. It was so thick and pushing in so deep I knew that I was crying in my sleep. I tried to wake up to get away from the exquisite pain, but I couldn't open my eyes, I couldn't move.

It just kept dipping in and out almost in slow motion

until my pussy got adjusted, opened and spread willingly and the tingle of excitement stirred deep in my belly. It felt like my entire being was filled with this wonderful dick of my dreams.

I wanted to give back as good as I was getting, but still I could not move. Only the dick. That thing of my dreams that was torturing me with pleasure.

The first time I came that night, I was sure I had died. The intensity of my climax was so hard and powerful that my heart and my breathing stopped. But the dick didn't. It just kept going, kept pumping and rotating, twisting and turning in and out of me like it wasn't connected to anything on the other end.

And then I came again, and again. I lost count and probably my mind.

At some point it finally stopped and I fell into a deep, dreamless sleep.

When I woke up I could barely move. All my joints ached as if I'd been tied up in knots for weeks. The only thing I could move, in the beginning, was my head.

I turned to look at the bedside clock and couldn't believe that it was six o'clock in the evening. I'd slept for the entire day into the night. The sun was beginning to set. I felt a little chill and that's when I noticed that my sheets and comforter were on the floor. I sat up just a bit and realized that my nightgown was twisted up around my neck and I was sitting in a very big wet spot in the center of my bed.

I was wide awake then. I sat up and stared down between my legs. My clit was so swollen I could see it peek out from beneath my pubic hair. Not to mention the purple bruises that ran along the inside of my thighs.

"What the—?" I switched on the bedside lamp just to make sure my eyes weren't playing tricks on me.

I scrambled out of bed and darted to the full length bedroom mirror. I couldn't believe what I saw. Something resembling handprints covered both my breasts and the center of my stomach like the imprint had been seared into my skin.

I covered my mouth to stifle the scream that was making a beeline up my throat then I started running in frantic circles trying to figure out what the hell happened to my creamy smooth high-yellow body.

That's when it hit me. Mitch! That sonofabitch did this to me! "Shit, shit, shit. Wait till I talk to Mel. I'm never going to let her forget that she set me up with a fuckin' sadist. Christ, look at me." I faced the mirror. "And he didn't even make me come."

I frowned. All my thoughts started running together. Mitch...us on the couch...him exploding inside me like an atom bomb...me unfulfilled and pissed...someone fucking the hell outta me in my sleep.

I shook my head to dispel the images of my dream. That's all it was, a dream, and that bastard Mitch put his marks all over me like I was cattle or something. Guess I needed that wicked fantasy to offset the disappointment, I concluded.

I looked down between my bruised thighs and my swollen clit twitched and pulsed. A shiver of delight ran up my spine. I wanted to touch it but decided it had experienced enough action for a while.

It was all too crazy. Nothing made sense other than me cussing Mel out the very first chance I got. I marched off best as I could to the bathroom. It was at that point, when my clit kept brushing against my pussy hairs and sending shock waves through my system, that I wondered how in the world men managed to walk around all day with dicks and not be in a constant state of hardness.

I started to run a tub of water when the phone rang. I turned the water off then went to pick up the phone in the bedroom. I sat down on the side, the telltale wet stain staring back at me.

"Hello?"

"Hey girl, what in the hell did you do to that boy last night?"

"What did *I* do to him?" I snapped with indignation.

"Tony has been running his mouth all day about how his boy won't stop talking about you and can't wait to see you again. You must have put something on him."

I frowned. "Listen, your friend—" Something brushed against the back of my neck. I whipped my head around and swatted the air. Then something stroked the crack in my ass.

"Shit!" I dropped the phone and whirled around.

"Chris! Chris!"

I was down on all fours, searching the room like a hunter on Safari. Somebody was in my room.

The next thing I knew I was flipped over on my back and my legs got pushed apart. I tried to scream but I was paralyzed. The room grew dark, not like lights going out but more like me not being able to see.

And then it was inside me again. That same big thing that was in my dream. I couldn't wake up, couldn't move, all I could do was lay there and suffer in silent ecstasy.

Then all of a sudden it stopped and I could hear Mel

screaming into the phone like a madwoman. My vision slowly began to clear and the room came back into focus.

I reached across the floor and pulled the phone toward me. My hands were shaking like leaves in winter.

"M-Mel, I...I gotta call you back."

"What the hell is going on over there? I heard you squealing and moaning like... Is Mitch there? Girl you should have told me you had company. Damn. I'll catch you later. You go get yours." She giggled and hung up.

I lay there on the floor with the dial tone humming so long that the operator came on the line to tell me I had a phone off the hook.

I crawled to my hands and knees and finally stood up. My head spun. What the hell was going on? Was I hallucinating? Did that bastard slip something in my drink last night? Whatever was happening it was scaring the shit out of me but I knew if I told anyone, even Mel, they'd think I was nuts. For that matter, *I* thought I was nuts.

But I wasn't.

I managed to get through what was left of my day without further incident. I even managed to read a few chapters of a book I'd had laying around for a while and caught a rerun of *Girlfriends* before I got so sleepy I could no longer keep my eyes open.

I took out a clean set of sheets from the linen closet and changed my bed. That night I slept like a baby, and for several weeks after all was right and well with my world. Mitch tried to get me to go out with him again, but I turned him down. Mel was right on one count, you might as well get the sex thing out of the way early and know if it's worth your time. He wasn't.

So of course, Mel took it upon herself to find Mr. Dick for me. I went through a series of three of her most eligible men—all with the same outcome as Mitch. They all fucked like superstars and I didn't feel a damned thing.

By this point I was getting antsy. The way I'd been made to feel in my dreams was beginning to haunt me all the time. Sex was all I could think about. I wanted that feeling again. I longed for nightfall to see if it would happen, but it didn't.

I resigned myself to my fate of never meeting Mr. Right or ever having an orgasm again.

That's where I was so very wrong.

chapter FIVE

"You sure you don't want to join me and Bruce tonight? We're going to a movie and we'll probably have some Chinese afterward. You're welcome to come," Mel said when she pulled her car to a stop in front of my building.

Bruce was her latest beau.

"No. Thanks. I'm good. I'm going to veg out in front of the TV and relax. It's been a long week."

"You need to get out. Ever since Lenny you don't do anything but work and go home. There's more to life, you know."

Lenny was my last fiasco. I gave her a wan smile. "So I've heard. But I'm fine. Really."

She shrugged. "Okay but if you change your mind, I'll be home until eight."

I opened the car door and got hit with a blast of cold air. "Thanks. Have a good time." I shut the door and walked to my building entrance, bracing myself against the chill.

It felt nice and cozy inside my apartment and I quickly stripped out of my clothes, took a shower and got ready for bed even though it was only five-thirty. I knew that night was *the* night. *It* would be back. I could tell.

For the past few days I'd started getting that funny feeling again, like someone or something was following me, touching me ever so gently. I wanted to be prepared.

I slipped in between my new sheets, turned off the light and waited.

I guess I must have finally drifted off. I was dreaming about one of our new clients, a young actor with plenty of potential. I dreamed that I'd found him the perfect job and he got hired.

Then all of a sudden I couldn't breathe. A weight like an anvil was sitting on the middle of my chest. I tried to wake up to get some air. I couldn't.

A slow heat moved along my limbs until I felt like I was on fire from the inside out. I gasped for air. The pressure on my chest increased.

Shockwaves of delight shot up my center. My pussy was being eaten like it was homemade apple pie. Oh, my God. The pleasure was so intense it was almost painful. I tried to squirm away, but the bliss and the pressure only grew.

There'd been men who'd gone down on me before. But never anything like this. It's what you can only dream about a man being able to do to your cunt with his mouth and tongue. Sucking, licking, teasing, stopping, starting, bringing you to the brink of fulfillment only to start all over again. And when you have a tongue that is long enough to slide up in your trap and tickle it… Lord have mercy!

I came so hard I thought my insides had popped out. But it didn't stop, not for the entire night. The incident went on for hours, fucking me every which way but loose. I came and came and came. I was delirious.

When I finally broke free of my dream I found myself on the floor and had no idea how I'd gotten there. I crawled back up on my bed and drew my knees up to my chest.

I looked around my empty room, felt the stickiness between my legs, inhaled the scent of sex in the air, listened to the silence in my apartment, and I knew I'd lost my mind because whatever this was that was happening to me, I never wanted it to end. Ever.

That Monday I called in sick. I did the same thing on Tuesday, Wednesday, Thursday and Friday. I took my phone off the hook so I wouldn't be disturbed by phone calls and I refused to answer my door because I knew it would be Mel.

All I wanted to do was lay in bed and wait for the "incident" to begin pleasuring me, having its way with me. The most I did in that week was bathe and soak away the soreness. I drank water but food wouldn't stay on my stomach.

I was like a junkie, hooked on dick. A dick I couldn't see, only feel.

I was losing my mind a little bit more day by day, but I didn't care as long as the feeling never stopped. I was willing to sacrifice anything to have it.

By the end of that first week, I was so drained, I could barely get out of bed to bathe, but *it* didn't seem to mind. It came to me anyway, and when it got tired of licking and fucking my pussy, it took me from behind.

I never thought I'd enjoy that kind of sex but I did. I

loved it, craved it, gave it up with pleasure and begged for more. I'd found my Mr. Right.

That Sunday I finally dragged myself out of bed and took a long hot bath. I felt tired but calm inside. This was my world now. I'd come to accept that.

Just as I was coming out of the bathroom, there was a pounding on my door.

"Chris open this door or I'm coming in. The super is with me. Open the door, Chris!"

I fastened the belt of my robe. My house was a mess, I noticed for the first time. Padding to the front door, I pushed the hair away from my face and opened it.

"Hi," I croaked.

Mel pushed the door open. My super tried to peek inside but I shut the door in his face.

Mel whirled toward me. "What the hell is going on with you?" She looked wildly around then sniffed the air. Her gaze zeroed in on mine. "Chris …what is going on? You haven't been to work, you won't answer the phone and your apartment smells like a fuckin' brothel."

Trancelike I turned away from her and sat down on the couch, tucking my feet beneath me.

"I've been fucking," I said in a deadpan voice.

"What?"

"I've been fucking, for hours and hours every night." I smiled and I'm sure I must have looked like a loon when I did. "I finally found Mr. Right."

Mel slowly lowered herself into a chair opposite me. "You mean to tell me that you haven't been to work in a week because of some good dick? You have got to be kidding me."

I shook my head, no.

"Chris, let's be reasonable. Is he going to pay your rent, your bills and buy your food when you lose your job?"

I blinked, trying to clear my head. I hadn't had a conversation with anyone in days and I'm sure what I was saying must sound crazy, but it was true. However, Mel did have a point. I couldn't afford to lose my job.

"Listen," she leaned forward and took my hands. "I don't know who this guy is that has blown your damned mind but unless his dick is dipped in gold and he can cash that bad boy in, you need to get a grip and get back out into the world. When I told you that you needed to find a good dick to change your life I didn't mean for you to ruin it in the process.

"All of us find that one good fuck in our lifetime. Makes your head spin. But the key is, control. You have to be in charge. You still have to live your life, girl. Make him want it," she huffed. "Who is he anyway and how come I don't know anything about him?"

'Cause he's all in my head, I wanted to say, but I'm sure she would have made the call and the men in the white suits would have been at my door.

"His name is Lucas. Lucas Daniels. We met a few weeks ago," I went on, surprising myself with my own made-up bullshit. "And one thing led to another." I shrugged.

"So where is he now?"

"Uh, he had to go back to...L.A. That's where he lives."

Mel leaned back, a slow smile crept across her mouth. "I get it. He was only here for a short time so you wanted to get it while you could! Girl you should have told me. I would have understood instead of making myself crazy worrying about you. You need to talk to a sista!" She slapped my thigh.

"I'm sorry. Really. I should have told you. But…well it was all so new and exciting."

"Well, well, well, my girl has finally found Mr. Dick. I'll be damned. We need to celebrate." She hopped up from her chair and hurried off to the kitchen. "I'm going to make us dinner," she called out. "You look like you could use a meal. And you can tell me all about your new man."

There wasn't much to choose from in my fridge, but Mel being the cook that she is, whipped up some stir fried rice and left over chicken and from somewhere found the makings for a salad. She boiled some teabags she found in my cabinet and made iced tea. It was the first time I'd eaten a meal in a week and suddenly I was ravenous.

"Damn, take it easy. When is the last time you ate?" She peered at me, a mixture of awe and curiosity.

"I don't remember," I garbled over a mouthful of rice.

She shook her head. "Humph, he must be hung, that's all I can say." She took a delicate sip of her iced tea. "So, what's he like, what does he do for a living?"

"He's really nice. Works on computers in, uh, L.A."

"He's not married is he?"

"No." I gobbled down some more food.

"Kids?"

"No."

"When's he coming back?"

"Uh, in a few weeks."

"Good. I want to meet him."

"I don't know…he's really shy."

"Too shy to meet your best friend. Humph. I'll fix dinner and you can bring him over. It's settled."

Whatever, I thought. When Mel made up her mind it was a waste of time trying to change it. I'd just deal with it when the time came. "Fine," I eventually answered.

She looked around. "We really need to clean this place up," she said, rising from her seat to put her plate in the sink. "And you definitely need to do something with yourself. You look a mess."

Absently I brushed my hair with my hands. "I guess."

"Now that Mr. Magic is gone, do you plan to come back to work on Monday?"

I nodded.

"Good." She marched off to the living room and began straightening up. I just sat there. Tired, drained and horny as hell. I simply wanted her to leave just in case Mr. Dick made an early appearance. I forced myself to get up and help with the clean up project. The quicker I got Mel out of my apartment the better.

I went into the living room and she wasn't there. I wandered into my bedroom and she was standing over my bed holding up the soiled sheets. She turned to me, her pert nose wrinkled in dismay.

"Girl, when was the last time you changed these funky sheets? Dayum!" She pulled them from the bed. "These will never come clean." She stuffed the sheets into a pillowcase and tossed them in the corner then strode off to my linen closet for a clean set.

While I sat in the chair, Mel cleaned dusted and mopped. She was a regular black Martha Stewart. In no time, my apartment actually looked like someone lived there.

She turned in slow circles to observe her handiwork. "This is more like it. No man likes to come to a nasty apartment and if he does, you don't need him." She wagged a finger at me. "Don't ever forget that."

"Okay," I muttered then yawned.

She stared at me, hands on her hips. "Are you sure you're all right?"

"Fine. Just tired, that's all."

"I guess so. If I was screwing non-stop I would be, too." She chuckled. "Christine Jones, who would have thought that you would get turned out." She huffed. "Well, I gotta run. See you on Monday?"

"For sure. Thanks for everything."

"Anything for you, Sis. I just want you to be all right and happy." She kissed my cheek.

Any other time I would have had all manner of erotic thoughts about Mel if she'd kissed my cheek. But I could care less. I walked her to the door. "See you Monday."

She turned to me. "Don't ever worry me like that again, Chris. We're friends, remember? You can tell me anything."

"I'll remember that."

She walked out and I closed the door behind her.

I went to my bedroom to prepare for my nightly visit. But it didn't come, not that night or any night for almost a week.

My next visit was that day at the office. And it didn't just fuck me, it made love to me, bound me to it forever with sex that was so sublime as to be inexplicable. All I could think about was that I had to have it like that again, just once that's all I asked. Just one more time. So there I was, soaking in the tub. Waiting. Hoping. Waiting and praying that it would come back and satisfy this raging need that consumed my every waking and sleeping moment.

chapter six

Somehow I managed to go to work everyday, although concentrating on anything was growing increasingly difficult.

I hadn't had an incident in nearly a month and I was slowly losing whatever sanity I had left. I spent all of my free time surfing the internet looking for erotic toys, any new gadget to feed the lust that raged inside me; from vibrating panties to ten-inch rubber dicks. Nothing helped. I couldn't cum. I didn't even get close.

Then one day in a moment of lucidity I actually started paying attention to Mel. She looked different, worn out, something totally foreign to Mel. And when I really thought about it, she hadn't stopped by, called or asked me to join her on a double date in weeks.

I stopped by her desk. She was staring at a stack of papers and barely noticed me.

"Hey," I said. "What's up?"

Mel glanced at me and all the fire was out of her eyes, replaced with something crazed and distant. I instinctively took a step back.

"You look…I don't know…strange."

She giggled. "Do I? Well I feel…incredible."

She was a mess. Her usual expertly styled hair was thick and undone, her nails were chipped and her suit looked like she'd slept in it. And there was a strange odor wafting around her…the scent of old sex.

I flinched. My heart started to pound in my chest. "Um, what have you been up to lately? We haven't talked much in a while," I said, my thoughts running around like crazy.

She shrugged. "Nothing much." She giggled again. "You know how it can be sometimes." She started staring at the papers again, then all of a sudden she said, "I think I'll leave early today." She pushed up from her chair, grabbed her coat and purse from the hook and walked away without so much as a goodbye.

I stood there for a few moments, trying to put it all together in my head. I'd seen that look, I'd smelled that scent. I'd been where Mel was.

It couldn't be. It simply couldn't.

I managed to make it through the rest of that day. But my mind was on Mel and the growing possibility of betrayal.

I went home that night and made sure that my apartment was spotless and inviting. I ran a bath and soaked in my favorite bath wash. I didn't bother to put on any clothes when I was done bathing. I went straight to my bedroom, pulled back the sheets and got in bed, legs spread, eyes closed. I waited. Tonight it would come to me. It would come to me and put out the fire, stamp out the doubt.

But it didn't. And with each passing day I grew more desperate, more unhinged and Mel grew more distant.

One night, weary with waiting I turned on a late night

movie. It was called *The Entity*. I watched, transfixed as the woman was ravaged night after night by some unseen thing called a Incubus. No matter where she went it followed her, sexing her until at times she lay unconscious.

She was me. I was her. Her story was my story. For months I'd believed that what was happening to me was some depraved twisting of my mind, so desperate for sex that it had concocted the perfect dick. But it wasn't in my mind. It was real. However, unlike the victim in the movie that wanted the pillaging of her body to end, I never wanted it to stop. Never. Ever. And in that one moment of madness I understood that the only way to get it back was to take it.

In the ensuing days I became consumed with getting my incubus back in my bed. I started doing research on the entity, searching through all the articles, photographs and victim accounts of attacks, books on demons, anything I could find in the hopes of uncovering some clue that would help me. Finally, I realized that I only had one choice.

It was bitter cold that night. The moon was full, the night still. Nothing moved on the snow-covered streets except me.

In my oversized tote I had a meat cleaver, plastic gloves and several heavy duty black garbage bags, some sponges and bleach.

My boot-covered feet crunched against the ice and snow. I smiled. Soon it would be over.

I stood in front of her house. The lights were out. I went around back and peeked in the window. Through the light of the full moon I saw her, elevated slightly above her bed—arms and legs spread eagle. Her head was tossed back, her mouth wide open. Her hips moved up and down as if by force. Her fists clenched and her teeth bared. Something unseen squeezed her breasts and she howled, the sound drifting off into the night.

To anyone else they may think that they were sleep-walking, hallucinating. But I knew better. My best friend was being fucked by *my* Mr. Dick. Somehow, she'd managed to steal him from me, turn him against me. Now it was Mel who was experiencing the ultimate in sexual pleasure, taken to heights most will never know. But he was mine. Mine!

For years I'd lusted after Mel, thinking that one day she would see how much I loved her. But then I found something that loved me...that made me feel complete in a way that loving Mel never could. And she took that from me. Mel, the woman who had everything—looks, personality, money, clothes, her own house and men tripping over themselves to get between her legs. She even had to have the one thing that was finally mine.

An irrational rage built inside me, clouding my vision, muddying my thoughts. There was a part of me that said what I was about to do was wrong. But the other part of me, the part that had already descended into the depths of decadence understood only one thing—revenge.

I made my way around to the side of the house. I knew she kept the side window to the kitchen cracked. I pushed the window up, tossed my tote bag inside and crawled in.

The house was totally dark, but the smell of demon sex cast a hazy glow to the rooms, leading me to them like a beacon.

Quietly, I approached her bedroom. The door was open. Through the light filtering in from the moon I saw Mel. She was on her stomach now, ass raised in position and grunting as the unseen thing thrust in and out of her pussy.

Did he do it as good to her as he did to me? Did she thrill the way I did every time that knobby, surreal cock pushed up inside her?

She cried out. A long aching wail. Whether it was in pain or pleasure I didn't know, but something inside me snapped. I drew the cleaver out of my bag and went to work.

I took a deep breath and looked across the table at the two detectives. One was sweating profusely, totally red in the face as if he'd been in an oven. The other was standing against the wall staring at me and holding his dick as if he thought it was something I might snatch if given the chance.

The detective at the table turned off the tape recorder. He cleared his throat, took out a handkerchief from his pocket and mopped his brow.

"Is there anything else you want to add, Ms. Jones."

I shook my head with great effort. "No," I whispered.

He got up from the table, walked over to his friend and whispered something before they both walked out.

I sat there staring into nothingness. It was done. All I had to do now was wait.

Several moments later, two men in white jackets came into the interrogation room, followed by the officer who took my statement. The officer unlocked my handcuffs from the table. He then cuffed my hands behind my back and helped me to my feet.

"You're going to go with these two men," the officer said.

I nodded. That was fine.

They led me out and through the office filled with desks and burly cops. Each one that I passed stopped what they were doing to look at me. I heard the whispers but I couldn't make out what they were saying.

I wanted to laugh. But then they would really think I was crazy. I wasn't. I did what any woman would have done in my situation.

The two men put me into the back of an ambulance and we drove off.

They say I'm crazy, but I know better. So they did to me what they do to most crazy people—especially people who've hacked someone to death—they put them away in a safe place where they can't harm themselves or anyone else.

But, shit, this fucking room is the pits. Padded walls, no mirrors, everything bolted down. I can't go anywhere without an escort and they are forever shoving some kind of medication down my throat. They say it will help keep me calm, keep the delusions away.

Ha! They think I'm delusional.

I know they're watching me, watching me through the tiny little window on my padded door. Let them, because one of these nights they are going to get the show I was telling them about.

I really shouldn't be here. The fact of the matter is that everything I did was justified. Anybody would have done the exact same thing, given the circumstances. But of course no one understands.

Listen, if you would have asked me six months ago if I'd

ever lose my head over a man, I would have laughed in your face and then kicked your ass for asking. Except that, well Lucas isn't really a man, not like how you and I understand what a man is. He's sex, raw, ragged, unquenchable sex. A thing with a wicked dick and a deadly tongue that did things to me that made me lose my natural mind.

Everyone has heard of a man being pussy whipped, but I was dick whipped. Still am. I'll never get it again like he gave it to me. And the only one I have to blame is Melody. But Melody ain't getting it no more either. That's the only good thing that came outta this mess.

Besides, he'll come back. He always does. And I'll be waiting...

Donna Hill began her career in 1987 with short stories. Her first novel was published in 1990. Since that time she has 25 novels and 16 novellas in print. Three of her novels have been adapted for television. She has received numerous awards for her work. She has edited two award-winning anthologies and works as an editorial consultant. She is presently published in mainstream women's fiction and contributed to the vampire anthology, *Dark Thirst* (Pocket books). Donna lives in New York. Find out more about Donna online at http://donnahill.com

VAMPED

by Monica Jackson

Dedicated to my readers, without whom no words could be written and shared.

chapter one

The bouillabaisse was sublime, but I was too tense to enjoy it. Somehow I had to get my brand-new fiancé, Andre, to the Black Hole nightclub tonight for my coworker's birthday get-together. The heifers at work think I'm just making him up.

My problem is Andre never goes anywhere but to work and back. He wouldn't even come to my place. Our entire relationship has taken place in this town house, other than our first meet in his restaurant when I was there on a date with another guy.

Thank goodness he complimented the chef. Andre came to our table and at first glance, I was hooked. I had to slip him my digits.

He's a tad eccentric, but otherwise he is too good to be true. I can almost understand those cows at work not believing me.

Since he's a chef, he can throw down in the kitchen, which is a good thing, because when it comes to cooking, the microwave is my best friend. He's also fine, not in a pretty-boy way, but *stop-a-bitch-in-her-tracks* fine with his bad-boy perpetual five o'clock shadow and long, thin dreadlocks that he usually wears in a ponytail.

The hottest thing about him though, is his cool. He's a product of the Oakland streets and has dealt with stuff I can't imagine—crime and desperation, blood and death. It showed in the lethal grace of his walk, the confidence of his moves and the alertness in his stance.

After two gunshot wounds and a stint in prison, he decided to change his life, went to cooking school and got a prestigious job as junior sous chef-in-training at one of the best restaurants in San Francisco.

With a man like that, a woman is willing to put up with a few eccentricities, you know what I mean?

"Andre, I want to ask you a favor."

He looked at me over the rim of his wine glass. "What do you need, babe?"

I swallowed hard and stiffened my resolve to get him out of this damn house, but it was hard to stiffen anything under his sexy, irresistible gaze. His eyes were arresting, gold, green and blue mixed together, like a tumble of precious gems, framed by impossibly long lashes in a face that was chiseled, lean, and covered with pecan-brown skin. Yum.

"I want you to take me out tonight. Some friends of mine will be at the Black Hole and the jealous female dogs are dying to meet you," I said.

He took another sip of wine, the expression on his face unchanging.

I bit my lip, urgency filling me. I just had to get him to go or I couldn't show my face at work tomorrow. "Please, Andre. You know I don't ask you for much." I kept my tone low to ensure the whine I was feeling inside didn't show in my voice.

"I know." He grinned at me, sudden and boyish, and my heart twisted. I loved him so much.

"I can think of an alternate activity that's much more…gratifying, than some noisy, crowded club," he said.

There was a rush of heat between my thighs as I anticipated our lovemaking. Then I stifled a sigh. That's what Andre always does. He's a master of distraction.

"I want us to go out tonight," I repeated.

He bent over his plate and speared an asparagus stalk in his fork. "I don't like clubs. Too many people."

He wasn't going to go. It had been months since I'd been anywhere. *Months.* Other men always loved to take me out and show me off. I'd put up with Andre's undercover ways without a complaint, and this one time I wanted him to compromise for me, he was going to say no?

Anger, tinged with insecurity rippled, though me. I know how good I look. I should be totally secure, a high maintenance bitch, right? But something inside me was crooked. I'd let too many men do me wrong, misuse me.

I was crazy about Andre, because while he superficially resembled the thuggish types I favored, he wanted more for himself and for me. There was something fundamentally good about him too. I know he'd never hurt me for fun, games or power. His word was gold; he always meant what he said.

But the broken, insecure part inside me was scared. I wasn't sure that he loved me or would continue to love me. I wasn't sure if anyone could.

Sure, men wanted me for how I looked, but I know it's

like when they buy a new car. After a while the new smell fades, the excitement wanes, and all of a sudden, it's just another car like the one you had before.

I stared at my three-karat engagement ring. We'd been walking past a jewelry shop and I'd oohed and ahhed. He told me to go on in and try it on. I was floored when he bought it and slipped it on my finger. No formal proposal, just the action.

That was Andre, all action, little talk.

But I swear I'd heard the words *cubic zirconia* from those bitches at work. It was small, it was petty, but I wanted to gloat when they had a fit over the fine piece of man I'd bagged. And if I didn't show, I'd lose so much face at work, I might as well wear a brown paper bag on my head from now on out.

"Sometimes I wonder if you like people at all," I said to Andre.

He picked up his wine and shrugged with a ghost of a smile on his face. "I like you."

His composure raised my blood pressure. "You go to work and then rush to your car to come home and don't leave your house until it's time to get into the garage and go to your car again. I can't even pry you out of here on weekends. You even have your freaking groceries delivered!"

"You never considered that a problem before."

"I'm considering it a problem now. I want to get out. I want us to go out, have some fun and see my friends."

He said nothing.

"We're going out tonight, to the Black Hole." I clenched my hands together in my lap under the table. "I can't see being married to you and living like this. I'm starting to feel like a prisoner."

His slightly narrowed eyes were the only sign of emotion on his face. "Joy, I understand. We'll get out, I promise. But right now, I'm enjoying it being only you and me."

"I've spent all my time at your place, doing what you want to do. If you want this relationship to continue, you need to compromise too." I looked away, unable to meet his too-calm gaze. "A marriage needs to be a mutual effort," I said, my voice soft, barely drowning out what felt like the broken part cracking inside me. What if I lost him?

I'd never challenged him before, never tried to be anything but the good girlfriend. And here I'd just thrown down my gauntlet and had no idea if he'd pick it up or not. It could be over, just like that.

Silence. Silence. Silence. Tears filled my eyes and blurred the food on my plate. I willed that one not drop into it. I couldn't show that weakness. I wouldn't go out crying.

He sighed and pushed his plate away. "Fine. Fine, I'll go, but..."

"But what?"

He ran his hand over his locks. "Nothing."

The music was bumping and the club was as crowded as always on a Friday night. When I walked in with Andre, some of the men almost got whiplash as they swiveled their necks to stare at me. I'd dressed to impress, in a short tropical looking, designer halter dress that accentuated every curve I have, along with some high-heel fuck-me shoes.

I'm used to the reaction, but the way the women stared and preened as Andre passed them disconcerted me. I dismissed the niggles of jealousy and took Andre's hand. I plowed through the dancers to the table at the back, where I knew my bitchy coworkers would be.

I must say their reaction to my man was gratifying. "Pick your jaw up off the floor, something might fly in," I murmured to Tina as I made introductions and soaked in their reactions—admiration, jealousy, resentment, envy, lust for my man—*ah, yes,* it was sweet.

Four women had asked Andre to dance by the time I finished with the initial introductions and hellos. I was getting irritated enough at all the attention the female dogs were giving to my man that I didn't mind when he suddenly grabbed my arm and dragged me away from the group.

I thought we were leaving the club, but was surprised when he took me into the thick of the dancers. I slid into the beat and undulated my body while he fell into the *cool dude shuffle,* that little back and forth movement that's hardly moving at all but still looks incredibly hot.

The song was sexy as hell, so I started to move in to him with a little grind. I stared into his eyes and almost lost the beat when I saw the fear in them. Adrenaline raced through me as I looked around, alarmed. Was it one of his old gang members? Somebody come to shoot him up?

The song stopped and eased into a slow groove. "What's wrong? Do we need to run?"

He swallowed, shook his head. "She's here. I knew she'd come, but not so quickly."

Who the fuck was she? "She? Point her out to me." What kind of bitch could get Andre shaking in his boots? The flickers of jealousy inside me flared into an inferno as I looked around with my eyes narrowed.

"You won't see her unless she wants you to."

"Let's get out of here then."

He sucked air through his teeth. "No, we can't. Not now. *Fuck,*" he said with a savagery I'd never heard from him before.

It was as if somebody took the floor out from under my feet. I swayed with the realization that the man I loved felt that strongly about *another woman.* Oh God. I had to get out of here.

"I'm going to the bathroom," I said.

"No!"

I looked at him. Had he lost his damn mind? I eluded his wild grasp and disappeared into the crowd.

There was a blonde putting on lipstick in front of me in the line that snaked out of the woman's bathroom. Men streamed in and out of the lineless men's room. "Another unfair advantage of their basic equipment," she said with a laugh, snapping her compact closed.

I looked at her and almost gasped at the electric blue intensity of her eyes. She laid her hand on my arm. Her fingers were hot. The intimacy of her touch on my bare arm was almost as if she had touched me...*there.*

She leaned toward me, her lips close to mine. "No need for you to wait. We can share a stall."

It's evidence of my confusion that I didn't say a word, but as soon as she got to the head of the line, I let her lead me into a sticky stall, smelling of urine. She leaned me up against the wall, as if I were a doll, and pressed her body to mine. Her breasts were soft. It was a strange sensation.

"You're a sweet-looking plaything," she said. I fell into

the ice-blue heat of her gaze and gasped as I felt her fingers run up the inside of my thigh, beneath my panties and into the too-damp crevice.

My eyes closed of their own volition as her fingers stroked my clit. The smell of sex rose and I shook, no more able to pull away from her clever fingers than a starving man could pull away from a chicken wing. Her fingers were magic. It was unbelievable.

The world narrowed to electric blue eyes and body shaking, shuddering, craving satisfaction. There was no thought, just sensation, as if I was under a spell.

I whimpered as she drew her fingers away, bereft, but she fell to her knees and fastened her mouth in between my legs. My knees buckled as I felt her tongue, the warm wet pressure even more intense than her fingers. Over-whelming sensations washed through me. Her tongue teased my clit with incredible skill. She kept me from falling, holding me erect with one strong hand.

My hips bucked and I grabbed her hair as the feeling blew up like a balloon, expanding and expanding until it filled the world and crashed over me like a tsunami.

She silenced my cries with her mouth, tasting of my own salty juices.

How could this be happening? This wasn't happening. I wasn't gay. The thought of making out with a strange woman in a nasty bathroom stall had never crossed my mind before. It had to be a weird dream. She drew away and in a blink she was gone.

I heard somebody trying the stall door, but I couldn't move. Not just yet. I didn't even know her name. I trembled in reaction. I always try to approach problems in a logical way and figure stuff out. There's an explanation that makes sense for everything under the sun.

I'm not gay. I'd deal with it if I were, but I know I'm not. I've never had a sexual experience with a female in my life, but more important, I've never had the urge to do so before. Not when there was a man around. No way could any pussy appeal when there was hot, hard dick aplenty, wanting nothing more than my attention and body.

But, I've never cum so hard in my life and I've had head before, excellent head. So how was this different? Stunned didn't even begin to describe how I felt over what I allowed to happen to me.

I reached to pull up my panties and stared at the red blood on my fingers. Had I started my period? That was crazy too. I just finished my period last week. I wadded toilet paper between my legs, and reached out a shaking hand to the door. I needed a drink to help figure this shit out.

I made my way to the bar, ordered a double Vodka tonic and tossed it back like lemonade. Scanning the crowd, I saw no sign of the blonde. No sign of Andre either. I eased off the bar stool to look for him. I decided what just happened was so bizarre, it simply cancelled itself out as if it never was.

I'd forget about it. A blip on the experience screen of my life. I blinked, but couldn't dim the clear recollection of her eyes, her scent, her hands…how much she turned me on and how hard I'd come. I couldn't wait to find Andre, and lose my funky weird lesbian experience in the reality of my desire for him.

But Andre was nowhere to be found.

His car was gone too. "Did you see a guy leave with long

dreadlocks, wearing black and a small silver hoop in his left ear, quite good-looking?" I asked the guy at the club exit.

"Yeah. He was with some blonde chick."

chapter TWO

Panic curled through me. He'd left me here and split with a blonde? I thought about the blonde in the bathroom. Poetic justice? No. It didn't make sense. I hailed a taxi.

His townhouse was dark. I fumbled in my purse for the key he'd given me and let myself in. I dropped my purse to the floor as I heard the tell-tale sounds of the mattress springs pounding. Oh, God, Andre was fucking somebody. He'd brought some blonde bitch to his home from the club to fuck and left me there without a word.

My blood turned to adrenaline as I rushed to the bedroom. I almost tripped on my own feet as I stopped short, frozen by the gleam of ice-blue eyes. She was here, the lesbian bitch in the bathroom. Her white thighs were splayed wide. My man between them, his smooth brown ass pumping up and down, not missing a beat of working his big, hard dick in and out of her, a trickle of sweat running down his back.

I growled, deep in my throat, primal. I wanted to rip him off her, and then rip her to shreds. But I couldn't move. The dreamy lethargy I felt in the bathroom stall stole over me as she stared at me and pinned me in place.

She smiled a little, then bared impossibly long fangs and buried them into Andre's neck. He didn't miss a beat, just kept on pumping.

She bit my man in the neck! Just like a fucking vampire. I had to be dreaming. This freaky sex and vampire shit could not possibly be happening. I'd watched some bad vampire movie and fallen asleep after eating too much of Andre's high-fat cooking.

My fingers curled, and my nails bit into my palms as I clenched my fists. The pain was anything but dreamlike.

Time passed. How much, I'm not sure. I couldn't move, but my rage didn't subside as I watched her suck blood from my man's neck. I wanted to kill her, do the same thing to her.

Andre's thrusts were less powerful, slowing, and a thin trickle of blood ran from where her mouth connected to his neck.

I bit my lips, fighting the jungle urge to tear the throat-biting vampire bitch's head off.

He slowed, slower, slower, stopped. She broke her gaze from mine, but her mouth still moved on his neck. I roared and sprinted to the bed. I grabbed him by the hair and pulled him off her. He fell to the side, unconscious.

She laughed and rose from the bed, like some mythical goddess from the sea-foam of white sheets.

"Your timing is excellent," she said. "I wasn't quite finished, but you will make a lovely dessert."

She reached for me, but I punched her in the face. It was like hitting a stone. I winced and she grabbed me as if were I doll and pulled me closer, her breath metallic, fetid. She bared her fangs.

I let her draw me close, then I made a quick movement

and she yelped. I'd bitten her jugular vein as hard as I could. It was like biting through rancid rubber. Hot, salty liquid filled my mouth, tasting truly awful, but I was determined not to let go.

With the way she was shrieking and trying to knock my head away, she clearly wasn't happy. Bitch didn't know as far as fighting with other bitches, she'd picked on one of the best. I'd been fighting since first grade, 'cause for some reason girls didn't like me much. As far as bitches fighting bitches, in the real deal, there are no rules except winning. Vampire, right? How do you like getting some of your own medicine, skanky vamp whore?

Saying the words aloud would have been far more satisfactory, but it was hard to do anything but clamp my jaws on tight to her nasty vampire throat while enduring what felt like sledgehammer blows to my head and back.

But vamp bitch was at a bad angle and I have a rock-hard head. The worst part was I had to gulp down the funky blood that ran into my mouth before I choked on it. I gagged, but held on, willing myself not to puke.

Then sparks flew in front of my eyes as she struck me with a blow that knocked me off and slammed me into the far wall.

She snarled, her neck torn open and oozing. She crashed through the closed bedroom window, shards of glass flying. I felt my body slide down the wall and land on the floor. Staring at Andre's unconscious form, I willed myself to move, but he faded to black.

I opened my eyes to the glint of pale dawn sunlight coming through the broken window, and groaned. It burned. I rolled away on the hard floor from the painful rays and struggled to my feet. Andre hadn't moved, but any sign the vampire had bitten him had vanished. Please, let him be alive.

I pressed my head to his chest and listened for his heart. It pounded slow and faint. Too faint.

"Andre?" No response. Panicked, I called 911.

The paramedics wanted to know if we had a fight. I looked way worse for wear, the room was in disarray with the window broken and glass shards everywhere. I told them I'd come home after a night of partying and drinking and he'd been asleep. This morning I couldn't wake him up.

I could almost hear them thinking *drugs*. I wanted to scream at them to give him a blood transfusion. But I didn't know how to tell the paramedics that he'd been bled out since he had no discernible wound on his body.

They wouldn't let me ride with him in the ambulance. I had to follow. I pulled on a pair of jeans and pulled my hair back into a ponytail and rushed to the car. As soon as I stepped outside the door I almost fell down. The morning sun burned. What the fuck? I could almost feel my skin blistering.

I ducked back into the house and went into the bedroom to look for the keys to his Lincoln Navigator in the slacks he'd discarded on the floor to fuck that vampire bitch.

Bile roiled through my stomach. I felt sick, nauseous, hungry. But that was nothing compared to how I'd feel if Andre died. I promised myself that I'd hunt down that bitch and kill her.

I changed to a long-sleeved shirt, grabbed some big

shades and almost tore up Andre's bathroom cabinets looking for the sunscreen. I thought I'd seen some somewhere. Finally, I found a tiny tube of SPF 50. I stepped into the cool, dark attached garage of his townhouse, slathering sunscreen on my face and exposed skin.

I steeled myself against the sun as the garage door rolled up. Yeah, I've watched enough vampire movies and read enough books to know the deal, but I really hadn't processed it yet. I was only thinking about Andre.

I squinted as I rolled out into the street. The sun was hot, but not nearly as painful as before, when I was fully exposed. The hospital had covered parking and an elevator straight to the lobby.

When I got to the emergency room, I told them I was Andre's wife. They escorted me to his curtained cubicle and sheer relief zoomed through me when I saw Andre conscious, laying on a gurney with fluids dripping in his arm.

I slipped my hand into his, and he squeezed. Words were unnecessary.

"Don't you know I'm invulnerable?" he said. "Two gunshots couldn't bring me down."

But a vampire almost did. "You need blood," I said.

He nodded. "I told them I was anemic. When my initial blood work came back, they drew a cross-match for a transfusion right away."

Then his eyes widened, as he realized the implications of what I said, his brain reacting more sluggishly than usual from the loss of blood.

"You saw her?"

I nodded.

His eyes closed. "I couldn't help—"

"Shush." I laid my finger across his mouth. "I know. It's all right. Everything's all right."

"I wish."

His words were so full of despair, I ached for him.

"Did she touch you? Tell me she didn't touch you," he said, his voice urgent.

I could smell the anxiety roiling off him. I hesitated.

"Tell me!"

"No." The lie rolled off my tongue. I wasn't going to level with him. I was too afraid of what was happening to me, the sickness I felt at a cellular level. "You were unconscious. It was—it was terrible." The time difference, how could I account for it? "I was terrified. I fainted. I didn't come to until this morning." I studied my hands gripping the silver sidebars of his gurney. "I'm sorry."

The fear and worry didn't fade from his face. "There was nothing you could have done, baby. It's a blessing that she didn't kill you. But she probably marked you." He looked away from my searching gaze.

"Marked me?"

"That's what she did to me, years ago. She marked me with her scent, bit me. Then as far as she's concerned you're nothing but food in the refrigerator. She can come and get you at will. She kills most, but some she chooses to play with—for years."

It was if a light turned on. I understood Andre's eccentricities. He'd only been trying to survive. "That's why you never wanted to go outside."

"That's right. Apparently some vampire rules hold true, they can't come in unless invited. They also hesitate to feed in crowded places. The restaurant is very strict about letting in unauthorized personnel to the kitchen area."

"How long have you been marked?"

"Since I was a teenager. She comes and goes, never quite killing me. I thought she was going to kill me last night. She wasn't happy about my impending marriage."

He was her lover, my fiancé was that blonde bitch of a vamp's regular squeeze. My feelings must have showed on my face.

"She has a way of coercion. I—I couldn't help it," he said, looking away.

My stomach twisted. He remembered making love to her.

I didn't trust myself to say anything. But it would be more than all right when I killed the bitch. If I had to put her in an industrial size hamburger grinder and torch the meat, I would do whatever it took to lay her un-dead ass to rest.

I started shaking, tears leaking from my eyes. I hate to cry, especially in front of people, but this was all too much.

"Baby, c'mere." Andre offered me comfort, but right now I couldn't take it. I hurt too bad physically, mentally and emotionally.

I turned away and grabbed a box of tissues. "I think I'm in shock." That was the understatement of the century. The deal is that I think I'm turning into a vampire.

chapter three

Two nurses came in the emergency room cubicle, one carrying a bag of dark fluid. They went through an elaborate ritual of checking and rechecking to make sure he was the right patient and that was the right bag of blood before they hung it. Finally, the dark red fluid seeped slowly through a filter and down the tubing. My mouth watered.

"We're going to take him up to his room now," one of the nurses said. "The doctor is going to admit him overnight for observation."

"Don't leave. I don't want you going back to my place alone," Andre said. "It's not safe."

"Don't worry, I won't." I swallowed back a rush of nausea. At that moment, I felt too sick to do much of anything but follow his stretcher.

But I made the effort to pull a nurse aside and ask to close the blinds and curtains to the windows in his room before I entered.

Sick or not, I don't want to burn.

* * *

The chair next to Andre's hospital bed reclined and the nurse told me it converted into a bed. As soon as he was settled, I collapsed on it and nodded my thanks to the nurse for the blankets and pillow she handed me.

I was shaking inside, feeling cold and feverish. I wanted nothing more than to go to sleep, but there were some things I had to ask Andre first. Things about vampires.

"Why didn't you want me to go back to your place?"

Andre stared at the silent figures moving on the television screen. "I invited her in. She'll be back."

"So it's true that vampires can't come into a residence unless invited? Are we safe now?"

"She called it human magic. A human's body or their shelter, whether a cave, tent, car or a hole in the ground, can't be invaded by evil unless invited. Even this room, since we're sheltered from the outside, is considered our home and can't be invaded."

"A human's body can't be invaded? Doesn't that defeat the whole vampire purpose?"

"Unless invited or allowed. She has powers of coercion and seductiveness. She has no problem being invited."

My lips tightened as I remembered how I complied in that bathroom stall when she slipped her fingers between my legs. I wouldn't normally allow any woman, short of an OB-GYN, to do that.

"If she marked you, it's as if she put a tracking device on you. She'd know exactly when you were back at my place, vulnerable and alone."

I had a lot of questions, but a spasm started in my stomach, shivered over my body. "Andre, we've been through a lot. I need to sleep, and I think you do, too."

He nodded. "Leave the door open."

"So nobody will have to knock and be invited in? How can we live like this?" It was a rhetorical question, full of worry.

"I hate it. I hate feeling helpless, I hate being afraid and most of all, I hate vampires."

I opened my eyes, startled by the vehemence of his words. "Surely she can't help being what she is?"

"Evil is always a choice and she's pure evil. She needs to die." He turned his head and met my gaze. "I've got to figure out a way to kill her and any other stinkin' vampire I ever run across."

I murmured my agreement and closed my eyes, hurting both body and soul.

I opened my eyes to the darkened hospital room. A nurse was there, standing over Andre. "Hello sleepy-head," she said.

I stretched. Andre was sleeping and a tray of food was on the bedside table beside me. "You missed lunch and dinner. I had them leave your dinner tray in case you woke up hungry."

The new-fangled way to take vital signs only involved pressing a button. The cuff in place on his arm hissed as it filled with air.

"What time is it?"

"A little after midnight."

I was stunned at her answer. I'd slept more than sixteen hours straight. I never slept that long at night. "Could you take the tray? Thank you."

I was relieved when she left. I could smell her and I

never smelled people before unless they were actively
funky, which this nurse was not. Her smell was weird and
appealing. But the smell of the food was disgusting. It was
surprising considering how hungry I was.

They'd hung more blood on Andre. Drip, drip, drip. I
watched it, fascinated. Amazing how well I could see in
the dark. More amazing was how I could smell. Andre's
delicious personal scent wafted over me and it was all I
could do not to start making love to him. I heard the drop
of the blood from the needle to the filter that connected
to the tubing filled with dark, red...

Blood. I wanted it. I wanted it bad. I rushed to the
bathroom and stood in front of the mirror and opened my
mouth. Even my gums were sore. I couldn't believe my
eyes when my incisors started to protrude, razor sharp.
Oh *fuck*. I was a vampire for real or I'd lost my freaking
mind for goddamn real.

I considered my weird hunger. It was something like
sex, the hunger, this incessant craving. I wanted to slip into
bed with Andre and take him inside me, pounding with
blood and life and just...taste.

My eyes closed with pain. That was one thing I could
never, ever do. He hated vampires. I heard the truth in his
voice. If he ever realized that I was a vampire, he'd hate
me, too. And he would want to kill me.

My knees buckled. I grasped the edge of the sink. *I was
a vampire*. I'd been sick, as if I had a mild virus. I felt a
little better now, but deep in my cells something about me
had changed.

My senses were sharper. I could feel the strength in my
muscles. They'd changed somehow. I knew I was stronger,

probably faster, too. What had changed most was the way I handled food, my entire gut. The thought of eating solids made me feel nauseous. Food didn't smell good and if I could bring myself to taste it, I was sure it wouldn't taste good. My new hunger craved something different. Lord help me.

Was vampirism nothing more than a blood-borne virus? I cast a reflection in the mirror. I was definitely not undead. Hot blood pounded in my veins and rushed through my body as always. I drew air in and out of my lungs, bathing the blood that rushed through those capillaries in air. I was breathing, warm and alive. But I had no doubt I was a vampire.

I stared at my incisors in the mirror. They were evident if I smiled, but they appeared retractable according to my hunger and reaction to my circumstances. I was alive but very, very different.

I'd become extremely photosensitive to sunlight and my circadian rhythm had changed to adapt to that. I'd always been a morning lark, now I was going to be a creature of the night.

The immortality bit was probably too good to be true, also the magic powers. Just my luck that the first person in my life that I'd bit the fuck out of was a vampire. The shit was apparently a blood-borne virus. It could be worse, I suppose. She could have had AIDS.

The thought of food nauseated me, but hunger gnawed at the pit of my stomach. My fangs extended again when I thought of that delicious blood dripping into Andre. But I wasn't up to bite somebody to *eat*. Gross.

I frowned as I remembered how Andre's wound disappeared. That seemed like magic. But it could be some enzyme in my newly vamped saliva. There was no such thing as magic, ghosts, demons, werewolves and other beasties.

Okay, there was such a thing as vampires, but it had to have a perfectly scientific explanation.

The hunger roared through me, almost bending me double. I had to get out of here, away from the smell of the man I loved.

I staggered out of the room. It was worse out here. The air was sharp and metallic with blood. The hunger sharpened into pain.

I took the elevator downstairs to the basement. A lone janitor was mopping the floor. He didn't look human anymore. He looked like a giant donut, cinnamon crusted. "Where's the blood bank?" I asked, trying to stand as far away from him as I could.

"We don't have no blood bank I know of."

"Where do you keep your blood? I need to pick some up for a patient."

"That would be the lab," he said, pointing.

I raced down the hall.

I went through the door marked "Laboratory." There was nothing but a little cubicle with a young man behind glass.

"Can I help you?"

"I need a bag of blood for Andre Moore, room 417. Um, make it a double."

He stared at me. "Where's your blood requisition? And I need your RN badge to scan for pickups."

The hell with that. I stared into his eyes and made a mental demand. *Get me my blood, dammit!*

His face went slack and he went to work. "I want three," I called after him.

That was pretty cool, how he skedaddled on my mental command. But I was unsettled. My neat virus theory was shaky. Wasn't mind to mind coercion some kind of magic? But people hypnotize others all the time and don't call it magic. There had to be a scientific explanation for it.

But what else had Andre said? If the vampire bites you, she marks you and can somehow find you anywhere? That had to be duplicated in nature somewhere. As soon as I got home, I'd hit the Internet hard.

The man returned and slid three bags of blood through the bottom opening of the glass, much like a bank withdrawal.

"Hey, thanks."

He nodded, not looking happy. I hoped he wouldn't get into trouble, but hey, I have needs.

There was a woman's bathroom right down the hall. I felt my incisors extend.

As soon as the door of the stall closed, I raised one of the bags to my lip, intending to rip it open with my incisor. Then I felt the stall tremble. An earthquake? It was San Francisco. But then a clear, bright white beam of light from nowhere fell on my blood. I looked around wildly but I couldn't see where it came from. I clutched the bags to my chest.

All of a sudden I heard a deep voice say, "It is forbidden, a mortal sin."

What the fuck?

"But the flesh of life, which is the blood, you shall not eat," the deep male voice said in my ear, way too close for my comfort.

"Um. Is this God?"

"Hardly. You're not *that* important."

A smart-ass disembodied voice. Just what I needed. "But I'm hungry! What else can I eat?"

"Nothing else." The voice was lower. Did I detect a note of sympathy? "...to abstain from pollutions of idols, and from fornication, and from what is strangled, and from blood."

"If I don't eat, I'll die."

Silence. I moved my hands away from my chest, and the beam of light illuminated the bags of blood. The life. *My life*.

"You know most people on the verge of committing mortal sins don't get supernatural visitations with dire warnings, or at least not that I've heard."

Silence. Then the voice said, "Vampires get a choice because you humans have the gift of free will. But you've made your choice harder." The note of sympathy was pronounced. "Most vampires have to also make the decision to hunt and often make a messy kill to obtain their first meal, not merely tear open a clean, plastic bag."

"So what will happen if I drink this blood?" Every cell in my body was screaming for me to ignore the hallucination and satisfy my hunger.

"You will be damned by God."

I gave a bitter laugh. "Is that what you call free will? To either satisfy my natural hunger or be damned by the Lord Himself or die an agonizing death in good standing?"

"Yes, now you understand."

The light clicked off as if somebody flicked a switch. I was left alone with my choice.

chapter FOUR

Hours had passed while I curled on the floor of the bathroom floor, racked with pain. The blood was tossed in the far corner, my back to it. I really, really didn't want to be damned by the Lord.

I think I'm a fairly ordinary black chick for my age as far as religion goes. I'm not the overly religious or church-going type at this point in my life, but my religious indoctrination runs deep, you know?

My three sets of foster parents were all churchgoing people where the family income was supplemented by taking in foster kids. Sunday school was a requirement. Some of my happiest times were at Bible school and singing with the church choir.

Although my unhappiest times were at home with the people charged to raise me, it seemed God cared and would eventually set things straight. It wasn't until I grew up that my faith started to crack a bit and I'd wonder sometimes where He really was and what He was doing while we suffered.

Cold sweat coated my body and sharp pains shot through me. I was dying. I'm only twenty-three years old, just out of college. I don't want to die. I've only started to get it together and live.

I used to be a model, not the high fashion type, but the type that's shot in scanty bikinis and sometimes less. I appeared in a few rap videos, trying to live the glamorous life, full of men, sex and drugs.

But I tasted the funky aftertaste of that life real quick. I found out that bling and flash doesn't make me happy, that the men who fucked me were unsatisfying and only considered me at most an accessory and, at least, another wet hole, that getting high only made me lose myself and feel worse in the end.

Like Andre, I decided to make a change. I went back to school, graduated and got a job in an ad agency doing graphic art. My job was just all right, very routine, but I'd only just begun. I loved my art.

When I met Andre, everything clicked. I looked into his eyes and it was like seeing my other half. All of a sudden, I wasn't alone anymore. And I'd only just realized how deep the bruises of my past ran. I was working on trying to stop tromping on my inner wounds so they could heal and trusting that Andre cared.

Now, after all this, with happiness touching my fingertips, I was going to die? *It wasn't fair.*

And on top of everything, it hurt like hell on goddamn fire, too. What if I stopped cussing and went to church three times a week, stopped fornicating until Andre married me, then would God let me take a little sip of blood? Please?

I wept. *I don't want to die. I hurt so bad. I can't bear it.* I don't know how long I sobbed, but it must have been a long time.

When I came back to myself and lifted my head, a bag of blood was in my hand, my mouth wet.

It seems I'd made my choice. I wasn't strong enough to die.

I sucked all three bags dry in what seemed like a few minutes. The pain receded and I could feel the life pulsing within me. I hoped it was worth it.

I wiped my mouth and stood swaying. The world was two shades darker. The air was thick, dark and full of shadows. I opened the bathroom stall, afraid.

I sensed presences all around me. Malevolent, twisted presences. Oh, God, I thought. Then I remembered with despair that He was no longer mine to call upon.

I looked into the mirror and gasped. I didn't have a reflection. I heard a scream in the distance followed by the grunts of what seemed like an animal in pain.

I was in the same place, but somewhere different too. The shadows weren't the same. Along with the darkness, everything seemed covered with some sort of scum. There was a faint foul odor hanging in the air, like something decaying.

I reached to touch a shadow and jumped back. The darkness opened. I backed away, staring into another place where people floated as if they were lost, and a variety of monstrous and twisted creatures moved, fought, fucked and killed.

The doorway closed after a moment. Was I now on the edge of hell? How much would it take to push me completely in?

Beyond worried, I buried the empty bags of blood in the bottom of the trash. The clock on the wall said 5:00 a.m. I needed to get back to Andre, hell or no.

In the elevator, I saw a sign, "Hospital Chapel, 3rd Floor." I took the detour because I had to know for sure. The chapel was close to the intensive care and surgery units, appropriately near death. The delicious metallic smell of blood grew more intense.

A glow emerged from under the chapel door. It was from no human light source. A feeling of awe filled me as I realized the place was sanctified by the light of the Lord. I approached, trembling and fearful. Through the glass window, I could see two people, kneeling in prayer in front of the altar.

As I edged closer to the glow, it felt like sunlight. You understand that wasn't a good thing, but I pressed toward it anyway. I touched the chapel door and jerked my hand away, staring at the painful burn marks on my inner fingers.

I touched the outside of the wooden door. The heat was intense, like there was a fire on the other side. Probably for me, there was. If I opened that door and went in, I'd be incinerated and be cast straight into hell.

Fat tears dripped off the tip of my nose. This was too much. Holy places were forbidden to me. Crosses, ankhs, stars of David and any other symbol sanctified to the Most High would probably burn me, too. Blessed water would feel like acid. It was true, all true about vampires because we drank blood—stole sacred and forbidden life. I was damned by God.

I knew if Andre found out about my choice and what I'd become, it would be over between us. *Evil is a choice.*

All vampires need to die, he'd said. He could never know, would never know. His love was the only lifeline to humanity I had left.

Andre was awake when I walked in the room. "The nurses thought you'd gone home," he said. "I saw you left your purse and cell, but I was worried."

"I couldn't sleep. I went to the hospital gym to work out." The lie rolled off my tongue easily, as if it was second nature. I guess for damned creatures, it was.

"My doctor is going to discharge me once he gets here to make rounds. Apparently he has office hours in the morning and that won't be until afternoon," Andre said.

I squeezed his hand. "Good."

"We can't go back to my place. Dahlia will return."

"I know. We can stay at my apartment."

"We'll get something bigger soon, maybe across the Bay."

"It's only a place to live. What matters is that we still have each other. Look, I'm a mess and I need to go home and change. I'll get you some clothes and be back in a few hours to pick you up."

"Don't go back to my house, I mean it. Take care of yourself, Joy." His gaze met mine, serious. "I couldn't bear it if anything happened to you. It was as if I spent my entire life alone until you came to share it with me."

Emotion washed through me. I thought I was drained, that my prior storm of emotion had washed me clean of grief, regret and mourning for what was, but his words filled me like the swell of an ocean. He'd voiced exactly what I felt.

Andre was my soulmate and finding one was rare as

diamonds. But now I was a vampire, living on the edge of hell and damned by God, with human joys beyond and behind me. But somehow I'd figure out how to manage. I wasn't going to lose him.

I kissed him again to hide any truth in my face and eyes from his searching gaze. "I love you."

chapter FIVE

As I left the hospital, I saw that ghosts walked the now dark and shadowy halls, confused spirits that thought they were sick or dreaming rather than dead. I was in a hurry to get home, but stopped short when I saw a ghost of a little brown girl, probably around seven, with huge bruises and terrified eyes.

Other than the ghost of the girl being semitransparent, she reminded me of myself as a child, sadder than any kid should be, alone, lost. She wore Sesame Street pajamas. Sesame Street had been on a long time. I wondered how long she'd been wandering the hospital halls. I wonder how she died.

I kneeled in front of her. "You're lost, honey?"

She nodded and opened her mouth, but I couldn't hear her words.

"Look around. Do you see a light that doesn't seem to come from anywhere?"

She pointed to her left. I squinted at where she'd pointed, and saw the faint glow emerging from the shadowed mists. It must be an entranceway to a place forbidden to me now.

"Go, run to it. The ones you love and who love you are there. They're waiting for you."

She hesitated, looked at me and tried to take my hand. Her hand passed through mine. "No honey, you can't come with me. Go over there now. Hurry. It's the right thing to do, I promise. I'll wait here."

She looked at it again.

"Don't be scared. It'll be all right."

Finally, she nodded and made her way to the light. I saw it envelop her and got a glance at the sudden excited and happy expression on her face.

I dashed my sleeve across my wet eyes, got to my feet and brushed my jeans off. The security guard stared at me as if I'd lost my mind. I suppose it looked like I had, crouching on the floor, talking to nothing. "I just sent the ghost of a little girl off to heaven," I told him as I passed.

I went to Andre's house, no longer scared of the blonde vampire. In fact, I hoped she showed. I'd love to beat her slutty ass down and saw her fiancé-stealing head off. I visualized the knife I was going to get to do the deed. I dug out an outfit I'd hidden, something I bought as a gift for Andre and hadn't given him yet. It was expensive and leather, not something I'd normally wear, but I hoped it would suffice.

I took out my contacts, which were starting to feel like boulders in my eyes and went to get a new pair. I blinked as I realized that I could see perfectly. My contacts were no longer needed. That was one reason things looked so blurry and different. A vampire virus cured my near-sighted vision? Had to be some research possibilities there.

I could understand my vamp kin wanting to stay on the

down low though. The whole being damned and blood drinking thing was a bummer.

When I got to my place, everything seemed normal, other than the weird shadows, otherworldly chatter and occasional ghost hanging on the street. FYI, ghosts look just like anybody else, only not as solid.

I parked Andre's car in front of my door and covered up as well as I could with a blanket I'd swiped from the hospital. I dashed to my front door as if the sunlight was acid rain, which was how it felt. I put my key in the door lock and turned. The door opened and I started to step through the door and was knocked flat on my ass.

It was as if the air had thickened to some hard substance blocking the doorway. I tried to push through, but I wasn't getting into my apartment. If this wasn't magic, what was? My logical orderly world and my neat little vampire theory was crumpling all around me, ripped to shreds by angels, ghosts and magic. I couldn't get into my own fucking house.

I sprinted back to the car, my skin burning at the on-slaught of sunlight. Once behind the filtered glass, I punched numbers on my cell phone, angry. Loretta would come through, she always did. Sure enough, she answered on the first ring.

"Girl, I need you to do me a major favor," I said. "It's a little strange, but I'll owe you big time."

"Whazzup? You know I got your back, though I've hardly seen your hide lately. Where is that fine-ass man of yours anyway? Never mind. I likes to keep my man from the other bitches too. I get it."

"Could you come over to my place? The key is under

the front mat. I'll be over in a little bit. I've got something important to tell you."

"You won the lottery?"

"Naw, not that good, but if you need some bucks you know I'm good for it."

"Cool. I'll be right by."

Loretta was always broke. But she was my girl from way back. She was also in the foster care system, the same agency as me. She'd had too many bad men, too many pregnancies, too many disappointments and heartbreaks, and I knew it broke the girl.

A pang went through me as I thought of her kids, my godchildren. Loretta was the same age as me, 23, but she had three kids. The oldest was eight, named Joy after me. Everybody called her JJ for Joy Junior and I thought that was great. My little man Jackson was six and the youngest girl was named Chai, she had just started kindergarten.

I looked after those kids, bought them shoes and coats and most important, kept them out of the goddamned system. If I died or changed profoundly over this vampire shit, I didn't want to think about what might happen to them.

The most important thing in the world to Loretta used to be her kids. But now... She'd needed something to get by, to help her to feel different. I understood. After the world treats you like a piece of shit for so long it's hard not to believe that's what you are. Loretta had needed not to feel like a piece of shit, at least for a little while.

But now she was a slave. She didn't even want to be herself anymore; all she wanted was to be high. Once that stuff possessed you, it often crowded everything else out, even your soul.

Loretta was a good friend despite everything. Because of Andre, I'd been the self-absorbed one lately, and I didn't have despair and drugs to blame. I didn't know what else to do for her but take care of her kids as I could. She said that was enough and sometimes she'd cry and thank me out of nowhere. But it didn't seem like enough. Even if I managed to save her kids, which I wasn't sure I could do, I knew I couldn't save her, my only true friend.

I sighed and steeled myself to brave the sun. I darted to my apartment door and secreted my key under the front mat.

Loretta pulled up a few minutes later and I crouched down into the seat. She wouldn't recognize Andre's car since we never went anywhere together.

I peeked as she got the key and went in. I waited a moment before I got out of the car and rang the doorbell.

"You don't have your key?" Loretta said, as she pulled open the door.

"Invite me in."

"What are you talking about? This is your own place. Invite you in where?"

"Humor me, Loretta, and invite me in."

"Why you all wrapped up in a blanket like that? You look like a crazy woman. Looks like you slept in those clothes too."

"Invite me in, Loretta! Dammit, I'm burning!"

"Shit. Well, come on in then."

I held my breath as I stepped through the doorway and exhaled a sigh of relief when the wall of air was gone.

"What you high on and can I have some?" she asked.

I ignored Loretta, and shivered with pain. My skin felt

burned and blistery like I imagined a severe sunburn would feel.

"Do me another favor, Lou. Please close all the blinds and curtains. Hang blankets and quilts behind the curtains if you can. Make it as dark as you can in here. Lately, I'm allergic to the sun."

"Allergic to the sun?"

"Just do it girl, please?" I made my way to my windowless bathroom, dropped my clothes on the floor and stepped into the shower to cool my feverish skin. The chilled water against my skin felt real good.

When I got out, I checked the mirror and did a double take. No reflection. Dang, it was freaky. I stared at the air that was where the image of my face was supposed to be.

Being damned caused one to lose their reflection? I frowned. Reflections were caused by light bouncing off a reflective surface. Was the fact that I could cast no reflection emphasizing the point that I was now damned? that my light gone?

The burning church thing was enough. I didn't need any more reinforcement of the fact. How was I going to get my make-up on right and tell how I was dressed? But that was small potatoes compared to being damned in the sight of God, I suppose.

But I couldn't dwell on that or I'd go crazy. Maybe I was crazy already. There was the possibility of that and frankly, a life on anti-psychotics was looking like the better option.

"There was fourteen dollars in your purse," Loretta said when I went into the kitchen.

I know Loretta would steal money from me in a heartbeat, but we had a tacit agreement that if I was so careless to leave my purse out, it was fair game as long as she told me what she'd taken.

"I gotta go to the bank. But now we need to get rid of all the mirrors."

"You into some vampire shit deep, huh?"

I blinked and stared at her. How could she know?

"What do they call that shit? Goth. That's it, Goth. I didn't know any black folks went for that dumb shit, but you always been different."

"Thanks, Loretta."

I never said that Loretta was stupid. She wasn't. "C'mon, I'm going to get the mirror off the dresser, and I need you to take it out. The sunlight, you know."

She followed me to the bedroom and jumped a step away from me. "Dang, I know I ain't smoked anything, but have you noticed you ain't casting no reflection in that motherfuckin' mirror?"

Uh-oh. "Uh, yeah, I know."

"It's reflecting everything else, including me, just fine, but your vampire ass isn't showing up." She waved her hands in front of her eyes. "Maybe I'm having a flashback."

"No, you're okay. It's me. You're right. I accidentally turned my silly self into a vampire last night."

"Oh."

There really wasn't much else she could say, I guess.

"Tell me this. How do you accidentally manage to turn yourself into a goddamned vampire?" she added.

"You get in a fight with the vampire fucking your boyfriend and bite the shit out of her, thus sucking her blood."

"Oh."

"Yeah, it's not much of a plan, but it works."

"You done moved on over to crazytown with me." She sucked her teeth. "It's nice to have some company."

I handed the mirror to Loretta forgetting to account for my increased strength and it crashed to the floor, shattering.

"Shit!" I reached to pick it up and promptly speared my hand with a shard of glass. Blood welled from a good three inch gash. What got me was it didn't even hurt.

"That's going to need stitches," Loretta said.

But as she spoke the words, the wound was closing, healing before my eyes.

"I'm going to put a Band-Aid on it. I think it's going to be all right."

By the time I got to the bathroom, every trace of the wound was gone. I stuck a Band-Aid over the place anyway for Loretta's benefit.

Instant healing powers were apparently a vamp benefit too. No wonder everybody was so quiet about this virus. I wondered about the immortality part. Extreme long life suddenly didn't seem so far-fetched.

As we worked, I noticed Loretta had smelled funny—like something decaying. It was very off and abnormal. Was it cancer?

"Go to a doctor, Lou. Get yourself checked out. I'm worried about you."

"Yeah, like I have health insurance. You know folks like me don't get to see doctors. I'm just grateful those greedy motherfuckers who get the world handed to them on a silver platter let my kids see the doctor when they're sick."

"There's a free clinic. Promise me you'll go."

"With all the backed-up patients they have, you gotta

be damned near dead for them folks to give you a second glance. Why you think I should see the doctor?"

"I just think you should. I'll pay. All right?"

She shrugged. "It's your money to waste."

"I'll make an appointment."

I dug my last twenty from my emergency hiding place and gave it to Loretta, giving her a kiss goodbye. The rank odor lingered in my nostrils. I sensed my friend was dying and there wasn't a damn thing I could do. I didn't have the money for much more than a doctor's visit. Andre made a decent salary, but he didn't have that kind of coin either.

After she was gone, I felt let down. I'd confessed my biggest, darkest secret to Loretta and she'd discounted what her eyes told her about my reflection a few moments before. Instead, she decided I was crazy.

Anybody I told would think that, unless they'd had contact with a vampire before. Andre would believe me, but that was no comfort at all because I feared his belief would be in a package deal along with rejection.

But my apartment was now suitably dark with no mirrors other than the one on the medicine cabinet. I felt confident I could avoid that mirror when Andre was in the room.

I dressed in tight black spandex jeans, a black baby tee that showed my belly button and, what the hell, a black leather jacket.

I didn't blow out my relaxed mane after my shower and I hadn't neglected that since I could remember. I knew it would shade my face better than a hat. I rubbed some conditioner on my hair and let it dry in wild and frizzy corkscrew curls. My ensemble called for dramatic make up. It was going to be me, eyeliner and mascara with no mirror. Life as a vampire is nothing but an adventure.

Then the phone rang. Andre was ready to come home.

chapter six

Andre was pacing a groove in his hospital room floor. I was fascinated and a bit disturbed by how the gaze of a ghost of the old woman sitting on the empty bed next to his, followed his ass.

He grabbed the clothes out of my hands and disappeared in the bathroom before I could say hello. The woman floated behind him. Dirty old peeping Tess.

"I'm dying to get out of this place," he said from the other side of the cracked bathroom door. "I've finished all the discharge paperwork and we can book."

He stepped out of the bathroom. Damn, he looked good in black leather. The nurses almost tripped over each other to tell him good bye with full body hugs, pressing all their jiggly bits into him. I snapped my mouth closed as my fangs extended. I know I'm a jealous bitch, but I can't seem to help it.

He wanted to drive. In close quarters of the car, my mouth watered over how good he smelled. I wanted him so bad.

"Your new look is interesting," he said.

"You don't like it?"

"No, I do like it. It's just different."

"Hmm." Whatever. I couldn't think about anything but getting him home and getting those clothes off him.

But he was going in the wrong direction.

"Where are you going?"

"I need to buy a few things. I thought we could do a little shopping first."

"I'd rather not. I'm really tired." I was mainly worried about burning up in the sun, but it was true, I was tired. It felt like three o'clock in the morning. I suppose since I'd been up all day, it was way past my bedtime.

"Let's go home. I'll go out later and get everything. You need to rest."

"Baby, that's all I've been doing."

But thank goodness he turned to go back to my place. I ducked in, feeling my exposed skin sizzle.

"You've made some changes in here," he said. He'd only been over a few times. His place was a lot more comfortable than my tiny one bedroom.

His scent blossomed in the small space, making me wet and my nipples hard. I pressed my body against his. His mouth met mine, and our tongues tangled. He tasted as good as I imagined.

He tangled his fingers in my hair and inhaled. "Your hair is so soft. Don't change it, okay?"

"The frizz turns you on?"

"Everything about you turns me on, baby." He ran his hands along my waist, under my jacket, easing it off my shoulders and dropping it to the floor.

His fingers played up my back, expertly unsnapping

my bra and pulling it and my top over my head, exposing my breasts.

"You're fucking beautiful." His voice was hoarse with sex.

I flooded, wet and ready. He cupped my breasts, circling his tongue around one nipple then the other, his warm, moist breath making them hard peaks.

Then he sucked them hard, drawing a response from my creaming core. I threw my head back and moaned, my hips rotating, my fingers in his locs.

It felt damn good. And this was only the beginning.

He unbuttoned my jeans, his hand slipping between my legs and under my lace thong. Caressing my clit, he rubbed my flowing juices over it in time to the hard draws he made on my nipples.

My pussy contracted in warm waves. I wanted to feel his hard dick inside me. I needed to be fucked. He backed me up to the bed, slipping my jeans down over my hips. I was naked, splayed open and creamy.

He was clothed, his bulge huge, hard and straining.

"Give it to me. Give it to me now," I said, panting.

He ran his hand over his bulging dick with a devilish grin. "You mean this? How bad do you want it?"

My hips were rotating in anticipation. "I want it bad."

"Come get it then."

He didn't have to ask twice. I fell to my knees, unbuckling his belt, unzipping his jeans and pushing them down with frantic fingers.

His ten, gorgeous inches popped out, rock hard, veins distended.

The sex now had another dimension, with my hunger and how delicious he smelled and tasted. I cupped his balls in my hands, and swirled my tongue around his plum like glans, massaging the head of his dick with my tongue and mouth, while I worked my hand, wet with saliva, up and down his shaft. He tasted so good, my head spun.

It was his turn to moan and grasp my hair. My incisors extended and I had to take care not to graze his sensitive skin.

His distended veins throbbed, the scent of blood filling my nose. Just a little taste. What could it hurt? A tiny nip. *Yessss*.

No. I can't. Not Andre. One of the hardest things I'd ever done was to pull my head away from his big, delicious dick.

He tumbled me back on the bed and pinned my arms over my head, parting my wet folds with his dick, moving it back and forth over my dripping pussy and swollen clit.

I went wild. "C'mon, give to me. Slide that sweet dick home. Please, please."

He bared his teeth, suddenly looking like a vampire himself and gave it. He pumped it deep with hard, fast strokes. My pussy clasped his dick like a glove as he shoved in and out of my slick walls. His swollen cock head felt too good shoving and slamming in and out of my pussy.

We beat against each other's bodies like animals, straining. My nose filled with his scent and my mouth with blood. I'd bitten the inside of my own cheek.

My attention concentrated down to the hard, thick dick banging in and out of me, hard and tight, our bodies reaching, reaching, reaching.

Then my pussy snapped and convulsed on his dick, spasming. Waves of ecstasy crashed though me, keen as a razor, rolling in painful pleasure.

He stiffened and with a yell, I felt a hot wetness flood into me like light.

Food. Life. My pussy convulsed again, draining every drop of life. Suddenly the edge of my hunger was gone.

He collapsed against my body. I ran my fingers over his sweat-slicked back, fully satiated in more ways than one.

chapter seven

I reached for Andre, disoriented. I must have fallen asleep after our lovemaking. He was beside me, sleeping. The house smelled of food, he'd cooked. The clock read midnight. Hours had passed and again, I'd slept my evening away.

I was hungry again. My incisors extended as I became acutely aware of Andre's pulse, his aroma, his blood—my food.

I rolled out of the bed and jumped in the shower. It was a little better in there, because under the spray of water, I couldn't smell.

When I got out, I slapped some conditioner on my hair and got dressed in record time. I grabbed my purse and fled before I did something I'd regret for however long I'd exist as a vampire.

I stopped at another hospital and made a withdrawal, easy-peasy. I got a dozen bags of blood, and a few kits to take blood from people and put them in the bags. If bums would sell their plasma for a measly sum to the blood bank, why couldn't they sell a pint or two to me?

My problem was I didn't know how I could store the blood in the refrigerator where Andre wouldn't find it since he did most of the cooking.

I drank crouched down in the car watching the shadows. What looked like demons and the ghosts who never slept hang out on the street.

I remembered the taste of hot chicken wings, Mama Lee's special lo mein, Ben and Jerry's New York Fudge Chunk ice cream. Blood was one-dimensional and flat compared to my remembered human pleasures. It nourished my body and kept the pain at bay, that's all. It seemed that what I had left of pleasure was sex. No wonder vampires had the rep of fucking so much.

A man drove past my car slowly, in a Jag. The hairs at the back of my neck rose, my inner alarms went off. He stared at me, his eyes glinting and somehow I knew we were of a kind, human predators, damned by God. He was pretty good-looking. Apparently vampires don't mess with turning ugly humans.

Doesn't seem like we vamps could suffer each other's company that well. Competition, I guess.

I stuffed the used blood bags into a plastic bag. What could I do now? Go cruise the clubs, shake my booty, enjoy my solitary pleasure of getting fucked by hot men and sip on their blood?

Once it would have been interesting to me, but now the notion wasn't nearly as interesting as marrying Andre in a church, having his babies and for the first time in my life, having a family.

I sighed and started the car. I'd stash the rest of my blood at Loretta's, it was my only option.

I banged on her door for a few minutes before she opened up. "Bitch, do you have any idea what time it is?"

"Almost two. Here, I need you to put this in the refrigerator."

"What is this? Blood? Are you out of your mind?"

"So you said. Just take good care of it. There are two good meals left there. Thanks." I pressed a twenty in her hand that I'd taken from Andre's wallet.

"You're really off the deep end, girlfriend."

"Undoubtedly."

I went home. Andre was sleeping, peaceful. I was wide awake as if it was midday but I had nothing to do. I ended up finishing a novel I was dying to read. Shadows kept covering the damn print and obscuring my vision at the good parts. It was incredibly annoying so far, the whole creature of the night thing was annoying when it wasn't as boring as hell.

I gave up on the book and cleaned the apartment. I watched Andre closely, dropped my clothes and hopped into bed as soon as he stirred.

He reached for me before he opened his eyes. This is why I love Sundays. It's our day of lazy lovemaking, great food and easy conversation. We rarely get all the way dressed.

He rolled over and inside me, not fully awake. Luscious. We moved slow and sensuous, our own slow dance.

I moved on top. He grasped my hips, opened his eyes and smiled. "Good morning."

"Good morning, baby," I said with a like smile as I rolled my dripping pussy over his dick. I wasn't going to last too long, my clit bumping against his dick shaft and his crisp pubic curls.

His hand traveled leisurely over my body, his thumbs massaging my sensitive nipples. I could feel the big head of his dick swell inside me and catch on my walls.

I bent down and kissed him, our tongues tangling, stroking in and out with the rhythm of his dick in me.

Pressure built within me. I was too greedy to savor the sweetness of this scrumptious fuck. I tightened and relaxed my pussy walls on his dick, heightening every move we made.

He groaned. "Fuck, baby."

His thrusts got deeper and wilder, his lower abdomen hard, his balls pulling tight. It tipped me over the edge and I yelled with the force of the orgasm ripping though me.

Only with an edge of my conscious did I discern the delicious splashes of life in my pussy, stretching my shuddering orgasm out to unbearable pleasure.

"I think I have a virus," I said to Andre. "I feel like crap. I'd like to stay in bed today."

"Do you want some orange juice and chicken soup?"

My stomach roiled at the thought. "No. I don't have much of an appetite."

"Want me to take your temperature?"

"Go back on the computer, I'll be fine."

"I know what happened is a lot to take in, but I'm going to kill that vampire."

Determination was in his voice. I closed my eyes so he wouldn't see whatever was reflected there.

"How? Isn't she supernaturally strong? With one glance she took my will away."

"She has weaknesses. Evil can be overcome. It's the rules."

"Whose rules?"

He smiled. "My rules."

"Let it go. We can avoid her. We're doing fine. I don't want you killed."

"I haven't felt like the man I used to be since she marked me. But now she's threatened my woman. I have to do this. You understand?"

I didn't want to, but I did. Andre and I were barreling down a short road to a dead end. I sensed he had no particular problem fucking the vampire when he had nothing to live for. But now I was in his life and it had changed things irrevocably for him.

My mind spun with worry and fear, but I must have fallen asleep, exhausted after my long night awake.

When I woke up, it was dark. I sensed the passage of hours and I knew Andre was on to something.

He'd left the kitchen uncharacteristically messy and cooked nothing, just ate sandwiches, the remains stacked around my computer.

I booted it on and checked the history. He'd done dozens of searches on vampires from every angle.

I saw a scratch piece of paper sticking out from under the CPU and pulled it out. My blood froze as I saw Andre's rudimentary notes on his plan to ambush and kill Dahlia.

I stayed up the night looking for more clues to his plan. I went to bed early in the morning and pretended to sleep until he left for work. Then I called in to my job. I was going to have to start looking for night shift work because it seemed as if there was no way I could stay awake for the entire day.

Andre woke me after he came home from work. "You

must really be sick, baby. I've never seen you sleep like this before."

"I must need the rest."

"You're not eating either. I'm going to take you to the doctor."

My stomach contracted with hunger. "I'm on the mend." I looked at the clock. "I'm late! I need to make a quick run."

"Where?"

"To Loretta's." He didn't have to know I needed to get my fix of blood.

He frowned. "It'll be dark soon. I don't want you out."

Some of the notes he'd written and the searches he did indicated that he planned to go out late tonight to draw and confront the vampire. He wasn't wasting time.

I might lose him over this vampire shit, but I couldn't lose him to death. I wanted him to go forward, to marry, to belong to somebody, to finally have a family. Even if it was out of my grasp now, I wanted his happiness.

I was going to make sure of it. I planned to kill Dahlia myself, but fuck, he wasn't giving me much time.

chapter EIGHT

"Aunt Joy!" Loretta's daughter JJ cried as she let me in.

The other children ran to me, Jackson trying to be cool, and turning his face away from my kiss but lingering in my arms for the hug. Chai snuggled in, feeling so soft and sweet. I breathed deep the sweet scent of their life and their warm, childish forms before I dug in my purse for the treats I always carried for them.

"Hey girl," Loretta called from the kitchen. "C'mon in, I'm cooking dinner."

"I've gotta get mine," I said opening the refrigerator. "Where did you put it?" I was on the verge of panic when I didn't see the blood.

"On the bottom shelf, way back, in a plastic bag wrapped in aluminum foil."

I exhaled in relief as I moved leftovers to the side and saw what looked like a huge ball of aluminum foil.

Loretta made a face as I pulled it out. "You know there's medication that can help you."

"I wish." I tore away the foil.

"I know you're not going to drink that stuff in front of me."

"Uh, okay."

Somehow I always thought being a vampire would be more romantic than sitting on a toilet guzzling blood from a plastic bag.

But I drank it all. I'd need my strength for tonight.

The cell phone vibrated. It was Andre. "It's almost dark," he said.

"I'm over at Loretta's. I'll be home in a few moments."

"If you aren't, I'm coming to get you."

If only he knew how much more dangerous the dark was for him than me.

"I'll be home shortly."

"You staying for dinner?" Loretta called through the door. "I'm making catfish and coleslaw. Got corn bread and potato salad too."

"See what I'm missing?"

"Sounds good. But I ordered Chinese. It's waiting." He clicked off.

It sounded like coagulated dead fish flesh, weeds, roots and grease to me. Catfish used to be my favorite, but my stomach recoiled. "No, thanks," I hollered to Loretta. "I better get. Andre is expecting me back home."

"We need to talk," Andre said as soon as I walked through the door. Every inner alarm I had went off because from most men, hearing those words are rare unless it's dire. Andre is more of a doer than a talker.

I sank on the sofa. He sat down beside me and took my hand. "I'm going to kill the vampire tonight."

I could have cried with both relief and trepidation. He wasn't going to break the engagement or something equally awful because of my new weirdness. Now all I had to do is to talk him out of his wild scheme and kill the bitch myself.

"How are you going to do that?"

"I'm going to blow her head off."

I swallowed hard. That might do it. With my new powers of instant healing, even a gunshot might not stop me...or her. But if he took off her head...

"I can't let you die."

"I'm not going to die," he said.

I started. I didn't realize I said it out loud.

"We could find out where she sleeps. Don't vampires sleep very soundly?" I asked.

He shook his head. "We're not going to be able to find her. I've tried for years. The only way to get her is to draw her out. I'm going back to my house, Joy. Tonight."

"One look and she can make you do whatever she wants you to do."

"She's not going to see me."

"How is that?"

"I've had this idea in my head for a while. I have a high-powered sniper's rifle. I'll be on the roof with it when she comes."

I drew in a breath. "It's too risky."

"It's the only way. She's a cold-blooded killer and she's toyed with me for years. But now she's threatening my family."

A giant lump lodged in my throat. His family. He considered me his family. It was everything I ever wanted, but it was too late. I was the thing that he hated most, damned and unnatural. I took a breath, held it, and let it out slowly. I had to tell him. I couldn't live a lie with the man I loved.

"I have something to tell you, too." He opened his mouth to say something, but I held up my hand. "Let me finish first. This is hard… Dahlia did more than touch me, that night in the club. She…she…"

He sat down beside me and caught my hands. "Shhh. I know. You couldn't help it any more than I could."

"There's more."

The caressing motion of his fingers stilled.

"When I came in the house you were on top of her. Fucking her. She looked at me and I couldn't move. Then she bit you on the neck."

Tears dripped from my eyes as I relived the moment.

"Eventually she broke her gaze, just for a moment, but that was enough. I jumped on her and Andre, I—"

I was unable to go on. Saying it was too hard.

He lifted my chin and wiped my wet cheeks with a tissue. He dropped a feather-light kiss on my lips. "Tell me what happened."

"I bit her. I bit her hard."

"You did what?"

"Okay, basically I ripped her throat out with my teeth. There was a lot of blood."

He looked aghast. "Why?"

"She bit your throat. At the time payback seemed like a good idea. And it was really the only way I could get to her and hold on. She was incredibly strong."

He looked worried, but said nothing. He turned to me, waiting for more. He was smart enough to know there had to be more.

"Her blood seems to have uh, turned me into a vampire."

"What?"

"I think it's a blood-borne virus."

"Slow down. What do you mean, turned you into a vampire?" He was pacing now.

"Uh, the whole sunlight will burn you up, blood drinking, vampire thing."

He stood still and stared at me. "Is that why you've been sleeping all day and not eating?"

"Yes. Food smells disgusting."

He sighed, running his hand over his head.

I couldn't seem to shut up. "I see ghosts now. What might be demons too, but I'm not about to focus on that with all the crap I'm going through right now."

He sank down in a chair across from the couch and stared at me.

"When were you going to tell me?"

"I was sort of hoping I wouldn't have to, but it's hard to hide with the blood drinking and all."

"*Blood drinking,*" he echoed. "Are you telling me you're biting people and drinking their blood?"

"Heavens, no! That would be gross. I'm getting it from the hospital blood banks."

"Gross?"

"Hell, yeah."

Silence lengthened between us.

"So, I'm going with you," I said, too brightly. "I better find some weapons."

I left him sitting on the edge of my recliner, staring into space and went to look to see what lethal items I had around the house. I wished I had a sword or something equally stylish, but I dug around in my closet and found a hatchet that I'd taken camping once and a big knife. I had some Mace, and I had intended to buy a gun, but I kept putting it off because I was ambivalent about the whole gun control issue and it would also mean I'd have to learn to shoot the thing.

Andre started cooking up a storm. He always cooked when he was upset.

Why couldn't I tell him about my choice? About how things had changed, about how I was teetering on the edge of hell, able to peer in if I wanted to?

I needed his strong shoulder and his strength to lean on, but I knew why I didn't tell him—because I was scared he'd reject me. I know he loves me, but how can I put it? He's bad, but he doesn't respect evil. Andre spent time in jail, but it wasn't for doing anything evil, he's not capable of it.

He got on the wrong side of a drug sweep. He was working. In East Oakland, what other work is there?

I could see how he'd be irresistible to a vampire, and he could hang with one, but he'd never love one back. Never. My eyes wet up again and I sniffed. I never heard of a crying vampire, but it seemed like that was all I did.

The important thing was that we were going to kill Dahlia together. Then we'd figure out what was going to come next.

chapter NINE

Andre didn't protest when I said I wanted to stay outside the house and keep her eyes on me and away from him. I was fairly sure I was immune to her powers. A frisson of fear ran through me when I realized that then he could take me out as readily as he took out Dahlia.

He got his equipment and settled in position while I hid myself in some shrubbery on the side where I could see both the front and back entrances. We'd been in place only twenty or thirty minutes when a white Mercedes SL 450 pulled up.

I tensed. This was it. She stepped out, then reached and pulled something out of the backseat. Somebody else.

I hissed as I recognized Loretta. She dragged my friend in front of her, keeping her close. Dahlia wasn't dumb. She'd been watching us and knew it was a set-up.

I stepped out of the bushes, hatchet in hand. "Let her go."

"Gladly." She plunged a knife in Loretta's back. My friend's eyes widened and she went down without a sound. I was frozen, unbelieving and stricken at what had taken place.

"She wasn't worth eating," she said and threw the knife on the body. All this time she didn't stop moving, swaying back and forth, making her a poor target.

"That's Andre's knife, by the way. His prints are all over it." She held up her latex gloved hand, pulled it off and dropped it into her jacket pocket. "Looks like my boy Andre is going back to jail. Such a shame for a pretty boy to spend the rest of his life there. But he'll have lots of friends, won't you, Andre?"

I heard a muffled pop from Andre's silencer and Dahlia's shoulder exploded in a large rosette of blood. She looked up. With a cry Andre fell off the roof.

I charged. We met like freight trains, and knocked each other to the ground.

"Vamp slut, you're going to die tonight," I swore, scrambling to my feet. Her shoulder was healing before my eyes, but she still favored it, wheeling to face me with her other side.

"You're judging me, fool? I see you made your choice. Nice that the Most High makes it so black and white, huh? Die or be damned. You're as damned as I am, blood drinker. We're both together in hell and you know what? We're going to be here forever."

I raised my hatchet and started to charge at her again, but another silenced shot rang out. This time it was her head that bloomed and disappeared.

Vampires just don't turn to dust and drift away. I wish it was that easy. But we do have powers and we're close to the astral, or hell on earth, as I call it.

I reached into a nearby shadow and it opened. I picked

up Dahlia's body and slid it into hell where it belonged. It disappeared into the darkness.

I jumped as I saw a light shining behind me. There was Loretta, looking again like the girls we'd once been together, all the past years and mistakes gone. "Make sure my kids are all right. Keep them out of the system. Please, girl. If you can't, I know your man will."

I nodded.

She turned away. A look of joy was on her face as she let the light take her to the place I'd never be able to go.

Sorrow filled me.

Andre approached, his steps slow and weary. He picked up the knife off Loretta's body. "Get rid of this and the gun."

"It's over," I said.

He nodded, but didn't look at me.

I stashed the knife and gun in hell, where they would never be found.

Then I went to get Loretta's children. I packed their little bags, told them I'd answer their questions later, but for now they were coming over Aunt Joy's house. It was testimony to the upheaval in their lives that they weren't too fazed.

I tucked them into our one bed. Andre would have to sleep on the couch. Me, I don't need to sleep at all.

Andre walked in an hour later, looking exhausted and drawn.

"I got Loretta's kids. They're in our bed."

He sighed with what sounded like relief and went to the kitchen. He returned with a bottle of wine and a glass. "I was worried that Dahlia had disposed of them."

He poured a glass. I missed that before he'd never drink

without offering me some. There was a chasm between us that wasn't there before my confession.

"What happened at the house with Loretta?" I asked.

"Later. I need to shower."

I flicked channels on the television as I waited. Of course Andre was freaked out, but we'd work it out. We had to.

He came out a little later, completely dressed.

"Aren't you going to bed?" I asked. "I made up the sofa."

He didn't answer. "I told the police that I was looking out the window because I heard loud fighting," he said instead. "Somebody pulled up in a white Mercedes. All of a sudden Loretta ran out toward my house and a man followed her. He grabbed her. Then she crumpled to the ground and he ran away." Andre ran his hand over his hair. "Dahlia's gone and they'll think her car was stolen. There's nothing to connect her and me. Loretta's system is full of crack so they'll assume she was in for the ride doing what crack hoes do."

"Loretta wasn't just a crack ho."

"No?"

I shook my head.

"Wake the kids, I'm taking them home," he said.

"You want us to go back to your place tonight?"

"No. Just the kids and I are going. You're a vampire. You made your choice."

"Andre?"

"I'm sorry, but I've lived in the thrall of a vampire for the past ten years, since I was seventeen. How can I tell if you're not controlling me? I can't deal with that for the rest of my life."

"I've never considered controlling you. Never. Do you really think I'm evil? I love you, Andre."

"I heard what Dahlia said to you. You made a choice, the same one as she made. You didn't tell me."

"No. No."

"Was she lying?"

I was silent.

"Did you willfully choose to go against God? Did you drink human blood?"

I stared at him with wide, wet eyes. My throat was dry, my tongue paralyzed.

"So she wasn't lying. I'm sorry, Joy, but I can't. I've been to the dark side and I don't want to live there any more. I love you, but I can't trust you. So it's got to be goodbye."

He stood. Something inside me broke. He was leaving and there was nothing I could say or do, because he had the right to live without fear.

"Are you going to turn Loretta's kids over to foster care?" He wasn't taking them if he was. I'd live here on the edge of hell if I had to, but I'd get those kids raised somehow.

"No. I'm going to raise them. I've seen the look on your face when you talk about them. You love those kids and I'm going to love them too."

All the breath went out of my body as I realized it was his final gift to me. I knew he would love Loretta's children, not only because he said so and he was a man true to his word, but because they were lovable. Andre finally had his family.

"Thank you," I whispered.

The pain in his gaze was raw as he inclined his head, looked away and turned to go into the bedroom.

I slipped out the door because the last goodbye was one that was too hard for me to do.

I walked the night streets of San Francisco. Andre was right to leave and take the kids. I was mad to think I could have raised them. I was a blood-drinking, night walking vampire, an innately evil thing, burned by the sun and anything holy. I saw ghosts and demons and could open portals to hell. Who knew what I'd draw to the kids?

I looked into the shadows of hell and the evil creatures it held and I knew what I had to do. There was one other choice I could make.

I ran through the night mists with sudden exhilaration. I enjoyed the harsh breaths panting through my laboring lungs, the pounding of my heart and the ache of my muscles—reveling in being alive. I ran to St. Anthony's Cathedral, blazing with holy white light that lit up the night and kept the other night creatures at bay. But I picked up speed and sprinted up the steps. I pushed through the door and flew into the blazing white fire of God.

"Wake up, child."

I looked into the eyes of an older man with white hair and rheumy blue eyes.

"Wake up. It's morning," he said.

I sat up. I was lying on a hard marble floor in front of an altar, the statue of Jesus looking down at me.

Morning sun blazed through stained glass windows and on my skin. I held up my hand and looked at the light reflected in it. It didn't burn.

"Is there someone we can call to get you, young lady?"

"Do you have a mirror? Um, in the bathroom? I need

to use the bathroom." I was afraid to hope what I suspected could be true.

He led me to a room. There was a small mirror over the sink. I approached it slowly, scared at the enormity of my hope. I stared and started to laugh.

My reflection laughed back.

I washed my hands and used the bathroom. The priest was waiting outside the door.

"Yes, I have someone for you to call," I said.

I stood in the blazing sun as Andre pulled up in front of the church looking worried. He ran up the cathedral steps. "Are you all right? The priest said he'd found you on the church floor, unconscious."

I grinned. "I'm more than all right. Look Andre, I'm in the sun."

"You're not…?"

"I'm not. I thought I'd die and go to hell when I ran into the church, but He restored me back to what I was before."

Andre folded me in his arms. "I never thought I'd be the type to say this, but Praise the Lord."

I echoed his words, my heart shining, full of light and love.

A week later, Andre and I stood side-by-side in a church in Nevada. JJ and Jackson were beside us and Andre held Chai in his arms. We'd gone through the ritual that legally bound us.

We all left the church, skipping, laughing and whooping, our happiness at being the Moore family. Our love for each burst out and overflowed. I was secure in Andre's love, and I knew we'd always be there for each other and all our children—the ones we had now, and the ones to come, because the Lord in His grace and mercy was the glue that would hold us together forever.

Monica Jackson is the national bestselling and award-winning author of ten novels and has participated in nine anthologies. Two of her novels were optioned for screenplay adaptation and one appeared on television. She contributed work toward the African American vampire anthology, *Dark Thirst* and is presently published in paranormal romance and erotica. Find out more at her website at http://monicajackson.com.

Balancing the Scales
by J. M. Jeffries

To the wonderful women in this book who share our passion for the otherworldly. What a pleasure it is to be bad with all of you.

From Jackie: To Miriam, welcome to the naughty girls' club.

From Miriam: To Jackie, it could have been worse.

chapter one

Paloma Alexander pushed open the front door of her home, dragged her suitcase in after her and walked into the enormous marble foyer. She started to call out to her husband, Keith, to let him know she was back in Las Vegas from her meeting in Los Angeles two days earlier than expected, but decided she would just surprise him. She and Keith hadn't had time alone together in forever. He would be delighted with the unexpected bonus of having her all to himself for two complete days.

She dropped her house keys in the crystal bowl on the side table and frowned at the sight of Keith's cell phone. How strange, Keith never let his cell phone out of his sight, even taking it into the shower with him.

The cell phone blinked announcing two messages waiting for him. She checked and saw they were both from her—one while waiting for her plane and the other after she'd landed. But now she was happy she hadn't caught him, anticipating the surprised look on his face when she appeared so unexpectedly.

She erased the messages and put Keith's phone back on the table. As she glanced up at the curving staircase, the heavy silence weighed on her. Where was the staff? In fact, she realized she hadn't seen any of the gardeners who seemed to be forever puttering around the huge mansion.

Paloma started up the steps. A muted sound came to her and she stopped, one hand resting on the balustrade, and head tilted to listen. The sound wasn't repeated.

She frowned as she walked up to the second story and down the long hallway, peering into open doors as she passed. The mansion was huge and she never understood Keith's need to own so pretentious a showplace when only the two of them lived in it.

Keith wasn't in his office though she could see a sports jacket tossed carelessly over the arm of a high-backed wing chair. The room smelled faintly of cigar smoke. Paloma wrinkled her nose. She didn't like Keith's cigars and liked even less that he'd been smoking in the house when she'd asked him not to.

She backed out of Keith's office and again heard a sound. She tried to locate it, but found nothing. She headed toward the end of the hall and the double doors that opened to her sitting room. Once again she heard a sound.

Had that been a groan?

Her feet sank into thick white carpet, her steps soundless. Another moan sounded. The door to her bedroom was slightly ajar and she hesitated before pushing it open another inch.

What the hell? Her husband of fifteen years lay in the center of the bed, butt-naked, his legs apart and his eyes rolling back in his head. An equally naked woman sat on him, long braids hiding her dark face as she pumped up and down making little moans and groans as though she were dying.

Paloma caught her breath. Keith was screwing another woman!

The woman flung her braids back and Paloma saw the face of Keith's newest protégé, Syrah. Syrah straddled him pumping up and down like an oil rig. Her firm, man-made breasts barely bounced. Her eyes were closed and though she moaned and groaned, she had a look on her face that made Paloma think she wasn't having as much fun as Keith.

How dare they! In her house! On her bed! Paloma took a step forward wanting to yank that woman's hair so hard the damn weave would come off. Hurt. Rage. Betrayal. She could barely breathe.

A scream built in Paloma's throat, but she forced it back. Her fists clenched so tight, her nails cut through her skin. How could he, she thought. Hurt spiraled through her. The betrayal of what he was doing dug into her and she closed her eyes. Great, gulping sobs started in the back of her throat, but she put a fist over her mouth and swallowed hard.

She warred with the idea of storming into the room and giving him and that bitch the Lionel Richie treatment. But some innate caution stopped her. A voice in the back of her head sounded. *Paloma,* the voice said, *stop and think*.

Keith gripped Syrah's hips and thrust one last time deep inside her. "Go, baby, go." He shouted as though urging a horse on the race track. "That's good. You're the best."

When they'd first married, Keith had told Paloma he

wasn't much interested in sex. At first, she'd been startled because their sex life before marriage had been so passionate. But she had been in love and didn't care. She thought then if she loved him enough, he'd change for her. Fat chance! And here he was in her bed with Syrah. Damn him. Damn his lying, cheating heart to hell. Damn. Damn. Damn. Tears started in Paloma's eyes as she fought not to make a sound.

Keith pushed Syrah off, his penis slick with wetness. He rolled to his knees, pushed Syrah down until her rear end was in the air and then he smacked her hard. Not once, but several times, the sound cracking through the room like a whip. Syrah moaned and wriggled her big, bubble butt in the air while Keith gripped her hips and started going at her from behind. Sweat poured down his dark sepia skin as he worked himself inside her and reached around her waist to grab at her breasts, squeezing and kneading them with his big hands while his butt pounded back and forth.

"That's right baby. Work me hard," Syrah cried.

Paloma wanted to leave, but found her feet rooted to the spot not wanting to watch, yet unable to look away. He pushed and shoved at Syrah, battering her like a ram.

How could he bang that low class cow? They did it animal style because that's what they were. Animals. Syrah reached between her legs and grasped his balls. Keith cried out as he pushed inside her one more time. His buttocks clenched and he came with a roar, yelling his release and bucking against her.

Finally, Keith pulled out of Syrah and fell on the bed next to her. He ran his hands down her mahogany-colored skin, pinched her nipple and then reached between her legs to push a finger inside her. Syrah lay back, legs spread as he worked her with his fingers. Obviously, this was one bitch who needed a lot of satisfying.

Paloma felt bile rise in her mouth. She swallowed. When her husband finished with Syrah, he lay back and started stroking himself. Syrah leaned on her elbow and watched him. At one point, she checked her watch and Paloma could only stare. Syrah was in the middle of having hot and horny sex with Paloma's husband and she was checking the time. Did she have a bus to catch?

Paloma couldn't watch anymore. She backed away from the door, turned and ran down the hall to the stairs. She needed her mother. Her mother would help.

In the foyer, she grabbed her suitcase and let herself out after resetting the alarm. She stalked down the driveway trying to keep her rage under control. How long had the affair been going on?

She wasn't going to let that bastard get away with this. He was going to pay for having the audacity to bring that bitch into Paloma's home, into Paloma's own bed. Bastard, she was going to rip his nuts off and have them as earrings. Forget she was a lady, she was going to have her revenge.

First she called a taxi and then she paced back and forth trying to decide what to do next. Her thoughts kept returning to the bedroom and the moans and groans, the slick bodies, the spanking. Is that what Keith had wanted to do to her? She knew their sex life was tame compared to what she had just seen, but had things been that bad?

Admittedly, Keith had spoken to her about her image.

He'd been nagging her to change her image from classy to slutty. He'd complained her music wasn't selling because she didn't appeal to the younger set who had all the discretionary income these days. Obviously, he'd found his audience.

She finally called her brother, Matthew.

"Hey sis," Matthew said.

Paloma took a deep breath. "Do you know a good divorce lawyer?"

"What's wrong Paloma?"

She told him about what she'd just seen. "That bastard is cheating on me with that skanky broad, Syrah, who wants to be a singer like me." What had Keith promised Syrah to get her to do him so thoroughly? Her own contract, an album and chance at the stardom Paloma had spent the last fifteen years working for?

"I'm going to kill him," Matthew said.

If anyone was going to kill him it would be her. "He's not worth jail time. You didn't answer my question. Do you know a good divorce lawyer?"

"I know one."

"Then you call him and get things started. After you call him, I want you to start shifting my money around. I'm not gonna give that bastard a penny of anything I've worked for." After all, what had he ever done but spend everything she earned on his precious Bentley, building his own recording studio and now on that tramp. How could she have been so blind? "Send Brandi to the bank to clear out the lock box. Make sure she gets all my jewelry." Brandi was Matthew's wife and Paloma's stylist.

A cab cruised down the street and when the driver saw

her, pulled to a stop. She got in and gave him her mother's address out in Henderson.

"I'll get Brandi to the bank ASAP. Where are you now?"

"In a cab, on my way to mom's. I need some down time to think about what I'm going to do next." Okay, she really wanted to hide. She wanted to lie in bed and eat bread pudding and have her mother fuss over her, just like she did when Paloma had been a child. That was the cure for every bad thing that had ever happened in her life.

Her brother laughed. "Good, I'll give you a call as soon as I loot your accounts."

"That isn't illegal or anything, is it? I don't want you to get into trouble."

"I'm your lawyer, not his. Keith doesn't have the balls to get dirty with me, so stop worrying."

Too true. At six foot five inches, her brother was a former linebacker at LSU and could pretty much intimidate Satan. "I love you little brother."

"I love you, too, big sis. Don't worry, we're going to get through this...together."

She needed to hear that. "Thank you." She disconnected and leaned back in the taxi. She was going to get through this. She would. She just didn't know how.

The taxi pulled up to her mother's house and Paloma paid the driver, grabbed her bag and got out. She was halfway up the stone path when her mother opened the front door.

Marianne Justin was a tiny, elegant woman with soft brown skin, a narrow face and hazel eyes. She was dressed in a beige Chanel suit, a gold necklace with matching bracelets and dainty Jimmy Choo shoes on her size five feet. Her mother dressed to go to the grocery store. Her dark brown wig was fashionably styled and her delicate face was the mirror image of Paloma even though Paloma was five inches taller and thirty pounds heavier.

At the sight of her daughter, Marianne Justin's welcoming smile faded. "Paloma, what's wrong?"

Paloma set her suitcase down on the stone flagstones, needing to feel her mother's embrace to take away the pain. She abruptly burst into tears.

Marianne reached up and stroke Paloma's face. "What happened?"

"Let's go inside, the neighbors don't need to hear me wailing away out here like a little kid."

Inside the cool, rambling ranch house, Paloma tucked her bag in the hallway closet as her mother walked to the kitchen to fix her some sweet tea. Sweet tea was her mother's cure all for life's every ill.

Paloma went into the living room and sat down in her mother's wicker rocker to stare at the rock garden that surrounded the patio.

Her mother's heels clicked on the tiles as she made her way back into the living room. She set down a tray containing two frosted glasses and a pitcher full of tea on the coffee table. "Now tell me what's wrong?" she asked as she poured tea and handed a glass to Paloma.

Paloma took a long sip and when she finished, she said, "Keith is cheating on me."

Her mother sat on the chair opposite her. "What do you intend to do?"

"My first thought was murder, but I don't want to go to jail. My second thought was revenge, but I don't know what to do. My third thought was divorce, but somehow that seems too easy. I want him to suffer, I want him to hurt." The pain inside Paloma grew and shattered until the tears filled her eyes again.

"Murder's a little drastic, revenge would work easily enough, and divorce is definitely the way to go, but..." Marianne's voice trailed away as she stared thoughtfully at the garden.

"Hell's bells, please don't suggest I try and work it out with Keith. You've never been his biggest fan. He had that bitch in my bed." Frankly she half-expected her mother to load her shot gun and head out with guns blazing. That's what Paloma wanted to do.

Marinane shook her head. "I'm not suggesting anything. I just want you to know I'll be supportive of any decision you make. Personally, I want to skin him alive, chop him into little pieces and dump the debris over the Hoover Dam."

Paloma laughed. No one was more classy and lady-like than her mother, but to hear her talk so savagely was... well, it was funny.

With one eyebrow raised, Marianne said, "You're surprised?"

Paloma nodded. "Where did you get this vicious streak?" *Note to self: stay on my mom's good side.*

"No one," Marianne said in a fierce tone, "hurts one of my babies and gets away with it."

Before Paloma could answer, her cell phone rang. She checked it seeing her brother's number on the display. "Hello, Matthew," she said.

"Paloma, I just checked with the banks. You're broke," he said without preamble.

"I'm what?" Had she heard him right? How could she be broke? This year alone had brought in almost fifteen million in song revenue alone.

"Everything's gone. The money markets, savings accounts, checking accounts, everything's gone. The house is mortgaged to the roof. He hasn't paid the car insurance on any of your cars in three months."

A numbness stole over her as she tried to make sense of what her brother was saying. "I have over forty-five million dollars in the bank. What the hell happened to all my money?" How could Keith do this to her? Fucking bastard. He was going to pay.

"I thought I'd call your accountant to ask what was going on, until I remembered he's a partner with Keith in the recording studio and because Keith wouldn't be able to get at your accounts with the accountant's help, I decided to bypass him. So I had to go through things on my own and from what I can tell Keith has been siphoning money for the last year. A lot has gone to his recording studio, but a lot is just missing and I don't see what he's spent it on."

She gripped the cell phone. "What about the safety deposit box at the bank?" She had stocks and bonds in the box along with her jewelry.

"Brandi's not back yet."

"When she gets back, call Christies and start arrangements to auction off my jewelry." That would give her a few hundred thousand dollars or so. "I'll call Harry Winston to let him know." She had a couple pieces Harry had been wanting to purchase and had been nagging her to sell them to him.

"That could present a problem. Since you and Keith were married in Nevada and that's a community property state, you'll have to make a gift of your jewelry to someone you trust to hold it for you until after the divorce is final. Otherwise, it's a marital asset."

Her stomach knotted. She was poor again. Oh, God. She couldn't be poor again, not after working so hard to get her and her family out of poverty. "Is there anything left at all?"

Her brother paused for a long moment. She could hear him breathing. Finally he said, "There's about a hundred and ten thousand dollars in one of the savings accounts."

"A hundred and ten thousand dollars! That isn't enough money for a shark divorce lawyer."

"Sis, don't worry about paying a lawyer. You put me through law school, and helped me start my practice, my money is your money. I'll pay for the damn divorce lawyer."

Paloma appreciated her brother's comment, but couldn't see through the anger. She reeled from the knowledge that fifteen years of albums, tours, Vegas shows and product endorsements was gone and she only had a hundred and ten thousand dollars. What the hell had Keith done with forty-five million dollars? No wonder he was dogging her into signing the new five-year contract for the casino. He needed more money to steal.

"Thanks, Matt." She disconnected and put her phone away and turned to her mother. "That asshole has taken all my money."

Her mother lifted her regal chin. "Your heart, your pride and now your money. What do you intend to do?"

A bitter taste laced her tongue. She swallowed it down. If nothing else now was not the time to be weak. "I'm going to make him pay. I don't know how, I don't know when, but he will answer for this."

Her mother picked calmly at a thread and then said in a sweet voice. "Kill him."

Paloma stared at her mother. "What? Did I hear you right?"

"You heard me dear, I said kill him."

She thought about getting Keith out of her life permanently. In a strange way that would be a blessing. But did she have the stomach to do it? She would be the first person that any sane person would suspect because she would have two strong motives. Besides, death would be too tidy. "I'm not going to kill him, I am going to punish him."

"How?" Her mother sipped her tea.

For a surreal moment, she wondered how her mother could act so self-possessed and tranquil. Anyone eavesdropping would think they were talking about what they'd scored on their latest shopping expedition. "I don't know how, but I do know I want him to suffer. For a long, long time." Was eternity long enough?

Her mother's perfectly groomed eyebrow rose. "How will you accomplish that?"

Paloma stood, her mind made up. "I'm going to New Orleans."

"No." Marianne shook her head, a look of fear in her eyes. "Don't do that. The price is too high."

"The price of my freedom is never too high." She took her cell phone out of her pocket and dialed information for the airline's number. She called and booked a flight to New Orleans that was taking off in five hours.

Paloma turned off the boat's motor, stepped out of the dinghy and tied it to an iron ring embedded in the rickety dock. As she walked down the dock, she could see through the planks to the murky water below. Somewhere in the distance an alligator roared. Overhead white egrets took flight, circling and then taking off for the Gulf.

As Paloma stepped off the dock, her feet sank into the thick bayou mud and she remembered all the times in her youth when she'd promised herself she would never return should she ever escape from this place.

She hesitated before walking up to the gray, weather-beaten shack. She'd come this far. Now was not the time to turn back. She scanned the area surrounding the shack, searching for her great-aunt Odile.

Miss Odile was the local voodoo woman for all the inhabitants of Bayou La Lune. If anyone could help Paloma with her predicament, it would be Miss Odile.

The ramshackle house was set back from the water, and surrounded by towering live oaks drooping with Spanish moss. The house looked as though it was going to fall down any second, but she couldn't tell if that was the normal appearance or the after-effects of last season's terrible hurricane.

Paloma hitched her black tote over her shoulder and set off, her sneakers slapping against the dirt of the path. Was Miss Odile even home?

She glanced around and saw a small garden to one side of the clearing. A dovecote sat under one of the trees and she could hear the cooing of the birds inside.

Having left for good, Paloma only returned for the odd family reunion and never stayed more than a few days. Now that her life was in shambles, she was back where she started.

A shaft of sunlight pierced the trees. A brown pelican landed on a log and stared at her. Nothing like having the wildlife eyeball her like they knew she'd been played by her husband.

"What you want, chile?" Miss Odile said in a raspy voice.

Paloma started. Where had Miss Odile come from? One second the porch had been empty and the next Miss Odile stood on the gray wood slats with a broom in her hand as though she'd been there all along.

Miss Odile had been old when Paloma had been a child. Except for a more shrunken stature, she seemed pretty much the same. Beautiful coal-black hair was wrapped around her head contrasted with the wizened look of her walnut-colored face. Shrewd brown eyes studied Paloma with a sharpness that seemed to see right into her soul.

Not sure how to get down to business with her aunt she went for good manners. "Good morning, Miss Odile," Paloma held out the tote bag.

Miss Odile took the bag and peered inside. "What you bring an old woman, chile?"

"Chocolates." Miss Odile's sweet tooth was legendary. "Tea, toilet paper, flour and cornmeal."

"Chocolates! From Paris?" Miss Odile pulled the gold foil box out of the tote. "You so fancy now."

Paloma wondered if her statement was a thank you, but remembered her great-aunt did things in her own time. "Only the best for you."

Miss Odile peered at her. "I remember you running barefoot on my bayou. Your mama brought you and asked me to make you special." The old woman's gaze raked Paloma from head to toe, taking in the designer jeans, T-shirt, expensive Nikes and gold watch. "Your mama's sacrifice was well made. You're mighty fine, girl. But, I sense your heart is heavy."

Paloma said nothing for the moment.

"You have troubles." Miss Odile reached up to touch Paloma's throat, running her gnarled fingers down the smoothness. "You'd best come in and set a spell. You can fix me a cup of this fine tea and we'll have us a talk."

Paloma entered the shadowed interior. Inside a pungent spice smell slid into her senses. She didn't recognize the smell, but caught the scent of sage mixed with rosemary and thyme.

The room was small, but tidy. Despite herbs hanging from the ceiling and bottles crowded on the bookshelves along one wall, the room had an airy feel. Two over-stuffed chairs sat in front of the fireplace next to a Tiffany style lamp on a rosewood claw-footed side table, a silver Reed and Barton tea service on a sideboard and any number of other treasures on tables and shelves throughout the room. Miss Odile didn't appear to have lost anything in the hurricanes. Paloma wondered how she'd kept her house intact.

Something must have showed on her face because Miss Odile cackled as she sat down. "Live in balance with nature, chile, and nature respects that."

A big raccoon walked in through the front door. Miss Odile smiled at the animal. She opened the box of choco-lates and pulled one out. She handed it to the raccoon who grabbed the chocolate and ran out again clutching the treasure in its mouth.

Miss Odile held out the open box of chocolates, but Paloma shook her head. "No thank you, I'm watching my figure."

Miss Odile chuckled. "Everyone watches your figure, you take the day off."

What the hell, Paloma thought and reached into the box, took a chocolate square and popped it in her mouth. The sweet, rich taste running down her throat made her feel decadent.

"Now about that tea." Miss Odile dug into the tote, handed Paloma the tin of imported tea and pointed to the kitchen.

Obediently, Paloma walked into the kitchen. The water was already boiling and for a second, she wondered if her great-aunt had known she was going to have company. Paloma dropped loose tea leaves into the silver teapot, set two dainty Meissen cups and saucers on a tray, poured boiling water into the teapot and returned to the small living room.

Miss Odile watched with such intensity, Paloma almost dropped the tray. She managed to set it on a low table, which she would bet her last hit record was a Chippendale in pristine condition. She poured tea into a cup and handed it to Miss Odile. She poured her own tea and sat down across from her great-aunt.

"How's your mama?" Miss Odile popped a chocolate into her mouth.

"She's fine. Still complaining about her lack of grandchildren from me."

Miss Odile tilted her head and studied Paloma with sharp eyes. "And you, child. What about you?"

"Fine." But she knew she didn't sound convincing.

Miss Odile gave a very unladylike snort. "How come you don't have babies? You been married fifteen years to that man."

Having babies with Keith had never seemed like the right decision. And now that she was going to end her marriage, there would never be any babies. "My life is fine without babies." Keith liked playing celebrity husband and hadn't wanted anything to distract her from her career or his personal pursuit of happiness.

"What that man do to you?" Miss Odile leaned forward, her piercing eyes never leaving Paloma's face.

She thought about how to answer, about where to start and realized that his dissatisfaction with her had been going on a long time. She might as well start at the beginning. "He told me a few months ago my music CD sales were down. He suggested that if I changed my image, dressed like a slut and strutted half naked on a stage like a bimbo, I'd start selling better." Class to trash, all in one easy lesson.

Miss Odile looked disapproving. "Your mama raised you to be a lady."

Once started Paloma couldn't stop. All the other things he'd said to her suddenly made sense in a way. "Look at my face, do you think I need a lift?" She touched her eyebrows and her chin. "He says I look tired and haggard. I'm only thirty-six years old. What does he want? I spent half my life making more money for him and he still wasn't happy. No, he still has to have other women fawning over him, making him feel good. Someone like Syrah who bangs him in my bed, in my house, in my..." She stopped and took a deep breath struggling for control. "And now he's stolen all my money. All my hard work has been for nothing."

"What you want to do about it?"

She struggled for an answer, knowing once she said the words, there would be no turning back. Searching deep inside her, searching for balance, she finally said, "I want everything back." The more she thought about it, the greater her fury became. "That bastard doesn't deserve anything I gave him." Paloma wanted to hit something. She clenched her fist and tried not to pound the arm of the chair. "I want him to pay."

Miss Odile chose another chocolate and bit into it. Chocolate oozed over her fingers. "You had the look when you walked up the dock."

"What look?"

"Revenge."

Paloma took a breath. "Yes, I want revenge."

"You want him to suffer." Miss Odile's voice dropped to a whisper.

"Yes." Did she ever want him to suffer.

Miss Odile smiled. "All the angry wives come to me." She stroked her long neck a few times. "What you willing to pay?"

Anything. "I don't have much now, but..."

Miss Odile ate another chocolate. "I don't need money."

"I have several fur coats. They're yours."

Miss Odile shrugged. "Who I gonna impress in the swamps?"

Paloma ran through the list of her possessions. What did she have to tempt the old voodoo woman with? Paloma's throat started to burn and she gasped with pain.

Miss Odile raised one of her thin gray eyebrows. "I don't need things. I have all I want." She touched her black hair. "But, I've always wanted a voice like an angel."

The burning in Paloma's throat grew until she thought she would die. Her voice! Miss Odile wanted her voice. Her voice was the one thing that made her special.

Miss Odile patted her hand. "You take your time and think about it. I'll be back in a couple minutes."

With Miss Odile gone, Paloma finished her tea. In her unsteady hands, the cup rattled against the saucer. Could she give up her voice? She didn't know. But she did know she had given her husband loyalty and he had betrayed her. She'd not only taken care of her family financially, but his as well. And he'd repaid her with infidelity and theft.

She didn't know how many minutes passed before she sensed Miss Odile standing in front of her. "I know how troubled you are, but you don't need to make a decision right this second." She held out her palm and nestled against her skin was a sea shell of some sort with a velvet cord threaded through it.

Paloma started to take the shell, but jerked her hand back. The shell turned its pointy end toward her.

Miss Odile draped the cord about Paloma's neck. The shell nestled deep in her cleavage. She carefully touched it surprised the shell wasn't smooth but ridged.

"Once you call this in motion," Miss Odile said, "you cannot call it back."

Could she really give up her voice? Never be special

again? Her heart raced. Was the loss of her voice the price of her freedom? "How does the charm work?"

Miss Odile jiggled her eyebrows. "Sex got you into this, sex will get you out."

What the hell did Miss Odile mean?

"Whatever you decide, chile," Miss Odile continued, "I'll know." She clutched Paloma's chin. She stared deeply into her eyes. "You're a good chile, and you'll do." She kissed Paloma on the forehead, the tip of her nose, and then her lips and then sat herself down heavily in the chair and waved at the door. Paloma had been dismissed.

As she made her way back to the dinghy, the burning in her throat increased. She started the motor and headed back to New Orleans.

chapter TWO

Paloma sat in the first class lounge waiting for her plane, relieved that her visit with Miss Odile had ended. The voodoo cursed shell hung heavy around her neck and she resisted the urge to touch it. Every time she did, the burning in her throat intensified. And she worried that she didn't have the fortitude to set the hex in motion, despite her fury over Keith's treachery. How could she have been so deceived? Again, the image of her husband spanking "Miss Thang" returned.

The PA system called her plane and she opened the door to the lounge and started toward her gate. She bumped into a young man who smiled apologetically, then gave her a huge, megawatt smile. He was tall, taller than Paloma, and slender, with cafe-au-lait skin and pleasant brown eyes.

"Excuse me," he said enthusiastically, "you're Paloma Alexander, aren't you?"

How the hell had he seen past her sunglasses and big, floppy brimmed hat? She tried to stay anonymous, but someone always seemed to recognize her. The last thing she needed was for someone to recognize her in New Orleans.

Should she deny it or not? She took off her sunglasses and gave him a full view of her face. "Yes, I'm Paloma Alexander and you are—" She held our her hand inviting him to introduce himself.

He enfolded her hand in his two big ones. His fingers were long and slender. He didn't yank on her as if she were a water pump, but just held her. "Darius Montgomery, your biggest fan."

The name sounded familiar. "Thank you. I'm so—"

"You…are gorgeous." His dark brown eyes were wide with admiration and his full lips were curved upward with a smile that made Paloma feel warm and fuzzy inside. She hadn't felt so esteemed in a long time. Maybe if Keith…she shied away from her thought.

Darius Montgomery had probably had a face full of pimples the first time he heard her sing. He looked around twenty-nine, maybe thirty. But hell, his open appreciation made her day after the drumming her ego had taken. "Thank you so much."

"I'd recognize your gorgeous mouth anywhere." His enthusiasm was refreshing and he didn't seem to want anything from her. He took a business card out of his pocket and handed it to her. "You have a face for movies." The loudspeaker called another flight number. "I wish we had more time, but that's my plane. Call me sometime. I think we could—" The rest of his sentence was cut off by another loudspeaker announcement.

Darius Montgomery rushed off toward his gate and Paloma headed for hers. A second later, she turned around and saw him standing at the door to the jetway ready to board. As he waited, he stared at her. When he lifted his hand and waved, she smiled and waved back, before turning around to board her own plane.

As she walked along the jetway, she read the business card. Darius Montgomery, producer, director, Camelot Productions, Los Angeles, California. Now she remembered. A small independent film maker, Darius Montgomery was the darling of the film critics. His latest film, debuting at Cannes, had been done on a shoe-string budget, opened to rave reviews and decent box office revenues. The little film was even being considered an Oscar contender.

How interesting. Paloma shoved the card into her purse. She doubted she'd ever call. She was a singer, and doubted she could act her way out of a paper bag.

Not wanting to go back to the house, Paloma went to the Penthouse suite that the Istanbul Hotel provided for her to live in. The Istanbul casino and hotel was modeled to look like the city from which it had taken its name. It had gold minarets and towering spires. A grand bazaar took up one whole floor and sold carpets, jewelry, leather goods and other exotic imports from Turkey. Intricate mosaics decorated the casino and as Paloma walked through to the elevators, she felt as though she'd entered a foreign world.

Employees dressed in red fez hats and white tunics over floppy red pants rushed back and forth. Cocktail waitresses in brief harem costumes delivered drinks and took more orders as they moved along the rows of slot machines. The constant chimes of slots gave Paloma a headache.

She reached the penthouse elevator and stood for a

moment watching the people sitting at the slots wondering what their lives were like. Did they have spouses who cheated on them? Did they care? The elevator opened, she stepped inside and inserted her key card to identify that she belonged in the elevator. As the elevator lifted, she contemplated what Keith had done to her. He had done more than betray her; in his own way, he'd destroyed her and unknowingly destroyed himself.

The burning in her throat and the heaviness of the charmed shell on its velvet cord worried her. Was she doing the right thing? Was Miss Odile's solution Paloma's curse or miracle? And did she really want to analyze the answer too closely? All she knew was that she needed her pound of flesh no matter the cost.

The elevator stopped, the doors opening to the penthouse. She stepped into the hall and inserted her key card into the door. Inside, she heard a sound and entered the elegant penthouse suite to find her mother standing in the center of the black and white living room talking on the phone. Marianne smiled, said a few more words and then closed the phone.

"Mama," Paloma said, "what are you doing here?"

"Waiting for you. I figured you'd come here." Marianne's gaze searched her as she sat in the overstuffed easy chair in the middle of the penthouse living room. "How is Miss Odile? She have everything she needs?"

"Miss Odile is always fine. You know how it is, the bayou folk take care of her." Paloma was too agitated to stay still. She paced back and forth, fingering the shell on its velvet cord. Was she angry enough to pay the price? She tried to think, but realized she was too tired.

Marianne patted the spot next to her. "Sit down before you wear a path in the carpet."

Paloma sat. "Please," she said, holding up her hand, "don't lecture me."

Her mother's eyes shifted as she seemed to gather her thoughts. Finally, she sighed. "I'm not going to lecture you. From the day he slipped the ring on your finger, I've been waiting. I knew he was a taker. I saw a lot of men like him growing up in the bayous. Men who let their women do all the work while they took the money. Men who..." Her voice trailed away and her eyes grew hard with old memories that probably had something to do with Paloma's father. He'd been gone a lot of years and even though Paloma wondered about him, she'd never had the courage to ask.

"Why didn't you warn me," Paloma said, though even as the words tumbled out, she already knew the answer.

Her mother patted Paloma's hand. "You wouldn't have listened. I made a decision to keep quiet and just be around to pick up the pieces. And I thank God every day, you didn't have children with that man."

Paloma looked at her mother surprised. "I beg your pardon. You have nagged me every day of my marriage about children."

Her mother held up a hand, smiling. "You are so stubborn and so defiant, I knew if I nagged you every day, you'd never have a baby."

Paloma glared at her mother. "You played me."

Her mother smiled. "Nobody on this earth knows you better than I do."

Keith had never liked Marianne and begrudged Paloma

every minute she spent with her family. The harder he tried to pull her away, the harder she'd clung to her family.

"Are you upset with me?"

"I was, for about five minutes, until I realized all you've ever done or said had my best intentions at heart."

She'd wasted fifteen years with Keith. Why hadn't she seen him for what he was earlier? She tried to think back to what about him had first captured her attention. She remembered the fiery ambition he'd had and how they would set the world on fire with her music. When had that changed? As the years went by, she'd stopped listening to him as he became more interested in her money and motivated by her success.

"What did Miss Odile give you?" her mother inquired.

Automatically, Paloma's hand went to the charm. She removed the cord and held the shell out to her mother. "This."

Marianne shrank away from Paloma. "Put it back. If I touch it, the magic will be broken. Only you can activate its power."

Paloma replaced the cord about her neck. She jumped to her feet to gaze out the giant picture window overlooking the city. Las Vegas sprawled outward encroaching on the brown desert in colorful ribbons. Traffic poured down Las Vegas Boulevard and pedestrians flocked along the sidewalks stopping to admire the water show at the Bellagio, or going into the M&M museum. Paloma turned away to face her mother. "The price I have to pay is my voice."

"There's always a price," her mother said sadly as she touched her head. Her fingers probed at the wig, her eyes unfocused for a second, then sharpened to look at Paloma.

"This isn't how I wanted things to work out. I wanted life to turn out better for you and Matthew."

Paloma stared at her mother remembering the gloriously thick, black hair Miss Odile sported. "You went to Miss Odile, too. You sacrificed your hair, didn't you?"

Her mother's bottom lip trembled. She seemed to turn inward for a second, as though looking down a long tunnel from the present to the past. "My hair was beautiful, but you and Matthew were so much more important."

"What did you want for us?" Paloma asked, humbled by her mother's sacrifice.

"What every mother wants, my children's happiness and success."

Paloma touched her throat. Her voice had brought her mother security, could she take that away from her? She glanced around the penthouse. Her voice had brought all this, as well, but the apartment was a thing, a possession she didn't really need, yet something that Keith so dearly prized.

"Paloma—" Marianne touched her daughter's arm "—I will take care of you if—"

The door to the penthouse was flung open and Keith entered. A shaft of sunlight touched him as he walked into the living room and Paloma's breath caught in her throat. He was so handsome with his cocoa-colored skin, brown eyes and well-built body. And for just a second, she remembered the way he'd been when they'd first met and his dreams had coincided with hers.

He flashed a grin. "Your flight landed an hour ago and when you didn't show up at home, I thought I'd check here."

He didn't even know she'd come back and left again. "Yes, I'm here." *Been bouncing on top of that bitch again?*

"I'll leave you two alone," Marianne picked up her purse and headed to the door. "We'll talk later."

Keith turned to kiss Marianne on the cheek, but she ducked and his kiss landed on air. He set his briefcase down on the table and studied Paloma. Something was different about her. Her eyes glowed and her skin seemed almost iridescent. A flush of desire radiated through him, reminding him of the blatant sexuality that had first attracted him to her. He remembered the first time he'd seen her on a side stage at the Texas State Fair, belting out an over-wrought ballad and looking like a reject from a second hand consignment store. Even then, he'd seen the talent and knew he'd found his meal ticket.

He opened his briefcase and pulled out the contract. He also removed a small gift box and handed it to her. "I brought you a coming home present." She loved jewelry. Maybe now she'd sign the damned contract. His palms itched with the need to smash the pen into her hand. "Baby, you know I miss you when you're gone."

She opened the box thinking he hadn't missed her enough to stay away from Syrah. "I was only gone for five days." She pulled out a gold pendant shaped like a summer daisy. "How nice." She replaced the pendant in the box. "How is Syrah's recording coming along?"

Did he sense something in her voice? "Taking longer than I want, but everything must be perfect." More than perfect. Syrah wasn't Paloma and he had to work harder at bringing her image up to the standards he exacted of his girls.

"Whatever you need to do, get the job done right." She smiled. "God knows, you brought out the best in me."

Didn't he know it. But she was aging. He thought he detected crow's feet at the corners of her eyes, and when she smiled, did he see a little too much chin? He wished she'd do as he'd asked and get some work done. She needed to look fresher, dress younger, update her look to appeal to a younger audience. Her body was fine and she could wear the midriff baring fashions without being ashamed. Her breasts were perky but too small, implants would solve that. Thank God, he'd resisted her desire to have children. Another mouth to feed with a hand out for his money. Besides, a baby would have ruined that almost perfect body.

She reached out to touch his cheek, eyes sparkling. Heat came off her like a furnace and he felt himself hardening. Keith couldn't remember a time when she hadn't been anything more than booty call for him in between his mistresses. She was his last cookie in the jar, but he suddenly wanted her like never before. And he'd just spent the last five days with Syrah humping her as often as he could.

Was he possessed? What was so different about Paloma tonight? He ran his finger down Paloma's shoulder to her breast. A little too soft, unlike Syrah whose breasts were hard and easy to grab with nipples he loved to suck and bruise.

Paloma raised her lips to kiss him and he covered her lips with his. She was warm and willing and all he could think of as he led her to the bedroom was wild, animal sex in as many positions as he could coax out of her.

For some strange reason he found himself so hard, he could barely walk. Her skin burned next to his. And a sultry, musky scent surrounded her. She smelled like sex. Hot, sweaty, nasty sex. Perhaps, he ought to send her to L.A. more often.

* * *

Paloma flung the door to the bedroom open. She wanted to fuck him. Which totally surprised her. She hadn't wanted to even touch him for months. Now her body craved him.

She pushed Keith toward the bed, making quick work of unfastening his belt and unzipping his pants. His pants fell and she yanked his briefs down. His erect cock sprang free. He was swollen and the veins popped out. He was so hard for her. A smoldering expression filled his eyes and for an instant she had to fight the urge to attack him instead of fuck him. But as the excitement built, she knew she had him in her power. Cheating on her was gonna cost him everything he valued.

Paloma pushed him down to lay spread-eagle on the bed. She knelt next to him and cupped his penis. "I haven't seen you in a while."

Keith gulped. "He's happy to see you, baby."

"Poor baby, nobody's been taking care of you." For a second Keith looked uncomfortable.

"He misses you, baby." Keith twisted his hips a little, bringing the head of his penis closer to her lips.

"We don't want him to be lonely," Paloma said as she gently licked the head of his penis, skimming her lips up and down before she sat back. The voice in her head egged her on. And amazingly she wanted him in her mouth. Until this moment she never understood that giving a man a blow job gave her all the power. His most precious possession was this close to her teeth. Just a little pressure and John Wayne Bobbitt would be his new best friend. "I'm going to eat you all up."

Sweat popped out on Keith's forehead. And his eyes grew wide. Paloma loved the glimmer of fear in his eyes and couldn't prevent the smile that tugged at her. This was gonna be good. She ran her fingers around his balls and they clenched under her touch.

His whole body spasmed. Slowly she slid her lips over his cock, taking the tip inside her mouth. His salty taste rolled over her tongue. A heady sensation surged through her body. Heat and ache overwhelmed her.

At this moment she couldn't get enough of him. Did she still want him or was this a fringe benefit of revenge? They said revenge was best served cold, but no one ever told her it would be this sweet. Her hand caressed his balls making them tingle. Her manicured nails lightly brushed over his sack.

Her head began to swim as blood rushed to her vagina. She wanted to fuck him. Hell, she wanted to fuck him until he screamed in submission. As her heart rate sped up she opened her mouth wider and took him deep inside.

Keith moaned as her tongue caressed the slit of his cock's head. She squeezed him, milking him. *How come sex had never been this good before?* In the past, Keith always acted as though he was directing traffic. Do this. Do that. Move faster. Move slower. She didn't even know what to do anymore when they had sex. Not like he'd touched her in the last several months.

He nearly bucked her off the bed when she sank her teeth into the hard flesh of his dick. *Where had this side of her been all their married life?*

She'd never felt so strong a need to fuck him before. Her

256 J. M. Jeffries

head bobbed up and down as she worked his shaft between her lips and tongue.

For an instant, she swore she heard her aunt laughing in the background, but quickly dismissed the thought as she bent back down and her greedy tongue moved down the length of his penis. She worked her lips around his testicle and took it inside her mouth while she stroked his cock with her hand.

"Shit, honey," he said, "welcome home."

She'd never been so…so free before. She took the other testicle into her mouth and gave it the same treatment.

Keith yanked on her hair and she brought her mouth back to his penis. Part of her wanted to raise up her skirt and plunge right onto him as though she were still a teenager and the sex was fresh and mysterious, yet she held back to keep control and remembering that this was about revenge.

Sweat poured off his skin. And she could tell he wanted to come, but she wouldn't take him over the edge just yet. She wanted him to feel as powerless as she did.

Paloma was on fire to her very core. The rough texture of the skin of his balls caressed her hot tongue. She could hear her own slurping sounds coming from her. God that kicked up the temperature another few degrees. Keith let out a tormented wail.

Good she thought as she raised her head. "Enjoying yourself, baby?" she asked in a low, mysterious voice.

"Hell, yeah," he panted, "where did you learn that trick?"

"Isn't this what you want? A wife who fucks like a

whore." Her voice was hot and sultry and filled with promise.

"This is more than I ever hoped for."

The tip of her tongue begin to glide along that seam on the sack as he tightened up. She followed the seam until she was at the base of his hard, throbbing cock. Then she deep throated him taking the entire length of his penis in her mouth. His jaw fell open. Her sucking quickened and his hips started thrusting.

She grabbed him, digging her nails into his skin. He wasn't going to last much longer. When she reached for his testicles and palmed them, it was over. She sucked his cock and squeezed his balls and he came. His hot juices sped through his hard shaft and exploded in her mouth.

Keith couldn't hold on any longer. The sweetness, the pain, the pleasure gathered inside him and erupted like a fireworks display. He pumped hard, harder and finally his whole body tensed, then shuddered.

Something in him shattered. His whole body went into a spasm and still he pumped into his wife's mouth.

He could barely breathe. A black wave crashed over him hitting against him like a jackhammer. Deep in the recesses of his orgasm, he thought he heard a woman laughing. The laugh was harsh and cynical, and finally finished, his body went limp and he stared at Paloma with his semen on her mouth as she sat back on her heels and stared at him. Again her eyes took on an odd light. Blackness hovered at the edge of his vision and before he could gasp or collect his thoughts, he passed out.

* * *

Paloma sat in her brother's office staring at her hands. Her wedding ring winked back at her. She'd wanted to take if off, but worried that Keith would notice and demand an explanation. He might be banging Syrah, but he still considered Paloma his wife—lock, stock and barrel.

What had just happened to her? Not an hour ago, she'd gone down on her husband, and here she was perfectly composed as though that little scene had been nothing but a brief, somewhat unpleasant interruption to her day.

She couldn't shake the heady sense of power she had felt giving Keith a blow job. She tried to analyze her feelings, but numbness spread through her and she worried at the state of her soul. Did being bad always make a person feel so out of control?

Matthew's office was plush, but not ostentatious. His wife, Brandi, had a way of making things look expensive when they weren't. Her brother sat on a sofa with a folder in his hands. His wife sat in a wing-backed chair, a carton on the floor next to her. She was a tall, slender woman with caramel-colored skin and large brown eyes dominating a heart-shaped face.

"I paid your car insurance," Matthew said. He handed her a bill and she glanced at it. "So at least you can drive again."

"Thank you," Paloma said, glad to know she wouldn't have to rely on cabs anymore. She turned to Brandi who sat across from her, a sad expression on her pretty face. "What do you have for me?"

"The jewelry is gone." Brandi held out an open necklace box. A diamond necklace lay nestled against the red satin. "At first I thought everything was there, but then I thought things didn't look quite right. So I took every piece to a jeweler I know at the Bellagio and he confirms your jewelry has been replaced with fakes. Excellent replicas, but still fakes."

Paloma wasn't the least bit surprised. If Keith was bold enough to empty her back accounts, he would be bold enough to take her jewelry. She would never notice because she so seldom wore those pieces. Keith had chosen them and to Paloma they were vulgar.

She cradled an emerald bracelet in her hand. Now she knew—she could see that the luster of gems just wasn't there. How clever of Keith to have such excellent copies made. They probably had some value just because of their exquisite workmanship. "Can I sell these?"

"You can," Brandi said, "but do you want to? My jeweler friend says you'd get maybe eighteen, twenty thousand for everything, but I don't think you want to sell just yet. One piece on the market will probably bring attention from the tabloids and you know how ruthless they can be even when they don't have a shred of evidence to back up a story. Everything will break before you're ready to file the paperwork and then Keith will know what you intend to do."

She couldn't have the tabloids sniffing around her at the moment. Though she could feel the vultures hovering around her already. Paloma took a deep breath reeling from this second hit to her pride.

Brandi patted her hand, her face filled with empathy. "We'll get through this together."

A tear slid down Paloma's cheeks. "I know. Thank you."

"I hired a private investigator to look into Keith's affairs," Matthew said.

"I can't afford something so expensive."

"Reduced fee," Matthew said. "Cousin Jean-Luc from Baton Rouge volunteered. He's never liked Keith and when Keith dissed you, he dissed the family. Now he's going to deal with the family."

Paloma was overwhelmed. Her cell phone rang and she dug in her purse to answer it. Keith, her low-down, cheating, rat-bastard husband was on the other end. "Hello, Keith."

"Baby girl," he said, his voice choking as though he were crying, "I've been in an automobile accident. I'm at Sunset Hospital."

Strangely, Paloma felt nothing. "Are you hurt?"

He slipped into a sob. "My Bentley is gone."

Too bad, she thought. The Bentley was a manifestation of his pride. "We're insured. You can get another one." Silence from the other end spoke volumes. She thought he might fess up about the insurance, but he said nothing.

"Yes, of course," he finally answered. "Can you pick me up?"

"I'm in the middle of a business meeting." Did he really expect her to drop everything to take care of him?

"Are you talking about the contract?" The Bentley forgotten, he sounded a little too eager. "Don't worry then, I'll call someone else."

She didn't think so. Her voice softened, "Your welfare comes first. I'll be at the hospital as soon as I can." She disconnected and stood. A burning had started in her throat and she knew she needed a moment alone before she left for the hospital. "I need to use the bathroom."

Inside the bathroom, she wrapped her hand around her throat and fell on her knees. When she opened her mouth no sound came out. The burning grew until her throat felt on fire.

Sweat broke out on her body. Images of Miss Odile ran through her head. She heard distant chanting. The sound of drums throbbed on her skin and started an ache in her bones. In her mind, she saw a bonfire and a woman swaying to the snap of the flames and the pounding of the drums.

She grasped the shell around her neck. The shell was hot and slippery as the rough ridges undulated up and down beneath her fingers. She felt dizzy and disoriented. Her stomach lurched and her throat grew raw. She was paying the price of the curse. She rested her head against the coolness of the sink and slowly, the burning faded away. The movement of the shell beneath her fingertips slowed. The heat dispersed. When the shell was cool again, she fingered it and found that one of the ridges had smoothed down, only two were left.

Urgent knocking sounded on the door. "Paloma," Brandi called, "are you all right?"

She took a second to compose herself. "Yes," she answered, surprised at how normal her voice sounded. "I'll be out in a couple minutes."

She pushed herself to her feet and stared in the mirror, surprised at how normal she looked. Every hair on her head was in place and her face showed none of the turmoil she'd just experienced. She turned on the faucet and washed her hands and face. When she felt better, she opened the door and found Brandi hovering outside.

"Do you want a ride to the hospital?" Brandi asked.

"Thanks, but no. I need to take care of this myself."

"I'd like to take care of him myself."

Paloma hugged Brandi, unable to express in words her feelings of gratitude at her sister-in-law's loyalty. "Homicide is a felony and you're too pretty to go to jail."

"I grew up in the Cabrini Green Projects in Chicago," Brandi said. "I can find someone to take care of him and who can get rid of the body so it will never be found."

"Obviously," Paloma said in a dry tone, "you don't watch TV. They always find the body."

"Maybe, but if I had a .45 and an alibi—" Brandi grinned "—you'd be a free woman."

Paloma chuckled. "Thanks, but that's too quick and too painless. I want him to suffer." She touched the shell.

Brandi frowned. "I have never heard you talk like this before. What happened to my live and let live sister-in-law?"

What indeed? "She was stomped down too hard this time." She kissed Brandi again. "I'll talk to you later."

In the parking lot outside her brother's office Paloma hailed a cab and gave the driver orders to take her to the hospital. As she sat in the back seat watching Las Vegas pass by, her throat ached. She couldn't stop fingering the shell. Miss Odile's words kept repeating themselves over and over in her mind. *Sex got you into this and sex will get you out.*

The cab let her off in front of the emergency room entrance. Paloma was directed to a cubicle at the end of a long hall. When she pushed aside the privacy curtain,

Keith appeared overjoyed to see her despite the fact Miss Thang, also known as Syrah, was with him, clucking over him like a mother hen while her eyes shot daggers at Paloma. Paloma stiffened at the sight of the other woman, but decided now was not the time to make a scene.

Keith sat on the side of a hospital bed. A bandage had been applied to one cheek and a small spot of blood seeped through. A bruise shone on his chin. He held one hand awkwardly, though nothing else appeared to be wrong with him.

Paloma walked right up to Keith and gently folded him into a hug. "My poor baby," she crooned and wondered where she'd learned such acting skill. Maybe she should call Darius Montgomery after all and see if she could get a job acting in one of his films.

She stroked Keith's face. He closed his eyes and leaned into her touch, nuzzling her breast like a newborn and sliding a hand over her butt. "Do you want me to call your mamma?"

"I just want to go home," Keith said plaintively.

He looked up at her and she smiled as sweetly as she could at him, when she really wanted to gloat.

She started leading him to the door. She glanced back at Syrah standing alone in the center of the room. Paloma waved. "I can take it from here, Syrah. You go on home. Keith will call you later." *In another few days, he'll be all yours, anyway, honey. Just wait, be patient a little bit longer.*

"Tell me what happened," Paloma said once she had him settled in the cab and headed home.

Keith's face contorted as he held tight to her hand. "I don't know exactly. This old lady just stepped out in front of me and *wham*..." He leaned back on the headrest, frowning. "I swerved to avoid her and hit a tree." He paused, his frown deepening. "I don't know why, but that old bat reminded me of your crazy aunt. You know. The one who lives in the swamp. Miss...what's her face, I can't remember her name."

"Odile," Paloma said calmly, "and she's not crazy." She patted his hand. She noticed just the faintest tremor in his fingers as he held on to her.

"Anybody who brings a twelve foot python to a wedding is crazy," Keith snapped.

Paloma glanced away. She hadn't been amused either, but Miss Odile did what she wanted and like all the other members of her large family, Paloma simply ignored the old woman's eccentricities. "I'm glad you have so much respect for my family."

"Don't take it that way, baby." Keith took her hand, gripping it tightly. "I didn't mean to sound so...so..." he didn't finish his sentence.

"So...what was Syrah doing at the hospital?"

"I didn't ask her to come," Keith said quickly, defensively, "I just called to let her know I was all right. I didn't want her to see my accident on the news or something and have her worry. She rushed down to the hospital to hold my hand." He sounded pleased at Syrah's behavior.

"She's such a thoughtful girl." Paloma patted his hand. Her private thoughts about Syrah were much different. *The slut!*

"That's how girls are raised in South Carolina," Keith said as he patted her knee. "I just love Southern girls."

Don't you now, Paloma thought as the cab turned

down their street and pulled into the driveway. She helped Keith out of the cab and up the steps.

As Keith fumbled for the door key, Paloma found herself pausing, reluctant to enter this house that had been her home for the last four years.

The memory of Keith and Syrah in her bed rose to her mind as she helped him up the stairs and down the hall to the master suite. The room had been tidied, so obviously the servants had returned from their afternoon off.

She managed to get Keith into bed. He sank down on the mattress and closed his eyes. He looked soft and vulnerable as he fell into sleep and began to snore.

Paloma watched him for a moment, then went across the hall to the spare bedroom. She couldn't share a room with him anymore. Not after he'd desecrated everything she considered hers. He had no idea she knew anything and she felt a feeling of contempt creep over her.

The guest room was neat and tidy. Paloma sat down on the bed for a moment trying to decide what to do. The shell at her throat had grown warm again and she touched it hesitantly. So much power resided inside this innocent-looking object. The kind of power that most people feared.

She entered the bathroom and turned on the water in both the sink and the shower. She stood in front of the mirror and started singing scales. Her voice was hoarse and raw, as though she been screaming for hours, and wouldn't hit a high C, a note she'd always hit perfectly before. She did a few exercises to clear her throat and then started again. No high C. Her voice cracked and faded.

She clutched the shell fingering the smooth area where the third ridge had been.

chapter three

Richard Talmage, general manager and half-owner of the Istanbul casino, was a short, dapper man with a British accent. He wore a conservative dark blue suit, blue tie and a hard-edged manner. He sat across from Paloma in the Minaret restaurant, a place that tried hard to look like a Turkish bazaar, but couldn't quite complete the translation.

Most of the lunch crowd had departed and over half the tables were empty. The remains of lunch had been cleared away, except for Keith's who still picked at his sandwich complaining about his sore jaw and other assorted aches and pains from his car accident.

Finally, Keith ordered another bourbon and fell silent as he watched Richard and Paloma, a greedy glow in his eyes. Paloma sipped her red wine, grateful for the warmth.

Richard smiled at Paloma. "About the contract."

"She's ready to sign," Keith broke in as he balled up his napkin and signaled for the hovering waitress to take his plate.

Paloma covered Keith's hand with hers. "A lot has

happened in the last few days." Her voice was hoarse and both Keith and Richard studied her carefully. "Keith was in an accident, I had a family situation in Louisiana to attend to, and I just don't feel like I'm in a good place to sign a contract."

"I'm willing to go up another ten million," Richard said, his eyes regarding Paloma with something she didn't quite understand. What did he know that she didn't?

Keith held his breath. "That's generous, Richard. I know Paloma appreciates your offer."

Paloma smiled. "I do, but again I need a bit more time to handle my personal life." Keith's hand squeezed her knee. "You know I'd sign the contract just to live in the penthouse."

Keith's hand tightened on her knee. She was going to have a bruise.

"Are you all right?" Richard stared intently at her. "You sound a little hoarse."

"I just need to rest my voice. A singer can only stress vocal chords for so long. And I've been doing six shows a week for most of four years now." She had Mondays off.

"She'll be fine," Keith interrupted. "I'll see that she goes to the doctor."

Richard nodded. He gathered up his copy of the contract and packed it away in his briefcase. "I'll make the changes. I don't think an extra ten mil will break the bank." He and Keith shook hands and Richard left.

"What the hell are you doing?" Keith hit his palm on the table. "The casino just handed you another ten million dollars for a year's worth of work. You just turned away forty million dollars."

"Honey, it's only money. And we have plenty." Okay, maybe not plenty, but if Keith hadn't drained her accounts, she would definitely have enough to live on for the rest of her life.

Keith opened his mouth, but for a second no sound came out. Finally, he sputtered, "That's…that's not the point."

"Don't be greedy, Keith." She shook her finger at him. "You're courting bad luck or karma, or whatever. Greed always comes back at you."

"Don't give me any of that backwoods, bayou, voodoo bull shit," he sneered. "Money is the only thing that matters."

"Really? Is money the only thing keeping us together? Am I nothing but an ATM machine to you?" She really enjoyed seeing him squirm. He didn't have the balls to tell her the truth, though she could see the indecision on his face. Tell her, not tell her.

Paloma stood and adjusted the strap of her purse across her shoulder. "I don't want to deal with this contract stuff right now." She left the restaurant, took a short cut through the grand bazaar heading toward the valet parking lot.

As she waited for her car, she knew she had to get away. Without a thought, she found herself on the road to Henderson and turning down the street where her mother lived.

When Paloma walked in the front door, her mother took one look at her and drew her into a tight hug.

"You look tired," Marianne said. "Sit down and I'll get us a glass of sweet tea."

Paloma lay back on the sofa and looked out over her mother's garden. A small bird sat on the edge of the bird bath and took little sips of water while eyeing the neighbor's cat warily. A lizard ran across the patio and disappeared beneath the ice plant. A humming bird stopped at the feeder, tiny wings tight against its little body as it thrust its long bill into the feeder.

When Marianne returned and handed her a glass of iced sweet tea, Paloma could only take a small sip. "It's happening." She touched her throat. "I can't even reach a high C."

Her mother, sadness reflected in her dark eyes, leaned over and kissed her on the cheek. "I'm sorry."

"Don't be." Paloma had made the decision and would stand by it for the rest of her life. "I need to know, can I be who I am if I'm a schoolteacher?"

Kindergarten. Paloma always thought she'd be a great Kindergarten teacher.

"If I told you once, I've told you a hundred thousand times." Her mother's voice was indulgent. "You can be whoever and whatever you want. I won't love you any less. No one in our family will."

Paloma closed her eyes. She didn't like the whining tone she heard in her own voice. "I know I sound petty, but I love being Paloma Alexander, headlining at the Istanbul, going on tour, recording CDs, having thousands of fans cheering for me every night." Maybe she was wrong to define herself by who she was on stage, but she had worked hard to get where she was and giving up her lifestyle would be difficult.

"You've spent a lot of years letting your career consume you," Marianne said. "I realize you had to give up a portion of who you are, but living in obscurity isn't a bad thing. You've made your mark on the world, time to move on."

"I don't know what I'm going to do with myself."

Marianne's eyebrows rose. "Go back to college and finish your degree."

Right. Paloma had keenly felt the lack of an education, but Keith had discouraged her from returning to school. *You don't need a college diploma, baby,* she heard in her mind. *You can get what you want without one.* Maybe, but as she'd just discovered she had no fall back position.

Paloma's phone rang. She rummaged through her purse searching for her phone and found the business card of the nice young man, Darius Montgomery, at the airport and how good he'd made her feel. The memory of his gushing adoration would have to last her the rest of her life. She tucked the card into a side pocket and answered her phone.

"Baby, come home," Keith said.

"I'm going to stay with my mom tonight."

"But, baby, I need you."

Yeah, you need me to sign that contract, she thought. "I want to spend some time with my mother. We have some family business to discuss. She got an offer for her house in New Orleans."

"Just sell it," Keith said, "people with property down there are making money, hand over fist."

Not hardly, Paloma thought sadly. The government was screwing them and most of them didn't even know it. "I bought my mother that house as security," Paloma said, her voice cool, "and she is not selling it."

"What about what I want? You ever think about that?" His voice sounded petulant and whiny. "I think about you every minute of every day. I want you home—now."

She studied her manicured nails. "Stop acting like a baby. I'll be home tomorrow. You can entertain yourself for one night."

Good, Keith thought, she was going to stay with her mother for the night, as he hung up the phone and looked around at the opulent penthouse. Not bad for a good ole boy from the wrong side of the tracks.

He didn't need Paloma when he had Syrah. He picked up the phone and called her. "Get your ass over here," he barked into the phone before Syrah had a chance to even say anything. He hung up and stood at the window looking down on the city lighting up the dark with a thousand colors. Las Vegas had the kind of energy he thrived on.

He loved Las Vegas. Never in his wildest dreams did he think he'd end up here. But Paloma had bought all this for him and damn if he was going to give it up.

Damn, he might have lost his car, but the second she signed that contract, he'd get himself something better with a little more prestige. A Rolls Royce Phantom, now that was a car.

He liked the way the girls sized him up when he stepped out of his car, as though measuring his bankroll by the size of his wheels. He just needed Paloma to sign the damn contract. He didn't understand why she was dragging her feet.

Thinking about the afternoon refueled his anger. How could Paloma just walk out and not come home? He wanted a little more of what she gave him earlier in the day. Sex with her had never been so wild before and he wanted more. But since then she'd been distant and cool.

What the hell kind of uppity bitch was she to deny him what he wanted? If not for him, for his foresight, she'd still be singing at county fairs and fending off unwanted advances from drunks. No wonder he always had to have something on the side. If Paloma ever found out, she'd hand him his tickets out of town.

Try as he might he never could make her do what he wanted. She'd insisted on being sophisticated and elegant which was all fine and good, but teenagers wanted hoes who showed their ass and sang about dirty sex and bad-ass hoodlums. That translated into dollars.

He thought about the major clothing endorsements, the shoes, the handbags, the everything that never came her way because she had to maintain her dignity, her class. Dignity never got a person anywhere. And Paloma never did anything if she thought her family would disapprove. Her family was at fault.

When he'd met Paloma, her family hadn't had two dimes to rub together. Big fucking deal that there had been some old money family back in the day, by the time he'd come along, they'd had nothing but their image, a run-down mansion with holes in the walls and the facade of still being the kind of powerful folk only money could buy. If not for him, they'd still be back in their big house, falling down around their ears, wishing for the old times.

Twenty minutes later, the door to the penthouse opened and Syrah stepped into the foyer. He smiled at her and she gave him a kiss. All he could think of was that this bitch was going to make it big. She talked like a ho, dressed like a ho and fucked like a ho. He was going to make a pile of money off her.

"Hey, baby." Syrah pressed her over-full breasts against his chest. She stuck her hand down his pants and fingered his flaccid dick. He leaned back waiting for her magic to bring him to life, but nothing happened.

Keith's eyes popped open and he stared at her. He should have been hard by the time she'd sashayed her way across the room, but nothing, his cock wasn't cooperating. He was as floppy as a dead fish on a mountain of ice.

Syrah, undaunted, unzipped his pants and pushed them down to his ankles. She eyed his limp cock and got down on her knees. "Well, let see what I can do to make my popsicle happy."

Finally, she was going to suck him off.

Syrah leaned over and kissed his penis and ran her horny little tongue around the tip and down the side.

Nothing happened. Keith fought panic. Never in his life had he ever failed to come to life.

She cupped his balls in one hand and then guided his penis to her mouth with the other and sucked on him.

Not even a hint of stiffness. *Goddamn Paloma,* she'd broken his dick. Fuckin' bitch!

Syrah stroked him. "Ain't you happy to see me, little boy," she crooned at his penis. She smiled at him revealing her gold grill with the sparkling wink of diamonds. She tugged on his penis, but it remained limp.

Keith's eyes narrowed. Was she laughing at him? Keith was getting angry.

Paloma had gotten a good enough rise out of him. Why was he being denied now? All he wanted was the same pleasure he'd found with his wife. "Come on, girl, is this the best you can do?" He grabbed her hair and pushed her face into his groin.

Syrah struggled for a second and then shoved his hand away. "Shit, man, this ain't my fault. Maybe you're gettin' old. Get you some blue pills."

He growled at her. "I don't need Viagra, bitch. I'm all man."

Syrah stood and rolled her eyes. "Sure you are. When you get it up again call and I'll come by to see it for myself." She picked up her purse and headed toward the door.

Stunned, Keith didn't know what to say. He'd never had a problem performing before. Syrah had to be at fault. She just wasn't doing him right. He started massaging his penis but still nothing happened. Not his boy. Limp pecker couldn't be happening to him. "Get back here," he screamed after Syrah but all he heard was her cackling laughter and then the slam of the door.

He was alone with his limp dick.

Keith was on his fifth glass of cognac when the penthouse door opened. The volume on the big screen was low, so he heard Paloma humming to herself.

He wasn't sure, but she sounded off key and a little rough. What had she been doing all night? That ticked him off. She was out having a good time and he was here suffering alone in the dark.

Checking his watch, he noticed the hands had stopped moving. One hundred and fifty grand for a Rolex and the damned thing just stopped working. He was going to call the jeweler who sold him this piece of shit and get a new one.

Rage coursed through him. He got up from the bed and put on his silk robe. He tied the sash as he walked out of the bedroom. He found Paloma in the kitchen making herself a cup of coffee.

"Where you been?"

She turned around and smiled sweetly at him. "I told you, I was spending the night at my mother's. You look terrible. Are you ill?"

His mouth fell open. Sshe looked radiant. Her skin glowed with life. She shimmered. He couldn't talk. A stirring in his groin brought him back to life.

Paloma walked over to him and put her hand on his forehead. "You don't seem hot?"

His penis came to instant attention.

"Let me fix you some tea," she said, "or would you like something to eat?"

He couldn't talk as all the blood from his head had raced down to his crotch. He'd never remembered ever going from zero to raging boner with her before. His lips moved but nothing came out.

"Baby," Paloma said, "are you okay?"

Keith clenched his fist. All he could think about was getting between her legs and relieving his ache.

Paloma stepped back and glanced down at him. "Oh, no wonder you can't talk." She laughed.

Keith couldn't understand why he was so hot for her and he couldn't even get it up for Syrah. This was too strange. All he wanted to do was have sex with his wife. "Paloma..."

"You want me to help you with that?" She slid her hand inside his robe and touched his rock-hard prick.

He nodded. He was on fire. If he didn't get relief he was going to pop. Well, maybe not pop, but something traumatic was bound to happen.

Paloma led him to one of the chairs in the breakfast nook. The desire to fuck him was way strong. This time she wanted to see what she would get from the sex. But she wanted to be in control again.

She yanked the chair away from the table and turned it around, then she shoved him down. They were going to do it in the kitchen, in the morning with the sun shining through the window. Shit, how hot was this?

Paloma bent over, untied the sash of his robe, and flipped it over her shoulder. The silky material parted revealing his massive erection.

Licking her lips she almost laughed at his determined expression. Silly man, he thought he was in control and that she was doing this all for him.

Without speaking, she walked behind the chair and grabbed one wrist and then another. He tried to pull away but she was so strong he couldn't. "Hey I don't—"

She bent over and whispered in his ear. "Either do it my way or no way at all."

Keith glanced at his rock hard shaft and all the fight went out of him.

The silky sash slid along his skin and he relaxed. The fabric whispered and she secured his hands behind the chair, tying him a little too tight, but hell she didn't care.

After she was done she walked around and stopped in front of him. He was hoping she was going to give him head like she had the other night, but she lifted up her skirt, whipped her panties off and tossed them across the tiled kitchen floor.

Paloma positioned her body above his and lowered herself until the head of his cock touched her nether lips. She bit her lip as his hard cock slid in her. She gripped him inside, feeling her own heat and wetness on the tip of his cock. He leaned forward his lips puckered.

Pulling back, she lifted herself off his penis. "I don't want to kiss."

He shrugged, then tried to thrust up to get inside her, but she pulled herself away and shook her head.

"Beg for it," she ordered.

His mouth dropped open for a second.

She laughed. "Don't you want it?"

"I don't beg for pussy."

She stood. "Guess you don't want it bad enough." Getting off him left her feeling empty and wanting.

He stared at his dick again. She could tell he was weighing his pride or his hard-on. Still not speaking he pulled at his ties. As much as she wanted to fuck him, she wasn't going to do it until he pleaded. She wanted his pride more than his dick. Searching the kitchen, she wondered where she tossed her panties.

"Please," he said.

"You can do better than that?"

Keith gritted his teeth. "Please, I'm begging."

She had him where she wanted him. He needed to fuck her and he needed to do it now. Sex as a weapon was a wonderful thing. Smiling with a superior glint in her eyes, she lowered her body.

She felt his heavy cock at the entrance of her pussy and

he grunted as she pulled him into her. Clenching her muscles, she let her hot wet flesh encircled him.

Keith closed his eyes and a sigh escaped his mouth. "Thanks, baby."

All her nerve endings tingled as he throbbed inside. If he could do this to her all the time, she'd have nothing to complain about and the divorce wouldn't happen.

Keith watched her face as she plunged deep onto him. He trembled beneath her.

He pulled against his restraints as she grinded down on him. With each stroke he hit her hard clit. The relentless need to cum drove her on. She tweaked his hard nipple and he groaned. Her own nipples poked out from the lacy cups of her bra. She leaned forward and rubbed herself on his chest trying to get some relief.

Rotating her hips she forced her clit against his cock. She bit her bottom lip to stop the moan of pleasure wanting to escape her mouth. She knew she was close.

Paloma raked her nails down his chest. He yelped in pain, she didn't care. Paloma strained against him, her body undulating over his crotch. The chair scraped on the floor. She ground down on him as his body jerked with the harsh rhythm and Keith thrust up and she exploded with pleasure.

In her mind a fire wave rolled over and she heard a distant laugh. She rode out her orgasm until she felt him shoot his load inside her.

Wave after wave of pleasure filled her. She slumped forward. After a minute, she had the strength to stand. She pushed herself up, sliding off his still throbbing cock. Quickly she adjusted her skirt and looked at him. He'd passed out. It figured.

chapter Four

Paloma sat in a chair at the foot of the bed watching Keith. A small smile curved his lips. He lay with one hand tucked beneath his ear.

She was almost done. Almost free.

He rolled over and his eyes fluttered open. "Hey, baby, come back to bed."

That was the last thing she wanted to do. "I'm hungry. I want breakfast, how about you?"

"I want you." Lazily, he patted the empty area next to him and gave her a sensual smile.

She stood and stretched. "Let me eat something and I'll be so much more fun."

She drew her robe around her shoulders and left the bedroom for the kitchen. The penthouse kitchen had been designed for a cook. Though the appliances were all upscale and the brown granite counter tops were top of the line, Paloma always felt like a fraud in it. Her best dish was macaroni and cheese out of a box. Though she liked the look of the cheerful yellow walls contrasting with the chrome appliances, she always felt like she would never live up to the kitchen's expectations.

When she cooked, she used every pan she owned which meant she needed extra counter space, and extra counter space was at a premium in the small kitchen.

As she chopped strawberries for strawberry pancakes, Keith entered wearing his pajamas and carrying his cell phone. He grabbed her from behind and nuzzled her neck. *Please God,* she prayed, *don't let me throw up in the pancake mix.* That would really ruin her day.

Keith's cell phone rang and he let go of her to answer it. "Yeah," he barked into the phone. He listened for a second. "What? What do you mean my recording studio burned down? It can't burn down."

Paloma's throat started to sting. She clutched the base of her neck and tried to swallow. The burning grew until she almost whimpered in pain.

The shell grew heated as her fingers caressed the two remaining ridges. The shell undulated beneath her fingers and slowly the second ridge smoothed down. Only one was left. "What's wrong, honey?" she asked in a honey-sweet tone.

"Shut up," he snarled.

Paloma wondered if she had a bottle of champagne, she felt like celebrating. She went back to slicing the strawberries. Keith rampaged around the kitchen as he talked on the phone. Finally he hung up. "I don't believe it."

"What's going on, Keith?" Did she have the right amount of concern in her voice? Probably not, but he was so upset, he'd never notice that she was gloating again.

"Didn't you hear me? My recording studio burned down. I have to go."

"Was anyone hurt?"

He snarled at her. "Do I care?" He headed toward the hall. "I need to borrow your car."

"When are we going to go down to the dealership and buy yourself a new Bentley?"

As he stared hard at her, rage crossed his face and was gone in an instant. "I don't have time for that right now. I have to see how bad the fire was and what was lost."

"I can call the insurance agent if you want."

"No," he said too quickly.

"Do you want me to come with you?"

"No."

For a second she thought he was going to cry. *Too bad, so sad,* she thought as she popped a strawberry into her mouth. Should she show more compassion? No, she didn't think so.

She sighed and put the griddle on the stove to heat. "I'll save you some pancakes," she called after his retreating back.

I should feel bad, she thought, but I don't. She dropped batter onto the griddle and stood with the spoon in her hand watching it sizzle.

She didn't feel bad about using sex as a weapon, or that his life was crashing around him. A good wife would support her husband, but then again he wasn't a good husband.

When her brother had almost died in an accident, Keith had come to the hospital one time. When the hurricane hit New Orleans, he'd simply shrugged as though he couldn't be bothered.

He'd begrudged her time to go to New Orleans and help handle family business, and when she'd given two concerts and donated the proceeds to the relief effort, he'd gone ballistic. He hated when she spent money on her family. He hated when she spent money on anyone but him.

Her pancakes cooked, little bubbles rising to the surface. When the pancakes were done, she heated maple syrup in the microwave and sat down to eat. When bad things happened to bad people her grandmother used to make the comment that the elephant would dance among the chickens. Paloma would ask what that meant, saying that the elephant would stomp the chickens. And her grandmother would smile and reply, exactly. Paloma realized the elephant was warming up to stomp on her husband's chickens.

Was there a special place in hell for her? Getting back at him for what he'd done to her was worth it. She forked bites of pancake into her mouth and chewed thoroughly. Damn, she was a good cook. At least she could take care of herself.

The phone rang and she picked up to find her cousin Jean-Luc on the other end.

"I have some interesting information for you," he said.

"So tell me." She pushed the plate away.

"I did some checking on Syrah. How long has your man been working that girl?"

"I'm not totally sure, but I think about three years." She remembered when Keith had bought and paid for voice lessons for her, a make over, and her new clothes. He did all the same things for Syrah he'd once done for Paloma. He even spent thousands of dollars getting Syrah's teeth fixed and she put on a gold grill.

"How old is she?"

"I think around twenty-two or twenty-three."

"Not yet, she ain't."

Paloma sat up straight. "What do you mean, Jean-Luc?"

"I found her birth certificate, she's barely eighteen."

Shocked, Paloma tried to make sense of what her cousin was saying. "Oh, my, God," Paloma said as the implication finally set in.

"Your husband was going at her when she was fifteen. That girl is from South Carolina and you know what that means."

"No," Paloma said, "but I'm sure you'll tell me."

"Let's just say, your husband has not only committed a felony, but he took her across state lines before she was eighteen and that makes his action a federal crime."

Paloma did some rapid math. "But she's at least eighteen now."

"But the statute of limitations clock is still tickin'. And I talked to that gal's grandmama who is a sweet church-going lady. She's looking to press charges. She was so happy to know her baby was all right and not dead. She filed herself a missing person's report and those small town police officers were thinking she was dead. No one had any idea she'd shown up in Sin City. I'm sure everyone would like to close the case."

Paloma reeled. What the hell had Keith been thinking? An underage girl! That made Paloma a co-conspirator. She was going to need a criminal lawyer as well as a divorce lawyer. That bastard, that lying, cheating, money-sucking bastard.

"Your man is learnin' his first big reality lesson about women, *cher*," Jean-Luc said.

"And what's that?

"Hell hath no fury like a woman scorned." Jean Luc chuckled. "You think about what you want to do."

What she wanted to do was call her cousin, Tyrone. Tyrone would make the body disappear. Bull sharks, snapping turtles and alligators, the rumor was that Tyrone used all sorts of wild life to clean up his messes. Damn, but she was already in league with the black magic. She didn't want to make a deal with Satan and compound her sin. She was going to be doing penance the rest of her life. But being free of Keith made it all worth while.

"Thank you, Jean-Luc." She hung up the phone and took a long sip of her coffee. Her throat felt tight and raw.

The silence in the penthouse gnawed at her. She turned on the TV and found that the news of Keith's loss had already spread to the media. A camera panned the devastation as the fire crews poured water on the smoldering building. A close-up of Keith showed him staring at the fire, his face devastated.

Paloma's heart almost went out to him. Maybe she'd made a mistake. As she fingered the shell nestled against her breasts, she thought maybe she had been too harsh on him.

Keith obviously loved his studio. Everything had been state of the art and from the look of some of the people he'd signed, he had found some real talent. But then he turned and the camera followed him as he headed back to Paloma's Lexus. Just before the camera swung back to the fire, Paloma saw Syrah sitting on the passenger side as though she owned the damn Lexus.

Paloma's heart hardened. She frowned, her hands curling into fists as she resisted the urge to pound the table. That bastard, he had his hoochie girl with him when he hadn't wanted Paloma. Paloma's throat burst into an inferno of burning.

She hadn't been too harsh on the bastard. He deserved everything he got. As the camera swung back to the reporter, an old woman darted out of the crowd viewing the fire. Paloma leaned forward trying to see, but the old woman blended back into the crowd and had disappeared before Paloma could identify her. Had she just seen Miss Odile? No. Not possible. Miss Odile never left the bayou.

The news ended and Paloma switched off the TV and the phone rang. Paloma answered to find her mother on the other end.

"Paloma," Marianne said, "I'm sitting here eating my poached egg watching your husband's studio burn. I just wanted to call and extend my condolences." Sarcasm laced her voice.

Paloma chuckled. If nothing else, her mother understood the value of proper manners. "You could always call him."

"But then he might think I really care."

"So you called me, instead."

"I'd rather talk to you. Besides, I'm worried about you. Are you having any regrets?"

"I did a few minutes ago. For about five seconds," Paloma said, "and then I saw Syrah sitting in my car…in my car." Paloma's voice rose. "Any regrets I might have considered were all gone."

Richard Talmadge agreed to meet her in his office. She walked in feeling sad that she was about to give up so much of her future. She hated what she was about to do because Richard had been nothing but respectful and kind.

"Thank you for seeing me on such short notice." She approached his desk.

"I have the contract right here." He held up a folder in one hand and a pen in the other.

"Richard," she said, "more than anything I would sign this contract, but I can't."

"Is it the money?" Panic crossed Richard's face.

"No, it's me."

"Are you having a personal crisis?" His face was creased with concern. "Do you need a shrink? My son goes to the best one in Vegas and I can get you in today."

"My voice is gone."

He looked shocked. "What?"

"I can't sing. The damage to my vocal chords is permanent."

"What damage? Did you get hurt?"

She patted his fist. It really bothered her to hurt him like this. He'd been nothing but a friend to her. And a fan. "I've overtaxed it singing non-stop."

"I don't care what it costs, I'll get the best doctors. I'll pay for it." He gripped her hands tightly.

"I swear to God," Paloma said with a fond smile, "I will never tell anyone that the most cut-throat businessman in Las Vegas is really nothing more than a sentimental man with his heart on his sleeve."

He actually blushed. "The first date I ever had with my wife was at one of your concerts. Every time I hear *Tender is My Lover's Way,* I still cry. We played that at our wedding."

Tears sprang into her eyes. Wrapped in her own problems she'd forgotten how important music, her music, was to other people. "After what happened today, Keith is going to need me."

Richard's eyes filled with anger. "You're not giving up your career because of him?"

In a way, she'd done exactly that. "Richard..."

"That man never deserved you. He's a user. As soon as you stop being a paycheck, he'll leave."

My God, she thought, was I the only person who didn't see Keith for what he was? "I don't understand."

Richard gazed fiercely at her. "Keith hits on every woman under the age of twenty-five who works here. And I'm going to tell you something, which says a lot about you and the quality of person you are. Most of those girls turned him down because of you. You have always treated everyone with so much respect, as though they were special. Not only are you a great singer, but a great lady."

Paloma felt humbled by his statement, but knew she wasn't worthy because of what she was doing to Keith. She patted Richard's hand. "Thank you, Richard."

"If you need anything...anything at all, you call me. I don't care if you need money, a job, a shoulder to cry on, you call me."

"I might take you up on the job, though my waitress skills are a little rusty." She'd been working as a waitress when she'd first met Keith. "I can be out of the penthouse in a week."

He kissed her on the cheek. "You take all the time you need. I don't care if you're still in the penthouse next year."

His thoughtfulness moved her to tears. She almost wanted to confide in him that she was broke, but she didn't. He'd been more than kind and she felt grateful for his generosity. She was in a lot better straits than most women getting divorced. She had her family.

"You're a good friend, Richard." At least she didn't need to worry about a place to live for the time being. Though she wouldn't stay long. Just long enough to get herself organized. "I haven't discussed my decision with Keith yet. With everything that's happened to him in the last few days, I didn't want to add to his troubles. I want to give him my decision when he's best able to understand."

"He won't hear anything from me." Richard kissed her on the cheek.

Her throat felt tight and hoarse from unshed tears.

She went back to the penthouse to find Keith sitting on the sofa crying.

"Keith," she said quietly.

"My studio," he gulped, "is gone. The fire took everything."

She patted his hand trying to show sympathy, but she knew she was just going through the motions. In reality, she felt absolutely nothing and wondered if she were really a bad person. "Tell me what happened."

"The police think the fire was arson and they're acting like I set the fire myself."

"Really!" she said as she sat down next to him.

"They kept asking me where I was last night."

She smiled. "Be nice to me, since you need an alibi."

He turned tearful eyes on her. "Oh, baby, you know you love me."

"Oh, yeah," she answered, "bunches." All she could think of was the sarcasm that she was wasting on him—stupid jerk.

He slung an arm around her and pulled her into a tight hug. "Love me," he said in a plaintive tone.

She ran her hand down the front of his trousers. "I know what you need."

Keith moved his hand between her legs and Paloma trapped his hand between her thighs. "Ask me nice."

"Give it to me, baby. I need it."

"Of course you do." She relaxed her grip on his hand.

Keith positioned her over the arm of the sofa and then yanked her skirt up and ripped her panties off. He stuck his hand between her legs and rubbed her labia, amazed that she was already wet. His cock hardened. At least one thing in his life was going good. If he could only get her to sign that contract.

She wiggled her ass. "Let's go."

Damn she was hot. Good, he thought, this would be a fun ride for him. He plunged one finger inside her and then two. He was so on fire, he knew he wouldn't last long.

Quickly he moved his fingers in and out of her. He could feel her tightening up around him. The hot smell of musky sex wafted around the room. He started rubbing himself against her. Up and down, he ground his cock against the crease of her ass, enjoying how she writhed under him. She was teasing him. "You are so good to me."

He heard her laugh.

For a second he swore he heard a trace of meanness behind that laugh, but then she thrust her butt up to his cock and he forgot everything but his fingers inside her and the feel of her ass up against him. His finger sank a bit deeper inside her and he swore the heat coming from her was going to burn him.

His heart raced and the sweat poured off him. He wanted to be inside her so he could forget about the crap his life had turned into.

Easing his fingers out of her drenched channel, he spread her legs and positioned his cock at the entrance of her vagina. He swirled the tip around her entrance getting the head wet. Her ass twitched and he ran the blunt tip of his cock up and down her wet slit.

He liked the hot wetness surrounding him. Part of him wanted to play with her and make it last, but his cock screamed out for satisfaction. Slowly he slid inside her, she was so tight. Keith started to thrust into her, holding her hips.

Paloma thrust her hips back and sucked him inside her. He got into a rhythm. The pressure started to build and all he could think about was cumming and he started moving faster, faster pumping all the way in and out. His balls slapping up against her skin. Her internal muscles gripped his cock.

Keith could hardly breathe as he continued to thrust. She groaned and thrashed. He couldn't hold out any longer. He pulled out so that just the tip was inside and then shoved all the way back in as hard as he could. As he came he heard a woman's laughter and the room started spinning.

Then everything went black.

chapter FIVE

The doorbell chimed and Paloma answered it to find Syrah standing in the hall. "Yes?" What the hell did she want?

"May I come in?" Syrah asked in her breathless, little girl voice. "I need to talk to you."

Paloma debated slamming the door in her face, but curiosity got the better of her. She stood aside and Syrah sashayed into the penthouse. "What can I do for you?"

"I have a confession to make," Syrah said.

"And what would that be, dear?"

She hooked a hand on her hip. "I had a call from my grandmama and we had us a long talk. She says I have to start living my life right. So I'm starting with you."

Cautiously, Paloma eyed the young woman. "Okay. What do you want to start with?"

"The truth," Syrah said. "I've been sleeping with your man for the last three years."

Paloma's eyebrows arched. "And…"

"You don't seem surprised."

"I'm not that dumb," Paloma answered.

Syrah tilted her head. "How come you didn't stop him?"

"Why should I?" Paloma could only hope Syrah intended to take what was left of him off her hands.

Syrah looked surprised. "You never struck me as a woman who'd be understanding about her husband's straying."

Paloma pointed a finger at her. "You don't know me."

Syrah stepped back.

"I'm going to give you a piece of advice," Paloma said, "learn to handle your own money. In the beginning, Keith was a great manager and a decent husband but somehow the fame and money went to his head. If he cheated on me, he'll cheat on you."

Syrah rolled her eyes. "I'm not taking him away from you."

"I was hoping you would." Paloma sighed.

Syrah shrugged. "He was just a means to an end."

Paloma grinned. "You're smarter than you look."

"I rode the gravy train as far as it could go. He can't get it up, the studio is gone, and from what I hear the money is gone, too. What do I need him for?"

Paloma could barely contain her smile. "My sentiments exactly."

"I came here to tell Keith, I'm signing with Epic tomorrow. I thought he should hear it from me first."

Paloma covered her mouth. "Let him hear through the grapevine." She bit her tongue. "Do you want to get an early dinner?"

"You want to eat dinner with me?"

"Why not," Paloma said with a shrug, "we have so much in common. Let me just get some clothes on and then we'll go."

"Thank you for the invite, but I'm having dinner with the rep of my new label."

"Okay." Paloma hugged Syrah. "Good luck, dear. And next time, choose a man a little more wisely."

Syrah gave an impish smile. "You, too." She turned and left.

Alone again, Paloma touched the shell. Her throat felt barren. Her voice was gone. The last ridge had smoothed itself out while she'd been listening to Syrah's confession and she knew everything had finally come to an end.

She loosened the cord from around her neck and held the shell in her hand. The shell slowly started to glow and grow hot. She was about to drop it, when the shell suddenly shattered, the pieces flying out of her hand and onto the floor. A small bit of blood welled from a cut in her palm. She licked her palm and stared at the shell on the carpet.

Paloma walked back into the bedroom. Keith sat in the middle of the bed, the sheet draped over him as he stared at her. She remembered when things had been right between them, when they'd been young and foolish and filled with dreams and ambition. But he'd given everything away, including her.

She pulled a suitcase from the closet and started packing her clothes.

"What are you doing?" Keith asked.

"I'm leaving you, Keith. My brother found a divorce lawyer who will be filing the divorce papers tomorrow."

"Where are you going? You can't divorce me. What will you do with yourself?"

"I'm going to Henderson to stay with my mom. I am

divorcing you and I can look after myself. I did a pretty good job long before you met me."

"But why, things have been so good between us, baby."

Paloma shook her head. "Your life is in the toilet and I'm rescuing myself."

"You can't leave me now."

She put her hands on her hips. "You've sucked me dry. I have no money. I have no career. I have no marriage."

He looked puzzled. "What do you mean no career?"

She turned to face him, feeling a deep sadness. "Funny, you didn't ask about our marriage and you didn't ask about the money."

The magic had taken all the things away from him that he'd prized the most, and she realized she had not been on his list of favorite things. So she was leaving now before she got sucked into anything else.

Keith frowned at her. "Half your money is mine."

"Half of nothing is nothing. I had a meeting with Richard this afternoon and I told him I wasn't signing the contract."

Keith jumped to his feet. "What do you mean you aren't signing the contract?"

"I have no voice left." She tried to sing. Nothing but croaks came out. "That's what you did to me."

Keith went gray. "What happened to your voice?"

She paused and looked at him. She could barely keep the contempt out of her tone. "My voice was the price I paid to get rid of you."

He stared at her for a long moment. "Damn, bitch, just put a bullet in my head and get it over with."

She smiled. "That would have been too easy, too

painless and too quick. You get to have a long life with nothing but suffering. That's what I want for you."

She grabbed the suitcase and left. She had what she needed for the moment. She would send for the rest of her stuff later. She needed to get out, to get away.

As the elevator door closed behind her, she saw Keith standing in the open doorway shouting her name, but she didn't answer. For the first time in years, she felt free and clean. She may have paid a high price, but Keith's suffering was worth it and she still had her self-respect.

As she fumbled with her purse trying to find her car keys, her fingers closed on the business card. She took it out. The card seemed to be edged in light.

When one door closes, she heard her grandmother's voice from a long ago afternoon in her childhood, *another one opens.*

She walked out into the hot Nevada sunshine, the card clutched in her hand. She wasn't quite ready to call Darius yet, but she would before the week was over. For the moment, she just wanted to get as far away from Keith as she could get.

She tucked the card back in her purse as the valet brought her car. She turned onto Las Vegas Boulevard and she felt a new lightness, a new hope for her future.

epilogue

Eighteen months later

Keith sat on the rumpled bed in his seedy hotel room in Los Angeles. He hadn't shaved in days and he needed to do laundry, but he just couldn't get up the energy to do much of anything. He rubbed his chin with one hand while he idly flicked through the channels on the TV.

He'd been trying to get back into the music business, but all the doors Paloma had opened for him in the past were now closed. His reputation was his ruins.

He was lucky he'd managed to avoid jail time over that thing with Syrah. She didn't care that she was only fifteen. Why should he? That was a prize piece of ass. She fucked like a woman. He wasn't a judge of age, just ability. And she'd had ability in spades.

His thoughts drifted to her inventiveness at sex. He looked down at his limp dick. He couldn't get hard since Paloma walked out on him. He'd tried, but nothing worked. Damn bitch had cursed him.

Both those bitches got their pound of flesh. They'd left him nothing. He looked at the .44 caliber on the night stand. He couldn't even put one in his head. What did his wife say to him? She wished him a long life, because she wanted him to suffer. He was suffering. A black man without his dick working right was nothing.

He landed on a station showing a theater and a line of limousines at the curb. The door to one opened and a young man stepped out, who turned and held his hand out. Paloma stepped out of the limo as though she were visiting royalty. She paused and waved at the crowd behind the barricades then she turned to walk the red carpet. Squinting at her, his dick started stirring. Great he thought. He was jonesing for her.

A TV reporter gushed as Paloma glided down the red carpet heading toward the doors of the theater for the premier of her movie. She wore a red designer gown that hugged her curves in a way that brought Keith's erection to a painful point. He could drive this through concrete.

The reporter pushed a microphone in Paloma's face. For a second she looked startled, but then the reporter said, "A new movie and a new husband, you must be flying high tonight."

Paloma hung on the arm of a young man who looked barely out of the cradle. He was a lot younger than Paloma, if Keith was any judge. So she'd left him and robbed the cradle for what? Obviously, for a role in a new movie.

He felt a twist of bitterness as Paloma gazed lovingly up at the young man who was her new husband who gazed just as lovingly back at her. Keith remembered when she'd looked at him the same way.

How had his life gone down the tubes? What had he done to deserve this? He'd made Paloma a superstar and what did she do? Throw him over for a younger man.

Paloma smiled and turned to look at the baby brother by her side. "I have never been so excited about the turn my life has taken in the last few months. I have everything I ever wanted. I'm so blessed."

"Oh, my!" the reporter gushed pointing at Paloma's stomach. "Is that what I think it is?"

Paloma covered her middle with her hand. "Yes, I guess this is my official announcement. This is a baby bump."

Keith dropped his head in his hands. A baby! Fucking bitch havin' another man's baby.

He lifted his head just in time to see Paloma staring into the camera. His eyes caught hers. It was as if she was staring right at him. The cackling of an old woman's laughter ran through his head. And Paloma's eyes glowed. Her beautiful lips curved into a satisfied smile. The laughter grew louder. Chilled to the bone, his body started to shake. She'd won. He was nothing and he knew that was all he would ever be.

By day, Miriam Pace and Jacqueline Hamilton are two mild-mannered, Inland Empire book ladies running a book store for book lovers searching for their favorite novels. But at night, they become the dynamic writing duo known in the publishing world as author J. M. Jeffries.

"It's the local community's ardent appetite for funny, fast-paced books that makes the writing especially fun," says Miriam Pace. And Jackie Hamilton, the other half of J. M. Jeffries, quickly adds, "Few authors have more constant contact with readers than we do. We are lucky to have such a fabulous book-reading community! We owe much of our literary success to our community's strong base of readers...their love for humor...and their vocal demands for more action and romantic suspense."

Miriam Pace began writing in grade school when she started making up stories about her favorite storybook characters and television heroes. Her passion continued through high school where she sat in the back of the classroom writing furiously while all her teachers were thinking she was a terrific, conscientious student. All the while she lived in another world dreaming up stories and filling up notebook after notebook. By the time she finished her MFA in creative writing, Miriam was a full-time writer with five published novels under her own name.

Jackie Hamilton came late to writing. Even though she always had stories running around in her head and characters demanding to be heard, she ignored them during the first part of her life while she was running around Europe in her early twenties. An Air Force brat, Jackie has lived all over the world. Her best trait is observation and the ability to immerse herself in her characters. Not until she graduated college with a bachelor's degree in sociology did she decide to try her hand at writing the stories that wouldn't leave her alone.

Miriam and Jackie met in a critique group. Before the group met, they would walk around the neighborhood brainstorming and eventually decided that they needed to collaborate. They sold their first books, *Road-Tested* and *A Bride to Treasure,* to an electronic publisher and then sold their first romantic comedy to ImaJinn Books. After three romantic comedies with ImaJinn, they sold their first suspense thriller, *A Dangerous Love,* to Genesis Press. Since then, they have published six books with Genesis with two more being released in 2006. Recently, their romantic comedies, featuring Cupid and Venus as matchmakers to modern day lovers, have been optioned by Tivoli Productions as a possible TV series.

Miriam and Jackie love to write and have a ton of stories still seeking the light of day. They figure they have enough story material to last until the next millennium.

Avenging Angel
by Janice Sims

When men began to increase on the earth and daughters were born to them, the divine beings saw how beautiful the daughters of men were and took wives from among those that pleased them. The Lord said, "My breath will not abide in man forever, since he too is flesh; let the days allowed him be one hundred and twenty years." It was then, and later, too, that the Nephilim appeared on earth—when the divine beings cohabited with the daughters of men, who bore them offspring. They were the heroes of old, the men of renown.

—*Genesis* 6:1-4

Thank you, Monica Jackson, for phoning and asking me to write a story for this anthology. It's a real pleasure to share a book with you, L. A. Banks, Donna Hill and J. M. Jeffries. I couldn't ask for more talented company.

This story is for DRK who could have told me to bug off sixteen years ago when I wrote him to tell him I'd chosen him as my literary mentor. Instead, he shared his work and his wisdom with me. For that I will be forever grateful.

chapter one

3:00 a.m.

Trailing him was a nauseating experience for Sarai. To her sensitive olfactory senses his soul smelled like road kill left to marinate in the sun on an Arizona highway.

He led her through side streets and back alleys of a rundown South Side neighborhood. He couldn't have known he was being watched. Even the beating of Sarai's wings against the cold Chicago air currents was nearly silent. Yet, he kept looking behind him.

Just paranoid, she guessed.

Finally, he arrived at a tenement house whose heyday must have dated back to the 1920s, four stories of brick and mortar. The paint had worn off the woodwork years ago. All of the windows were boarded up, and the doors had padlocks on them.

Sarai sensed the building was empty except for his prey. She could hear the girl's heartbeat somewhere in the labyrinth—the lair of "road kill". In contrast, the girl's soul smelled like vanilla-mocha coffee.

Lauren Taylor was under the age of twelve. Humans lost their sweet scent after twelve. If their souls remained innately good, they started smelling like freshly cut grass or pine needles. Any clean, pleasing scent found in the natural world. They only started smelling rotten when they allowed evil to make a home in their hearts.

Old road kill had been evil for a long time. He took one more look behind him before quickly shoving a key into a padlock on the back door, unlocking it and going inside. He shut the door behind him.

Sarai touched down in the shadows, waited a few seconds for her wings to recede. She waited until the only indication that she'd ever had wings was a dark-hued tattoo of a wing below each shoulder blade. Otherwise the golden-brown skin of her back was unmarred.

She walked heedlessly into the dark building, following his scent. She didn't care if he heard her. She had no need to be stealthy any longer. In fact, she hoped he would hear her and try something foolish, like attacking her.

Her acute hearing picked up his footfalls directly ahead of her. He was running. Good, he *had* heard her. She didn't hurry. Haste led to mistakes. She would be as cool and calculating as this child-killing pedophile was. He'd killed four other little girls that the police knew of. He had choked the life out of them, molested them, and then had taken his sweet time mutilating their pitiful bodies. Sarai was going to be just as methodical with him.

It was pitch-black in the building, but she didn't need a flashlight. Her eyes had grown accustomed to the darkness within seconds of entering the building. He was using a miniature flashlight to help him find his way. Still, he stumbled and fell as he took a corner too quickly.

Breathing like the fox in a foxhunt, he scrambled to his feet, staggered a bit, got his bearings and took off running again, this time toward the stairs. Sarai could have had him in a split second but was curious to see where he was going. Surely not to Lauren Taylor. No, he would lead her away from the girl. Perhaps he had a weapon stashed somewhere in the tenement house. Cornered now, he might try to fight his way out.

She hoped he would. It would give her great pleasure to hurt him.

John Michael Young's heart was beating so fast he thought he'd pass out. He knew he'd been careful coming here. No one could have followed him. Tonight was the night he had planned to finish her. With anticipation, he had planned his time for killing her and carving intricate designs all over her lovely, fresh body. She would be his masterpiece.

He'd devoted the last two months to hunting and trapping Lauren Taylor. He first saw her as she walked home from school with three of her girlfriends. She'd outshone all of them with her vivacity, her spirit, her *essence*. One look and it was love.

He loved all of his girls. He treated them tenderly up until they took center stage in his three-act play of death. First, he strangled them. Then, he made love to them. Then, he left his personal signature on their bodies. He immortalized them. He was sure they would thank him if only they weren't dead.

Now, there was a wrinkle in his plans—an interloper. He would just have to deal with him. Hand-to-hand combat was out. He was slightly built, five-seven and well under a hundred and fifty pounds. His stalker appeared to be at least five-ten and must have weighed at least a hundred and fifty. No, things would go better for him if he could reach the gun before the stalker pounced on him.

He didn't for one second assume the person who was following him was a policeman. A policeman would identify himself. He would tell him to halt, and try to arrest him.

This person had a sinister air about him. It was as if he'd come here specifically to do him bodily harm. The thought made his bowels quiver.

For possibly the first time in his life, John Michael Young was afraid. He ran faster, hoping to reach the apartment on the third floor where he kept his instruments of torture.

It was not the same apartment where he'd held Lauren Taylor captive for the past eight days. That was on the fourth floor.

Lauren thought she heard someone in the building. Her bladder, overly full, burned painfully. No one ever came except that man. And he only came once a day to bring her food and drinks, to let her use the bathroom, and to say terrible things to her. He hadn't shown up today. She wondered if that meant something bad was going to happen now.

In the sparsely furnished room there was only the bed to which she was handcuffed, a table with a single lamp on it, and a broken down chest of drawers. She was lying on her back with both wrists pulled over her head and handcuffed to the iron headboard.

Her arms were numb from having been in an uncomfortable position all day. She could move her legs to keep them from going to sleep, and she did so at regular intervals.

The man left a radio on low all the time. The lamp was left on all the time, too. She didn't know where she was. All she remembered was being snatched into a car several days ago by a man with dark hair and dark glasses covering his eyes. He'd been prepared because in a matter of seconds he'd taped her mouth shut, tied her hands behind her back, tied her ankles together, and thrown a dark pillowcase over her head. She'd never been so scared in her life. And nobody heard her muffled screams.

Her mouth was not taped shut now. There was no need for it. The first night she had screamed until her throat was raw, and no one had come. On the second day, she knew that there was no one else in the house, or wherever she was being kept. There were no nosy neighbors like Mrs. Dempsey back home who noticed strange people in the neighborhood and was always calling the police. What she wouldn't give for somebody like Mrs. Dempsey now.

She was eleven, but small for her age. Much too scrawny. No matter how much her mother tried to feed her, she wouldn't gain weight. The mean kids called her Shrimp. Her friends called her Tiny. She had dusky brown skin and dark eyes, usually sad eyes, because she was a deep thinker for an eleven-year-old and life's vicissitudes hadn't escaped her notice. Her father had died in Iraq. Her mother worked two jobs, and it was her job to take care of her baby brother, Jamie, after school.

She worried most about her mother and Jamie. They must think she was dead. They had already grieved for her daddy. Now, they were probably grieving for her.

As she lay there, looking at the ceiling and fighting the urge to pee, she wished she had super powers and could beat up that man when he finally got here because she knew he was coming. Whenever she heard somebody in the house, it was nobody but him.

John Michael Young burst into the apartment and tried to lock the door behind him but the person following him prevented his doing so by throwing his full weight against the door like a battering ram.

John Michael was thrown ten feet across the room and landed hard on the floor. He dropped the flashlight when he fell and, now, he picked it up and pointed it at his assailant, his hand trembling so badly the beam danced.

His heart lurched when he saw that it was a woman, a beautiful black woman with long dark hair and dark eyes that had hit him so hard. And she was angry. Her eyes blazed, and her white teeth were bared in a feral snarl. She was looking at him as if she thought he was the filthiest human being ever to draw breath. And she wished him dead.

He was too afraid to breathe, let alone attempt to get up. She ordered him to get up, nonetheless.

He stood on wobbly legs. "Who are you?" he asked, sounding pitiful even to his own ears. "What do you want?"

He knew he'd made a mistake by speaking when she grabbed him by the collar and lifted him off the floor with one hand. Legs dangling, he wet his pants. She held him away from her so that the urine wouldn't get on her shoes. "I want you to rot in prison, you evil bastard." Her voice was deep and commanding. He felt the timbre of it in the pit of his stomach. It felt like an indictment of all his sins. It felt like the voice of God.

His bowels let loose.

She dropped him, turned him over, handcuffed him, removed his belt and used it to bind his ankles together, then read him his rights. "I'll be back for you."

She shut the door behind her.

John Michael Young lay on the floor writhing in his own filth.

Sarai got on the radio as soon as she left the third floor apartment. "This is Detective Sarai Wingate. I need back-up." She went on to give the dispatcher her location as she ran up the flight of stairs to the fourth floor. She didn't need Young to show her where Lauren Taylor was. She could hear her breathing. As she got closer to the apart-ment door, she could hear the poor girl's heart racing in panic. She undoubtedly thought John Michael Young was coming to torment her again.

The door was locked.

Sarai kicked it in.

Upon entering, she smelled urine and feces. The living room was not furnished. The windows were boarded up so that no one could see inside. The tiny kitchen could be seen in its entirety from the living room. The garbage can was overflowing with empty food and drink containers.

Sarai walked further into the apartment. "Lauren!"

In the bedroom, Lauren listened carefully. The man didn't like it when she spoke.

He wanted her to be quiet. He'd slapped her once when he'd come into the house and she'd thought it might be someone else, and had begun yelling for help. She had to be sure he wasn't disguising his voice this time and trying to test her. Therefore, she didn't immediately respond to that feminine-sounding voice.

Sarai followed the sound of Lauren's beating heart.

The bedroom door was locked as well. She leaned close. "Lauren, if you're anywhere near the door, try your best to cover your eyes. I'm going to have to break in."

She kicked the door in, and the lock popped open. She pushed her way inside.

Lauren immediately started crying in relief when she saw that it was not the scary man after all, but a woman. Sarai rushed to her side, removed the standard-issue handcuffs with a key on her key ring and tossed them aside, then pulled Lauren into her arms. "It's all right, now, honey. I'm with the police. More are on the way. We're going to have you back in your mama's arms soon."

Lauren cried harder. "Where is he?" she asked, sniffling.

Sarai rocked her in her arms. "He's been dealt with. He won't hurt you anymore."

"Oh, God, oh, God," Lauren suddenly cried.

"What is it?" Sarai asked, bending close, concerned.

"Let me up before I pee all over both of us," Lauren explained, laughing through her tears.

Sarai sprang up and Lauren went to the adjacent bathroom, moving a bit slower than she would have liked due to her limbs being lethargic from lack of use.

Sarai shook her head at the resilience of youth. Lauren was laughing already even after going through a harrowing ordeal of this magnitude.

Half an hour later, Lauren was being treated on the scene by a very sympathetic paramedic. She sat in the back of the ambulance with a blanket wrapped around her thin shoulders, behaving with the serene dignity of someone much older than she was.

A few minutes later she saw a patrol car pull up. Her mother and brother spilled out of it and she behaved like the eleven-year-old she was by running into her mother's open arms and receiving all the love she'd been missing.

Sarai watched with a warm feeling suffusing her.

But when she turned her gaze on John Michael Young who was being driven away in a squad car, her eyes turned as cold as ice. There was one less pedophile roaming free.

Twenty minutes later, the Captain tore her a new one.

"Wingate, have you lost your damn mind?" he ground out, pacing his office. "Going in there without calling for back-up first?"

"He could have grabbed Lauren and gotten away before back-up arrived," was Sarai's explanation. "I had to go in and catch him with the girl."

"He says you didn't identify yourself," Captain Holden stated. He paused to level a censorious stare at her. That stare usually made his subordinates tremble with fear.

Sarai simply smiled at him. "I didn't at first. I scared the shit out of him, literally," she told him. "But I did read him his rights. I did everything by the book."

Captain Holden sucked in the gut that lapped over his

belt and looked her straight in her big brown eyes. Wingate was one of his best detectives. She always got her man, even if she sometimes used unorthodox methods. Hell, she hadn't killed the son-of-a-bitch. That was good enough for him.

"Get out of here, Wingate," he shouted at her. "And stop dragging my ass out of bed at four o'clock in the morning. Learn to catch the bad guys at a decent hour!"

"Yes sir, Captain," Sarai said, smiling. She strolled to her desk.

Jim Ford, her partner and best friend, had also been awakened in the middle of the night. He had news for her. He'd been interviewing Young's parents while the Captain had been yelling at her. "That building you cornered him in?" he began. "Belongs to his parents. They own several abandoned buildings in the city.

"They're waiting until property values go up and then they're gonna make a bundle."

This was disturbing news to Sarai. She could think of only one thing: "What if he's used those other buildings as his killing grounds?" Frowning, she sat down in the swivel chair behind her desk, and threw her head back in exhaustion. "We've got to search every last one of those buildings."

Jim panicked. "Tonight?"

"Yeah, tonight," Sarai said as if the answer were obvious.

"But there are three of them and only two of us," Jim said.

"I'll help out," Serena Abraham, an African American officer in her early thirties, volunteered. Her desk was right next to Sarai's and she was known for eavesdropping on their conversations, and vice versa. "I ain't got nothin' going on at the moment."

"Okay," Jim said, sounding skeptical. "I guess we could each grab a desk jockey to tag along with us for back-up."

That's how they found two more missing girls. One of whom hadn't yet been reported missing by her family. Luckily, both were still alive, although they were suffering from dehydration and exposure. The buildings were not heated, and Young hadn't taken as good care of them as he had Lauren Taylor.

As Sarai finally dragged herself home after being up for twenty-four hours, the news on every radio and TV station in Chicago was about the capture of John Michael Young, and the rescue of three of his victims.

She drove her bike too fast through the streets, heading to Rogers Park, Chicago's most racially diverse neighborhood, where she shared an apartment with her husband of two years, Daniel. As a member of the House of Representatives, Daniel spent a lot of time in the nation's capital. She didn't expect him home until tomorrow night.

Rogers Park had some of the best vintage apartment buildings in the city. In the 30s many of the buildings near the lakefront were hotels. Folks from Chicago used to summer in Rogers Park. Today, those hotels were distinctive apartment buildings.

Sarai and Daniel Wingate's building was a renovated grand hotel. Their unit had ten-foot ceilings, oak floors, and spacious rooms. Because they lived on the top floor, their walled terrace was open to the night sky.

Sarai found this very convenient when she had to fly home. She would lightly touch down on the terrace and enter the apartment through the French doors.

Tonight, though, she was enjoying the feel of the

powerful Harley Davidson between her legs. The October air was cold but there were no ice crystals present in it. The cold didn't bother her. Nephilim loved the cold, which was why there were so many of them in Chicago. That, and the tall buildings. They delighted in both.

Tall buildings were ideal for jumping off and catching an air current. It felt kind of like surfing, but without the water. As for the cold air, somewhere in the sense memory of the angel, a part of their genetic makeup, it reminded them of heaven.

If hell were hot, heaven was the direct opposite. Sarai, who was the offspring of two Nephilim, looked as if she was in her early twenties but was actually closer to one hundred and twenty. Nephilim lived an average of four hundred years, so their ability to change their appearance came in handy.

Since Sarai was married to a human, she had opted to age alongside him. She hoped they would enjoy a long life together. When he was in his eighties, she would appear to be in her seventies.

Her parents had frowned on her marrying a human. Not because they thought Nephilim were somehow superior to humans, but because Sarai would have to pretend to be something she was not 24/7.

It would be difficult, if not impossible, they warned, to lead a double life. When it came to marriage, Nephilim usually chose partners from their own group.

Nephilim were divided into two groups: The Sons of the Morning Star, who were loyal followers of Lucifer; and the Grigori, who were devoted to God. Sarai's family was Grigori. Of course, since all of God's creatures were given free will, it wasn't unknown for a Grigori to cross over to the dark side.

Some years ago Sarai had had an unfortunate brush with the dark side but she'd managed to escape with her soul unscathed and had turned her life around.

All of this occupied her thoughts as she rode through the nearly deserted streets. A stop at a red light had her warily observing her surroundings. This would be an ideal place for someone to come out of the shadows, knock her over the head, and steal her bike right out from under her.

Human predators were not her enemies tonight, though. She felt a swish of air on her left cheek just before a pair of strong hands grasped her underneath the arms and lifted her into the night sky.

She didn't struggle, knowing that a drop from this height, when she hadn't had time to sprout wings, could cause severe injuries. It wouldn't kill her. Only two things could kill a Nephilim and a fall from a great height wasn't one of them. But she didn't relish having to wait for broken bones to mend. Sure, they healed fairly swiftly, but she would be off her feet for a couple of days, and she had work to do. Now that Young was in custody, she was free to move on to another pedophile she had in her sights.

Her captor effortlessly held her in his arms as he rose straight up and then turned in the direction of the heart of Chicago, Uptown.

"I hear congratulations are in order," he said smoothly, as if they were in the middle of a pleasant conversation and this was not the first time they'd seen each other in years.

Armaros, or *Nighthawk* as most Nephilim knew him.

Sarai didn't have to look at him to remember his bold

features. He had black, hooded eyes that could be as hard as obsidian one instant and as warm as molten lava the next.

Humans knew him as Nicolas Armaros, power-forward for the Bulls. He was a perfect specimen. Tall and muscular with a body honed in the gym and already a step above a human male's anatomy due to his Nephilim genes.

His dark brown skin was smooth and unblemished except for the tattoos he was fond of. Sarai looked at his profile, the proud African nose, square chin and wide mouth with full lips. Lips whose feel she was very familiar with.

"If my bike is stolen there's gonna be hell to pay!"

Nighthawk laughed. "Don't worry. One of my men will take it to your place and park it in its usual spot."

Sarai sighed. "What do you want, Armaros?"

"I want *you*. The question is, are you prepared to give yourself to me?"

"You know I'm married. Grigori mate for life. What you want is impossible for me to give you. And you know it!"

"Foolish girl," he said in placating tones. "You married a human on the rebound. I admit I made a mistake. I can see that now. You and I should have married. Instead, I listened to my family and chose not to shame them with a mixed marriage."

Mixed in the sense that he was a Son of the Morning Star, and she was a Grigori.

"No," Sarai said, disagreeing. "I didn't marry Daniel on the rebound. I met him, I fell in love with him, and I made a very wise decision to marry him."

"An ex-boxer turned politician!" Nighthawk almost spat out the words. "He's human. If you had married another Nephilim, then maybe you could be mated to him for life. But their lives are pitifully short. You're cheating yourself. You can't even tell him what you are. Humans never understand us. We're freaks to them."

"Really, Armaros," Sarai said sarcastically. "It's been eons. You should let go of the stigma attached to us because our ancestors were fallen angels. You have a choice."

"We're not dreamers like you Grigori," Nighthawk said resignedly. "We know that the only thing waiting for us is hell. You believe God can change His mind and pardon you. We believe the sins of the fathers are visited upon the sons."

"We have free will. If we do good, then we *are* good," Sarai countered.

She felt Armaros's arms tighten around her. She didn't want to upset him while he was flying 10,000 feet above the ground.

"I didn't snatch you off your bike to talk politics," Nighthawk told her. "*I want you.* I can't state it any plainer than that. Leave the human, and marry me."

"You'd just as well drop me and then cut my head off," Sarai said with conviction. "Because I'm never leaving Daniel."

Nighthawk thought for a moment. "Grigori take fidelity to new heights. You're probably the only sentient beings who do. He'll disappoint you."

"Daniel loves me. He may not be Grigori, but he has the heart of one."

"I *could* rip his heart out and eat it," Nighthawk threatened. He didn't raise his voice. The softness of his tone made the threat all the more believable, and horrifying.

"If you harm one hair on his head, you'll be in for a world of hurt!" Sarai said, and pushed out of his embrace. She fell like a stone, hurtling toward earth at such a velocity that it left her breathless.

She had to concentrate in order to quickly sprout wings. But she managed to remove her leather jacket and her blouse, grasping them tightly, and her wings began to grow, widen, lengthen, then finally sprang free, beating wildly to slow her descent.

Nighthawk flew beneath her and allowed her to stand on his back as she gained control. He could have allowed her to continue her headlong rush to meet the ground. But it wasn't his intention to let her come to harm. He'd only wanted to set his proposition before her.

Sarai's wings, the exact color of her midnight hair, and with a six-foot wingspan, were now bearing her weight. She rose straight into the air. Nighthawk followed.

"You're still too impulsive. You could have hurt yourself," he complained.

She looked at him through narrowed eyes. "What could have possibly changed your mind about me after nearly three years? Why come after me now?"

"That's simple," he said, looking her in the eyes. "When I was a boy, I let others dictate my actions. I'm a *man* now. And I go after what I really want. I dream about you every night."

It made Sarai's skin crawl to hear him admit that. Unlike humans' dreams which were random and not controlled by the dreamer, Nephilim had the power to choose what they wished to dream about.

"You'd better not have me doing anything nasty in

them," she said and she swiftly turned back in the direction they'd come.

She heard his laughter for a long time as she flew toward home. But he didn't follow her this time.

Sarai landed on the terrace, found the potted plant under which they kept a spare key to the terrace door, opened the door, and went inside. She immediately heard the shower in the master bedroom, and uttered a curse. If Armaros were still up to his tricks and had broken into her home with the notion of seducing her, he was in for one hell of a disappointing night!

She rushed into the bathroom and pulled the shower stall door aside to reveal Daniel holding his smooth, bald head under the shower's spray. He looked at her with his usual calm. Anyone else would have shown shock or surprise to have a crazy person yank open their shower stall door, but not him.

"Babe!" he said, grinning, happy to see her.

Still unconvinced it wasn't Armaros posing as Daniel, Sarai looked closely at his back. There were no tattoo-like images of wings under the shoulder blades of his broad, dark brown back. She realized he must think she was behaving strangely, and forced a smile. "I can't believe you're home!" she cried. "You didn't call, or anything."

"When was the last time you checked your cell phone?" he asked, looking at her with a smile curving his full lips. "Get in here!"

It was true. She hadn't checked her cell phone in a while. "I've been kinda busy catching a killer," she said as she began peeling off her clothes.

"It was the first thing I heard about after we landed," Daniel said, rinsing his head underneath the shower's spray. "I'm so proud of you."

When he said that, Sarai let go of the pent-up emotions that had been threatening to spill over all night long. Suddenly, she was trembling. Fear was not something she had the luxury of displaying in her line of work. She could not go into a house where a killer could be lurking and feel anything except *confident* that she would emerge the victor. Sharpness of intellect didn't go hand in hand with abject cowardice. Even though fear was a human emotion and not part of the angelic range of emotions, as a Nephilim, Sarai was also part human and she went through all the attendant pains, failings and insecurities that humans experienced.

So, now, when she was alone with the person she loved most in the world, she felt safe enough to let go. "Daniel, it was a nightmare."

Daniel turned off the water and stepped out of the shower stall, onto the bath rug.

He pulled her into his arms. She was naked from the waist up and still wearing her boots and jeans. His body, wet and warm from the shower, was hard and utterly masculine. He was six-three to her five-ten and muscular with a broad chest, a flat belly, long well-built legs, and big hands and feet. He made her feel protected.

Cradling her in his arms, he said, "It's okay, baby, I'm here. Let it out."

Suddenly, words that she hadn't been able to say, even to her partner, were coming out of her mouth. "I've never encountered such evil. I don't believe we'll ever find all of

the bodies of the children he's killed. I think what we discovered was just the tip of the iceberg. Those poor kids."
A sob tore from her, and she buried her face in his chest.

Daniel held her securely against him. "The important thing, right now, is that he's been stopped. He won't kill again."

"I wish I had killed him!" She looked up at him, her dark eyes glittering with hatred. "You should have seen the two girls we found at the other buildings. They were hollow-eyed, nearly catatonic with fear and had lost all hope of being found. And one of them, poor kid, had the bad luck of being born to a drug addict. Her mother hadn't even reported her missing and she'd been gone for four days. Four days, Daniel!"

She wept anew. She wept for that little girl. She wept for the state of the world and she wept for how useless she sometimes felt because no matter how much she did to eradicate the danger that pedophiles posed for children, she didn't think she was doing enough.

It was that very sentiment that had led her to follow Young tonight. He'd been their suspect for weeks but they'd never been able to catch him with any evidence whatsoever. His circumspection was what had kept him from being caught. He left behind no evidence at the kidnapping sites. No DNA linking him to the girls was found on their bodies. They had nothing, except the belief that he was guilty. On her own, Sarai decided to follow him around the clock. Her Nephilim metabolism allowed her to forego sleep, so she never let up on him. From the apartment where he lived the good life with his rich, elderly parents, to the school where he worked with special needs children, to a bar after work where he didn't drink any alcohol but played the pinball machine for three solid hours, then to a Chinese restaurant for something to eat.

Finally, he went home. His parents had gone to bed hours before. He stayed inside for a couple of hours, then got up and left the house again. That's when Sarai had hit pay dirt.

After relating all of it to Daniel, she peered up at him and smiled. "Thank you. Talking to you always helps me put things in perspective. He's off the streets and that's what counts."

Daniel smiled. "And you did scare the shit out of him. That was a little payback for all the fear he's caused his victims."

"A little," Sarai agreed, and tiptoed to kiss his mouth.

Daniel didn't need further encouragement. He kissed her back, after which he helped her out of her boots, jeans and panties. In the shower together, now, they continued to kiss and fondle each other. Then, Daniel took control and began to gently wash her body with the soapy sponge, taking his time and enjoying every minute of it.

"God, I missed you so much," he told her as he soaped her all over. "I'm definitely *not* going to seek reelection. Anything that takes me away from you is a bad thing."

"Well, you have another year to think about it," Sarai said softly. She didn't want to talk about it right now. Having his hands on her body was all she wanted to think about. She wanted him inside of her with nothing separating them.

Because they were trying to have a baby they were not using any type of birth control. She had to admit: she liked having sex with him without using a condom.

Daniel set the sponge aside and used only his hands. They lingered on her nipples, making both of them instantly harden against his palms. He bent and took one of them in his mouth and suckled gently, but not too gently. Sarai sighed happily and reached down to grasp his long, hard, thick penis.

Her vagina was already wet, slick and throbbing. Daniel gingerly lifted her. The tile in the shower stall was not slippery. And the shower spray had washed away all the suds from the floor, so he was confident that picking her up in his arms wouldn't result in both of them crashing through the shower stall door.

Besides, they were old hands at making love in the shower. She opened her legs and guided him to the mouth of her vagina where his engorged penis kissed her clitoris and made her convulse with pleasure. He pushed, her vaginal muscles contracted around him and, soon, he was inside of her.

He moved forward until her back was against the shower wall. "Tell me if you're uncomfortable."

"I'm fine," she said, panting.

"You're better than fine," he said. "You're beautiful." And he thrust deeper, pumping her hard, just the way she liked it. His penis grew harder and thicker, filling her up.

Sarai gave him thrust for thrust. Each time they pushed, his huge penis rubbed against her clitoris, providing her with voluptuous pleasure. So rich, so fine, that she instinctively knew that nothing this sublime had ever before existed this side of heaven.

It was his love for her, shining in his eyes, that was the strongest aphrodisiac. That, and the fact that he'd long since learned just where to touch her to make her body sing.

She came, a strangled scream escaping.

He didn't hold back. He yelled with his release, his voice reverberating off the shower stall walls.

Sarai laughed. "You sound like a Chimera demon."

"Have you known many of them?" Daniel asked, amused.

"Not in the biblical sense, but, yes, I've known a few."

chapter TWO

"How long is he in town for this time?" Edina Shaw, Sarai's mother, asked.

Sarai and Daniel had gone to her parents' Lincoln Park apartment for Sunday dinner. The judge, Sarai's father, Andrew, and Daniel were in the study discussing politics while she and her mom, who taught philosophy at Northwestern, saw to the meal.

Sarai, dressed in a fitted navy skirt suit with a white silk blouse, and expensive black leather pumps was bent over the oven removing a pan of vegetarian lasagna.

"I really think you should give the man who made you a grandmother a break," she said. Sarai carried the steaming dish over to the counter and set it atop a wooden cutting board. Her mother was staring at her, mouth agape. "When did you find out?"

"I haven't been to a doctor, but I know my body. I'm pregnant. I'm not going to tell Daniel until after he returns in time for the holidays. It'll be his early Christmas present."

Her mother, a tall, shapely woman with skin the color

of roasted almonds and dark eyes like her daughter's, pursed her lips. "You're only waiting because you don't want him to change his schedule. Which you know he'll do if he finds out you're expecting. You're *pregnant*. You deserve to be selfish for once in your life. Tell him now, and let him spoil you."

Edina walked over and hugged Sarai. "You know we don't have morning sickness and tender breasts like humans. Your libido will increase and you'll have disturbing dreams."

"So far, I'm not having any symptoms at all," Sarai told her. "I'm hoping they won't begin until after Daniel gets back home. It's only a few weeks' wait."

"A lot can happen in a few weeks," Edina said. "God made the world in less time."

Sarai frowned at her mother who'd been born with the gift of prophecy. Was she trying to say something bad would happen if she didn't tell Daniel she was pregnant right away?

"You don't *see* anything, do you?" Sarai asked worriedly.

Her mother smiled at her reassuringly. "No, baby. It's just experience talking. Husbands don't take well to wives keeping secrets, and vice versa."

Sarai was about to say that she was certain Daniel would forgive her anything once she gave him the news he was going to be a father, when her own father stuck his head in the kitchen doorway, and said, "Feel like a little bout before dinner, baby girl?"

Sarai immediately began taking off her apron. Turning to her mother, she said, "Mind if I borrow a pair of your athletic shoes and your sword?"

"Of course not, honey," said Edina, smiling.

This was just like old times when Andrew, who had been both Edina's and Sarai's fencing instructor, would challenge one or both of them to a match at the drop of a hat.

The library, which was in the center of the house, was soundproof in order to mask the loud clashing of their heavy swords. They didn't want the neighbors calling the police to complain about barbaric swordplay in their exclusive building.

Sarai hurried to her parents' bedroom to raid her mother's closet, giving Daniel a smack on the lips as she passed him. Daniel, looking handsome in black dress slacks, a white silk shirt open at the collar and with the sleeves rolled up, and black leather wingtips, only smiled.

In the three years since they'd been committed to one another and Sarai had divulged everything about herself and her family, these bouts had become common occurrences.

He understood that they were not just for fun. Although they were certainly fun to watch, they were a necessity. Traditionally, disputes between Nephilim were settled with a sword fight. And every Nephilim had to be capable of defending himself.

He watched Sarai as she sprinted away, eager to get changed and meet her father in the library. Andrew reached over and affectionately squeezed Daniel's shoulder. "You really should take lessons, too, Daniel. One day, you're going to be the father of a half-Nephilim child. He'll grow up in the human world *and* the Nephilim world. He'll need to be taught."

Daniel smiled at Andrew, who was a couple inches taller, and in excellent physical condition for a guy who had to be nearly two hundred years old. He looked around fifty. His black, curly hair only had gray at the temples.

"I'm a boxer, not a fencer. Sarai will have to teach him or her how to fight the Nephilim way."

Andrew smiled patiently as they walked slowly to the library. Edina had outpaced them and was already in the large wood-paneled room when they got there. A couple of minutes later, Sarai entered the room. She'd removed her jacket and her pumps, replacing the pumps with a pair of her mother's athletic shoes. The soles of the shoes gave her better traction on the hardwood floor of the library. In her hand was her mother's personal sword. It was a three-foot long broadsword made of polished steel and it weighed two and a half pounds.

Her father also wielded a broadsword, although his was heavier by half a pound.

The play area was twenty by thirty feet. Daniel and Edina sat on the arms of the leather couch that had been moved to the corner of the room. Sarai and Andrew faced one another in the play area.

As was tradition, each of them held their sword firmly in their hand, the tip pointing heavenward. Eyes momentarily closed, they kissed the broadside of the sword.

After which, it was *on*. Andrew, believing his daughter's mind was not entirely on their bout, lunged and aimed the first thrust at her left shoulder. Sarai, anticipating his move, met his thrust with a parry, and sparks flew as steel scraped against steel.

This sort of sword-fighting was not as civilized as fencing. Foils with blunted tips were not allowed, and there were no rules to speak of.

Andrew was six inches taller than Sarai and about fifty pounds heavier. He did not go easy on her because to do so would be shortchanging her. Always, in the back of his mind, was the thought that if he were remiss in her training, it could very well cost her her life should she actually be challenged to a duel.

Andrew aggressively advanced, forcing Sarai to retreat. "Where is your mind?" he shouted above the noise of the swords clashing. "You know my style of fighting better than I know the back of my hand. What am I going to do next, now that I have you on the run?"

You're going to get cocky any minute now, Sarai thought. *Then, you're mine.*

"Talk me to death?" she said to her father with a smirk.

Andrew didn't like her impertinence. She was joking while he was trying to teach her a valuable lesson, how to read her opponent.

Angry, he raised his sword to deliver a mighty blow. Sarai blocked the blow, her sword raised high, as well. As they leaned in close to one another, grimacing, muscles straining, swords ominously scraping together, she suddenly slipped underneath his raised arms and kicked his legs out from under him.

Andrew fell backward, and Sarai held the tip of her mother's sword at his throat.

"Never fight while you're mad, if you can help it," she said sweetly. "That's the first lesson you taught me."

Andrew burst out laughing.

Sarai helped him to his feet, whereupon Andrew attacked her again.

Edina rose from her perch on the arm of the couch.

"I'd better go make sure dinner doesn't burn. This might take a while."

Daniel acknowledged her words with a nod of his head, his eyes on Sarai and Andrew as Sarai executed a stylish riposte in response to her father's thrust. He couldn't take his eyes off her. A thin layer of perspiration covered her glowing brown skin. Her eyes were narrowed in concentration. She looked *hot*. It must have been the athlete in him, but Sarai never looked sexier than she did when she was engaged in physical combat. He couldn't wait to get her home.

"Tell me again what the prophecy says about me and Sarai," Nighthawk said to the wizened sorceress.

He sat in a dank, cold room far underground in the oldest cemetery in Chicago. The mortuary boasted the remains of some of Chicago's finest families. Of course, death being the great equalizer, the dead rich were no better off now than the dead poor.

The woman's face crinkled in irritation. "For *what?* You won't take my advice, anyway. Four years ago, I told you to marry her, and you ignored me."

Nighthawk blew air between his lips. He'd committed murder for lesser insults to his intelligence. Unfortunately, the woman was of his bloodline, and one of the Sons of the Morning.

Nighthawk tried not to kill blood, if at all possible.

"Just tell me, woman!" he said irritably.

"The prophecy says that through her you will sire a son who will be the most powerful Son of the Morning Star to ever walk the earth," she said this so softly that Nighthawk had to strain to hear. Her beady eyes were insolent when she raised them to meet his.

He leaned forward. "Give me the other half."

"Or, she will be the death of you." Humor sparkled in her eyes now.

Nighthawk pounded his hand on the stone slab that served as a table for the woman's many candles. Candles fell over, and hot wax spilled onto the stone slab. "Why are prophecies always so damned ambiguous? Either she will make me great through a special son, or she'll *murder* me? Is God so facetious?"

"You know the answer to that," the woman said with a cackle. "You're down here consulting a witch. It certainly didn't do Saul any good when he had the witch of Endor summon the ghost of Samuel in order to ask him for advice."

"Are you saying your advice is no good?"

She shook her head, pity evident in her expression. "My advice is what it is. I told you what I saw in your future. I can't be sure whether the information came from above or below. My receptors aren't what they used to be."

"You're a Son of the Morning Star," Nighthawk said. "Your allegiance is to Lucifer."

"Yes, but what if Lucifer's allegiance isn't to me? We both know that we're living on borrowed time. We haven't been tossed into the lake of fire yet because it pleases God to carry on this experiment. It's an age-old question: Did he kick us out of heaven to spend eternity on earth in order to punish us, or to give us the opportunity to change our ways and return to the fold?"

"What you're saying could be ruled seditious if it got back to Lucifer," Nighthawk warned her. "You talk as if we have that option. We don't."

She cackled again. "I'm nearly four hundred years old. I don't care what he thinks. It'd be a mercy if he would put me out of my misery. Besides, no punishment Lucifer could devise would be as horrible as an eternity of being separated from God. *I* know!"

Nighthawk abruptly stood up. He placed a rolled up wad of cash on the stone slab. Even an old witch had expenses. It couldn't be cheap to keep her crypt livable.

He looked at her again. She didn't even try to maintain the illusion of youth. She obviously didn't care that she looked like the Crypt-Keeper's sister. The skin on her face was so papery thin, her skull was in sharp relief.

No wonder she didn't go out in public anymore. The humans would have a field day with her. Imagine, they thought that a one-hundred-and-fifteen year-old woman who had died last year had been the oldest living human being on earth.

She turned her rheumy eyes on him. "Why don't *you* kill me? I can't change the prophecy. It is such as it is. I'm of no further use to you." She sounded hopeful.

"Sorry, I didn't bring my sword," Nighthawk said with a note of apology. "Maybe next time."

He quickly got out of there. Cemeteries gave him the creeps.

A few minutes later, he stepped outside into a bright Sunday afternoon. His stride was confident as he hurried to his Jaguar. He knew what he had to do now.

* * *

Sarai and Daniel were barely inside their apartment before they started undressing each other. "I'm not leaving until tomorrow afternoon," Daniel said. "Take the morning off so we can spend it in bed together. This has got to last us for nearly a month."

"You mean phone sex isn't leaving you satisfied?" Sarai joked. She'd gotten his shirt open, now, and bent to kiss his hairy chest. She licked his nipples.

"Baby, you know phone sex is never as good as the real thing," Daniel said as he grasped her face between his big hands and kissed her sweet mouth.

Sarai, being a multi-tasking kind of gal, was busy unbuckling his belt and slipping her hand inside his pants to lay hold of his hardened penis. She felt him throb in her hand.

Daniel moaned with pleasure and raised her skirt. Pantyhose and panties were dispensed with in a hurry, pumps with them. In an instant, they found themselves in a passionate clench on the foyer rug, Sarai on her back with her legs wrapped around him. Daniel was on top, giving her the full length of his manhood with every flex of his powerful leg, butt, and thigh muscles.

Sarai arched her back, welcoming him deep inside of her. Her golden-brown breasts, full and round, their tips hard, beckoned Daniel. He couldn't help touching them, gently twisting the nubs, which heightened her pleasure.

He momentarily bent to lick her nipples, the taste of her skin delicious to him. This added sensation made him swell even more. Sarai felt it at once. Her body was so attuned to his that even a minute change was detected by her. His penis pressed against the walls of her vagina.

She felt the urge to push harder and did so. Daniel, whose first desire when making love to her was to give her all the pleasure she could take, pushed, but slowly, making certain she felt every inch of him.

Soon, though, he could no longer hold back and both of them were in the full sensual grip of lust. He pulled her closer and pumped her with long thrusts, his penis pulling almost out of her and going back inside, feeling cooler to her each time due to momentarily being in the air. Sarai, as athletic as her husband, gave him back thrust for thrust.

Daniel was watching her face intently. He loved observing her when she was close to orgasm. Her eyes changed colors. Usually a very dark brown, the irises turned the color of brandy and the pupils turned a fiery red. Everything about her fascinated him.

As he watched, her eyes changed colors. He felt her vaginal muscles contract at that very instant, and knew she had cum.

With the knowledge of her completion, he came seconds later. He held her in his arms a few moments before rising and helping her to her feet. "We haven't done that in a while," he said jokingly of their lovemaking on the foyer rug.

Sarai craned her neck, trying to see her backside. "I'm gonna have rug burns on my behind."

Daniel laughed. "Probably on my knees, as well. But it was worth it."

The next day, Sarai didn't go to work until after Daniel had left for the airport. Dressed in jeans, a sweater, leather jacket and her favorite motorcycle boots, she rode the elevator downstairs, daydreaming about their lovemaking earlier that morning.

She sighed happily as she stepped off the elevator and right smack into Nighthawk's chest. His theme was black: a designer suit and overcoat, and sharp designer boots.

Sarai peered curiously up at him. "What are you doing here?"

Then, she saw the moving men, loaded down with boxes, coming into the building. Beyond the glass doors stood a semi-trailer belonging to a local moving company.

Her eyes narrowed as she regarded him once more. "You're moving in?"

"Lovely *and* astute," said Nighthawk, flashing white teeth roguishly.

Other residents were coming into the building, and getting off the elevator behind her. Now was not the time to get into a heated conversation. She yanked him away from the bank of elevators and around the corner. "I don't know what you're up to, Armaros. But, quit it, I love my husband and your moving into our building isn't going to make me leave him for you."

Nighthawk inclined his head. An amused expression sat in his black eyes. "My moving here has nothing to do with you, darling. I simply wanted a different venue. I'm tired of that big, old drafty penthouse. I wanted something homier. The apartment I've chosen is a tad smaller and down the hall from you and that rain-on-newly-mowed-grass smelling husband of yours."

Nighthawk had crashed their wedding. He hadn't made a scene, but his being there had been intrusive enough for Sarai. When he'd shaken Daniel's hand at the reception she hadn't known then that he'd been sizing him up. Remembering his smell.

Nephilim often joked about how they could smell a human's soul and know what type of person he was. Nephilim didn't have a detectable scent to one another. To the Sons of the Morning Star this was further evidence that God had stripped them of souls when he'd banished them to earth. Grigori thought that reasoning was ridiculous. Nephilim didn't have a scent because they were more angel than human. To them, it was proof that they were closer to God in genetic make-up, than to man.

But Sarai didn't have time to talk politics now. "Just stay away from me and Daniel," she warned, preparing to leave. "This is a free country. As far as I'm concerned, you can live anywhere you want. But you're not allowed to encroach upon my privacy! Stay out of my life, Armaros!"

"Of course," Nighthawk said calmly. "I would never impose on anyone. But should you get lonely in the middle of the night, remember that I'm just down the hall. I would be more than happy to accommodate you."

"It'll never happen," Sarai said, smartly tossing her bag onto her shoulder and walking away. "What a monumental ego," she said in a low voice as she pushed open the lobby door.

"I heard that!" Nighthawk said with a short laugh.

"Of course you did," she said in an equally low voice, knowing he could hear her. "Go screw yourself."

"I'd much prefer screwing you."

He knew *she* had heard that, too.

She didn't respond, though. She just got out of there as fast as she could.

chapter Three

Angry, Daniel tossed the newspaper he'd been reading into the wastebasket beside his desk and reached over to press the intercom button. "Maya, would you get me that reporter on the phone?"

"Mark Houston?" Maya asked cautiously.

"You know which one I'm talking about," Daniel said irritably.

"Just a minute, Daniel," Maya said.

Daniel sat back in his chair and impatiently drummed his fingers on the surface of the desk. This would be the last time a reporter referred to *him* as the Mike Tyson of Capitol Hill simply because he was an ex-boxer.

He and Mike Tyson had nothing in common except that they were both ex-pugilists.

He had started boxing when he was twelve. His father, a man who thought a black kid had only one way off the mean streets—by using his fists—had been his first trainer.

But his father hadn't been able to resist the streets himself and had turned into a drunk who knocked around both his wife and his kid when the spirit hit him.

One night, when the old man had come in looking for a fight, Daniel had given it to him. Beaten and humiliated, his father had thrown him out of the house while his mother had looked on helplessly.

He'd been only sixteen, but he'd been a man even then. He made a vow never to do two things—consume alcohol or hit a woman, no matter the provocation.

He moved in with his mother's brother, Jake, who took him to his neighborhood gym where one of the trainers immediately recognized his potential. By the time he was nineteen he was a two-time Chicago Golden Gloves champion.

For the next ten years he trained like a madman and steadily rose in the heavyweight rankings until he achieved the ultimate goal: Heavyweight Champion of the World.

His Uncle Jake had been in his corner all the way. His father died of liver cancer five years ago. His mother was now living in a mansion in Florida.

At thirty, he retired from boxing. He'd already been doing it for eighteen years and had enough money to live on for the rest of his life. He would have to be a fool to risk brain damage for money and glory. He went back to college instead and majored in political science. The news media ate it up. A boxer displaying intelligence? They were known for having brawn, not brains.

Daniel surprised them all by graduating in the top ten percentile of his class at Northwestern. Then, he shocked them again by announcing that he was going to run for the House of Representatives. There were a lot of young people, he said, who needed to know that hustling on the streets or becoming a famous athlete weren't the only two ways a person could be a success in life.

He went back to his old South Side neighborhood and opened a youth center. The people were skeptical at first. But when he moved into the neighborhood, they knew he was for real. They got behind him and got him elected. He felt duty bound to represent their interests in Washington, D. C. Now, he felt having reporters always referring to him as the Mike Tyson of Capitol Hill detracted from his purpose, which was to have his constituents' concerns heard and taken seriously in this town.

Maya knocked quickly but came into the room before he could say "come in" as was her normal routine. Smiling, she placed a fresh cup of coffee in front of him, and went to sit on the chair across from him. "Do we really want to antagonize Mark Houston? He works for the biggest paper in D.C. Can't we simply ignore that comment at the end of the piece? The rest of the article was complimentary. He said you were effective, smart, and devoted to your constituents. He didn't mean anything by the Mike Tyson comment, I'm sure. It's just that you and Mike are the most popular ex-heavyweight champions. You for who *you* are and Mike for who *he* is," she said, grimacing. "I mean, I'm sure Mike gets tired of them reminding him about the past, too. But as long as you used to be the Champ they're going to remind you." She smiled. "Wouldn't you much rather talk to Sarai? I have her on line one."

"You're fired," Daniel said, pointing to the door as he reached for the phone. "Out!"

Maya, smiling happily, rose and left the room. She knew she wasn't really fired.

Daniel always thought twice before letting her go after she disobeyed a direct order.

Although she had a huge crush on Daniel, she would never dream of letting him in on the secret. For one thing, she loved working for him, and for another, she knew he adored Sarai who was the only person who could talk sense into him, which she hoped was what was going on in his office right now.

Tell Mark Houston off, indeed! Houston was just waiting for Daniel to fall flat on his face. The thing about Washington, D.C. was that the only thing more interesting than politics was the politicians making fools of themselves in the media. Daniel was a good man, and way too idealistic to recognize that not everyone in town had his best interests at heart. In fact, most of them didn't.

Sometimes, she had to step up and save him from himself.

She sat down at her desk, and took a sip from her coffee mug. She glanced at the red light on the phone denoting that line one was still in use. Smiling, she continued with her morning correspondence while the man sitting in the office waiting to speak with Daniel tried to be unobtrusive about staring at her breasts.

It was hard to do, though, because Maya Stephenson was quite a beauty. She had rich chocolate skin, sooty black-brown hair that she wore in a short, layered cut that flattered her heart-shaped face. Lips a man's eyes lingered on. And a tall, curvaceous body with legs that the guy sitting across from her had glimpsed only once when she'd gotten up to go into the inner office but now swore were the finest he'd ever laid eyes on. He was hoping she'd get up again so he'd get the chance to see if his eyes were deceiving him or not.

But, no, the buzzer sounded, and he heard Representative Wingate's voice say, "Maya, you can send Mr. Green in now."

Send him in. He sighed regrettably. He wasn't going to see those legs anymore.

In Chicago, Sarai replaced the receiver in its cradle on her desk. Speaking with Daniel only intensified her need to see him in the flesh. He'd been gone nearly three weeks now, and she missed him terribly.

Lord knows she'd done her best to stay so busy that when she returned to an empty apartment at night all she'd have the energy to do would be to take a shower and fall into bed. Still, she craved him so badly her dreams were filled with him. He was the only thing she *wanted* to dream about.

As for work, the case against Young was getting stronger every day. All three of the girls they'd rescued positively identified him as their captor. Even his parents were offering tidbits about his strange nocturnal habits. It seemed they didn't sleep as deeply as their son had assumed and were awakened many nights by the sound of his either leaving the apartment, or returning to it.

They were appalled that he could have done such horrible things, and while they would pay for his defense, if he were found guilty, they thought he should be punished to the full extent of the law. If that meant life imprisonment, then so be it.

Fortunately for Young, in 2000, then governor, George

Ryan imposed a moratorium on the death penalty in Illinois. The present governor hadn't seen fit to lift the moratorium. Therefore those who would have formerly been put to death were instead sentenced to life in prison.

Sarai could understand why the death penalty didn't work. However, animals like Young were benefiting because of a flawed system, and that rankled her.

She turned her attention to her next case: that of Sean White. As was the modus operandi of many pedophiles, Sean had chosen a career working with children. He was a kindergarten teacher at a private school. The city's wealthiest families inadvertently sent their little darlings to school to be fondled by him.

He first came to the police's attention in 2005 when the mother of one of his students filed a complaint against him saying her son, Peter, age five, had told her that Mr. White had touched him "down there."

At the time, Sean White explained, and quite believably, he had only been trying to assist Peter with a stubborn zipper. Peter admitted that he *had* been trying to get his zipper down in order to use the toilet.

A five-year-old makes a very bad character witness. His own character is not yet fully formed, and he is bound to make poor judgments. The school wanted to drop it.

It would be bad publicity to have their name dragged into the news. Peter's mom simply removed Peter from the school. The school then terminated Sean White on general principle.

In their opinion, he was probably innocent. But it wouldn't do for the source of rumors to still be on their exalted staff. They gave him a nice severance package.

Today, Sean White, brought down a peg or two by the incident, was working at a lowly public elementary school. Once again, a mother lodged a complaint against him.

The school, less worried about its reputation than the welfare of its students, brought the police in and the mother pressed charges. White was arrested, spent the night in jail but disappeared the next day after being bailed out by his brother.

Sarai was just happy that White had not thus far shown a propensity for murder like John Michael Young. So what if she had to track the big doofus down? She had a good feeling that he hadn't gone far. His bank account couldn't support a flea, and it wouldn't be the first time a fugitive from justice tried to get lost in the city of Chicago.

Therefore, she and Jim were focusing on all of White's friends and family. They figured someone he knew had provided him with a hideaway.

"Wanna grab some lunch?" Jim asked, looking up from his computer monitor.

"Not hungry," Sarai said. "You go. I want to go through White's employment record again."

"You've already been through it with a fine-tooth comb."

"Yeah, but I keep thinking I might have missed something."

Jim smiled as he pushed himself up from his desk. He was a good-looking guy with dark brown hair and eyes. He was five-eleven, and had a fit, but not overly muscular build.

At forty he had been a policeman for fifteen years. He'd been a Marine before joining up. Sarai had met him the first day on the job more than ten years ago and he'd treated her with respect from the beginning. It was not something she could say about some of her other male colleagues who either treated her like a Barbie doll, as if an attractive woman had to have been born without a brain in her head, or as a sex object.

"Okay," Jim said finally. "I'll bring you back a sandwich."

He was always looking out for her.

"Thanks," she said, and returned her attention to the thick file on her desk.

What had struck her about White's work history was that there was a lapse of two years between one position at an elementary school and employment at another. She didn't think he had not had to work those two years. She figured he must have gotten a job where he was paid under the table. That meant he was paid in cash and the employer neglected to report it to the proper governmental authorities.

Taking into account his need to be near children, she narrowed his options down to neighborhood daycare centers whose proprietors didn't care whom they hired as long as they got cheap labor.

She got on the phone with a friend in Social Services. Ten minutes later she received a fax with the list of all the daycare centers in the city that had been written up for violating labor laws in the past twelve months.

When Jim returned with her sandwich, she rose and handed him a copy. He gave her the sandwich, a turkey on rye. "What's this?" he asked, peering down at the sheet of paper.

"I'll tell you on the way," she said, putting on her jacket. "I'll drive."

* * *

"I need two things from you," Nighthawk told Embeth, which was the name of the ancient sorceress. "If you provide them, I'll do what you wish."

Her eyes, the only lively feature in her face, shone with excitement. "You promise?"

"I swear," said Nighthawk. "But I want your assurance that the enchantment will last as long as I wish it to. Not just for a few days as most of your spells do."

"This spell will last as long as I draw breath," Embeth promised. "And I'm still a few years away from my four-hundredth birthday."

Nighthawk smiled his pleasure. "Wonderful. You have eight days to work your magic."

"More than enough time," Embeth said in anticipation of her impending death. "I need to know one thing, though."

"What's that?" Nighthawk asked, nervous about any stipulation she might insist upon. Lately, she was more concerned about her spells not causing harm to others.

She used to be a stand-up gal. Always willing to kill or maim in the name of Lucifer.

Now it seemed the closer she got to death, the more she wanted to make sure that the tote board that kept count of her bad deeds and her good deeds had a vastly superior number on the good side.

Frankly, that made him nervous.

However, one didn't come by a powerful sorceress every day. They were as rare as a faithful husband, which reminded him why he was there.

"What's that?" he patiently asked again.

"I would feel better about it if I knew you were doing

this because of true love and not as another bid in your quest for power," she told him boldly.

"I love her," he said with sincerity.

Embeth studied his face for several minutes before agreeing to his request. "Come back tomorrow," she said at last.

Sarai and Jim's search for White proved fruitless for four days. On the fifth day they went to a daycare center in an old South Side neighborhood.

The building was a large renovated frame house painted a loud blue as if the application of a bold primary color was the first indication to prospective clients that children would naturally be happy there. Sarai went to the front door and introduced herself while Jim went around back to prevent White from skipping should he be on the premises.

The black woman who answered the door was big, tall, gray-haired, and from the expression on her mocha-colored face, had little time for visitors. The noise level was in the upper registers, infants screaming, other children ripping and running all over the place, plus a dog barking. Sarai guessed the woman's nerves were frazzled.

She held up her ID and the woman looked at it through the screen door.

"Police?" she said, frowning. "What y'all want 'round here?"

"Hopefully, nothing," Sarai said with a reassuring smile. "There is a very dangerous pedophile who's on the lam. We're checking every daycare center in the city because he usually gravitates toward children." She tiptoed, peering behind the woman. Most of the children Sarai saw were either African American or Hispanic.

Two women were trying to corral the ones who were causing havoc. They were also African American.

"Pedo-what?"

"Pedophile," Sarai said. "It's a person who molests children."

This was obviously distressing news to the woman. Her eyes stretched wide. "Listen, this is my business. I've been running this place for nearly thirty years. Now, I had a problem with somebody who worked here falsifying papers in order to stay in the country and I got in trouble because of it. But since then, I check out everybody who works here. Everybody!"

"That's good," Sarai said calmly. "That's excellent, in fact."

The woman suddenly looked embarrassed. She smiled tentatively as she held the screen door open for Sarai. "Come on in, child," she said. "Come on back to the kitchen. We ain't gonna be able to hear ourselves *think* in here."

They walked through the melee toward the back of the house. The kitchen was a big, clean room with a huge oak table in the center and the south wall had a huge picture window. The backyard looked deep, and beautifully manicured. A large yellow dog romped in it.

"Sit down," the woman offered.

Sarai sat down.

"You're Mrs. Davenport, then," Sarai assumed. A Nora Davenport was the owner of Wee Heaven Daycare Center.

"That's right," said Nora proudly. "Up until last year,

I didn't have any problems from anybody about the operation of this place. It scared me. Now, I request a résumé and I call the references every time. I don't just ask for them and never phone to check them out."

"That's a good habit to have," Sarai complimented her. While she was talking she was pulling out a manila folder with copies of White's mug shot in it. She opened the folder and handed Nora a copy.

"Have you seen this man?"

Nora's skin went pale underneath her mocha coloring. Her large brown eyes looked frightened. "Oh, God, that's the new guy. I just hired him two weeks ago."

Sarai contained her excitement. There would be time to celebrate after White was in custody. "Is he here now?" she asked softly.

Nora shook her head. "No, he won't get here until noon. He works from noon until six when the last of the kids who stay longer because their parents work late go home. I've never seen him in a car. I think he walks to work."

Sarai glanced at her watch. It was fifteen minutes until noon. She had parked the unmarked police car down the street, thinking that if White was there he'd be jumpy and seeing any car pulling up to the daycare center might make him bolt out the back.

Now, she wasn't confident that she'd parked far enough away. Criminals on the run were among the most paranoid people she'd ever encountered. It was almost like some of them had special antennae when it came to detecting the law nearby.

She abruptly rose. "Thank you, Ms. Davenport. Please lock the door and keep all of the children inside. Don't let them go in the backyard. My partner and I are going to wait for Mr. White outside."

Nora rose, too. "Y'all get that boy. Coming here, giving me all kinds of excellent references just so he could get next to my kids!" she cried indignantly. "Y'all get him, because if *you* don't, I will!"

"Don't worry, Ms. Davenport, we'll catch him," Sarai said as she quickly walked to the exit. She got on the radio. "Jim, this is the place. The owner says she hired him a couple of weeks ago. She expects him any minute now."

"I'm still around back," Jim responded. "Where will you be?"

"I'm going to change my appearance a bit and take a stroll down the sidewalk."

"But he's seen you before," Jim said worriedly.

"Only once, and then I had my hair drawn back and was wearing all black."

Jim laughed shortly. "Lucky you. You only wear a dress once every blue moon and today there happens to be one."

"Ha, ha," Sarai said dryly. "I'm going now." She dropped the compact radio into her shoulder bag, reached up and took the clasp off her heavy fall of hair and shook the waves out as she stepped onto the front porch.

Nora locked the door behind her as she'd been instructed.

Sarai casually sashayed down the sidewalk, occasionally glancing at her watch as if she were waiting for someone to come pick her up in a car, and they were running late.

It wasn't long before she spotted Sean White lumbering in her direction.

He was a tall man with straight red hair and watery

blue eyes. Just short of being obese, he was awkwardly formed. His arms seemed too long for his body, and he was knock-kneed. When he walked his thighs rubbed together. Sarai heard him coming in his brown corduroy slacks a block away.

As he drew closer, she got her cell phone out of her shoulder bag and keyed in her home number. When the answering machine kicked in, she pretended she was talking to the imaginary person who'd forgotten to pick her up. "Look, if I can't depend on you to be here when you say you're going to be here, then forget you! I don't need this hassle. I'm going to be late to work because of you."

She was standing in the middle of the sidewalk, so Sean had to either walk around her or ask her to move aside. She hung the phone up and put it away as soon as he was within five feet of her.

She smiled at him, and said, "Hi, Sean!"

Sean went still. He squinted at her, confused by the fact that a stranger had called him by his name. He was sure that he didn't know her. He wasn't the type of man who collected beautiful women as friends.

If they didn't give him disdainful looks, they gave him pity-filled ones. Either way, he never got anywhere with them. "Do I know you?" he asked, a little flattered by, but a lot suspicious of her apparent interest in him.

"Sure, you do," Sarai said softly, still smiling. "My partner and I arrested you about three weeks ago."

All bets were off then. Sean hauled off and tried to cold clock her.

Sarai ducked, went low, and quickly came back up with a punch to his mid-section. As she'd suspected, Sean didn't work on his abdominal muscles. He doubled over in pain and yowled like a kicked dog.

By that time, Jim was there, and Sean didn't give him any trouble as he forced him to the grass on his belly and handcuffed him.

"Next time, I'll wear the dress," Jim joked.

"You've got the legs for it," Sarai said, grinning at him.

She helped him get Sean to his feet, then they walked him down the sidewalk to the waiting car. Sarai was more than pleased with the outcome.

It had taken them four days, but her hunch had paid off. Plus, there were only three days left before Daniel would be coming home. And now that Sean White was in custody, she could concentrate more fully on her man.

She would make sure that his first night back would be a night to remember.

chapter four

"Are you sure you don't want me to drop you off on my way?" Daniel asked Maya one last time before they parted at the airport.

Maya, already heading in the opposite direction toward a line of waiting taxis shook her head. "I've got a date, boss," she said. "And if I grab a taxi I can be home in time to get all dolled up for him. Your taking me home would take you out of your way. You've kept Sarai waiting long enough!"

Daniel couldn't argue with that. He still innately felt it was his duty to deliver her home safely, though. It was undoubtedly the Boy Scout in him.

"Okay," he finally conceded. "Take care of yourself."

They waved and he trotted the rest of the way to the waiting town car. He used the same limousine service every time. And they usually sent the same driver: Titus. The guy standing next to the back door of the car wasn't Titus this time.

He recognized Daniel right away, though. "Good

evening, Representative Wingate. I trust you had a pleasant flight?"

"I did. Thanks," Daniel replied, his keen eyes taking in the tall, muscular black man. "Titus couldn't make it, huh?"

"Afraid not, sir," said the man as he held the door open. "I'm Malcolm."

Daniel held out his hand. Malcolm shook it. "Good to meet you, Malcolm. Mind if I see some identification?"

"No problem," Malcolm said good-naturedly as he reached into his inside jacket pocket and produced a billfold. He showed Daniel his driver's license and the I D that the limousine service provided for all of its drivers.

Satisfied, Daniel climbed onto the backseat and relaxed, his mind already anticipating his reunion with Sarai.

Sarai was in the kitchen when she heard Daniel's key in the door. A delicious thrill of longing shot through her. She closed the refrigerator door, and hurried to the living room, the soft, sheer fabric of the negligee she was wearing floating in her wake.

The negligee was red. Her hair was piled on her head in a sexy twist. She smelled good enough to eat, and she was barefoot.

Daniel saw her the moment he opened the door, and he didn't have time to either close the door or drop his bags before she was in his arms. The bags fell to the floor.

Lips immediately locked in deep, ravenous kisses.

Tears of relief sat in her eyes when he set her back down. His eyes devoured her as if he was seeing her for the first time. The love, the lust, the palpable emotions were all exposed for her to witness.

"Welcome home, baby," she said, grinning.

He shut the door, locked it, and enfolded her in his arms again. "You're a vision," he said, his voice husky. He couldn't take his eyes off her. Or his hands, it seemed. He picked her up, heading to the bedroom. Sarai wrapped her arms around his neck.

"I cooked dinner for you," she said.

"Thank you," he smiled, kissing her chin. "Later. Right now, all I want is you."

Sarai buried her nose in his neck, loving the scent of his skin. "The bed's already turned down."

In the bedroom, he dropped her onto the bed and immediately began removing his clothing as she watched. He removed his shoes and socks first, which made her wonder when he'd started doing that. He usually removed his jacket, shirt and tie first.

Then he would turn his attention to his shoes and socks, which he usually took off before taking off his slacks.

She missed so much when they were apart.

She wondered what else he was doing differently lately.

Soon, he was down to his boxer briefs. She got up and went to him. "Let me give you a nice relaxing massage."

"Okay," he said, surprising her. His dark eyes were alight with sensual promise. "But, ladies first."

Sarai's brows drew together in a frown. As an athlete, Daniel enjoyed a massage but only *after* physical exertion, not before. She didn't say anything, though. Maybe he was simply following her cues. She'd brought up the massage, after all. Maybe it'd slipped his mind that she sometimes teased him by offering him a massage to relax. Relaxing was the last thing on their minds when they were about to make love. Relaxing was for later when they didn't have any energy left to pleasure each other. *Then,* it was time for a leisurely bath and a soothing massage.

He insisted on taking the sexy negligee off her and had her lie down on her stomach. Sarai scooted over to the middle of the bed, her golden brown body long, lithe and gorgeous.

Daniel began by gingerly straddling her and beginning the massage at her shoulders. Sarai smiled knowingly when she felt his penis, heavy, and approaching a full-on erection, brush the backs of her thighs.

She gave him two minutes, tops, before he was trying to penetrate her. The old Daniel would have had her on her back by now.

"That feels good," she said.

Indeed, his big hands felt wonderful on her. She could get used to this.

She didn't see Daniel's face, though. He'd closed his eyes with sheer satisfaction and he had to remember to breathe because the feel of her skin excited him so much.

His penis continued to harden until he was in pain with the desire to pin her to the bed with it. He held himself in firm control, though, because a husband's, a good husband's, first duty to his wife was to assure her pleasure. He would get his afterward.

"Daniel?" Sarai said after several minutes of silence.

"Yes, baby?"

"Would you screw me already? I'm enjoying this new you, but you know I'm a ride 'em cowboy kind of girl. I'm horny as hell."

It was true. A couple of days ago, she'd begun having those symptoms her mother had warned her about. She felt like she could make love to Daniel all night long. "Baby," Daniel breathed, none too gently turning her over in bed, "you read my mind." Sarai opened her legs wide and he guided himself inside of her.

"Oh, *God,* you feel good!" he gasped roughly.

Sarai smiled up at him. "That's the idea." She arched her back, driving him deeper. Daniel screamed with a powerful orgasm.

Sarai was astonished, but schooled her features so that he wouldn't see the surprise on her face. Daniel had never had a premature ejaculation. *Never.*

He collapsed on top of her and nuzzled her neck. "I'm sorry, baby. I guess I've been away from you for too long."

She turned her head to kiss him softly. "It happens to the best of men," she told him, a mischievous gleam in her eye.

Daniel surprised her again by rolling over onto his back and throwing his arm over his face in an apparent moment of self-disgust. "But not to me."

Usually, whenever Sarai made a comment about human males, Daniel would assume she was comparing humans to Nephilim and he'd come back with something like, "Oh, I guess a Nephilim never lost control of *his* dick in bed!"

Then they'd have a spirited debate about human sexual prowess versus Nephilim sexual prowess.

Sarai cuddled closer to Daniel. "We've got all night," she said, kissing him in the middle of his back.

When Daniel felt her mouth on his back, he was startled as if she'd touched him with a red-hot poker.

Sarai sat up in bed. "What's going on with you tonight?"

Daniel sat up and regarded her with a tired expression. "I guess I'm more stressed out than I thought. I need to take my mind off work." His eyes were pleading. "Talk to me, Babe. Tell me something funny that's happened to you lately."

They got comfortable in bed, with her lying in Daniel's arms. "Okay, well, my ex moved into the building a few weeks ago. You remember him. He crashed our wedding."

Daniel appeared stumped for a moment, then said, "Oh, you mean Nicolas Armaros?"

"Who else crashed our wedding?" Sarai asked, really concerned, now, that Daniel had indeed been working too hard. He normally had a mind like a steel trap. Anything that went in it remained firmly in there for easy future reference.

"Anyway," she went on. "He's been making a nuisance of himself."

"In what way?"

"Leaving orchids and other exotic flora on the terrace for me to find when I come home from work. He never leaves a note. He doesn't have to. No one except someone who can fly would have access to the terrace."

"What do you suppose he wants?" Daniel asked, his tone calm.

"He wants me to leave you for him," Sarai told him.

Daniel laughed. "He's got big balls."

"To match his ego," Sarai said with a short laugh of her own. "Nighthawk is the most powerful Nephilim in the city. He can have any woman he wants. Yet, he wants a woman who's already taken. He's like a spoiled kid in a candy store—Gimme, gimme, gimme! I detest him."

"You never loved him?" Daniel asked.

His tone was serious, and that gave Sarai pause. She had been in a joking mood until then. Having a bit of fun at Nighthawk's expense.

But she and Daniel never lied to each other. So, her tone got serious, as well. "I did love him, Daniel. I loved him so much I wanted to marry him and have his children. That kind of behavior goes against everything I've been taught about the Sons of the Morning Star and the Grigori. But I was willing to forget all that just to be with him. Then, he broke my heart by telling me he couldn't see me anymore for those very reasons. His family had found out about us and demanded that he drop me. So, he did."

"Just like that?" Daniel asked incredulously.

"That was the cruelest cut," Sarai admitted. "I thought I meant something to him. Apparently, I was dispensable." She sighed. "Luckily for me, a year later I met a guy who has the heart of a lion and the loyalty of a Grigori." She smiled into his eyes.

"Did you fall for this guy?" Daniel asked, smiling back.

"Hard," she said.

Then, they were kissing again, and Sarai could feel his arousal on her thigh.

That night they fell asleep, naked, in each other's arms. The bedroom curtains were open and moonshine spread its benevolent light over them as they slept.

Sarai was awakened, quite pleasantly, before daybreak when Daniel took one of her nipples in his mouth and began to suckle.

She opened her eyes to clearly see his face in the moon-light. A mischievous grin curled his lips. "I woke up hungry for you."

Smiling, Sarai grasped his hardening penis. "You're a growing boy. You need your nourishment. Eat up."

Straddling her, he licked her nipples with obvious relish, his tongue, wet, hot and insistent.

Sarai moaned with pleasure and arched her back.

Daniel ran his tongue between her breasts, straight down to her bellybutton where he made a wet circle, then continued downward.

Grasping her by the hips, he roughly pulled her toward him and bent to plunge his tongue into the slick, swollen folds of her vagina.

"Daniel." His name was a breathless sigh on her lips.

Daniel didn't hear her. He was under the spell cast by the combination of her taste and her smell. It was a unique aroma that lovers emitted exclusively for each other.

"Daniel." She said his name again, this time more urgently. He looked up and saw what she was referring to: Her wings had begun sprouting.

She propped herself up on her elbows, allowing her wings room to grow. Once the transformation had started there was nothing to do except allow it to happen.

"Do you want me to stop?" Daniel asked, concerned.

"No, I want you inside of me."

This had never occurred before. She wondered if it was a symptom of her pregnancy: sprouting wings when sexually aroused. In which case, she would have to be careful not to become aroused in public.

Daniel straddled her once again and bent to kiss her.

Sarai squeezed his ass with both hands. Daniel moaned deep in his throat and entered her, his penis thick, hard, and pulsing. He grabbed her ass, too, and pulled her hard against him as he thrust deeper.

Sarai closed her eyes and gave herself over to the pleasure of the moment. Her arms were wrapped tightly around Daniel, as his were around her.

Suddenly, she began to rise from the bed, with Daniel on top of her. His eyes were closed too.

Daniel felt her convulse when she came. He followed soon afterward, and they continued to hold each other close as their bodies settled down.

They were so caught up in the passion that they were floating six feet above the bed before they realized that they were defying gravity.

Sarai was the first to come to her senses. "Oh, God, Daniel. Look what we're doing."

Daniel opened his eyes and looked down. "Shit!"

That broke the spell, and they plummeted to the bed.

"What was that?" Daniel asked of the strange phenomenon.

"I don't know," Sarai admitted. "Maybe my powers are evolving."

Daniel gently rubbed his hands over her wings which had grown to their full splendor. "You didn't hurt yourself when you fell, did you?"

Sarai smiled at the joke. "Oh, I get it, another fallen angel joke."

There were two delivery men in the truck as it pulled up to the gate that led to an exclusive estate in one of

Chicago's historic neighborhoods. Stan was the driver, a short, terse, pugnacious man whose personality was invariably sour when he thought that someone was trying to take advantage of him. He was in a sour mood tonight.

LaSalle Antiques was emblazoned on the side of the panel truck. Henri LaSalle had a reputation for finding anything a collector wished to pay for. He asked no questions. The customer was always right, especially if his credit rating was in good standing.

Stan looked around suspiciously as he yelled into the intercom, "LaSalle Antiques! We have a delivery for Mrs. Martin."

"Of course, you do," said a deep feminine voice fairly dripping with sex. "Come right in, gentlemen."

The ornate gates slowly opened.

Stan's partner, Charlie, said, "Man, they must have really good cameras. She knew there were two of us. And did you hear that voice? I can't wait to get a look at her."

"No ogling the customers," Stan warned. "You know how touchy that twit, LaSalle, gets if a customer complains. You do still want to be working during the holidays, don't you?"

At twenty-two, Charlie was half Stan's age and had only been working for LaSalle's Antiques a little over a year. He looked up to Stan, even though they were a Mutt and Jeff pair, and he was actually about six inches taller than Stan.

"All right," he hurriedly said, his head bobbing up and down. "I gotcha."

When they got to the front of the house they figured the butler would come out and direct them around back.

Instead, the front door opened and they could see the silhouette of a shapely woman standing in the doorway. "Bring it right through here, gentlemen."

Charlie and Stan moved with alacrity, getting out of the truck and quickly opening the back to reveal a very large wooden crate in the belly of it.

"What *is* that?" Charlie whispered to Stan as they climbed in back to fit the crate into the dolly so they could safely lower it on the lift.

"Hell if I know," said Stan. "But LaSalle promised both of us an extra C-note if we would deliver it to this address in the middle of the night. Customer's request."

"I wonder why?" Charlie said. "Do you think she's a vampire?" He laughed nervously.

"Less talk and more work," Stan said. His tone was firm, but without rancor. He liked the kid. Charlie just had a tendency to find everything worth commenting on and his incessant yammering got on his nerves.

Soon, they were rolling the crate through the double doors of the mansion. Curiously, there were no lights on in the house. Dozens of candelabras sat on tables, on floors, and anywhere else they could be set.

The woman who greeted them was so exquisite that each of them stood mesmerized for a few seconds before following her to an adjacent elevator.

"I'd like it in the basement," she was saying as she turned and began walking toward the back of the house. They followed, watching the sensuous movements of her hips in a tight white dress. She had flawless brown skin, large brown eyes, luscious red lips and slick black hair that fell to her waist.

They didn't even try to guess her age. Beauty like that was undoubtedly ageless.

They encountered no one else in the house as they followed her but were curious as to why the air was so damp and musty. Couldn't she afford central heat and air?

Stan figured she was another one of LaSalle's eccentric customers. At least that's how LaSalle described them. Stan thought they were nuts.

It was insane for a woman living alone to open her door to a couple of deliverymen in the middle of the night without asking for any identification whatsoever. It was insane for someone who could afford a house this big to neglect to turn on the electricity and to let mold grow in it instead.

Stan sneezed. Yeah, his allergies were acting up.

"Bless you," said Mrs. Martin.

They arrived at the elevator and got on it. It was a little cramped inside and too dim for Stan's comfort. He wondered how it worked without electricity.

"Don't worry, gentlemen," said Mrs. Martin, as if reading his mind. "This house was among the first built in the city with an elevator. This baby has never let me down. It works on the pulley system." She closed the cage door and released a lever. Down, they went.

Stan was pleased with how smooth the ride was. "I've never been in one of these," he said, his voice awe-filled.

"And I assure you, you won't ever see another one," Mrs. Martin said pleasantly.

In the basement, they placed the crate in the middle of the room as Mrs. Martin instructed. Then, they got back in the elevator.

"I do appreciate your coming out tonight," Mrs. Martin said as the elevator rose back to the main floor. She reached into a pocket in that skintight dress and produced two crisp hundred-dollar bills. Handing them to Stan whom she must have sensed was the lead man on the job, she said, "For your trouble."

"Oh, it was no trouble, Mrs. Martin," Stan said. "We're already being given a bonus for the job." Not enough of a bonus, but a bonus, nonetheless.

"You're a kind man," Mrs. Martin insisted. "I've always thought kindness should be compensated."

Stan looked into her eyes and somehow felt compelled to take the money. She placed it in his palm and when her hand inadvertently touched his, for a moment she appeared to be an old ugly hag in a deep red robe. Then, she smiled and stepped back a little and she was once more a vision of loveliness.

Stan's voice cracked when he said, "Thank you."

When the elevator arrived on the main floor, Stan hurried out of the conveyance.

Charlie had to nearly run to keep up with him. "Good night, Mrs. Martin!" Stan called over his shoulder.

Charlie, who was pushing the dolly, walked swiftly alongside Stan. "Hey, man, what's the rush?"

"Come on, Charlie, keep up!" Stan said angrily. Fear made him testy.

Stan ran down the steps and was standing at the back of the truck impatiently waiting for Charlie. He pressed the button for the lift. "Come on, come on," he growled.

Charlie, nervous now because of Stan's behavior, nearly

tripped as he rolled the dolly to a stop. He stepped onto the lift with the dolly and Stan operated the lift.

Charlie looked back at the house while he was going up on the lift, but the house was no longer there. They were suddenly in the middle of a cemetery. The only living beings in a cemetery at one o'clock in the morning!

Charlie screamed and shoved the dolly to the back of the truck, then jumped down.

"Close it, close it," he yelled at Stan as they attempted to close the roll-down door.

"Screw it," said Stan, turning to run to the driver's side. "It's empty anyway."

"Right!" said Charlie.

He beat Stan inside the cab of the truck because he was younger and had longer legs.

Stan was praying hard for the engine to catch without its usual trouble as he turned the key in the ignition. It did. He threw the truck in gear and sped through the huge wrought iron gates.

In his rearview mirror, he could now see the huge sign above the open gates: Heavenly Slumber Mortuary.

Charlie was sweating next to him. "What just happened, man?"

"Listen," said Stan. "When weird stuff like that happens the best thing to do is to tell yourself you just imagined it."

"I didn't imagine that!" Charlie cried, shaking. "We just delivered a crate to a ghost!"

"Yeah," said Stan. "But don't tell nobody about it, if you don't want to be spending time in a rubber room."

Several feet below ground, Embeth was happily

opening her lovely new toy. She'd returned to her normal appearance, having no patience for illusion. Inordinately strong, she handled the crowbar like a pro. When she finally got the top off, and had lowered all four sides of the wooden crate her new toy seemed to sparkle in the candlelight.

She stepped forward and lovingly touched the blade. Drawing her forefinger across her tongue, she tasted blood. That baby was sharp.

She threw her head back and laughed with glee.

chapter FIVE

It was the day after Thanksgiving, and Sarai had gone in to work to take care of a pile of paperwork that she and Jim had been unable to go through before the holiday. She had let him slide so he could spend quality time with his kids.

Sitting at her desk, she placed her hand on her belly. Soon, Jim wouldn't be the only one who could use that excuse. She still hadn't given Daniel the news!

Her neighbor, Serena Abraham, was working today, too. Serena was single with no kids. She was trying to get a well-earned promotion, so she worked as much overtime as she could get away with.

The two women had been there since seven that morning, and it was now after two in the afternoon. Neither had taken a lunch break. There had been intermittent small talk between them all day, but nothing substantial.

However, Sarai had noticed Serena giving her frequent surreptitious looks when she thought she wasn't looking.

Serena did it again, and Sarai called her on it. "What?" she asked, more curious than irritated by her friend's behavior. "Do I have a booger?"

Serena laughed shortly. "Now, you know I'd tell you if you had a booger."

"Then, what? And don't tell me it's nothing. You've been stealing glances at me all day. Have you gone gay on me all of a sudden?"

Serena laughed. "Girl, please, I love men too much for that." She frowned suddenly. "Didn't you tell me that Daniel was taking a few days off from work?"

"Yeah, that's right. He'll be home for another week."

"So, he and his assistant don't have any reason to be spending time together?"

"No, Daniel hasn't seen her since he got back. Why?"

Serena averted her eyes a moment, then looked Sarai straight in the eyes. "I'm telling on myself by telling you this because I was at the club with a married man. But night before last, I saw Daniel and Maya having a blast at The Inferno."

Sarai laughed shortly. "The night before Thanksgiving?"

"Yeah. It was late, around two in the morning."

"You couldn't have seen Daniel at The Inferno. He was in bed with me at the time."

Serena looked confused. She bent and got her purse from the bottom drawer of her desk. "Hold on," she said. "I knew you wouldn't believe me, so I took their photo with my cell phone."

Sarai stood up and walked over to Serena's desk. Serena handed her the cell phone.

Sarai looked at the photo, which was astonishingly sharp. The date on which the photo had been taken was clearly printed below it.

In it, Daniel was smiling into Maya's upturned face. It

looked as if they were going to kiss any second now. Sarai almost expected the photo to turn into a video and she'd have to watch them kiss right before her eyes.

She handed the phone back to Serena. "That looks like Daniel and Maya. But in order for him to have been at The Inferno at that time, he would've had to have gotten out of our bed, dressed, and left the apartment. I would have heard him."

"Were you awake at that time?" Serena asked, being the Devil's advocate.

Sarai shook her head, no. They had exhausted themselves with a great lovemaking session that night. There hadn't been any more premature ejaculations for Daniel.

Lately, he'd been insatiable. It suited her because her pregnancy symptoms had kicked in and she was equally unstoppable in bed.

"Daniel can't be having an affair with Maya," she stated bluntly. "Believe me, we've been making up for lost time. He hasn't got the energy to make love to anybody else."

"I hope you're right," Serena said. "But if I were you, I'd definitely find out what the hell he was doing there with her. I was just watching your back, girl."

"I know," Sarai said. "And I appreciate it."

"Really?" Serena asked, sounding skeptical.

"Yeah," Sarai assured her. "I'd rather know."

"Some women would just like to stay in the dark."

"I'm not one of them," Sarai said. "I believe in fidelity. If that's lost, then where does a couple go from there? Cheating ruins everything."

"Ain't that the truth," Serena said. "The married man I'm seeing? He keeps telling me he's leaving his wife, but never does anything about it. I know he's lying. And I wish to God I'd never met him, but now he's gotten under my skin, and I'm just letting it play out. I'm such a fool!"

"You're not a fool," Sarai told her sincerely. "You just got caught up. If you ever want to talk, I'm here."

Serena smiled. "Thanks, Sarai."

"I mean it," said Sarai, going back to her desk to retrieve her shoulder bag. "Now, I've got to have a conversation with my husband. See you!"

"Go on, girl, and handle your business," Serena said encouragingly.

Sarai rode her bike home, and by the time she got upstairs where she expected to find Daniel working in his home office, she was convinced that the couple Serena had photographed at The Inferno had been Nephilim.

They had obviously known that Serena had taken their photo. In fact, they had probably planned it that way. They had known Serena would show her the photo.

Although that part of the plan could have gone against them. Serena had apparently considered not mentioning it to her. Otherwise she would have told her first thing this morning instead of a few minutes ago.

Sarai walked through the apartment, calling Daniel's name. He wasn't there.

Then, she heard a loud thud on the terrace.

Hurrying to the terrace door, she turned the handle only to find that it was locked.

She opened the door and stepped outside. It was very cold, and the wind was biting.

Yet, Daniel was out there in his shirtsleeves leaning over the railing, peering down at something on the street.

"Daniel!"

He turned around. "I'm saved! I *thought* I heard your bike. At least I *hoped* it was your bike. I came out here to take a look at that patio chair you said needed repairing and I forgot and let the door slam behind me without disengaging the lock." He laughed. "Where was my mind?"

Looking at him curiously, Sarai propped open the door to prevent both of them from being locked out, then went and hugged him tightly. "You could have frozen to death!"

"I was only out here about half an hour," he said.

Sarai thought his body should have felt cooler to the touch if he'd been exposed to thirty-degree weather for that long, but didn't say anything. Instead, she looked into his eyes, trying to discern if this were truly Daniel. If that wasn't Daniel at The Inferno two nights ago, perhaps this wasn't Daniel, either. Maybe Daniel never came home from Washington. Daniel would have known about the key under the plant. Her heart thudded, but she tried to hold on to some semblance of calm.

They went inside, and she shut the terrace door and secured it. Daniel pulled her into his arms again. "You're home from work early." He grinned. "Couldn't stay away from me any longer, could you?"

"You guessed it," Sarai said, tiptoeing to kiss his cheek. She walked past him, and spun on her heels to face him. "But I also came home to deliver a message—your dad phoned. He's upset because you won't talk to him. He's sorry about arguing with you the last time you spoke." Her eyes were pleading. "He's so desperate for you to call him that he begged me to intercede on his behalf. Won't you call him, Daniel?"

She waited, her heart doing double-time, and her stomach muscles twisted in knots.

Daniel had a pained expression on his handsome face as he regarded her. He seemed to be at war with his conscience. Then, he sighed heavily, and said, "All right, I'll give him a call right now." He turned and left the room, utterly oblivious to the turmoil he'd thrown Sarai into when he'd said he was going to phone a dead man.

Sarai was wracked with indecision. She wanted to launch herself on him and tear his throat out with her teeth, she was so enraged. *Where was Daniel?* Had this impostor murdered him? Or did he have him stashed somewhere?

She'd never find out if she killed him.

But, her anger prevented her from thinking straight. She had to get out of there.

"Well, I've got to get back to work, babe!" she called to him, her voice sounding much more convincing than she expected it to under the circumstances.

The impostor jogged back into the room, looking like a laid-back Daniel in Daniel's skin and with Daniel's face, and gave her a peck on the cheek. "Okay, baby. How about I take you out to dinner tonight?"

"That sounds good," she said, smiling lovingly.

He patted her on the butt when she turned to leave.

Edina was lying on the chaise lounge in her bedroom reading her favorite book of poems by Paul Laurence Dunbar when her field of vision turned white, then bright blue. She recognized this as a precursor to receiving a running video in her mind.

After years of receiving them, she knew not to fight them. She calmly put the book down, lay back on the lounge in as comfortable a position as she could, then closed her eyes.

The images moved swiftly, however the vision was not simply a mini-movie in her brain. The sights were augmented by sounds and the sounds were intensified by emotions.

She saw Daniel and Maya being kidnapped. Daniel by a driver named Malcolm. Maya kidnapped by a man masquerading as her boyfriend. He picked her up at her apartment and took her to a house in Englewood.

Daniel had fought Malcolm when Malcolm had made him get out of the car at gunpoint at the house in Englewood. But Malcolm wasn't really a human and Daniel, though he fought bravely, was soon violently subdued.

Maya screamed so much that she was knocked out. In Edina's last glimpse of her, her face was purple and swollen.

While inside the vision, Edina strained to try to see Daniel again, but she was unable to. When the vision ended, she was physically drained. The visions always sapped her energy. Nonetheless, she got up and went to the phone on her nightstand and dialed Sarai's cell phone number. When Sarai answered, she instantly sensed her daughter's distraught state of mind.

"Sarai, I just had a vision. Daniel's been kidnapped."

Sarai's voice broke when she asked, desperately, "Is he alive?"

"They're both alive. Maya was kidnapped, too. I know where they are."

"Did you see anything at all about the son of a bitch who's been sleeping in my bed for the past five days?"

"No, I'm sorry," said Edina. "But don't worry. There's only one person who could cast a spell powerful enough to mask his identity for that long."

"Embeth!" Sarai said.

"Right," said her mother. "Your father and I will pay her a visit. In the meantime, you need to arm yourself and go to…" She gave Sarai the exact address of the house where Daniel and Maya were being held captive.

Edina had caught Sarai just as she was entering the parking garage where she'd earlier parked her bike. Now, instead of taking the bike, she took Daniel's late model SUV. Her favorite sword was stowed in the back.

Her first impulse, as she started the ignition, was to call her partner for backup. However, this was Nephilim business and she'd never confided in Jim. She was on her own.

When she arrived on the street where the house sat, she drove around the block and parked on the street behind it. As she approached the house from the back, her acute hearing picked up the sound of a television, and two people talking. She concentrated and was able to block out the sound of the television and leave the two voices in the foreground.

"Gin!" cried a female.

"Aw, damn, what are you, a card shark?" asked a male.

The female laughed delightedly. "Only with you. You're lousy at cards."

"I concentrate my energies in other areas," said the male with a lascivious note to his voice.

"Get real," said the female. "If I didn't have the hots

for Nighthawk, I wouldn't even be here. This is stupid. Why're we keeping them here? We should have killed them days ago. I ain't going down for kidnapping."

Outside, Sarai listened long enough to determine that Nighthawk had left only two of his goons to guard Daniel and Maya.

It was broad daylight. The neighborhood was teeming with people. Since it was the day after Thanksgiving, many people were off from work. Children were out of school, and they filled the streets on bikes, skateboards, and nearly thirty of them were playing ball in the vacant lot across the street.

She would have to move quickly and efficiently. She needed to go through the door on the first try. Constant battering of the door would draw attention to this house, and she didn't need the police to be summoned.

She was wearing her motorcycle boots, a pair of jeans that gave her freedom of movement, a T-shirt and her leather jacket. The key was the boots. They were heavy and well-made. They would protect her feet and ankles.

She got a good running start and threw herself at the door, feet first, putting all of her weight and prodigious strength behind it. The door vertically split in half.

The man and the woman sprang up from the table, picking up guns that had been lying on the tabletop within easy reach. Sarai kept moving.

She leaped onto the man and butted his head with hers. His forehead split and blood spilled into his eyes as her weight propelled both of them to the tile floor.

The back of his head connected with the floor and he ceased moving. Knocked out cold.

Human? Sarai thought. *He left humans to guard my husband?*

She was outraged. Then she thought how logical it was to have humans guarding humans. If, somehow, they were found out, and the police raided the house, Nighthawk didn't want any of the Sons of the Morning Star to be interrogated. Smart.

The woman, frightened beyond belief, held the gun on Sarai with shaky hands.

Sarai looked like a wild woman. Her long, black hair was in disarray. She had the man's blood on her forehead, and her teeth were bared in a fierce snarl. "Do you know who I am?" she asked the woman.

"You're her," the woman said nervously. "The wife."

Sarai nodded, satisfied. "That's right, I'm the pissed off wife. If you know what's good for you, you'll put that gun on the table and get the hell out of here."

The woman slowly lowered the gun, put it in the middle of the table, and ran through the splintered door. "Nighthawk can kiss my ass. I ain't dyin' for him!"

"Wise girl," Sarai called after her. The modest ranch house was only about 1500 square feet. It didn't take Sarai long to locate Daniel and Maya in a back bedroom. They were bound to separate twin beds.

They were fully dressed, and their eyes were covered with wide, black blindfolds.

Daniel called out, "Who's there?" when he heard her enter the room.

Sarai threw the light switch then ran to his side. "It's me, baby!" She removed the blindfold.

Daniel squinted in the bright light of the fixture

overhead. Sarai threw her arms around him and kissed his face repeatedly.

"I never thought I'd see you again," he said, his eyes moist with relief. Then, his expression changed to horror. "Sarai, check on Maya. I haven't heard her say anything for a couple of hours!"

Sarai quickly ripped apart the twine they'd used to tie Daniel's wrists to the headboard, and freed him. Then she hurried over to Maya who was lying perfectly still. She hadn't said a word since Sarai had shown up.

Sarai felt for a pulse. It was faint, but it was there.

She removed Maya's blindfold and peeled an eyelid back to look at her eye. It was dilated. Her skin felt cold and clammy. "She's passed out," she told Daniel.

"Oh, my God, she has a heart condition," Daniel said. He was busy removing the twine from around his ankles.

Sarai cradled Maya in her arms. "Can you walk?" she asked Daniel.

He stood on weak legs. "Yeah, they let us go to the bathroom a couple times a day. My legs are okay, just a little rubbery."

"Good, then you can walk to the car. I've got to get you two to a hospital."

Daniel slowly followed her through the house. When they got to the guy's prostrate body in the kitchen, he joked, "Was it something he said?"

"No," Sarai told him. "He just didn't get out of my way fast enough. I'll come back and take care of him after I know you're safe."

"We'd better get our stories straight before we get to

the hospital," Daniel said. "I'm guessing telling them we were kidnapped by Nephilim won't go over well."

"You were kidnapped, but you didn't see their faces. I backtracked from the moment you and Maya got off the plane and found you at an abandoned house in Englewood.

"You suspect it was political. Maybe they were going to photograph you and Maya in a compromising position. Anything to ruin you politically."

"I'm sure they'll believe that," Daniel said. "Everybody wants to believe the worst about politicians."

Sarai gently placed Maya on the backseat, then she removed the strap from across her chest, unclasping the sword in its sheath that had been strapped to her back the whole time, and stowed it on the floor in the back. She hadn't known whether she was walking into a nest of Nephilim or not. When her mother had told her to arm herself, she'd made sure she had her automatic *and* her sword.

At the hospital, Maya was placed in the capable hands of a heart specialist while Daniel was examined and told he was sound. Although he had some contusions on his head and face, they were healing and he didn't have a concussion.

He and Sarai were then left alone in the examination room. They held each other.

On the way to the hospital Sarai had phoned her parents, then she'd told Daniel that Nighthawk was behind his kidnapping. But she didn't know why he'd done it.

She had not mentioned the worst part, she hadn't told him the fact that she had been so deceived by him that she'd slept with him. It was ironic, really. Serena had nearly accused Daniel of cheating on her, when *she* had been the one cheating on Daniel. There was nothing left to do but to confess her sins to Daniel.

He was sitting on the examination table, and she was standing between his legs. He held her securely in his strong arms. Looking deeply into his eyes, she said, "I know I could claim to have been under a powerful spell, and that's the reason I did what I did when you were gone. But I've never been one to run from responsibility. I slept with him, Daniel."

Tears appeared in Daniel's eyes. In all the years they'd been together, she had never seen him cry. Of course, she had never hurt him as badly as her confession must have done before, either. Her eyes welled up in response to his pain.

"I'm sorry, Daniel."

He held her tighter. "He violated you!" he said against her neck. "You don't need to apologize for anything. You're only guilty of loving me."

He raised her chin with a finger and peered into her eyes. "I love you. I wish I could kill him for what he did, but a human is no match for a Nephilim."

"I love you," Sarai told him passionately. "I'd planned a special dinner for us the night you were supposed to return. I had something important to tell you. I never did find the right moment to say it while you were gone. Now, I know why. But here goes—we're going to have a baby."

Fresh tears came to Daniel's eyes as he rained kisses on her face and throat. They didn't have time for further celebration because the doctor whom they'd left Maya with came into the room at that moment. He was smiling. "Mr. and Mrs. Wingate, Miss Stephenson came to a few minutes ago. She's going to be fine."

Sarai burst into tears of relief.

Maya, as far as she was concerned, had nearly died because of her. She was such a sweet kid, only twenty-six, and so damned optimistic about life.

They thanked the doctor, after which he quietly left the room.

Daniel shook Sarai, trying to break her crying jag. "Listen to me, you can't afford to fall apart now. You've got a child to protect. What do you think Nighthawk is going to do when he finds out his plans have been foiled and instead of getting you pregnant, as was undoubtedly his goal, you're pregnant with *my* child?"

Daniel was back, Daniel with a steel trap of a mind. While she had been wracking her brain trying to figure out why Nighthawk would go to such lengths to pretend to be Daniel, Daniel had come to the logical conclusion.

"He wanted a child with me?" she asked incredulously, sniffling still.

She couldn't imagine why.

Several miles away, her parents were getting the whole story from the sorceress who had dreamed up the spell that had made Nighthawk's scheme possible.

Edina and Andrew had arrived at Embeth's crypt thinking that they were going to have to break in.

However, Embeth cordially greeted them at the door and asked them inside. She was not cloaking her true appearance. "What are a few wrinkles between old friends?" she joked as she led them down the stone steps to the main room of the large underground crypt.

In the center of the candlelit room sat a huge guillotine. She stood next to the monstrosity, her demeanor friendly if a little cocky. "I see you got my message," she said, looking at Edina.

"You mean *you* sent the vision?"

Embeth smiled slyly. "Of course I sent it. How else was I going to get you here? I told Nighthawk that with Sarai he would have a powerful Son of the Morning Star. To achieve this goal, he had to bed her. In order to bed her, I had to put a holding spell on him. Nephilim can shape-shift but not for more than a few hours at a time. I also had to make sure he smelled like Daniel. If he could get her pregnant he was certain she'd leave Daniel for him since you Grigori insist on birth parents raising their offspring."

"The Sons of the Morning Star obviously don't share that belief," Edina boldly said.

Embeth laughed. "You know, then?"

"That Nighthawk is your son?" Edina said. "Yes. I've known for years now. I found out when he and Sarai had a thing for each other, and his father insisted he stop seeing her."

"Lucifer is a jealous god. He couldn't bear the thought that he might one day have a grandson who was half-Grigori. It's not as if he doesn't have offspring that are half jackal or any number of other mutations. But, half-Grigori was not to be tolerated!"

Edina wisely knew that intellectual sparring with Embeth was a losing proposition.

The sorceress had her by at least two hundred years. "What do you want from us?"

"In order to break the spell, I have to die," Embeth stated.

"Isn't the spell already broken?" Andrew asked. "Sarai

told us only minutes ago that she knows it was Nighthawk who was posing as Daniel."

"You don't understand," Embeth said. "When Nighthawk finds out she is with child, he will kill her *and* the child. If he can't have her, no one shall. That's another thing he got from his father. The need to completely possess another being. They will fight, and unless the spell is broken, it will seem to Sarai that she is fighting her beloved, Daniel.

"That puts her at a distinct psychological disadvantage, don't you think?" Her confident smile told them that she knew she'd made her point.

"Kill her, Andrew," Edina said with resignation.

"I didn't bring my sword," Andrew said. "Did you?"

"I didn't think I'd need it," Edina replied.

Embeth shook her head in disgust. "You young ones never learn." She walked over and calmly positioned her tiny body in the embrace of the guillotine. She had even placed a basket in the proper spot to insure herself some dignity in death.

"If one of you would be so kind?" she said. "I bought the damned thing but could never figure out a way to release the blade without someone's assistance."

"It would be my pleasure," Edina said, and stepped forward and released the blade.

Embeth didn't have time to say "thank you" before her head fell into the waiting basket. The mouth was turned up at the corners in a grotesque smile.

The moment Embeth's head fell into the basket, Nighthawk was sent a grisly mental image of the deed. He knew the woman who had given birth to him was dead.

He'd never loved her, though, so he felt no grief. He might have felt more emotion if his butler had kicked the bucket. Embeth's passing meant only one thing to him: the spell was broken.

So he wasn't surprised when Sarai phoned him a few minutes later with, "Millennium Park, at Pritzker Pavilion, 2:00 a.m. Be there!"

That's all she had to say.

The word spread swiftly among the Nephilim, both Grigori and Sons of the Morning Star. There was going to be a sword-fight to settle a dispute with charges of rape, kidnapping and attempted murder on the table.

The combatants were from opposite camps. The male was the issue of Lucifer and a powerful sorceress. The female was the issue of the greatest swordsman of the Grigori and a talented seer.

The bout would take place at the Jay Pritzker Pavilion, a band shell with seating for up to 4000, plus enough room to accommodate 7000 more if they didn't mind sitting on the lawn. Wings only. No motor vehicles were allowed. Thousands of cars coming down Michigan Avenue, East Randolph Street, Columbus Drive and East Monroe Drive at 2 a.m. might awaken slumbering humans and alert them that something significant was going on, to say nothing of the police!

A sorcerer would provide an invisible shield around the entire assemblage at the stroke of 2 a.m., thereby masking the sounds of swords clashing and voices cheering and jeering. Anyone who arrived late would be prevented from entering by the same force field.

In the spare bedroom of her parents' apartment, Sarai and Daniel lay on the bed fully dressed, looking into each other's eyes. It was less than an hour before the duel and Daniel, who had been barred from attending because he was human, didn't want her to go.

"You all don't have a Nephilim prison, or something?" he asked against hope. "Yes, he deserves to die for what he did to you, but do you have to be the one to fight him?

"He's bigger than you and he's older than you, therefore he's probably more experienced at this sort of thing. He's probably pissed somebody off before."

Sarai smiled at him with her love for him shining in her eyes. "I wish I could tell you, yes, there is another form of justice among Nephilim. But there isn't. Our form of justice is simple and straightforward. The two who have a gripe against each other do the fighting."

Daniel still wouldn't give up. "Then, you can publicly announce that you forgive him for what he did."

"Forgive Nighthawk? He'd be humiliated. Believe me, if I tried that he'd toss my offer back in my face. He's too proud for that. He wants to fight. Right now he's so embarrassed to have been caught in the deception that the only way for him to gain any sense of honor among Nephilim, now, is to kill me in front of them."

Daniel pulled her into his arms and held her tightly. "I can't bear the thought of losing you and our child."

"You're not going to lose us," Sarai tried to reassure him. She gently kissed his mouth. Daniel leaned in and the kiss grew in intensity. It was as if both of them felt this might be the last time they got the chance to express their love for each other.

Finally, they drew apart. "Remember not to fight angry," Daniel said softly. "Don't let him distract you by trying to get you mad."

There was a knock on the door and they both sat up.

"Come in!" Sarai called.

Her mother entered. "Sarai, your escorts are here."

The judging council, who determined whether a grievance was worth fighting over or not, provided each combatant with two escorts who flew with them to the appointed fight venue.

Sarai and Daniel followed Edina down the hall to the living room where two male Nephilim, both the size of Chicago Bears linebackers, stood with Andrew discussing, of all things, football. After a closer look, Sarai realized that they did indeed play for the Bears.

Daniel recognized them too, and admired their prowess on the field, but he had no inclination to go over and play the fan tonight. His wife was getting ready to go into battle. Something he should be doing. He was the man, after all, the protector of his woman. He felt utterly helpless.

Sarai turned to him after the two escorts walked out onto the terrace with her parents in preparation for taking off.

"Daniel, this can't be easy for you, watching me leave like this. But I wouldn't have married you if I didn't think you could handle every aspect of this life we share. You're my hero." With this, tears fell. "I don't know how I lived without you all the years you weren't in my life. And I'll do my damnedest to get back to you."

"You *will* come back to me," Daniel said, his voice full

of conviction. His eyes were clear and determined. His mind could accept no other scenario.

They kissed briefly after which she joined the others on the terrace. One by one they flew away leaving Daniel behind, looking up into the night sky.

The Pritzker Pavilion was designed by world-renowned architect Frank Gehry and the band shell consisted of massive panels of stainless steel that looked somewhat like the sails of a Clipper ship folding in and out in continuous motion. Although, this effect was only when the light hit the stainless steel. During the day, or at night, the band shell was a magnificent example of architectural design.

Music lovers usually filled the seats. Tonight, the audience was no less enthusiastic about the spectacle to unfold before their eyes. They were divided. The Sons of the Morning Star claimed the seats and in order to keep the peace, the Grigori claimed the space on the lawn.

Sarai and Nighthawk began walking toward each other from opposite ends of the stage. The referee, a male Grigori of advanced age and wisdom, stood in the center of the stage awaiting them.

Once they arrived, the referee said for all to hear: "To my left is Sarai Wingate who accuses Nicolas Armaros of deceiving her to the extent that she made love to him, thinking he was her husband."

Gasps arose among the audience.

The referee raised his hand, and the audience immediately became silent.

"Mr. Armaros is also accused of kidnapping Mrs. Wingate's husband and his assistant who is in intensive care now due to heart failure. She is expected to live.

"Mr. Armaros, how do you answer to these charges?"

"We all know this is only a formality," Nighthawk said, his steely eyes on Sarai. "My sword will speak for me."

The referee gave the sorcerer who was standing off stage a signal with his eyes, and the sorcerer muttered an incantation under his breath. It was a spell that forces the accused to speak the truth.

The referee regarded Nighthawk once again. "I say once more—How do you answer to these charges, Mr. Armaros?"

Nighthawk clamped his mouth shut, but he was compelled to open it and say, "You don't have all the facts. If my people hadn't bungled the kidnapping and bruised both Daniel Wingate and his assistant, I had planned to drug them, put them in bed together, and let Sarai Wingate discover them. Such would have been her rage, she would have gladly killed them in an instant. Her husband would be dead, and her guilt would have driven her into my arms again. If my insane mother, a sorceress with suicidal tendencies, hadn't grown a conscience in her old age, I might have gotten away with it. But she no longer had the stomach for manipulating other peoples' lives."

"You wanted to trick me into killing my own husband?" Sarai screamed at him.

The referee stepped back as the two of them drew their swords. He flew up and out of range. Once again he cued the sorcerer. It was time to amplify the voices of the combatants so that everything they said could be heard by the audience.

"After that," Nighthawk told her, "it would have been easy for you to join the ranks of the mighty."

The Sons of the Morning Star cheered on their hero.

Swords held defensively, he and Sarai circled each other. They were both attired in all black. Sarai in leather—a bolero jacket, slacks and motorcycle boots.

A duster with a split tail covered Nighthawk's sleeveless T-shirt, jeans and combat boots. They were still taking the measure of each other when he said, "After I cut your head off, I'm going to cut that brat right out of your womb."

"What's the matter, Armaros, jealous of a human? You're never going to get that child your mother prophesied. She's not here to cloak your appearance now. I would never have let you near me if I had known it was you!"

"Liar!" he shouted back at her. "You loved me once. You told me that when you thought I was Daniel."

"There's a thin line between love and hate and, buddy, you've crossed it!"

Cheers from the Grigori.

"You didn't act like you hated me when I was giving it to you day and night. And I hate to disillusion you, darling, but that floating act happened only because you had another Nephilim in your bed instead of a puny human. Your powers are not evolving."

Cheers from the Sons of the Morning Star, along with lascivious laughter.

"Oh, shut up and fight!" Sarai said, and struck out at his mid-section.

Nighthawk easily deflected her thrust, and forced her backward with a series of rapid jabs of his own. Sarai, light on her feet, and with lightning reflexes, had no trouble withstanding the assault.

They danced back and forth across the stage, sometimes with him on the defensive and sometimes with her. They were equal in skill, and nothing either of them said to the other caused them to lose concentration.

Sparks flew from the heavy broadswords as steel bit into steel. Because they were Nephilim their strength did not desert them. Each hit, each thrust had as much force behind it as the first ones. Sarai realized they could go on like this until dawn.

Therefore, she decided to take Daniel's advice and offer forgiveness. "You can't beat me," she said.

"Just give me a little more time," Nighthawk said, gritting his teeth. He swung his sword in an arc that would have taken her head off at a 90 degree angle if he had succeeded.

Sarai blocked the blow, both hands firmly on the handgrip, and shoved him away from her. "We can be at this until the next Millennium," she said. "Or I can tell you that I'll forgive what you did as long as you leave the city and never come back."

Nighthawk growled as he ran toward her, his sword held high. When he was within two feet of her, he spun around, aiming the sword at her waistline in an attempt to cut her in half.

Sarai executed a perfect back flip from the standing position and landed on her feet. Whereupon, she knelt on one knee and drove her sword up to hilt into the belly of the charging Nighthawk. He gasped in pain, his breath suddenly gone from his body.

Their eyes met. His were astonished. He hadn't expected to be defeated by her. Hers were full of sympathy, but still determined. She hadn't wanted it to come to this. She'd offered him a way out but, like a fool, he had refused her gesture.

She slowly got to her feet, pulled the sword from his belly, and beheaded him.

It was done.

Sword held at her side, bloody tip pointed downward, she turned and walked away.

Since 1996 national best-selling author Janice Sims has published fourteen novels, including paranormal romance, and has had stories included in nine anthologies. And she's just getting started. She lives in Central Florida with her husband and daughter.

You can visit her on the Web at www.janicesims.com or write her at P. O. Box 811, Mascotte, FL 34753-0811.

A brand-new Kendra Clayton mystery
from acclaimed author...

ANGELA HENRY

Diva's Last Curtain Call

Amateur sleuth Kendra Clayton finds herself immersed in
mayhem once again when a cunning killer rolls credits on a
fading movie star. Kendra's publicity-seeking sister is pegged
as the prime suspect, but Kendra knows her sister is no
murderer. She soon uncovers some surprising Hollywood
secrets, putting herself in danger of becoming the killer's
encore performance....

"A tightly woven mystery."
—*Ebony* magazine on *The Company You Keep*

sepia™

*Coming the first
week of June
wherever books
are sold.*

tangled ROOTS

A Kendra Clayton Novel

ANGELA HENRY

Nothing's going right these days for part-time
English teacher and reluctant sleuth Kendra Clayton.
Now her favorite student is the number one suspect in a local
murder. When he begs Kendra for help, she's soon on the road
to trouble again—trying to find the real killer, stepping into
danger...and getting tangled in the deadly roots of desire.

"This debut mystery features an exciting new
African-American heroine.... Highly recommended."
—*Library Journal* on *The Company You Keep*

*Available the first week of May
wherever books are sold.*

KIMANI PRESS™
www.kimanipress.com

KPAH0680507TR

BETTYE GRIFFIN

A LOVE for All Seasons

Alicia Timberlake was the woman of Jack Devlin's dreams, but Alicia had always kept people at a distance, unwilling to let anyone close. Still, Jack isn't about to give up without a fight. But when a family tragedy reveals a secret that makes Alicia question everything she's ever known, she's suddenly determined to reassess her life and learn, finally, how to open herself to love.

Available the first week of May
wherever books are sold.

ARABESQUE®
www.kimanipress.com

KPBG0100507TR

A soul-stirring, compelling
journey of self-discovery…

journey
into My Brother's Soul

Maria D. Dowd

Bestselling author of
Journey to Empowerment

A memorable collection of essays, prose and poetry,
reflecting the varied experiences that men of color face
throughout life. Touching on every facet of living—love,
marriage, fatherhood, family—these candid personal
contributions explore the essence of what it means to
be a man today.

"***Journey to Empowerment* will lead you on a
healing journey and will lead to a great love of self,
and a deeper understanding of the many roles we
all must play in life."—*Rawsistaz Reviewers*

Coming the first week of May
wherever books are sold.

KPMDD0290507TR

Celebrating life every step of the way.

YOU ONLY GET *Better*

New York Times bestselling author
CONNIE BRISCOE
and
Essence bestselling authors
LOLITA FILES
ANITA BUNKLEY

Three fortysomething women discover that life, men and
everything else get better with age in this entertaining
three-in-one anthology from three award-winning authors!

Available the first week of March wherever books are sold.

KIMANI PRESS™
www.kimanipress.com

KPYOGB0590307TR

Pleasure SEEKERS

Part of the Hideaway Legacy

A sizzling, sensuous story about Ilene, Faye and Alana—
three young African-American women whose lives are
forever changed when they are invited to join the
exclusive world of the Pleasure Seekers.

Rochelle Alers

NATIONAL BESTSELLING AUTHOR

"Fans of the romantic suspense of Iris Johansen,
Linda Howard and Catherine Coulter
will enjoy [*Pleasure Seekers*]."
—*Library Journal*

Available the first week of January wherever books are sold.